STRAIGHT

STRAIGHT

DICK FRANCIS

G. P. PUTNAM'S SONS
New York

G. P. Putnam's Sons
Publishers Since 1838
200 Madison Avenue
New York, NY 10016

Library of Congress Cataloging-in-Publication Data

Francis, Dick.
Straight / Dick Francis.
p. cm.
I. Title.
PR6056.R27S76 1989   89-36492 CIP
823'.914—dc20
ISBN 0-399-13470-0

Printed in the United States of America
1 2 3 4 5 6 7 8 9 10

My thanks especially to
JOSEPH and DANIELLE ZERGER
of ZARLENE IMPORTS
Dealers in semiprecious stones

and also to
MARY BROMILEY—ankle specialist
BARRY PARK—veterinary surgeon
JEREMY THOMPSON—doctor, pharmacologist
ANDREW HEWSON—literary agent

and as always to
MERRICK and FELIX, our sons.

All the people in this story are imaginary.
All the gadgets exist.

STRAIGHT

1

I inherited my brother's life. Inherited his desk, his business, his gadgets, his enemies, his horses and his mistress I inherited my brother's life, and it nearly killed me.

I was thirty-four at the time and walking about on elbow crutches owing to a serious disagreement with the last fence in a steeplechase at Cheltenham. If you've never felt your ankle explode, don't try it. As usual, it hadn't been the high-speed tumble that had done the damage but the half-ton of one of the other runners coming over the fence after me, his forefoot landing squarely on my boot on the baked earth of an Indian summer. The hoof mark was imprinted on the leather. The doctor who cut the boot off handed it to me as a souvenir. Medical minds have a macabre sense of humor.

Two days after this occurrence, while I was reluctantly coming to terms with the fact that I was going to miss at least six weeks of the steeplechasing season and with them possibly my last chance of making it to champion again (the middle thirties being the beginning of the end for jump jockeys), I answered the telephone for about the tenth time that morning and found it was not another friend ringing to commiserate.

"Could I speak," a female voice asked, "to Derek Franklin?"

"I'm Derek Franklin," I said.

"Right." She was both brisk and hesitant, and one could

understand why. "We have you listed," she said, "as your brother Greville's next-of-kin."

Those three words, I thought with an accelerating heart, must be among the most ominous in the language.

I said slowly, not wanting to know, "What's happened?"

"I'm speaking from St. Catherine's Hospital, Ipswich. Your brother is here, in the intensive care unit . . ."

At least he was alive, I thought numbly.

". . . and the doctors think you should be told."

"How is he?"

"I'm sorry. I haven't seen him. This is the social worker. But I understand that his condition is very serious."

"What's the matter with him?"

"He was involved in an accident," she said. "He has multiple injuries and is on life support."

"I'll come," I said.

"Yes. It might be best."

I thanked her, not knowing exactly what for, and put down the receiver, taking the shock physically in lightheadedness and a constricted throat.

He would be all right, I told myself. Intensive care meant simply that he was being carefully looked after. He would recover, of course.

I shut out the anxiety to work prosaically instead on the practicalities of getting from the town of Hungerford in Berkshire, where I lived, to Ipswich in Suffolk, about a hundred and fifty miles across country, with a crunched ankle. It was fortunately the left ankle, which meant I would soon be able to drive my automatic gears without trouble, but it was on that particular day at peak discomfort and even with painkillers and icepacks was hot, swollen and throbbing. I couldn't move it without holding my breath, and that was partly my own fault.

Owing to my hatred—not to say phobia—about the damaging immobility of plaster of Paris, I had spent a good deal of the previous day persuading a long-suffering orthopedic surgeon to give me the support of a plain crepe bandage instead of imprisonment in a cast. He was himself a plate-and-screw man by preference but had grumbled as usual at my request. Such a bandage as I was demanding might be better in the end for one's muscles, but it gave no protection against knocks, as he had reminded me on other occasions, and it would be more painful, he said.

"I'll be racing much quicker with a bandage."

"It's time you stopped breaking your bones," he said, giving in with a shrug and a sigh and obligingly winding the crepe on tightly. "One of these days you'll crack something serious."

"I don't actually like breaking them."

"At least I haven't had to pin anything this time," he said. "And you're mad."

"Yes. Thanks very much."

"Go home and rest it. Give those ligaments a chance."

The ligaments took their chance along the back seat of my car while Brad, an unemployed welder, drove it to Ipswich. Brad, taciturn and obstinate, was unemployed by habit and choice but made a scratchy living doing odd jobs in the neighborhood for anyone willing to endure his moods. As I much preferred his long silences to his infrequent conversation, we got along fine. He looked forty, hadn't reached thirty, and lived with his mother.

He found St. Catherine's Hospital without much trouble and at the door helped me out and handed me the crutches, saying he would park and wait inside in the reception area and I could take my time. He had waited for me similarly for hours the day before, expressing neither impatience nor sympathy but simply being restfully and neutrally morose.

The intensive care unit proved to be guarded by brisk nurses who looked at the crutches and said I'd come to the wrong department, but once I'd persuaded them of my identity they kitted me sympathetically with a mask and gown and let me in to see Greville.

I had vaguely expected Intensive Care to involve a lot of bright lights and clanging bustle, but I found that it didn't, or at least not in that room in that hospital. The light was dim, the atmosphere peaceful, the noise level, once my ears adjusted to it, just above silence but lower than identification.

Greville lay alone in the room on a high bed with wires and tubes all over the place. He was naked except for a strip of sheeting lying loosely across his loins and they had shaved half the hair off his head. Other evidences of surgery marched like centipede tracks across his abdomen and down one thigh, and there were darkening bruises everywhere.

Behind his bed a bank of screens showed blank rectangular faces, as the information from the electrodes fed into other screens in a room directly outside. He didn't need, they said, an attendant constantly beside him, but they kept an eye on his reactions all the time.

He was unconscious, his face pale and calm, his head turned slightly toward the door as if expecting visitors. Decompression procedures had been performed on his skull, and that wound was covered by a large padded dressing which seemed more like a pillow to support him.

Greville Saxony Franklin, my brother. Nineteen years my senior: not expected to live. It had to be faced. To be accepted.

"Hi, guy," I said.

It was an Americanism he himself used often, but it produced no response. I touched his hand, which was warm and relaxed, the nails, as always, clean and cared for. He had a pulse, he had circulation: his heart beat by electrical stimulus. Air went in and out of his lungs mechanically through a tube in his throat. Inside his head the synapses were shutting down. Where was his soul, I wondered: where was the intelligent, persistent, energetic spirit? Did he know that he was dying?

I didn't want just to leave him. No one should die alone. I went outside and said so.

A doctor in a green overall replied that when all the remaining brain activity had ceased, they would ask my consent before switching off the machines. I was welcome to be with my brother at that crisis point as well as before. "But death," he said austerely, "will be for him an infinitesimal process, not a definitive moment." He paused. "There is a waiting room along the hall, with coffee and things."

Bathos and drama, I thought: his everyday life. I crutched all the way down to the general reception area, found Brad, gave him an update and told him I might be a long time. All night, perhaps.

He waved a permissive hand. He would be around, he said, or he would leave a message at the desk. Either way, I could reach him. I nodded and went back upstairs, and found the waiting room already occupied by a very young couple engulfed in grief, whose baby was hanging on to life by threads not much stronger than Greville's.

The room itself was bright, comfortable and impersonal, and I listened to the mother's slow sobs and thought of the misery that soaked daily into those walls. Life has a way of kicking one along like a football, or so I've found. Fate had never dealt me personally a particularly easy time, but that was OK, that was normal. Most people, it seemed to me, took their turn to be football. Most survived. Some didn't.

Greville had simply been in the wrong place at the wrong time. From the scrappy information known to the hospital I gleaned that he had been walking down Ipswich High Street when some scaffolding that was being dismantled had fallen on him from a considerable height. One of the construction workers had been killed, and a second had been taken to hospital with a broken hip.

I had been given my brother's clinical details. One metal bar had pierced his stomach, another had torn into his leg; something heavy had fallen on his head and caused brain damage with massive cerebral bleeding. It had happened late the previous afternoon; he had been deeply unconscious from the moment of impact and he hadn't been identified until workmen dealing with the rubble in the morning had found his diary and given it to the police.

"Wallet?" I asked.

No, no wallet. Just the diary with, neatly filled in on the first page, Next of Kin, Derek Franklin, brother; telephone number supplied. Before that, they had had no clue except the initials G.S.F. embroidered above the pocket of his torn and bloodstained shirt.

"A *silk* shirt," a nurse added disapprovingly, as if monogrammed silk shirts were somehow immoral.

"Nothing else in his pockets?" I asked.

"A bunch of keys and a handkerchief. That was all. You'll be given them, of course, along with the diary and his watch and signet ring."

I nodded. No need to ask when.

The afternoon stretched out, strange and unreal, a time-warped limbo. I went again to spend some time with Greville, but he lay unmoving, oblivious in his dwindling twilight, already subtly not himself. If Wordsworth were right about immortality, it was the sleep and the forgetting that were slipping away and reawakening that lay ahead, and maybe I should be glad for him, not grieve.

I thought of him as he had been, and of our lives as brothers.

We had never lived together in a family unit because, by the time I was born, he was away at university, building a life of his own. By the time I was six, he had married, by the time I was ten, he'd divorced. For years he was a semistranger whom I met briefly at family gatherings, celebrations which grew less and less frequent as our parents aged and died, and which stopped altogether when the two sisters who bridged the gap between Greville and me both emigrated, one to Australia and one to Japan.

It wasn't until I'd reached twenty-eight myself that after a long Christmas-and-birthday-card politeness we'd met unexpectedly on a railway platform and during the journey ahead had become friends. Not close time-sharing friends even then, but positive enough for telephoning each other sporadically and exchanging restaurant dinners and feeling good about it.

STRAIGHT

We had been brought up in different environments, Greville in the Regency London house which went with our father's job as manager of one of the great landowning estates, I in the comfortable country cottage of his retirement. Greville had been taken by our mother to museums, art galleries and the theater: I had been given ponies.

We didn't even look much alike. Greville, like our father, was six feet tall, I three inches shorter. Greville's hair, now graying, had been light brown and straight, mine darker brown and curly. We had both inherited amber eyes and good teeth from our mother and a tendency to leanness from our father, but our faces, though both tidy enough, were quite different.

Greville best remembered our parents' vigorous years; I'd been with them through their illnesses and deaths. Our father had himself been twenty years older than our mother, and she had died first, which had seemed monstrously unfair. The old man and I had lived briefly together after that in tolerant mutual noncomprehension, though I had no doubt that he'd loved me, in his way. He had been sixty-two when I was born and he died on my eighteenth birthday, leaving me a fund for my continued education and a letter of admonitions and instructions, some of which I'd carried out.

Greville's stillness was absolute. I shifted uncomfortably on the crutches and thought of asking for a chair. I wouldn't see him smile again, I thought: not the lightening of the eyes and the gleam of teeth, the quick appreciation of the black humor of life, the awareness of his own power.

He was a magistrate, a justice of the peace, and he imported and sold semiprecious stones. Beyond these bare facts I knew few details of his day-to-day existence, as whenever we met it seemed that he was always more interested in my doings than his own. He had himself owned horses from the day he telephoned to ask my opinion: someone who owed him money had offered his racehorse to settle the debt. What did I think? I told him I'd phone back, looked up the horse, thought it was a bargain and told Greville to go right ahead if he felt like it.

"Don't see why not," he'd said. "Will you fix the paper-work?"

I'd said yes, of course. It wasn't hard for anyone to say yes to my brother Greville: much harder to say no.

The horse had won handsomely and given him a taste for future ownership, though he seldom went to see his horses run, which wasn't particularly unusual in an owner but always to me mystifying. He refused absolutely to own jumpers on the grounds that he might buy something that would kill me. I was too big for Flat races; he'd felt safe with those. I couldn't persuade him that I would like to ride for him and in the end I stopped trying. When Greville made up his mind he was unshakable.

Every ten minutes or so a nurse would come quietly into the room to stand for a short while beside the bed, checking that all the electrodes and tubes were still in order. She gave me brief smiles and commented once that my brother was un-aware of my presence and could not be comforted by my being there.

"It's as much for me as for him," I said.

She nodded and went away, and I stayed for a couple more hours, leaning against a wall and reflecting that it was ironic that it was he who should meet death by chance when it was I who actively risked it half the days of the year.

Strange to reflect also, looking back now to that lengthen-ing evening, that I gave no thought to the consequences of his death. The present was vividly alive still in the silent diminish-ing hours, and all I saw in the future was a pretty dreary program of form-filling and funeral arrangements, which I didn't bother to think about in any detail. I would have to telephone the sisters, I vaguely supposed, and there might be a little long-distance grief, but I knew they would say, "You can see to it, can't you? Whatever you decide will be all right with us," and they wouldn't come back halfway round the world to stand in mournful drizzle at the graveside of a brother they'd seen perhaps twice in ten years.

[18]

Beyond that, I considered nothing. The tie of common blood was all that truly linked Greville and me, and once it was undone there would be nothing left of him but memory. With regret I watched the pulse that flickered in his throat. When it was gone I would go back to my own life and think of him warmly sometimes, and remember this night with overall sorrow, but no more.

I went along to the waiting room for a while to rest my legs. The desperate young parents were still there, hollow-eyed and entwined, but presently a somber nurse came to fetch them, and in the distance, shortly after, I heard the rising wail of the mother's agonized loss. I felt my own tears prickle for her, a stranger. A dead baby, a dying brother, a universal uniting misery. I grieved for Greville most intensely then because of the death of the child, and realized I had been wrong about the sorrow level. I would miss him very much.

I put my ankle up on a chair and fitfully dozed, and sometime before daybreak the same nurse with the same expression came to fetch me in my turn.

I followed her along the passage and into Greville's room. There was much more light in there this time, and more people, and the bank of monitoring screens behind the bed had been switched on. Pale greenish lines moved across them, some in regular spasms, some uncompromisingly straight.

I didn't need to be told, but they explained all the same. The straight lines were the sum of the activity in Greville's brain. None at all.

There was no private goodbye. There was no point. I was there, and that was enough. They asked for, and received, my agreement to the disconnection of the machines, and presently the pulsing lines straightened out also, and whatever had been in the quiet body was there no longer.

It took a long time to get anything done in the morning because it turned out to be Sunday.

I thought back, having lost count of time. Thursday when

I broke my ankle, Friday when the scaffolding fell on Greville, Saturday when Brad drove me to Ipswich. It all seemed a cosmos away: relativity in action.

There was the possibility, it seemed, of the scaffolding constructors being liable for damages. It was suggested that I should consult a lawyer.

Plodding through the paperwork, trying to make decisions, I realized that I didn't know what Greville would want. If he'd left a will somewhere, maybe he had given instructions that I ought to carry out. Maybe no one but I, I thought with a jolt, actually knew he was dead. There had to be people I should notify, and I didn't know who.

I asked if I could have the diary the police had found in the rubble, and presently I was given not only the diary but everything else my brother had had with him: keys, watch, handkerchief, signet ring, a small amount of change, shoes, socks, jacket. The rest of his clothes, torn and drenched with blood, had been incinerated, it appeared. I was required to sign for what I was taking, putting a tick against each item.

Everything had been tipped out of the large brown plastic bag in which they had been stored. The bag said "St. Catherine's Hospital" in white on the sides. I put the shoes, socks, handkerchief and jacket back into the bag and pulled the strings tight again, then I shoveled the large bunch of keys into my own trouser pocket, along with the watch, the ring and the money, and finally consulted the diary.

On the front page he had entered his name, his London home telephone number and his office number, but no addresses. It was near the bottom, where there was a space headed "In case of accident please notify" that he had written "Derek Franklin, brother, next of kin."

The diary itself was one I had sent him at Christmas: the racing diary put out by the Jockeys' Association and the Injured Jockeys' Fund. That he should have chosen to use that particular diary when he must have been given several others I found unexpectedly moving. That he had put my name in it made me wonder what he had really thought of me; whether there was much we might have been to each other, and had missed.

With regret I put the diary into my other trousers pocket. The next morning, I supposed, I would have to telephone his office with the dire news. I couldn't forewarn anyone, as I didn't know the names, let alone the phone numbers, of the people who worked for him. I knew only that he had no partners, as he had said several times that the only way he could run his business was by himself. Partners too often came to blows, he said, and he would have none of it.

When all the signing was completed, I looped the strings of the plastic bag a couple of times round my wrist and took it and myself on the crutches down to the reception area, which was more or less deserted on that early Sunday morning. Brad wasn't there, nor was there any message from him at the desk, so I simply sat down and waited. I had no doubt he would come back in his own good time, glowering as usual, and eventually he did, slouching in through the door with no sign of haste.

He saw me across the acreage, came to within ten feet, and said, "Shall I fetch the car, then?" and when I nodded, wheeled away and departed. A man of very few words, Brad. I followed slowly in his wake, the plastic bag bumping against the crutch. If I'd thought faster I would have given it to Brad to carry, but I didn't seem to be thinking fast in any way.

Outside, the October sun was bright and warm. I breathed the sweet air, took a few steps away from the door and patiently waited some more, and was totally unprepared to be savagely mugged.

I scarcely saw who did it. One moment I was upright, leaning without concentration on the crutches, the next I'd received a battering-ram shove in the back and was sprawling face forward onto the hard black surface of the entrance driveway. To try to save myself, I put my left foot down instinctively and it twisted beneath me which was excruciating

[21]

and useless. I fell flat down on my stomach in a haze and I hardly cared when someone kicked one of the fallen crutches away along the ground and tugged at the bag round my wrist.

He—it had to be a he, I thought, from the speed and strength—thumped a foot down on my back and put his weight on it. He yanked my arm up and back roughly, and cut through the plastic with a slash that took some of my skin with it. I scarcely felt it. The messages from my ankle obliterated all else.

A voice approached saying, "Hey! Hey!" urgently, and my attacker lifted himself off me as fast as he'd arrived and sped away.

It was Brad who had come to my rescue. On any other day there might have been people constantly coming and going, but not on Sunday morning. No one else seemed to be around to notice a thing. No one but Brad had come running.

"Friggin' hell," Brad said from above me. "Are you all right?"

Far from it, I thought.

He went to fetch the scattered crutch and brought it back. "Your hand's bleeding," he said with disbelief. "Don't you want to stand up?"

I wasn't too sure that I did, but it seemed the only thing to do. When I'd made it to a moderately vertical position he looked impassively at my face and gave it as his opinion that we ought to go back into the hospital. As I didn't feel like arguing, that's what we did.

I sat on the end of one of the empty rows of seats and waited for the tide of woe to recede, and when I had more command of things I went across to the desk and explained what had happened.

The woman behind the reception window was horrified.

"Someone stole your plastic bag!" she said, round-eyed. "I mean, everyone around here knows what those bags signify, they're always used for the belongings of people who've died or come here after accidents. I mean, everyone knows they can contain wallets and jewelry and so on, but I've never heard of one being snatched. How awful! How much did you lose? You'd better report it to the police."

The futility of it shook me with weariness. Some punk had taken a chance that the dead man's effects would be worth the risk, and the police would take notes and chalk it up among the majority of unsolved muggings. I reckoned I'd fallen into the ultravulnerable bracket which included little old ladies, and however much I might wince at the thought, I on my crutches had looked and been a pushover, literally.

I shuffled painfully into the washroom and ran cold water over my slowly bleeding hand, and found that the cut was more wide than deep and could sensibly be classified as a scratch. With a sigh I dabbed a paper towel on the scarletly oozing spots and unwound the cut-off pieces of white and brown plastic which were still wrapped tightly round my wrist, throwing them into the bin. What a bloody stupid anticlimactic postscript, I thought tiredly, to the accident that had taken my brother.

When I went outside Brad said with a certain amount of anxiety, "You going to the police, then?" and he relaxed visibly when I shook my head and said, "Not unless you can give them a detailed description of whoever attacked me."

I couldn't tell from his expression whether he could or not. I thought I might ask him later, on the way home, but when I did, all that he said was, "He had jeans on, and one of them woolly hats. And he had a knife. I didn't see his face, he sort of had his back turned my way, but the sun flashed on the knife, see? It all went down so fast. I did think you were a goner. Then he ran off with the bag. You were dead lucky, I'd say."

I didn't feel lucky, but all things were relative.

Brad, having contributed what was for him a long speech, relapsed into his more normal silence, and I wondered what the mugger would think of the worthless haul of shoes, socks, handkerchief and jacket whose loss hadn't been realistically worth reporting. Whatever of value Greville had set out with would have been in his wallet, which had fallen to an earlier predator.

I had been wearing, was still wearing, a shirt, tie and sweater, but no jacket. A sweater was better with the crutches than a jacket. It was pointless to wonder whether the thief would have dipped into my trousers pockets if Brad hadn't shouted. Pointless to wonder if he would have put his blade through my ribs. There was no way of knowing. I did know I couldn't have stopped him, but his prize in any case would have been meager. Apart from Greville's things I was carrying only a credit card and a few bills in a small wallet, from a habit of traveling light.

I stopped thinking about it and instead, to take my mind off the ankle, wondered what Greville had been doing in Ipswich. Wondered if, ever since Friday, anyone had been waiting for him to arrive. Wondered how he had got there. Wondered if he had parked his car somewhere there and, if so, how I would find it, considering I didn't know its license plate number and wasn't even sure if he still had a Porsche. Someone else would know, I thought easily. His office, his local garage, a friend. It wasn't really my worry.

By the time we reached Hungerford three hours later, Brad had said, in addition, only that the car was running out of juice (which we remedied) and, half an hour from home, that if I wanted him to go on driving me during the following week, he would be willing.

"Seven-thirty tomorrow morning?" I suggested, reflecting, and he said "Yerss" on a growl which I took to mean assent.

He drove me to my door, helped me out as before, handed me the crutches, locked the car and put the keys into my hand, all without speaking.

"Thanks," I said.

He ducked his head, not meeting my eyes, and turned and shambled off on foot toward his mother's house. I watched him go; a shy difficult man with no social skills who had possibly that morning saved my life.

2

I had for three years rented the ground floor of an old house in a turning off the main road running through the ancient country town. There was a bedroom and bathroom facing the street and the sunrise, and a large all-purpose room to the rear into which sunset flooded. Beyond that, a small stream-bordered garden, which I shared with the owners of the house, an elderly couple upstairs.

Brad's mother had cooked and cleaned for them for years; Brad mended, painted and chopped when he felt like it. Soon after I'd moved in, mother and son had casually extended their services to me, which suited me well. It was all in all an easy uncluttered existence, but if home was where the heart was, I really lived out on the windy Downs and in stable yards and on the raucous racetracks where I worked.

I let myself into the quiet rooms and sat on the sofa with icepacks along my leg, watching the sun go down on the far side of the stream and thinking I might have done better to stay in the Ipswich hospital. From the knee down my left leg was hurting abominably, and it was still getting clearer by the minute that falling had intensified Thursday's damage disastrously. My own surgeon had been going off to Wales for the weekend, but I doubted that he would have done very much except say "I told you so," so in the end I simply took another Distalgesic and changed the icepacks and worked out the time zones in Tokyo and Sydney.

At midnight I telephoned to those cities where it was already morning and by good luck reached both of the sisters. "Poor Greville," they said sadly, and, "Do whatever you think best." "Send some flowers for us." "Let us know how it goes."

I would, I said. Poor Greville, they repeated, meaning it, and said they would love to see me in Tokyo, in Sydney, whenever. Their children, they said, were all fine. Their husbands were fine. Was I fine? Poor, poor Greville.

I put the receiver down ruefully. Families did scatter, and some scattered more than most. I knew the sisters by that time only through the photographs they sometimes sent at Christmas. They hadn't recognized my voice.

Taking things slowly in the morning, as nothing was much better, I dressed for the day in shirt, tie and sweater as before, with a shoe on the right foot, sock alone on the left, and was ready when Brad arrived five minutes early.

"We're going to London," I said. "Here's a map with the place marked. Do you think you can find it?"

"Got a tongue in my head," he said, peering at the maze of roads. "Reckon so."

"Give it a go, then."

He nodded, helped me inch onto the back seat, and drove seventy miles through the heavy morning traffic in silence. Then, by dint of shouting at street vendors via the driver's window, he zig-zagged across Holborn, took a couple of wrong turns, righted himself, and drew up with a jerk in a busy street round the corner from Hatton Garden.

"That's it," he said, pointing. "Number fifty-six. That office block."

"Brilliant."

He helped me out, gave me the crutches, and came with me to hold open the heavy glass entrance door. Inside, behind a desk, was a man in a peaked cap personifying security who asked me forbiddingly what floor I wanted.

"Saxony Franklin," I said.

"Name?" he asked, consulting a list.

"Franklin."

"Your name, I mean."

I explained who I was. He raised his eyebrows, picked up a telephone, pressed a button and said "A Mr. Franklin is on his way up."

Brad asked where he could park the car and was told there was a yard round the back. He would wait for me, he said. No hurry. No problem.

The office building, which was modern, had been built rubbing shoulders to the sixth floor with Victorian curlicued neighbors, soaring free to the tenth with a severe lot of glass.

Saxony Franklin was on the eighth floor, it appeared. I went up in a smooth elevator and elbowed my way through some heavy double doors into a lobby furnished with a reception desk, several armchairs for waiting in and two policemen.

Behind the policemen was a middle-aged woman who looked definitely flustered.

I thought immediately that news of Greville's death had already arrived and that I probably hadn't needed to come, but it seemed the Force was there for a different reason entirely.

The flustered lady gave me a blank stare and said, "That's not Mr. Franklin. The guard said Mr. Franklin was on his way up."

I allayed the police suspicions a little by saying again that I was Greville Franklin's brother.

"Oh," said the woman. "Yes, he does have a brother."

They all swept their gaze over my comparative immobility.

"Mr. Franklin isn't here yet," the woman told me.

"Er . . ." I said, "what's going on?"

They all looked disinclined to explain. I said to her, "I'm afraid I don't know your name."

"Adams," she said distractedly. "Annette Adams. I'm your brother's personal assistant."

"I'm sorry," I said slowly, "but my brother won't be coming at all today. He was involved in an accident."

Annette Adams heard the bad news in my voice. She put a

[27]

hand over her heart in the classic gesture as if to hold it still in her chest and with anxiety said, "What sort of accident? A car crash? Is he hurt?"

She saw the answer clearly in my expression and with her free hand felt for one of the armchairs, buckling into it with shock.

"He died in hospital yesterday morning," I said to her and to the policemen, "after some scaffolding fell on him last Friday. I was with him in the hospital."

One of the policemen pointed at my dangling foot. "You were injured at the same time, sir?"

"No. This was different. I didn't see his accident. I meant, I was there when he died. The hospital sent for me."

The two policemen consulted each other's eyes and decided after all to say why they were there.

"These offices were broken into during the weekend, sir. Mrs. Adams here discovered it when she arrived early for work, and she called us in."

"What does it matter? It doesn't matter now," the lady said, growing paler.

"There's a good deal of mess," the policeman went on, "but Mrs. Adams doesn't know what's been stolen. We were waiting for your brother to tell us."

"Oh dear, oh dear," said Annette, gulping.

"Is there anyone else here?" I asked her. "Someone who could get you a cup of tea?" Before you faint, I thought, but didn't say it.

She nodded a fraction, glancing at a door behind the desk, and I swung over there and tried to open it. It wouldn't open: the knob wouldn't turn.

"It's electronic," Annette said weakly. "You have to put in the right numbers . . ." She flopped her head back against the chair and said she couldn't remember what today's number was; it was changed often. She and the policemen had come through it, it seemed, and let it swing shut behind them.

One of the policemen came over and pounded on the door

with his fist, shouting "Police" very positively, which had the desired effect like a reflex. Without finesse he told the much younger woman who stood there framed in the doorway that her boss was dead and that Mrs. Adams was about to pass out and was needing some strong hot sweet tea, love, like five minutes ago.

Wild-eyed, the young woman retreated to spread more consternation behind the scenes and the policeman nullified the firm's defenses by wedging the electronic door open, using the chair from behind the reception desk.

I took in a few more details of the surroundings, beyond my first impression of gray. On the light greenish-gray of the carpet stood the armchairs in charcoal and the desk in matt black unpainted and unpolished wood. The walls, palest gray, were hung with a series of framed geological maps, the frames black and narrow and uniform in size. The propped-open door, and another similar door to one side, still closed, were painted the same color as the walls. The total effect, lit by recessed spotlights in the ceiling, looked both straightforward and immensely sophisticated, a true representation of my brother.

Mrs. Annette Adams, still flaccid from too many unpleasant surprises on a Monday morning, wore a cream shirt, a charcoal-gray skirt and a string of knobbly pearls. She was dark-haired, in her late forties, perhaps, and from the starkness in her eyes, just beginning to realize, I guessed, that the upheaval of the present would be permanent.

The younger woman returned effectively with a scarlet steaming mug and Annette Adams sipped from it obediently for a while, listening to the policemen telling me that the intruder had not come in this way up the front elevator, which was for visitors, but up another elevator at the rear of the building which was used by the staff of all floors of offices, and for freight. That elevator went down into a rear lobby which, in its turn, led out to the yard where cars and vans were parked: where Brad was presumably waiting at that moment.

The intruder had apparently ridden to the tenth floor, climbed some service stairs to the roof, and by some means had come down outside the building to the eighth floor, where he had smashed a window to let himself in.

"What sort of means?" I asked.

"We don't know, sir. Whatever it was, he took it with him. Maybe a rope." He shrugged. "We've had only a quick preliminary look around up there. We wanted to know what's been stolen before we . . . er . . . See, we don't want to waste our time for nothing."

I nodded. Like Greville's stolen shoes, I thought.

"This whole area round Hatton Garden is packed with the jewel trade. We get break-ins, or attempted break-ins, all the time."

The other policeman said, "This place here is loaded with stones, of course, but the vault's still shut and Mrs. Adams says nothing seems to be missing from the other stockrooms. Only Mr. Franklin has a key to the vault, which is where their more valuable faceted stones are kept."

Mr. Franklin had no keys at all. Mr. Franklin's keys were in my own pocket. There was no harm, I supposed, in producing them.

The sight of what must have been a familiar bunch brought tears to Annette Adams's eyes. She put down the mug, searched around for a tissue and cried, "He really is dead, then," as if she hadn't thoroughly believed it before.

When she'd recovered a little I asked her to point out the vault key, which proved to be the longest and slenderest of the lot, and shortly afterward we were all walking through the propped-open door and down a central corridor with spacious offices opening to either side. Faces showing shock looked out at our passing. We stopped at an ordinary-looking door which might have been mistaken for a closet but certainly looked nothing like a vault.

"That's it," Annette Adams insisted, nodding; so I slid the narrow key into the small ordinary keyhole, and found that it turned unexpectedly counterclockwise. The thick and heavy door swung inward to the right under pressure and a light came on automatically, shining in what did indeed seem exactly like a large walk-in closet, with rows of white cardboard boxes on several plain white-painted shelves stretching away along the left-hand wall.

Everyone looked in silence. Nothing seemed to have been disturbed.

"Who knows what should be in the boxes?" I asked, and got the expected answer: my brother.

I took a step into the vault and took the lid off one of the nearest boxes, which bore a sticky label saying $MgAl_2O_4$, Burma. Inside the box there were about a dozen glossy white envelopes, each taking up the whole width. I lifted one out to open it.

"Be careful!" Annette Adams exclaimed, fearful of my clumsiness as I balanced on the crutches. "The packets unfold."

I handed to her the one I held, and she unfolded it carefully on the palm of her hand. Inside, cushioned by white tissue, lay two large red translucent stones, cut and polished, oblong in shape, almost pulsing with intense color under the lights.

"Are they rubies?" I asked, impressed.

Annette Adams smiled indulgently. "No, they're spinel. Very fine specimens. We rarely deal in rubies."

"Are there any diamonds in here?" one of the policemen asked.

"No, we don't deal in diamonds. Almost never."

I asked her to look into some of the other boxes, which she did, first carefully folding the two red stones into their packet and restoring them to their right place. We watched her stretch and bend, tipping up random lids on several shelves to take out a white packet here and there for inspection, but there were clearly no dismaying surprises, and at the end she shook her head and said that nothing at all was missing, as far as she could see.

[31]

"The real value of these stones is in quantity," she said. "Each individual stone isn't worth a fortune. We sell stones in tens and hundreds . . ." Her voice trailed off into a sort of forlornness. "I don't know what to do," she said, "about the orders."

The policemen weren't affected by the problem. If nothing was missing, they had other burglaries to look into, and they would put in a report, but goodbye for now, or words to that effect.

When they'd gone, Annette Adams and I stood in the passage and looked at each other.

"What do I do?" she said. "Are we still in business?"

I didn't like to tell her that I hadn't the foggiest notion. I said, "Did Greville have an office?"

"That's where most of the mess is," she said, turning away and retracing her steps to a large corner room near the entrance lobby. "In here."

I followed her and saw what she meant about mess. The contents of every wide-open drawer seemed to be out on the floor, most of it paper. Pictures had been removed from the walls and dropped. One filing cabinet lay on its side like a fallen soldier. The desk top was a shambles.

"The police said the burglar was looking behind the pictures for a safe. But there isn't one . . . just the vault." She sighed unhappily. "It's all so pointless."

I looked around. "How many people work here altogether?" I said.

"Six of us. And Mr. Franklin, of course." She swallowed. "Oh, dear."

"Mm," I agreed. "Is there anywhere I can meet everyone?"

She nodded mutely and led the way into another large office where three of the others were already gathered, wide-eyed and rudderless. Another two came when called; four women and two men, all worried and uncertain and looking to me for decisions.

Greville, I perceived, hadn't chosen potential leaders to

work around him. Annette Adams herself was no aggressive waiting-in-the-wings manager but a true second-in-command, skilled at carrying out orders, incapable of initiating them. Not so good, all things considered.

I introduced myself and described what had happened to Greville.

They had liked him, I was glad to see. There were tears on his behalf. I said that I needed their help because there were people I ought to notify about his death, like his lawyer and his accountant, for instance, and his closest friends, and I didn't know who they were. I would like, I said, to make a list, and sat beside one of the desks, arming myself with paper and pen.

Annette said she would fetch Greville's address book from his office but after a while returned in frustration: in all the mess she couldn't find it.

"There must be other records," I said. "What about that computer?" I pointed across the room. "Do you have addresses in that?"

The girl who had brought the tea brightened a good deal and informed me that this was the stock control room, and the computer in question was programmed to record "stock in," "stock out," statements, invoices and accounts. But, she said encouragingly, in her other domain across the corridor there was another computer which she used for letters. She was out of the door by the end of the sentence and Annette remarked that June was a whirlwind always.

June, blonde, long-legged, flat-chested, came back with a fast print-out of Greville's ten most frequent correspondents (ignoring customers), which included not only the lawyers and the accountants but also the bank, a stockbroker and an insurance company.

"Terrific," I said. "Can you now get through to the big credit card companies, and see if Greville was a customer of theirs and say his cards have been stolen, and he's dead."

I then asked if any of them knew the make and number of

Greville's car. They all did. It seemed they saw it every day in the yard. He came to work in a ten-year-old Rover 3500 without radio or cassette player because the Porsche he'd owned before had been broken into twice and finally stolen altogether.

"That old car's still bursting with gadgets, though," the younger of the two men said, "but he keeps them all locked in the trunk."

Greville had always been a sucker for gadgets, full of enthusiasm for the latest fidgety way of performing an ordinary task. He'd told me more about those toys of his, when we'd met, than ever about his own human relationships.

"Why did you ask about his car?" the young man said. He had rows of badges attached to a black leather jacket and orange spiky hair set with gel. A need to prove he existed, I supposed.

"It may be outside his front door," I said. "Or it may be parked somewhere in Ipswich."

"Yeah," he said thoughtfully. "See what you mean."

The telephone rang on the desk beside me, and Annette after a moment's hesitation came and picked up the receiver. She listened with a worried expression and then, covering the mouthpiece, asked me, "What shall I do? It's a customer who wants to give an order."

"Have you got what he wants?" I asked.

"Yes, we're sure to have."

"Then say it's OK."

"But do I tell him about Mr. Franklin?"

"No," I said instinctively, "just take the order."

She seemed glad of the direction and wrote down the list, and when she'd disconnected I suggested to them all that for that day at least they should take and send out orders in the normal way, and just say if asked that Mr. Franklin was out of the office and couldn't be reached. We wouldn't start telling people he was dead until after I'd talked to his lawyers, accountants, bank and the rest, and found out our legal position. They were relieved and agreed without demur, and the older man asked if I would soon get the broken window fixed, as it was in the packing and dispatch room, where he worked.

With a feeling of being sucked feet first into quicksand I said I would try. I felt I didn't belong in that place or in those people's lives, and all I knew about the jewelry business was where to find two red stones in a box marked $MgAl_2O_4$, Burma.

At the fourth try among the Yellow Pages I got a promise of instant action on the window and after that, with office procedure beginning to tick over again all around me, I put a call through to the lawyers.

They were grave, they were sympathetic, they were at my service. I asked if by any chance Greville had made a will, as specifically I wanted to know if he had left any instructions about cremation or burial, and if he hadn't, did they know of anyone I should consult, or should I make whatever arrangements I thought best.

There was a certain amount of clearing of throats and a promise to look up files and call back, and they kept their word almost immediately, to my surprise.

My brother had indeed left a will: they had drawn it up for him themselves three years earlier. They couldn't swear it was his *last* will, but it was the only one they had. They had consulted it. Greville, they said, pedantically, had expressed no preference as to the disposal of his remains.

"Shall I just . . . go ahead, then?"

"Certainly," they said. "You are in fact named as your brother's sole executor. It is your duty to make the decisions."

Hell, I thought, and I asked for a list of the beneficiaries so that I could notify them of the death and invite them to the funeral.

After a pause they said they didn't normally give out that information on the telephone. Could I not come to their office? It was just across the City, at Temple.

[35]

"I've broken an ankle," I said, apologetically. "It takes me all my time to cross the room."

Dear, dear, they said. They consulted among themselves in guarded whispers and finally said they supposed there was no harm in my knowing. Greville's will was extremely simple; he had left everything he possessed to Derek Saxony Franklin, his brother. To my good self, in fact.

"What?" I said stupidly. "He can't have."

He had written his will in a hurry, they said, because he had been flying off to a dangerous country to buy stones. He had been persuaded by the lawyers not to go intestate, and he had given in to them, and as far as they knew, that was the only will he ever made.

"He can't have meant it to be his last," I said blankly.

Perhaps not, they agreed: few men in good health expected to die at fifty-three. They then discussed probate procedures discreetly and asked for my instructions, and I felt the quicksand rising above my knees.

"Is it legal," I asked, "for this business to go on running, for the time being?"

They saw no impediment in law. Subject to probate, and in the absence of any later will, the business would be mine. If I wanted to sell it in due course, it would be in my own interest to keep it running. As my brother's executor it would also be my duty to do my best for the estate. An interesting situation, they said with humor.

Not wholeheartedly appreciating the subtlety, I asked how long probate would take.

Always difficult to forecast, was the answer. Anything between six months or two years, depending on the complexity of Greville's affairs.

"Two years!"

More probably six months, they murmured soothingly. The speed would depend on the accountants and the Inland Revenue, who could seldom be hurried. It was in the lap of the gods.

I mentioned that there might be work to do over claiming damages for the accident. Happy to see to it, they said, and promised to contact the Ipswich police. Meanwhile, good luck.

I put the receiver down in sinking dismay. This business, like any other, might run on its own impetus for two weeks, maybe even for four, but after that . . . After that I would be back on horses, trying to get fit again to race.

I would have to get a manager, I thought vaguely, and had no idea where to start looking. Annette Adams with furrows of anxiety across her forehead asked if it would be all right to begin clearing up Mr. Franklin's office, and I said yes, and thought that her lack of drive could sink the ship.

Please would someone, I asked the world in general, mind going down to the yard and telling the man in my car that I wouldn't be leaving for two or three hours; and June with her bright face whisked out of the door again and soon returned to relate that my man would lock the car, go on foot for lunch, and be back in good time to wait for me.

"Did he say all that?" I asked curiously.

June laughed. "Actually he said, 'Right. Bite to eat,' and off he stomped."

She asked if I would like her to bring me a sandwich when she went out for her own lunch and, surprised and grateful, I accepted.

"Your foot hurts, doesn't it?" she said judiciously.

"Mm."

"You should put it up on a chair."

She fetched one without ado and placed it in front of me, watching with a motherly air of approval as I lifted my leg into place. She must have been all of twenty, I thought.

A telephone rang beside the computer on the far side of the room and she went to answer it.

"Yes, sir, we have everything in stock. Yes, sir, what size and how many? A hundred twelve-by-ten-millimeter ovals . . . yes . . . yes . . . yes."

She tapped the lengthy order rapidly straight onto the computer, not writing in longhand as Annette had done.

"Yes, sir, they will go off today. Usual terms, sir, of course." She put the phone down, printed a copy of the order and laid it in a shallow wire tray. A fax machine simultaneously clicked on and whined away and switched off with little shrieks, and she tore off the emergent sheet and tapped its information also into the computer, making a print-out and putting it into the tray.

"Do you fill all the orders the day they come in?" I asked.

"Oh, sure, if we can. Within twenty-four hours without fail. Mr. Franklin says speed is the essence of good business. I've known him to stay here all evening by himself packing parcels when we're swamped."

She remembered with a rush that he would never come back. It did take a bit of getting used to. Tears welled in her uncontrollably as they had earlier, and she stared at me through them, which made her blue eyes look huge.

"You couldn't help liking him," she said. "Working with him, I mean."

I felt almost jealous that she'd known Greville better than I had; yet I could have known him better if I'd tried. Regret stabbed in again, a needle of grief.

Annette came to announce that Mr. Franklin's room was at least partially clear, so I transferred myself into there to make more phone calls in comparative privacy. I sat in Greville's black leather swiveling chunk of luxury and put my foot on the typist's chair June carried in after me, and I surveyed the opulent carpet, deep armchairs and framed maps as in the lobby, and smoothed a hand over the grainy black expanse of the oversized desk, and felt like a jockey, not a tycoon.

Annette had picked up from the floor and assembled at one end of the desk some of the army of gadgets, most of them matt black and small, as if miniaturization were part of the attraction. Easily identifiable at a glance were battery-operated things like pencil sharpener, hand-held copier, printing calculator, dictionary-thesaurus, but most needed investigation. I stretched out a hand to the nearest and found that it was a casing with a dial face, plus a head like a microphone on a lead.

"What's this?" I asked Annette, who was picking up a stack of paper from the far reaches of the floor. "Some sort of meter?"

She flashed a look at it. "A Geiger counter," she said matter-of-factly, as if everyone kept a Geiger counter routinely among their pens and pencils.

I flipped the switch from off to on, but apart from a couple of clicks, nothing happened.

Annette paused, sitting back on her heels as she knelt among the remaining clutter.

"A lot of stones change color for the better under gamma radiation," she said. "They're not radioactive afterward, but Mr. Franklin was once accidentally sent a batch of topaz from Brazil that had been irradiated in a nuclear reactor and the stones were bordering on dangerous. A hundred of them. There was a terrible lot of trouble because apart from being unsalable they had come in without a radioactivity import license, or something like that, but it wasn't Mr. Franklin's fault, of course. But he got the Geiger counter then." She paused. "He has an amazing flair for stones, you know. He just felt there was something wrong with that topaz. Such a beautiful deep blue they'd made it, when it must have been almost colorless to begin with. So he sent a few of them to a lab for testing." She paused again. "He'd just been reading about some old diamonds that had been exposed to radium and turned green, and were as radioactive as anything . . ."

Her face crumpled and she blinked her eyes rapidly, turning away from me and looking down to the floor so that I shouldn't see her distress. She made a great fuss among the papers and finally, with a sniff or two, said indistinctly, "Here's his desk diary," and then, more slowly, "That's odd."

"What's odd?"

"October's missing."

She stood up and brought me the desk diary, which proved to be a largish appointments calendar showing a month at a glance. The month on current display was November, with a few of the daily spaces filled in but most of them empty. I flipped back the page and came next to September.

"I expect October's still on the floor, torn off," I said.

She shook her head doubtfully, and in fact couldn't find it.

"Has the address book turned up?" I asked.

"No." She was puzzled. "It hasn't."

"Is anything else missing?"

"I'm not really sure."

It seemed bizarre that anyone should risk breaking in via the roof simply to steal an address book and a page from a desk diary. Something else had to be missing.

The Yellow Pages glaziers arrived at that point, putting a stop to my speculation. I went along with them to the packing room and saw the efficient hole that had been smashed in the six-by-four-foot window. All the glass that must have been scattered over every surface had been collected and swept into a pile of dagger-sharp glittering triangles, and a chill little breeze ruffled papers in clipboards.

"You don't break glass this quality by tapping it with a fingernail," one of the workmen said knowledgeably, picking up a piece. "They must have swung a weight against it, like a wrecking ball."

3

WHILE the workmen measured the window frame I watched the oldest of Greville's employees take transparent bags of beads from one cardboard box, insert them into bubble-plastic sleeves and stack them in another brown cardboard box. When all was transferred he put a list of contents on top, crossed the flaps and stuck the whole box around with wide reinforced tape.

"Where do the beads come from?" I asked.

"Taiwan, I daresay," he said briefly, fixing a large address label on the top.

"No . . . I meant, where do you keep them here?"

He looked at me in pitying astonishment, a white-haired grandfatherly figure in storemen's brown overalls. "In the stockrooms, of course."

"Of course."

"Down the hall," he said.

I went back to Greville's office and in the interests of good public relations asked Annette if she would show me the stockrooms. Her heavyish face lightened with pleasure and she led the way to the far end of the corridor.

"In here," she said with obvious pride, passing through a central doorway into a small inner lobby, "there are four rooms." She pointed through open doorways. "In there, mineral cabochons, oval and round; in there, beads; in there, oddities, and in there, organics."

"What are organics?" I asked.

She beckoned me forward into the room in question, and I walked into a windowless space lined from floor to shoulder height with column after column of narrow gray metal drawers, each presenting a face to the world of about the size of a side of a shoe box. Each drawer, above a handle, bore a label identifying what it contained.

"Organics are things that grow," Annette said patiently, and I reflected I should have worked that out for myself. "Coral, for instance." She pulled open a nearby drawer which proved to extend lengthily backward, and showed me the contents: clear plastic bags, each packed with many strings of bright red twiglets. "Italian," she said. "The best coral comes from the Mediterranean." She closed that drawer, walked a few paces, pulled open another. "Abalone, from abalone shells." Another: "Ivory. We still have a little, but we can't sell it now." Another: "Mother of pearl. We sell tons of it." "Pink mussel." "Freshwater pearls." Finally, "Imitation pearls. Cultured pearls are in the vault."

Everything, it seemed, came in dozens of shapes and sizes. Annette smiled at my bemused expression and invited me into the room next door.

Floor-to-shoulder-height metal drawers, as before, not only lining the walls this time but filling the center space with aisles, as in a supermarket.

"Cabochons, for setting into rings, and so on," Annette said. "They're in alphabetical order."

Amethyst to turquoise via garnet, jade, lapis lazuli and onyx, with dozens of others I'd only half heard of. "Semiprecious," Annette said briefly. "All genuine stones. Mr. Franklin doesn't touch glass or plastic." She stopped abruptly. Let five seconds lengthen. "He didn't touch them," she said lamely.

His presence was there strongly, I felt. It was almost as if he would walk through the door, all energy, saying "Hello, Derek, what brings you here?" and if he seemed alive to me, who had seen him dead, how much more physical he must still be to Annette and June.

And to Lily too, I supposed. Lily was in the third stockroom pushing a brown cardboard box around on a thing like a tea cart, collecting bags of strings of beads and checking them against a list. With her center-parted hair drawn back into a slide at her neck, with her small pale mouth and rounded cheeks, Lily looked like a Charlotte Brontë governess and dressed as if immolation were her personal choice. The sort to love the master in painful silence, I thought, and wondered what she'd felt for Greville.

Whatever it was, she wasn't letting it show. She raised downcast eyes briefly to my face and at Annette's prompting told me she was putting together a consignment of rhodonite, jasper, aventurine and tiger eye, for one of the largest firms of jewelry manufacturers.

"We import the stones," Annette said. "We're wholesalers. We sell to about three thousand jewelers, maybe more. Some are big businesses. Many are small ones. We're at the top of the semiprecious trade. Highly regarded." She swallowed. "People trust us."

Greville, I knew, had traveled the world to buy the stones. When we'd met he'd often been on the point of departing for Arizona or Hong Kong or had just returned from Israel, but he'd never told me more than the destinations. I at last understood what he'd been doing, and realized he couldn't easily be replaced.

Depressed, I went back to his office and telephoned to his accountant and his bank.

They were shocked and they were helpful, impressively so. The bank manager said I would need to call on him in the morning, but Saxony Franklin, as a limited company, could go straight on functioning. I could take over without trouble. All he would want was confirmation from my brother's lawyers that his will was as I said.

"Thank you very much," I said, slightly surprised, and he

told me warmly he was glad to be of service. Greville's affairs,
I thought with a smile, must be amazingly healthy.

To the insurance company, also, my brother's death
seemed scarcely a hiccup. A limited company's insurance
went marching steadily on, it seemed: it was the company that
was insured, not my brother. I said I would like to claim for
a smashed window. No problem. They would send a form.

After that I telephoned to the Ipswich undertakers who had
been engaged to remove Greville's body from the hospital,
and arranged that he should be cremated. They said they had
"a slot" at two o'clock on Friday: would that do? "Yes," I said,
sighing, "I'll be there." They gave me the address of the
crematorium in a hushed obsequious voice, and I wondered
what it must be like to do business always with the bereaved.
Happier by far to sell glittering baubles to the living or to ride
jump-racing horses at thirty miles an hour, win, lose or break
your bones.

I made yet another phone call, this time to the orthopedic
surgeon, and as usual came up against the barrier of his recep-
tionist. He wasn't in his own private consulting rooms, she
announced, but at the hospital.

I said, "Could you ask him to leave me a prescription somewhere, because I've fallen on my ankle and twisted it, and I'm
running out of Distalgesic."

"Hold on," she said, and I held until she returned. "I've
spoken to him," she said. "He'll be back here later. He says
can you be here at five?"

I said gratefully that I could, and reckoned that I'd have to
leave soon after two-thirty to be sure of making it. I told
Annette, and asked what they did about locking up.

"Mr. Franklin usually gets here first and leaves last." She
stopped, confused. "I mean . . ."

"I know," I said. "It's all right. I think of him in the present
tense too. So go on."

"Well, the double front doors bolt on the inside. Then the
door from the lobby to the offices has an electronic bolt, as

you know. So does the door from the corridor to the stock-rooms. So does the rear door, where we all come in and out. Mr. Franklin changes . . . changed . . . the numbers at least every week. And there's another electronic lock, of course, on the door from the lobby to the showroom, and from the corridor into the showroom . . ." She paused. "It does seem a lot, I know, but the electronic locks are very simple, really. You only have to remember three digits. Last Friday they were five, three, two. They're easy to work. Mr. Franklin installed them so that we shouldn't have too many keys lying around. He and I both have a key, though, that will unlock all the electronic locks manually, if we need to."

"So you've remembered the numbers?" I asked.

"Oh, yes. It was just, this morning, with everything . . . they went out of my head."

"And the vault," I said. "Does that have any electronics?"

"No, but it has an intricate locking system in that heavy door, though it looks so simple from the outside. Mr. Franklin always locks . . . locked . . . the vault before he left. When he went away on long trips, he made the key available to me."

I wondered fleetingly about that awkward phrase, but didn't pursue it. I asked her instead about the showroom, which I hadn't seen and, again with pride, she went into the corridor, programmed a shining brass doorknob with the open sesame numbers, and ushered me into a windowed room that looked much like a shop, with glass-topped display counters and the firm's overall ambience of wealth.

Annette switched on powerful lights and the place came to life. She moved contentedly behind the counters, pointing out to me the contents now bright with illumination.

"In here are examples of everything we stock, except not all the sizes, of course, and not the faceted stones in the vault. We don't really use the showroom a great deal, only for new customers mostly, but I like being in here. I love the stones. They're fascinating. Mr. Franklin says stones are the only things the human race takes from the earth and makes more beautiful." She lifted a face heavy with loss. "What will happen without him?"

"I don't know yet," I said, "but in the short term we fill the orders and dispatch them, and order more stock from where you usually get it. We keep to all the old routines and practices. OK?"

She nodded, relieved at least for the present.

"Except," I added, "that it will be you who arrives first and leaves last, if you don't mind."

"That's all right. I always do when Mr. Franklin's away."

We stared briefly at each other, not putting words to the obvious, then she switched off the showroom lights almost as if it were a symbolic act, and as we left pulled the self-locking door shut behind us.

Back in Greville's office I wrote down for her my own address and telephone number, and said that if she felt insecure, or wanted to talk, I would be at home all evening.

"I'll come back here tomorrow morning, after I've seen the bank manager," I said. "Will you be all right until then?"

She nodded shakily. "What do we call you? We can't call you Mr. Franklin, it wouldn't seem right."

"How about Derek?"

"Oh no." She was instinctively against it. "Would you mind, say . . . Mr. Derek?"

"If you prefer it." It sounded quaintly old-fashioned to me, but she was happy with it and said she would tell the others.

"About the others," I said, "sort everyone out for me, with their jobs. There's you, June, Lily . . ."

"June works the computers and the stock control," she said. "Lily fills the orders. Tina, she's a general assistant, she helps Lily and does some of the secretarial work. So does June. So do I, actually. We all do what's needed, really. There are few hard and fast divisions. Except that Alfie doesn't do much except pack up the orders. It takes him all his time."

"And that younger guy with the spiky orange halo?"

"Jason? Don't worry about the hair, he's harmless. He's our

muscles. The stones are very heavy in bulk, you know. Jason shifts boxes, fills the stockrooms, does odd jobs and vacuums the carpets. He helps Alfie sometimes, or Lily, if we're busy. Like I said, we all do anything, whatever's needed. Mr. Franklin has never let anyone mark out a territory."

"His words?"

"Yes, of course."

Collective responsibility, I thought. I bowed to my brother's wisdom. If it worked, it worked. And from the look of everything in the place, it did indeed work, and I wouldn't disturb it.

I closed and locked the vault door with Greville's key and asked Annette which of his large bunch overrode the electronic locks. That one, she said, pointing, separating it.

"What are all the others, do you know?"

She looked blank. "I've no idea."

Car, house, whatever. I supposed I might eventually sort them out. I gave her what I hoped was a reassuring smile, sketched a goodbye to some of the others and rode down in the service elevator to find Brad out in the yard.

"Swindon," I said. "The medical center where we were on Friday. Would you mind?"

" 'Course not." Positively radiant, I thought.

It was an eighty-mile journey, ten miles beyond home. Brad managed it without further communication and I spent the time thinking of all the things I hadn't yet done, like seeing to Greville's house and stopping delivery of his daily paper, wherever it might come from, and telling the post office to divert his letters. . . . To hell with it, I thought wearily. Why did the damned man have to die?

The orthopedist X-rayed and unwrapped my ankle and tut-tutted. From toes to shin it looked hard, black and swollen, the skin almost shiny from the stretching.

"I advised you to rest it," he said, a touch crossly.

"My brother died . . ." I explained about the mugging, and also about having to see to Greville's affairs.

He listened carefully, a strong sensible man with prematurely white hair. I didn't know a jockey who didn't trust him. He understood our needs and our imperatives, because he treated a good many of us who lived in or near the training center of Lambourn.

"As I told you the other day," he said when I'd finished, "you've fractured the lower end of the fibula, and where the tibia and fibula should be joined, they've sprung apart. Today, they are further apart. They're now providing no support at all for the talus, the heel bone. You've now completely ripped the lateral ligament which normally binds the ankle together. The whole joint is insecure and coming apart inside, like a mortise joint in a piece of furniture when the glue's given way."

"So how long will it take?" I said.

He smiled briefly. "In a crepe bandage it will hurt for about another ten days, and after that you can walk on it. You could be back on a horse in three weeks from now, if you don't mind the stirrup hurting you, which it will. About another three weeks after that, the ankle might be strong enough for racing."

"Good," I said, relieved. "Not much worse than before, then."

"It's worse, but it won't take much longer to mend."

"Fine."

He looked down at the depressing sight. "If you're going to be doing all this traveling about, you'd be much more comfortable in a rigid cast. You could put your weight on it in a couple of days. You'd have almost no pain."

"And wear it for six weeks? And get atrophied muscles?"

"Atrophy is a strong word." He knew all the same that jump jockeys needed strong leg muscles above all else, and the way to keep them strong was to keep them moving. Inside plaster they couldn't move at all and weakened rapidly. If movement cost a few twinges, it was worth it.

"Delta-cast is lightweight," he said persuasively. "It's a polymer, not like the old plaster of paris. It's porous, so air circulates and you don't get skin problems. It's good. And I could make you a cast with a zip in it so you could take it off for physiotherapy."

"How long before I was racing?"

"Nine or ten weeks."

I didn't say anything for a moment or two and he looked up fast, his eyes bright and quizzical.

"A cast, then?" he said.

"No."

He smiled and picked up a roll of crepe bandage. "Don't fall on it again in the next month, or you'll be back to square one."

"I'll try not to."

He bandaged it all tight again from just below the knee down to my toes and back, and gave me another prescription for Distalgesic. "No more than eight tablets in twenty-four hours and not with alcohol." He said it every time.

"Right."

He considered me thoughtfully for a moment and then rose and went over to a cabinet where he kept packets and bottles of drugs. He came back tucking a small plastic bag into an envelope which he held out to me.

"I'm giving you something known as DF 118s. Rather appropriate, as they're your own initials! I've given you three of them. They are serious painkillers, and I don't want you to use them unless something like yesterday happens again."

"OK," I said, putting the envelope into my pocket. "Thanks."

"If you take one, you won't feel a thing." He smiled. "If you take two at once, you'll be spaced out, high as a kite. If you take all three at once, you'll be unconscious. So be warned." He paused. "They are a last resort."

"I won't forget," I said, "and I truly am grateful."

Brad drove to a chemist's, took my prescription in, waited for it to be dispensed, and finished the ten miles home, parking outside my door.

[49]

"Same time tomorrow morning?" I asked. "Back to London?"

"Yerss."

"I'd be in trouble without you," I said, climbing out with his help. He gave me a brief haunted glance and handed me the crutches. "You drive great," I said.

He was embarrassed, but also pleased. Nowhere near a smile, of course, but a definite twitch in the cheeks. He turned away, ducking my gaze, and set off doggedly toward his mother.

I let myself into the house and regretted the embargo on a large scotch. Instead, with June's lunchtime sandwich a distant memory, I refueled with sardines on toast and ice cream after, which more or less reflected my habitual laziness about cooking.

Then, aligned with icepacks along the sofa, I telephoned to the man in Newmarket who trained Greville's two racehorses.

He picked up the receiver as if he'd been waiting for it to ring.

"Yes?" he said. "What are they offering?"

"I've no idea," I said. "Is that Nicholas Loder?"

"What? Who are you?" He was brusque and impatient, then took a second look at things and with more honey said, "I beg your pardon, I was expecting someone else. I'm Loder, yes, who am I talking to?"

"Greville Franklin's brother."

"Oh, yes?"

It meant nothing to him immediately. I pictured him as I knew him, more by sight than face to face, a big light-haired man in his forties with enormous presence and self-esteem to match. Undoubtedly a good-to-great trainer, but in television interviews occasionally overbearing and condescending to the interviewer, as I'd heard he could be also to his owners. Greville kept his horses with him because the original horse he'd taken as a bad debt had been in that stable. Nicholas Loder had bought Greville all his subsequent horses and done notably well with them, and Greville had assured me

[50]

that he got on well with the man by telephone, and that he was perfectly friendly.

The last time I'd spoken to Greville myself on the telephone he'd been talking of buying another two-year-old, saying that Loder would get him one at the October sales, perhaps.

I explained to Loder that Greville had died and after the first sympathetic exclamations of dismay he reacted as I would have expected, not as if missing a close friend but on a practical business level.

"It won't affect the running of his horses," he said. "They're owned in any case by the Saxony Franklin company, not by Greville himself. I can run the horses still in the company name. I have the company's Authority to Act. There should be no problem."

"I'm afraid there may be," I began.

"No, no. Dozen Roses runs on Saturday at York. In with a great chance. I informed Greville of it only a few days ago. He always wanted to know when they were running, though he never went to see them."

"The problem is," I said, "about my being his brother. He has left the Saxony Franklin company to me."

The size of the problem suddenly revealed itself to him forcibly. "You're not his brother *Derek* Franklin? That brother? The jockey?"

"Yes. So . . . could you find out from Weatherby's whether the horses can still run while the estate is subject to probate?"

"My God," he said weakly.

Professional jockeys, as we both knew well, were not allowed to own runners in races. They could own other horses such as brood mares, foals, stallions, hacks, hunters, showjumpers, anything in horseshoes; they could even own racehorses, but they couldn't run them.

"Can you find out?" I asked again.

"I will." He sounded exasperated. "Dozen Roses should trot up on Saturday."

Dozen Roses was currently the better of Greville's two

horses whose fortunes I followed regularly in the newspapers and on television. A triple winner as a three-year-old, he had been disappointing at four, but in the current year, as a five-year-old, he had regained all his old form and had scored three times in the past few weeks. A "trot-up" on Saturday was a reasonable expectation.

Loder said, "If Weatherby's gives the thumbs down to the horse running, will you sell it? I'll find a buyer by Saturday, among my owners."

I listened to the urgency in his voice and wondered whether Dozen Roses was more than just another trot-up, of which season by season he had many. He sounded a lot more fussed than seemed normal.

"I don't know whether I can sell before probate," I said. "You'd better find that out too."

"But if you can, will you?"

"I don't know," I said, puzzled. "Let's wait and see, first."

"You won't be able to hang on to him, you know," he said forcefully. "He's got another season in him. He's still worth a good bit. But unless you do something like turn in your license, you won't be able to run him, and he's not worth turning in your license for. It's not as if he were favorite for the Derby."

"I'll decide during the week."

"But you're not thinking of turning in your license, are you?" He sounded almost alarmed. "Didn't I read in the paper that you're on the injured list but hope to be back racing well before Christmas?"

"You did read that, yes."

"Well, then." The relief was as indefinable as the alarm, but came clear down the wires. I didn't understand any of it. He shouldn't have been so worried.

"Perhaps Saxony Franklin could lease the horse to someone," I said.

"Oh. Ah. To me?" He sounded as if it were the perfect solution.

"I don't know," I said cautiously. "We'll have to find out."

I realized that I didn't totally trust him, and it wasn't a doubt I'd have felt before the phone call. He was one of the top five Flat race trainers in the country, automatically held to be reliable because of his rock-solid success.

"When Greville came to see his horses," I asked, "did he ever bring anyone with him? I'm trying to reach people he knew, to tell them of his death."

"He never came here to see his horses. I hardly knew him personally myself, except on the telephone."

"Well, his funeral is on Friday at Ipswich," I said. "What if I called in at Newmarket that day, as I'll be over your way, to see you and the horses and complete any paperwork that's necessary?"

"No," he said instantly. Then, softening it, "I always discourage owners from visiting. They disrupt the stable routine. I can't make any exceptions. If I need you to sign anything I'll arrange it another way."

"All right," I agreed mildly, not crowding him into corners "I'll wait to hear from you about what Weatherby's decides.'

He said he would get in touch and abruptly disconnected, leaving me thinking that on the subject of his behavior I didn't know the questions let alone the answers.

Perhaps I had been imagining things: but I knew I hadn't One could often hear more nuances in someone's voice on the telephone than one could face to face. When people were relaxed, the lower vibrations of their voices came over the wires undisturbed; under stress, the lower vibrations disappeared because the vocal cords involuntarily tightened. After Loder had discovered I would be inheriting Dozen Roses, there had been no lower vibrations at all.

Shelving the enigma, I pondered the persisting difficulty of informing Greville's friends. They had to exist, no one lived in a vacuum; but if it had been the other way round, I supposed that Greville would have had the same trouble. He hadn't known my friends either. Our worlds had scarcely touched except briefly when we met, and then we had talked a bit about horses, a bit about gadgets, a bit about the world in general and any interesting current events.

He'd lived alone, as I did. He'd told me nothing about any love life. He'd said merely, "Bad luck" when three years earlier I'd remarked that my live-in girlfriend had gone to live-in somewhere else. It didn't matter, I said. It had been a mutual agreement, a natural ending. I'd asked him once about his long-ago divorced wife. "She remarried. Haven't seen her since," was all he'd said.

If it had been I that had died, I thought, he would have told the world I worked in: he'd have told, perhaps, the trainer I mostly rode for, and maybe the racing papers. So I should tell his world: tell the semiprecious stone fraternity. Annette could do it, regardless of the absence of Greville's address book, because of June's computer. The computer made more and more nonsense of the break-in. I came back to the same conviction: something else had been stolen, and I didn't know what.

I remembered at about that point that I did have Greville's pocket diary, even if his desk diary had lost October, so I went and fetched it from the bedroom where I'd left it the night before. I thought I might find friends' names and phone numbers in the addresses section at the back, but he had been frugal in that department as everywhere else in the slim brown book. I turned the pages, which were mostly unused, seeing only short entries like "R arrives from Brazil" and "B in Paris" and "Buy citrine for P."

In March I was brought up short. Because it was a racing diary, the race meetings to be held on each day of the year were listed under the day's date. I came to Thursday, March 16, which listed "Cheltenham." The word Cheltenham had been ringed with a ballpoint pen, and Greville had written "Gold Cup" in the day's space; and then, with a different pen, he had added the words "Derek won it!!"

It brought me to sudden tears. I couldn't help it.

I longed for him to be alive so I could get to know him better. I wept for the lost opportunities, the time wasted. I longed to know the brother who had cared what I did, who had noted in his almost empty diary that I'd won one of the top races of the year.

4

THERE were only three telephone numbers in the addresses section at the back, all identified merely by initials. One, NL, was Nicholas Loder's. I tried the other two, which were London numbers, and got no reply.

Scattered through the rest of the diary were three more numbers. Two of them proved to be restaurants in full evening flood, and I wrote down their names, recognizing one of them as the place I'd last dined with Greville, two or three months back. On July 25, presumably, as that was the date on which he'd written the number. It had been an Indian restaurant, I remembered, and we had eaten ultra-hot curry.

Sighing, I turned the pages and tried a number occurring on September 2, about five weeks earlier. It wasn't a London number, but I didn't recognize the code. I listened to the bell ringing continuously at the other end and had resigned myself to another blank when someone lifted the distant receiver and in a low breathy voice said, "Hello?"

"Hello," I replied. "I'm ringing on behalf of Greville Franklin."

"Who?"

"Greville Franklin." I spoke the words slowly and clearly.

"Just a moment."

There was a long uninformative silence and then someone else clattered on sharp heels up to the receiver and decisively spoke, her voice high and angry.

"How dare you!" she said. "Don't ever do this again. I will not have your name spoken in this house."

She put the receiver down with a crash before I could utter a word, and I sat bemusedly looking at my own telephone and feeling as if I'd swallowed a wasp.

Whoever she was, I thought wryly, she wouldn't want to send flowers to the funeral, though she might have been gladdened by the death. I wondered what on earth Greville could have done to raise such a storm, but that was the trouble, I didn't know him well enough to make a good guess.

Thankful on the whole that there weren't any more numbers to be tried, I looked again at what few entries he had made, more out of curiosity than looking for helpful facts.

He had noted the days on which his horses had run, again only with initials. DR, Dozen Roses, appeared most, each time with a number following, like 300 at 8s, which I took to mean the amounts he'd wagered at what odds. Below the numbers he had put each time another number inside a circle which, when I compared them with the form book, were revealed as the placings of the horse at the finish. Its last three appearances, all with 1 in the circle, seemed to have netted Greville respectively 500 at 14s, 500 at 5s, 1000 at 6/4. The trot-up scheduled for Saturday, I thought, would be likely to be at odds on.

Greville's second horse, Gemstones, appearing simply as G, had run six times, winning only once but profitably; 500 at 100/6.

All in all, I thought, a moderate betting pattern for an owner. He had made, I calculated, a useful profit overall, more than most owners achieved. With his prize money in addition to offset both the training fees and the capital cost of buying the horses in the first place, I guessed that he had come out comfortably ahead, and it was in the business sense, I supposed, that owning horses had chiefly pleased him.

I flicked casually forward to the end of the book and in the last few pages headed "Notes" came across a lot of doodling and then a list of numbers.

The doodling was the sort one does while listening on the telephone, a lot of boxes and zigzags, haphazard and criss-crossed with lines of shading. On the page facing, there was an equation: $CZ = C \times 1.7$. I supposed it had been of sparkling clarity to Greville, but of no use to me.

Overleaf I found the sort of numbers list I kept in my own diary: passport, bank account, national insurance. After those, in small capital letters farther down the page, was the single word DEREK. Another jolt, seeing it again in his writing.

I wondered briefly whether, from its placing, Greville had used my name as some sort of mnemonic, or whether it was just another doodle: there was no way of telling. With a sigh I riffled back through the pages and came to something I'd looked at before, a lightly penciled entry for the day before his death. Second time around, it meant just as little.

Koningin Beatrix? he had written. Just the two words and the question mark. I wondered idly if it were the name of a horse, if he'd been considering buying it; my mind tended to work that way. Then I thought that perhaps he'd written the last name first, such as Smith, Jane, and that maybe he'd been going to Ipswich to meet a Beatrix Koningin.

I returned to the horse theory and got through to the trainer I rode for, Milo Shandy, who inquired breezily about the ankle and said would I please waste no time in coming back.

"I could ride out in a couple of weeks," I said.

"At least that's something, I suppose. Get some massage."

The mere thought of it was painful. I said I would, not meaning it, and asked about Koningin Beatrix, spelling it out.

"Don't know of any horse called that, but I can find out for you in the morning. I'll ask Weatherby's if the name's available, and if they say yes, it means there isn't a horse called that registered for racing."

"Thanks a lot."

"Think nothing of it. I heard your brother died. Bad luck."

"Yes . . . How did you know?"

"Nicholas Loder called me just now, explaining your dilemma and wanting me to persuade you to lease him Dozen Roses."

"But that's crazy. His calling you, I mean."

He chuckled. "I told him so. I told him I could bend you like a block of teak. He didn't seem to take it in. Anyway, I don't think leasing would solve anything. Jockeys aren't allowed to own racing horses, period. If you lease a horse, you still own it."

"I'm sure you're right."

"Put your shirt on it."

"Loder bets, doesn't he?" I asked. "In large amounts?"

"So I've heard."

"He said Dozen Roses would trot up at York on Saturday."

"In that case, do you want me to put a bit on for you?"

Besides not being allowed to run horses in races, jockeys also were banned from betting, but there were always ways round that, like helpful friends.

"I don't think so, not this time," I said, "but thanks anyway."

"You won't mind if I do?"

"Be my guest. If Weatherby's lets it run, that is."

"A nice little puzzle," he said appreciatively. "Come over soon for a drink. Come for evening stables."

I would, I said.

"Take care."

I put down the phone, smiling at his easy farewell colloquialism. Jump jockeys were paid not to take care, on the whole. Not too much care.

Milo would be horrified if I obeyed him.

In the morning, Brad drove me to Saxony Franklin's bank to see the manager who was young and bright and spoke with deliberate slowness, as if waiting for his clients' intelligence to catch up. Was there something about crutches, I wondered, that intensified the habit? It took him five minutes to suspect

[59]

that I wasn't a moron. After that he told me Greville had borrowed a sizable chunk of the bank's money, and he would be looking to me to repay it. "One point five million United States dollars in cash, as a matter of fact."

"One point five million dollars," I repeated, trying not to show that he had punched most of the breath out of me. *"What for?"*

"For buying diamonds. Diamonds from the DTC of the CSO are of course normally paid for in cash, in dollars."

Bank managers around Hatton Garden, it seemed, saw nothing extraordinary in such an exercise.

"He doesn't . . . didn't deal in diamonds," I protested.

"He had decided to expand and, of course, we made the funds available. Your brother dealt with us for many years and as you'll know was a careful and conscientious businessman. A valued client. We have several times advanced him money for expansion and each time we have been repaid without difficulty. Punctiliously, in fact." He cleared his throat. "The present loan, taken out three months ago, is due for repayment progressively over a period of five years, and of course as the loan was made to the company, not to your brother personally, the terms of the loan will be unchanged by his death."

"Yes," I said.

"I understood from what you said yesterday that you propose to run the business yourself?" He seemed happy enough where I might have expected a shade of anxiety. So why no anxiety? What wasn't I grasping?

"Do you hold security for the loan?" I asked.

"An agreement. We lent the money against the stock of Saxony Franklin."

"All the stones?"

"As many as would satisfy the debt. But our best security has always been your brother's integrity and his business ability."

I said, "I'm not a gemologist. I'll probably sell the business after probate."

He nodded comfortably. "That might be the best course. We would expect the Saxony Franklin loan to be repaid on schedule, but we would welcome a dialogue with the purchasers."

He produced papers for me to sign and asked for extra specimen signatures so that I could put my name to Saxony Franklin checks. He didn't ask what experience I'd had in running a business. Instead, he wished me luck.

I rose to my crutches and shook his hand, thinking of the things I hadn't said.

I hadn't told him I was a jockey, which might have caused a panic in Hatton Garden. And I hadn't told him that, if Greville had bought one and a half million dollars' worth of diamonds, I didn't know where they were.

"Diamonds?" Annette said. "No. I told you. We never deal in diamonds."

"The bank manager believes that Greville bought some recently. From something called the DTC of the CSO.

"The Central Selling Organisation? That's de Beers. The DTC is their Diamond Trading Company. No, no." She looked anxiously at my face. "He can't have done. He never said anything about it."

"Well, has the stock-buying here increased over the past three months?"

"It usually does," she said, nodding. "The business always grows. Mr. Franklin comes back from world trips with new stones all the time. Beautiful stones. He can't resist them. He sells most of the special ones to a jewelry designer who has several boutiques in places like Knightsbridge and Bond Street. Gorgeous costume jewelry, but with real stones. Many of his pieces are unique, designed for a single stone. He has a great name. People prize some of his pieces like Fabergé's."

"Who is he?"

"Prospero Jenks," she said, expecting my awe at least.

I hadn't heard of him, but I nodded all the same.

"Does he set the stones with diamonds?" I asked.

"Yes, sometimes. But he doesn't buy those from Saxony Franklin."

We were in Greville's office, I sitting in his swivel chair behind the vast expanse of desk, Annette sorting yesterday's roughly heaped higgledy-piggledy papers back into the drawers and files that had earlier contained them.

"You don't think Greville would ever have kept diamonds in this actual office, do you?" I asked.

"Certainly not." The idea shocked her. "He was always very careful about security."

"So no one who broke in here would expect to find anything valuable lying about?"

She paused with a sheaf of papers in one hand, her brow wrinkling.

"It's odd, isn't it? They wouldn't expect to find anything valuable lying about in an office if they knew anything about the jewelry trade. And if they didn't know anything about the jewelry trade, why pick this office?"

The same old unanswerable question.

June with her incongruous motherliness brought in the typist's chair again for me to put my foot on. I thanked her and asked if her stock control computer kept day-to-day tabs on the number and value of all the polished pebbles in the place.

"Goodness, yes," she said with amusement. "Dates and amounts in, dates and amounts out. Prices in, prices out, profit margin, tax, you name it, the computer will tell you what we've got, what it's worth, what sells slowly, what sells fast, what's been hanging around here wasting space for two years or more, which isn't much."

"The stones in the vault as well?"

"Sure."

"But no diamonds?"

"No, we don't deal in them." She gave me a bright incurious smile and swiftly departed, saying over her shoulder that the Christmas rush was still going strong and they'd been bombarded by fax orders overnight.

"Who reorders what you sell?" I asked Annette.

"I do for ordinary stock. June tells me what we need. Mr. Franklin himself ordered the faceted stones and anything unusual."

She went on sorting the papers, basically unconcerned because her responsibility ended on her way home. She was wearing that day the charcoal skirt of the day before but topped with a black sweater, perhaps out of respect for Greville. Solid in body, but not large, she had good legs in black tights and a settled, well-groomed, middle-aged air. I couldn't imagine her being as buoyant as June even in her youth.

I asked her if she could lay her hands on the company's insurance policy and she said as it happened she had just refiled it. I read its terms with misgivings and then telephoned the insurance company. Had my brother, I asked, recently increased the insurance? Had he increased it to cover diamonds to the value of one point five million dollars? He had not. It had been discussed only. My brother had said the premium asked was too high, and he had decided against it. The voice explained that the premium had been high because the stones would be often in transit, which made them vulnerable. He didn't know if Mr. Franklin had gone ahead with buying the diamonds. It had been an inquiry only, he thought, three or four months ago. I thanked him numbly and put down the receiver.

The telephone rang again immediately and as Annette seemed to be waiting for me to do so, I answered it.

"Hello?" I said.

A male voice said, "Is that Mr. Franklin? I want to speak to Mr. Franklin, please."

"Er . . . could I help? I'm his brother."

"Perhaps you can," he said. "This is the clerk of the West London Magistrates Court. Your brother was due here twenty minutes ago and it is unlike him to be late. Could you tell me when to expect him?"

"Just a minute." I put my hand over the mouthpiece and

told Annette what I'd just heard. Her eyes widened and she showed signs of horrified memory.

"It's his day for the Bench! Alternate Tuesdays. I'd clean forgotten."

I returned to the phone and explained the situation.

"Oh. Oh. How dreadfully upsetting." He did indeed sound upset, but also a shade impatient. "It really would have been more helpful if you could have alerted me in advance. It's very short notice to have to find a replacement."

"Yes," I agreed, "but this office was broken into during the weekend. My brother's appointments diary was stolen, and in fact we cannot alert anybody not to expect him."

"How extremely inconvenient." It didn't seem an inappropriate statement to him. I thought Greville might find it inconvenient to be dead. Maybe it wasn't the best time for black humor.

"If my brother had personal friends among the magistrates," I said, "I would be happy for them to get in touch with me here. If you wouldn't mind telling them."

"I'll do that, certainly." He hesitated. "Mr. Franklin sits on the licensing committee. Do you want me to inform the chairman?"

"Yes, please. Tell anyone you can."

He said goodbye with all the cares of the world on his shoulders and I sighed to Annette that we had better begin telling everyone else as soon as possible, but the trade was to expect business as usual.

"What about the papers?" she asked. "Shall we put it in *The Times* and so on?"

"Good idea. Can you do it?"

She said she could, but in fact showed me the paragraph she'd written before phoning the papers. "Suddenly, as the result of an accident, Greville Saxony Franklin JP, son of . . ." She'd left a space after "son of " which I filled in for her "the late Lt. Col. and Mrs. Miles Franklin." I changed "brother of Derek" to "brother of Susan, Miranda and

[64]

Derek," and I added a few final words, "Cremation, Ipswich, Friday."

"Have you any idea," I asked Annette, "what he could nave been doing in Ipswich?"

She shook her head. "I've never heard him mention the place. But then he didn't ever tell me very much that wasn't business." She paused. "He wasn't exactly secretive, but he never chatted about his private life." She hesitated. "He never talked about you."

I thought of all the times he'd been good company and told me virtually nothing, and I understood very well what she meant.

"He used to say that the best security was a still tongue," she said. "He asked us not to talk too much about our jobs to total strangers, and we all know it's safer not to, even though we don't have precious stones here. All the people in the trade are security mad and the diamantaires can be paranoid."

"What," I said, "are diamantaires?"

"Not what, who," she said. "They're dealers in rough diamonds. They get the stones cut and polished and sell them to manufacturing jewelers. Mr. Franklin always said diamonds were a world of their own, quite separate from other gemstones. There was a ridiculous boom and a terrible crash in world diamond prices during the eighties and a lot of the diamantaires lost fortunes and went bankrupt and Mr. Franklin was often saying that they must have been mad to overextend the way they had." She paused. "You couldn't help but know what was happening all round us in this area, where every second business is in gemstones. No one in the pubs and restaurants talked of much else. So you see, I'm sure the bank manager must be wrong. Mr. Franklin would never buy diamonds."

If he hadn't bought diamonds, I thought, what the hell had he done with one point five million dollars in cash.

Bought diamonds. He had to have done. Either that or the

money was still lying around somewhere, undoubtedly care-fully hidden. Either the money or diamonds to the value were lying around uninsured, and if my semisecretive ultra security-conscious brother had left a treasure-island map with X marking the precious spot, I hadn't yet found it. Much more likely, I feared, that the knowledge had died under the scaffolding. If it had, the firm would be forfeited to the bank, the last thing Greville would have wanted.

If it had, a major part of the inheritance he'd left me had vanished like morning mist.

He should have stuck to his old beliefs, I thought gloomily, and let diamonds strictly alone.

The telephone on the desk rang again and this time Annette answered it, as she was beside it.

"Saxony Franklin, can I help you?" she said, and listened. "No, I'm very sorry, you won't be able to talk to Mr. Franklin personally. Could I have your name, please?" She listened. "Well, Mrs. Williams, we must most unhappily inform you that Mr. Franklin died as a result of an accident over the weekend. We are, however, continuing in business. Can I help you at all?"

She listened for a moment or two in increasing puzzlement, then said, "Are you there? Mrs. Williams, can you hear me?" But it seemed as though there was no reply, and in a while she put the receiver down, frowning. "Whoever it was hung up."

"Do I gather you don't know Mrs. Williams?"

"No, I don't." She hesitated. "But I think she called yesterday too. I think I told her yesterday that Mr. Franklin wasn't expected in the office all day, like I told everyone. I didn't ask for her name yesterday. But she has a voice you don't forget."

"Why not?"

"Cut glass," she said succinctly. "Like Mr. Franklin, but more so. Like you too, a bit."

I was amused. She herself spoke what I thought of as unaccented English, though I supposed any way of speaking sounded like an accent to someone else. I wondered briefly

[66]

about the cut-glass Mrs. Williams who had received the news of the accident in silence and hadn't asked where, or how, or when.

Annette went off to her own office to get through to the newspapers and I picked Greville's diary out of my trousers pocket and tried the numbers that had been unreachable the night before. The two at the back of the book turned out to be first his bookmaker and second his barber, both of whom sounded sorry to be losing his custom, though the bookmaker less so because of Greville's habit of winning.

My ankle heavily ached; the result, I dared say, of general depression as much as aggrieved bones and muscle. Depression because whatever decisions I'd made to that point had been merely commonsense, but there would come a stage ahead when I could make awful mistakes through ignorance. I'd never before handled finances bigger than my own bank balance and the only business I knew anything about was the training of racehorses, and that only from observation, not from hands-on experience. I knew what I was doing around horses: there, I could tell the spinel from the ruby. In Greville's world, I could be taken for a ride and never know it. I could lose badly before I'd learned even the elementary rules of the game.

Greville's great black desk stretched away to each side of me, the wide kneehole flanked to right and left by twin stacks of drawers, four stacks in all. Most of them now contained what they had before the break-in, and I began desultorily to investigate the nearest on the left, looking vaguely for anything that would prompt me as to what I'd overlooked or hadn't known was necessary to be done.

I first found not tasks but the toys: the small black gadgets now tidied away into serried ranks. The Geiger counter was there, also the hand-held copier and a variety of calculators, and I picked out a small black contraption about the size of a paperback book and, turning it over curiously, couldn't think what it could be used for.

"That's an electric measurer," June said, coming breezily into the office with her hands full of paper. "Want to see how it works?"

I nodded and she put it flat on its back on the desk. "It'll tell you how far it is from the desk to the ceiling," she said pressing knobs. "There you are, seven feet five and a half inches. In meters," she pressed another knob, "two meters twenty-six centimeters."

"I don't really need to know how far it is to the ceiling," I said.

She laughed. "If you hold it flat against a wall, it measures how far it is to the opposite wall. Does it in a flash, as you saw. You don't need to mess around with tape measures. Mr. Franklin got it when he was redesigning the stockrooms. And he worked out how much carpet we'd need, and how much paint for the walls. This gadget tells you all that."

"You like computers, don't you?" I said.

"Love them. All shapes, all sizes." She peered into the open drawer. "Mr. Franklin was always buying the tiny ones." She picked out a small gray leather slipcover the size of a pack of cards and slid the contents onto her palm. "This little dilly is a travel guide. It tells you things like phone numbers for taxis, airlines, tourist information, the weather, embassies, American Express." She demonstrated, pushing buttons happily. "It's an American gadget, it even tells you the TV channels and radio frequencies for about a hundred cities in the U.S., including Tucson, Arizona, where they hold the biggest gem fair every February. It helps you with fifty other cities round the world, places like Tel Aviv and Hong Kong and Taipei where Mr. Franklin was always going."

She put the travel guide down and picked up something else. "This little round number is a sort of telescope, but it also tells you how far you are away from things. It's for golfers. It tells you how far you are away from the flag on the green, Mr. Franklin said, so that you know which club to use."

"How often did he play golf?" I said, looking through the

less than four-inch-long telescope and seeing inside a scale marked *Green* on the lowest line with diminishing numbers above, from 200 yards at the bottom to 40 yards at the top. "He never talked about it much."

"He sometimes played at weekends, I think," June said doubtfully. "You line up the word *Green* with the actual green, and then the flag stick is always eight feet high, I think, so wherever the top of the stick is on the scale, that's how far away you are. He said it was a good gadget for amateurs like him. He said never to be ashamed of landing in life's bunkers if you'd tried your best shot." She blinked a bit. "He always used to show these things to me when he bought them. He knew I liked them too." She fished for a tissue and without apology wiped her eyes.

"Where did he get them all from?" I asked.

"Mail order catalogues, mostly."

I was faintly surprised. Mail order and Greville didn't seem to go together, somehow, but I was wrong about that, as I promptly found out.

"Would you like to see our own new catalogue?" June asked, and was out of the door and back again before I could remember if I'd ever seen an old one and decide I hadn't. "Fresh from the printers," she said. "I was just unpacking them."

I turned the glossy pages of the 50-page booklet, seeing in faithful colors all the polished goodies I'd met in the stockrooms and also a great many of lesser breeding. Amulets, heart shapes, hoops and butterflies: there seemed to be no end to the possibilities of adornment. When I murmured derogatorily that they were a load of junk, June came fast and strongly to their defense, a mother hen whose chicks had been snubbed.

"Not everyone can afford diamonds," she said sharply, "and, anyway, these things are pretty and we sell them in thousands, and they wind up in hundreds of High Street shops and department stores and I often see people buying the odd shapes we've had through here. People do like them, even if they're not your taste."

"Sorry," I said.

Some of her fire subsided. "I suppose I shouldn't speak to you like that," she said uncertainly. "But you're not Mr. Franklin . . ." She stopped with a frown.

"It's OK," I said. "I am, but I'm not. I know what you mean."

"Alfie says," she said slowly, "that there's a steeplechase jockey called Derek Franklin." She looked at my foot as if with new understanding. "Champion jockey one year, he said. Always in the top ten. Is that . . . you?"

I said neutrally, "Yes."

"I *had* to ask you," she said. "The others didn't want to."

"Why not?"

"Annette didn't think you could be a jockey. You're too tall. She said Mr. Franklin never said anything about you being one. All she knew was that he had a brother he saw a few times a year. She said she was going to ignore what Alfie thought, because it was most unlikely." She paused. "Alfie mentioned it yesterday, after you'd gone. Then he said . . . they all said . . . they didn't see how a jockey could run a business of this sort. If you were one, that is. They didn't want it to be true, so they didn't want to ask."

"You tell Alfie and the others that if the jockey doesn't run the business their jobs will be down the tubes and they'll be out in the cold before the week's over."

Her blue eyes widened. "You sound just like Mr. Franklin!"

"And you don't need to mention my profession to the customers, in case I get the same vote of no confidence I've got from the staff."

Her lips shaped the word "Wow" but she didn't quite say it. She disappeared fast from the room and presently returned, followed by all the others, who were only too clearly in a renewed state of anxiety.

Not one of them a leader. What a pity.

I said, "You all look as if the ship's been wrecked and the lifeboat's leaking. Well, we've lost the captain, and I agree we're in trouble. My job is with horses and not in an office. But, like I said yesterday, this business is going to stay open and thrive. One way or another, I'll see that it does. So if you'll all go on working normally and keep the customers happy, you'll be doing yourselves a favor because if we get through safely you'll all be due for a bonus. I'm not my brother, but I'm not a fool either, and I'm a pretty fast learner. So just let's get on with the orders, and, er, cheer up."

Lily, the Charlotte Brontë lookalike, said meekly, "We don't really doubt your ability . . ."

"Of course we do," interrupted Jason. He stared at me with half a snigger, with a suggestion of curling lip. "Give us a tip for the three-thirty, then."

I listened to the street-smart bravado which went with the spiky orange hair. He thought me easy game.

I said, "When you are personally able to ride the winner of any three-thirty, you'll be entitled to your jeer. Until then, work or leave, it's up to you."

There was a resounding silence. Alfie almost smiled. Jason looked merely sullen. Annette took a deep breath, and June's eyes were shining with laughter.

They all drifted away still wordlessly and I couldn't tell to what extent they'd been reassured, if at all. I listened to the echo of my own voice saying I wasn't a fool, and wondering ruefully if it were true: but until the diamonds were found or I'd lost all hope of finding them, I thought it more essential than ever that Saxony Franklin Ltd. should stay shakily afloat. All hands, I thought, to the pumps.

June came back and said tentatively, "The pep talk seems to be working."

"Good."

"Alfie gave Jason a proper ticking off, and Jason's staying."

"Right."

"What can I do to help?"

I looked at her thin alert face with its fair eyelashes and blonde-to-invisible eyebrows and realized that without her the save-the-firm enterprise would be a nonstarter. She, more than her computer, was at the heart of things. She more than Annette, I thought.

"How long have you worked here?" I asked.

"Three years. Since I left school. Don't ask if I like the job, I love it. What can I do?"

"Look up in your computer's memory any reference to diamonds," I said.

She was briefly impatient. "I told you, we don't deal in diamonds."

"All the same, would you?"

She shrugged and was gone. I got to my feet—foot—and followed her, and watched while she expertly tapped her keys.

"Nothing at all under diamonds," she said finally. "Nothing. I told you."

"Yes." I thought about the boxes in the vault with the mineral information on the labels. "Do you happen to know the chemical formula for diamonds?"

"Yes I do," she said instantly. "It's C. Diamonds are pure carbon."

"Could you try again, then, under C?"

She tried. There was no file for C.

"Did my brother know how to use this computer?" I asked.

"He knew how to work all computers. Given five minutes or so to read the instructions."

I pondered, staring at the blank unhelpful screen.

"Are there," I asked eventually, "any secret files in this?"

She stared. "We never use secret files."

"But you could?"

"Of course. Yes. But we don't need to."

"If," I said, "there were any secret files, would you know that they were there?"

She nodded briefly. "I wouldn't know, but I could find out."

"How?" I asked. "I mean, please would you?"

"What am I looking for? I don't understand."

"Diamonds."

"But I told you, we don't . . ."

"I know," I said, "but my brother said he was going to buy diamonds and I need to know if he did. If there's any chance he made a private entry on this computer some day when he was first or last in this office, I need to find it."

She shook her head but tapped away obligingly, bringing what she called menus to the screen. It seemed a fairly lengthy business but finally, frowning, she found something that gave her pause. Then her concentration increased abruptly until the screen was showing the word "Password?" as before.

"I don't understand," she said. "We gave this computer a general password, which is 'Saxony,' though we almost never use it. But you can put in any password you like on any particular document to supersede Saxony. This entry was made only a month ago. The date is on the menu. But whoever made it didn't use Saxony as the password. So the password could be anything, literally any word in the world."

I said, "By document you mean file?"

"Yes, file. Every entry has a document name, like, say, 'oriental cultured pearls.' If I load 'oriental cultured pearls' onto the screen I can review our whole stock. I do it all the time. But this document with an unknown password is listed under 'pearl' in the singular, not 'pearls' in the plural, and I don't understand it. I didn't put it there." She glanced at me. "At any rate, it doesn't say 'diamonds.'"

"Have another try to guess the password."

She tried 'Franklin' and 'Greville' without result. "It could be *anything*," she said helplessly.

"Try 'Dozen Roses.'"

"Why 'Dozen Roses'?" She thought it extraordinary.

"Greville owned a horse—a racehorse—with that name."

"Really? He never said. He was so nice, and awfully private."

"He owned another horse called Gemstones."

With visible doubt she tried "Dozen Roses" and then "Gemstones." Nothing happened except another insistent demand for the password.

"Try 'diamonds,' then," I said.

She tried "diamonds." Nothing changed.

"You knew him," I said. "Why would he enter something under 'pearl'?"

"No idea." She sat hunched over the keys, drumming her fingers on her mouth. "Pearl. Pearl. Why pearl?"

"What is a pearl?" I said. "Does it have a formula?"

"Oh." She suddenly sat up straight. "It's a birthstone."

She typed in "birthstone," and nothing happened.

Then she blushed slightly.

"It's one of the birthstones for the month of June," she said. "I could try it, anyway."

She typed "June," and the screen flashed and gave up its secrets.

5

WE hadn't found the diamonds.
The screen said:

JUNE, IF YOU ARE READING THIS, COME STRAIGHT INTO MY
OFFICE FOR A RAISE. YOU ARE WORTH YOUR WEIGHT IN YOUR
BIRTHSTONE, BUT I'M ONLY OFFERING TO INCREASE YOUR SAL-
ARY BY TWENTY PERCENT. REGARDS, GREVILLE FRANKLIN.

"Oh!" She sat transfixed. "So that's what he meant."
"Explain," I said.
"One morning . . ." She stopped, her mouth screwing up
in an effort not to cry. It took her a while to be able to
continue, then she said, "One morning he told me he'd in-
vented a little puzzle for me and he would give me six months
to solve it. After six months it would self-destruct. He was
smiling so much." She swallowed. "I asked him what sort of
puzzle and he wouldn't tell me. He just said he hoped I would
find it."
"Did you look?" I asked.
"Of course I did. I looked everywhere in the office, though
I didn't know what I was looking for. I even looked for a new
document in the computer, but I just never gave a thought to
its being filed as a secret, and my eyes just slid over the word
'pearl,' as I see it so often. Silly of me. Stupid."

[75]

I said, "I don't think you're stupid, and I'll honor my brother's promise."

She gave me a swift look of pleasure but shook her head a little and said, "I didn't find it. I'd never have solved it except for you." She hesitated. "How about ten percent?"

"Twenty," I said firmly. "I'm going to need your help and your knowledge, and if Annette is Personal Assistant, as it says on the door of her office, you can be Deputy Personal Assistant, with the new salary to go with the job."

She turned a deeper shade of rose and busied herself with making a print-out of Greville's instruction, which she folded and put in her handbag.

"I'll leave the secret in the computer," she said with misty fondness. "No one else will ever find it." She pressed a few buttons and the screen went blank, and I wondered how many times in private she would call up the magic words that Greville had left her.

I wondered if they would really self-destruct: if one could program something on a computer to erase itself on a given date. I didn't see why not, but I thought Greville might have given her strong clues before the six months were out.

I asked her if she would print out first a list of everything currently in the vault and then as many things as she thought would help me understand the business better, like the volume and value of a day's, a week's, a month's sales; like which items were most popular, and which least.

"I can tell you that what's very popular just now is black onyx. Fifty years ago they say it was all amber, now no one buys it. Jewelry goes in and out of fashion like everything else." She began tapping keys. "Give me a little while and I'll print you a crash course."

"Thanks." I smiled, and waited while the printer spat out a gargantuan mouthful of glittering facets. Then I took the list in search of Annette, who was alone in the stockrooms, and asked her to give me a quick canter round the vault.

"There aren't any diamonds there," she said positively.

"I'd better learn what is."

"You don't seem like a jockey," she said.

"How many do you know?"

She stared. "None, except you."

"On the whole," I said mildly, "jockeys are like anyone else. Would you feel I was better able to manage here if I were, say, a piano tuner? Or an actor? Or a clergyman?"

She said faintly, "No."

"OK, then. We're stuck with a jockey. Twist of fate. Do your best for the poor fellow."

She involuntarily smiled a genuine smile which lightened her heavy face miraculously. "All right." She paused. "You're really like Mr. Franklin in some ways. The way you say things. Deal with honor, he said, and sleep at night."

"You all remember what he said, don't you?"

"Of course."

He would have been glad, I supposed, to have left so positive a legacy. So many precepts. So much wisdom. But so few signposts to his personal life. No visible signpost to the diamonds.

In the vault Annette showed me that, besides its chemical formula, each label bore a number: if I looked at that number on the list June had printed, I would see the formula again, but also the normal names of the stones, with colors, shapes and sizes and country of origin.

"Why did he label them like this?" I asked. "It just makes it difficult to find things."

"I believe that was his purpose," she answered. "I told you, he was very security conscious. We had a secretary working here once who managed to steal a lot of our most valuable turquoise out of the vault. The labels read 'turquoise' then, which made it easy, but now they don't."

"What do they say?"

She smiled and pointed to a row of boxes. I looked at the labels and read $Cu\, Al_6(PO_4)\, 4\, (OH)_8 \cdot 4 - 5\, (H_2O)$ on each of them.

[77]

"Enough to put anyone off for life," I said.

"Exactly. That's the point. Mr. Franklin could read formulas as easily as words, and I've got used to them myself now. No one but he and I handle these stones in here. We pack them into boxes ourselves and seal them before they go to Alfie for dispatch." She looked along the rows of labels and did her best to educate me. "We sell these stones at so much per carat. A carat weighs two hundred milligrams, which means five carats to a gram, a hundred and forty-two carats to an ounce and five thousand carats to the kilo."

"Stop right there," I begged.

"You said you learned fast."

"Give me a day or two."

She nodded and said if I didn't need her anymore she had better get on with the ledgers.

Ledgers, I thought, wilting internally. I hadn't even started on those. I thought of the joy with which I'd left Lancaster University with a degree in Independent Studies, swearing never again to pore dutifully over books and heading straight (against my father's written wishes) to the steeplechase stable where I'd been spending truant days as an amateur. It was true that at college I'd learned fast, because I'd had to, and learned all night often enough, keeping faith with at least the first half of my father's letter. He'd hoped I would grow out of the lure he knew I felt for race-riding, but it was all I'd ever wanted and I couldn't have settled to anything else. There was no long-term future in it, he'd written, besides a complete lack of financial security along with a constant risk of disablement. I ask you to be sensible, he'd said, to think it through and decide against.

Fat chance.

I sighed for the simplicity of the certainty I'd felt in those days, yet, given a second beginning, I wouldn't have lived any differently. I had been deeply fulfilled in racing and grown old in spirit only because of the way life worked in general. Disappointments, injustices, small betrayals, they were everyone's lot. I no longer expected everything to go right, but enough had gone right to leave me at least in a balance of content.

With no feeling that the world owed me anything, I applied myself to the present boring task of opening every packet in every box in the quest for little bits of pure carbon. It wasn't that I expected to find the diamonds there: it was just that it would be so stupid not to look, in case they were.

I worked methodically, putting the boxes one at a time on the wide shelf which ran along the right-hand wall, unfolding the stiff white papers with the soft inner linings and looking at hundreds of thousands of peridots, chrysoberyls, garnets and aquamarines until my head spun. I stopped in fact when I'd done only a third of the stock because apart from the airlessness of the vault it was physically tiring standing on one leg all the time, and the crutches got in the way as much as they helped. I refolded the last of the $XY_3\ Z_6[(O,Oh,F)_4 (BO_3)_3\ Si_6O_{18}]$ (tourmaline) and acknowledged defeat.

"What did you learn?" Annette asked when I reappeared in Greville's office. She was in there, replacing yet more papers in their proper files, a task apparently nearing completion.

"Enough to look at jewelry shops differently," I said.

She smiled. "When I read magazines I don't look at the clothes, I look at the jewelry."

I could see that she would. I thought that I might also, despite myself, from then on. I might even develop an affinity for black onyx cuff links.

It was by that time four o'clock in the afternoon of what seemed a very long day. I looked up the racing program in Greville's diary, decided that Nicholas Loder might well have passed over going to Redcar, Warwick and Folkestone, and dialed his number. His secretary answered, and yes, Mr. Loder was at home, and yes, he would speak to me.

He came on the line with almost none of the previous evening's agitation, bass resonances positively throbbing down the wire.

"I've been talking to Weatherby's and the Jockey Club," he

said easily, "and there's fortunately no problem. They agree that before probate the horses belong to Saxony Franklin Limited and not to you, and they will not bar them from racing in that name."

"Good," I said, and was faintly surprised.

"They say of course that there has to be at least one registered agent appointed by the company to be responsible for the horses, such appointment to be sealed with the company's seal and registered at Weatherby's. Your brother appointed both himself and myself as registered agents, and although he has died I remain a registered agent as before and can act for the company on my own."

"Ah," I said.

"Which being so," Loder said happily, "Dozen Roses runs at York as planned."

"And trots up?"

He chuckled. "Let's hope so."

That chuckle, I thought, was the ultimate in confidence.

"I'd be grateful if you could let Saxony Franklin know whenever the horses are due to run in the future," I said.

"I used to speak to your brother personally at his home number. I can hardly do that with you, as you don't own the horses."

"No," I agreed. "I meant, please will you tell the company? I'll give you the number. And would you ask for Mrs. Annette Adams? She was Greville's second-in-command."

He could hardly say he wouldn't, so I read out the number and he repeated it as he wrote it down.

"Don't forget, though, that there's only a month left of the Flat season," he said. "They'll probably run only once more each. Two at the very most. Then I'll sell them for you, that would be best. No problem. Leave it to me."

He was right, logically, but I still illogically disliked his haste.

"As executor, I'd have to approve any sale," I said, hoping I was right. "In advance."

"Yes, yes, of course." Reassuring heartiness. "Your injury," he said, "what exactly is it?"

"Busted ankle."

"Ah. Bad luck. Getting on well, I hope?" The sympathy sounded more like relief to me than anything else, and again I couldn't think why.

"Getting on," I said.

"Good, good. Goodbye then. The York race should be on the television on Saturday. I expect you'll watch it?"

"I expect so."

"Fine." He put down his receiver in great good humor and left me wondering what I'd missed.

Greville's telephone rang again immediately, and it was Brad to tell me that he had returned from his day's visit to an obscure aunt in Walthamstow and was downstairs in the front hall: all he actually said was, "I'm back."

"Great. I won't be long."

I got a click in reply. End of conversation.

I did mean to leave almost at once but there were two more phone calls in fairly quick succession. The first was from a man introducing himself as Elliot Trelawney, a colleague of Greville's from the West London Magistrates Court. He was extremely sorry, he said, to hear about his death, and he truly sounded it. A positive voice, used to attention: a touch of plummy accent.

"Also," he said, "I'd like to talk to you about some projects Greville and I were working on. I'd like to have his notes."

I said rather blankly, "What projects? What notes?"

"I could explain better face to face," he said. "Could I ask you to meet me? Say tomorrow, early evening, over a drink? You know that pub just round the corner from Greville's house? The Rook and Castle? There. He and I often met there. Five-thirty, six, either of those suit you?"

"Five-thirty," I said obligingly.

"How shall I know you?"

"By my crutches."

It silenced him momentarily. I let him off embarrassment.

"They're temporary," I said.

"Er, fine, then. Until tomorrow."

He cut himself off, and I asked Annette if she knew him, Elliot Trelawney? She shook her head. She couldn't honestly say she knew anyone outside the office who was known to Greville personally. Unless you counted Prospero Jenks, she said doubtfully. And even then, she herself had never really met him, only talked to him frequently on the telephone.

"Prospero Jenks . . . alias Fabergé?"

"That's the one."

I thought a bit. "Would you mind phoning him now?" I said. "Tell him about Greville and ask if I can go to see him to discuss the future. Just say I'm Greville's brother, nothing else."

She grinned. "No horses? Pas de gee-gees?"

Annette, I thought in amusement, was definitely loosening up.

"No horses," I agreed.

She made the call but without results. Prospero Jenks wouldn't be reachable until morning. She would try then, she said.

I levered myself upright and said I'd see her tomorrow. She nodded, taking it for granted that I would be there. The quicksand was winning, I thought. I was less and less able to get out.

Going down the passage, I stopped to look in on Alfie, whose day's work stood in columns of loaded cardboard boxes waiting to be entrusted to the mail.

"How many do you send out every day?" I asked, gesturing to them.

He looked up briefly from stretching sticky tape round yet another parcel. "About twenty, twenty-five regular, but more from August to Christmas." He cut off the tape expertly and stuck an address label deftly on the box top. "Twenty-eight so far today."

"Do you bet, Alfie?" I asked. "Read the racing papers?"

He glanced at me with a mixture of defensiveness and defiance, neither of which feeling was necessary. "I *knew* you was him," he said. "The others said you couldn't be."

"You know Dozen Roses too?"

A tinge of craftiness took over in his expression. "Started winning again, didn't he? I missed him the first time, but yes, I've had a little tickle since."

"He runs on Saturday at York, but he'll be odds-on," I said.

"Will he win, though? Will they be trying with him? I wouldn't put my shirt on that."

"Nicholas Loder says he'll trot up."

He knew who Nicholas Loder was: didn't need to ask. With cynicism, he put his just-finished box on some sturdy scales and wrote the result on the cardboard with a thick black pen. He must have been well into his sixties, I thought, with deep lines from his nose to the corners of his mouth and pale sagging skin everywhere from which most of the elasticity had vanished. His hands, with the veins of age beginning to show dark blue, were nimble and strong however, and he bent to pick up another heavy box with a supple back. A tough old customer, I thought, and essentially more in touch with street awareness than the exaggerated Jason.

"Mr. Franklin's horses run in and out," he said pointedly. "And as a jock you'd know about that."

Before I could decide whether or not he was intentionally insulting me, Annette came hurrying down the passage calling my name.

"Derek . . . Oh there you are. Still here, good. There's another phone call for you." She about-turned and went back toward Greville's office, and I followed her, noticing with interest that she'd dropped the Mister from my name. Yesterday's unthinkable was today's natural, now that I was established as a jockey, which was OK as far as it went, as long as it didn't go too far.

I picked up the receiver which was lying on the black desk and said, "Hello? Derek Franklin speaking."

A familiar voice said, "Thank God for that. I've been trying your Hungerford number all day. Then I remembered about your brother . . ." He spoke loudly, driven by urgency.

Milo Shandy, the trainer I'd ridden most for during the past three seasons: a perpetual optimist in the face of world evidence of corruption, greed and lies.

"I've a crisis on my hands," he bellowed, "and can you come over? Will you pull out all stops to come over first thing in the morning?"

"Er, what for?"

"You know the Ostermeyers? They've flown over from Pittsburgh for some affair in London and they phoned me and I told them Datepalm is for sale. And you know that if they buy him I can keep him here, otherwise I'll lose him because he'll have to go to auction. And they want you here when they see him work on the Downs and they can only manage first lot tomorrow, and they think the sun twinkles out of your backside, so for God's sake *come.*"

Interpreting the agitation was easy. Datepalm was the horse on which I'd won the Gold Cup: a seven-year-old gelding still near the beginning of what with luck would be a notable jumping career. Its owner had recently dropped the bombshell of telling Milo she was leaving England to marry an Australian, and if he could sell Datepalm to one of his other owners for the astronomical figure she named, she wouldn't send it to public auction and out of his yard.

Milo had been in a panic most of the time since then because none of his other owners had so far thought the horse worth the price, his Gold Cup success having been judged lucky in the absence through coughing of a couple of more established stars. Both Milo and I thought Datepalm better than his press, and I had as strong a motive as Milo for wanting him to stay in the stable.

"Calm down," I assured him. "I'll be there."

He let out a lot of breath in a rush. "Tell the Ostermeyers he's a really good horse."

"He is," I said, "and I will."

"Thanks, Derek." His voice dropped to normal decibels. "Oh, and by the way, there's no horse called Koningin Beatrix, and not likely to be. Weatherby's say Koningin Beatrix means Queen Beatrix, as in Queen Beatrix of the Netherlands, and they frown on people naming racehorses after royal persons."

"Oh," I said. "Well, thanks for finding out."

"Any time. See you in the morning. For God's sake don't be late. You know the Ostermeyers get up before larks."

"What I need," I said to Annette, putting down the receiver, "is an appointments book, so as not to forget where I've said I'll be."

She began looking in the drawerful of gadgets.

"Mr. Franklin had an electric memory thing he used to put appointments in. You could use that for now." She sorted through the black collection, but without result. "Stay here a minute," she said, closing the drawer, "while I ask June if she knows where it is."

She went away busily and I thought about how to convince the Ostermeyers, who could afford anything they set their hearts on, that Datepalm would bring them glory if not necessarily repay their bucks. They had had steeplechasers with Milo from time to time, but not for almost a year at the moment. I'd do a great deal, I thought, to persuade them it was time to come back.

An alarm like a digital watch alarm sounded faintly, muffled, and to begin with I paid it no attention, but as it persisted I opened the gadget drawer to investigate and, of course, as I did so it immediately stopped. Shrugging, I closed the drawer again, and Annette came back bearing a sheet of paper but no gadget.

"June doesn't know where the Wizard is, so I'll make out a rough calendar on plain paper."

"What's the Wizard?" I asked.

"The calculator. Baby computer. June says it does everything but boil eggs."

[85]

"Why do you call it the Wizard?" I asked.

"It has that name on it. It's about the size of a paperback book and it was Mr. Franklin's favorite object. He took it everywhere." She frowned. "Maybe it's in his car, wherever that is."

The car. Another problem. "I'll find the car," I said, with more confidence than I felt. Somehow or other I would have to find the car. "Maybe the Wizard was stolen out of this office in the break-in," I said.

She stared at me with widely opening eyes. "The thief would have to have known what it was. It folds up flat. You can't see any buttons."

"All the gadgets were out on the floor, weren't they?"

"Yes." It troubled her. "Why the address book? Why the engagements for October? Why the Wizard?"

Because of diamonds, I thought instinctively, but couldn't rationalize it. Someone had perhaps been looking, as I was, for the treasure map marked X. Perhaps they'd known it existed. Perhaps they'd found it.

"I'll get here a couple of hours later tomorrow," I said to Annette. "And I must leave by five to meet Elliot Trelawney at five-thirty. So if you reach Prospero Jenks, ask him if I could go to see him in between. Or failing that, any time Thursday. Write off Friday because of the funeral."

Greville died only the day before yesterday, I thought. It already seemed half a lifetime.

Annette said, "Yes, Mr. Franklin," and bit her lip in dismay.

I half smiled at her. "Call me Derek. Just plain Derek. And invest it with whatever you feel."

"It's confusing," she said weakly, "from minute to minute."

"Yes, I know."

With a certain relief I rode down in the service elevator and swung across to Brad in the car. He hopped out of the front seat and shoveled me into the back, tucking the crutches in beside me and waiting while I lifted my leg along the padded leather and wedged myself into the corner for the most comfortable angle of ride.

"Home?" he said.

"No. Like I told you on the way up, we'll stop in Kensington for a while, if you don't mind."

He gave the tiniest of nods. I'd provided him in the morning with a detailed large-scale map of West London, asking him to work out how to get to the road where Greville had lived, and I hoped to hell he had done it, because I was feeling more drained than I cared to admit and not ready to ride in irritating traffic-clogged circles.

"Look out for a pub called the Rook and Castle, would you?" I asked, as we neared the area. "Tomorrow at five-thirty I have to meet someone there."

Brad nodded and with the unerring instinct of the beer drinker quickly found it, merely pointing vigorously to tell me.

"Great," I said, and he acknowledged that with a wiggle of the shoulders.

He drew up so confidently outside Greville's address that I wondered if he had reconnoitered earlier in the day, except that his aunt lived theoretically in the opposite direction. In any case he handed me the crutches, opened the gate of the small front garden and said loquaciously, "I'll wait in the car."

"I might be an hour or more. Would you mind having a quick recce up and down this street and those nearby to see if you can find an old Rover with this number?" I gave him a card with it on. "My brother's car," I said.

He gave me a brief nod and turned away, and I looked up at the tall townhouse that Greville had moved into about three months previously, and which I'd never visited. It was creamy gray, gracefully proportioned, with balustraded steps leading up to the black front door, and businesslike but decorative metal grilles showing behind the glass in every window from semibasement to roof.

I crossed the grassy garden and went up the steps, and found there were three locks on the front door. Cursing slightly I yanked out Greville's half ton of keys and by trial and error found the way into his fortress.

Late afternoon sun slanted yellowly into a long main draw-ing room which was on the left of the entrance hall, throwing the pattern of the grilles in shadows on the grayish-brown carpet. The walls, pale salmon, were adorned with vivid paint-ings of stained-glass cathedral windows, and the fabric cover-ing sofa and armchairs was of a large broken herringbone pattern in dark brown and white, confusing to the eye. I reflected ruefully that I didn't know whether it all reflected Greville's own taste or whether he'd taken it over from the past owner. I knew only his taste in clothes, food, gadgets and horses. Not very much. Not enough.

The drawing room was dustless and tidy; unlived in. I re-turned to the front hall from where stairs led up and down, but before tackling those I went through a door at the rear which opened into a much smaller room filled with a homely clutter of books, newspapers, magazines, black leather chairs, clocks, chrysanthemums in pots, a tray of booze and framed medieval brass rubbings on deep green walls. This was all Greville, I thought. This was home.

I left it for the moment and hopped down the stairs to the semibasement, where there was a bedroom, unused, a small bathroom and a decorator-style dining room looking out through grilles to a rear garden, with a narrow spotless kitchen alongside.

Fixed to the fridge by a magnetic strawberry was a note.

Dear Mr. Franklin,
    I didn't know you'd be away this weekend. I brought in all the papers, they're in the back room. You didn't leave your laundry out, so I haven't taken it. Thanks for the money. I'll be back next Tuesday as usual.
                                        Mrs. P.

I looked around for a pencil, found a ballpoint, pulled the note from its clip and wrote on the back, asking Mrs. P. to call the following number (Saxony Franklin's) and speak to Derek or Annette. I didn't sign it, but put it back under the strawberry where I supposed it would stay for another week, a sorry message in waiting.

I looked in the fridge which contained little but milk, butter, grapes, a pork pie and two bottles of champagne.

Diamonds in the ice cubes? I didn't think he would have put them anywhere so chancy: besides, he was security conscious, not paranoid.

I hauled myself upstairs to the hall again and then went on up to the next floor, where there was a bedroom and bathroom suite in self-conscious black and white. Greville had slept there: the built-in closets and drawers held his clothes, the bathroom cabinet his privacy. He had been sparing in his possessions, leaving a single row of shoes, several white shirts on hangers, six assorted suits and a rack of silk ties. The drawers were tidy with sweaters, sport shirts, underclothes, socks. Our mother, I thought with a smile, would have been proud of him. She'd tried hard and unsuccessfully to instill tidiness into both of us as children, and it looked as if we'd both got better with age.

There was little else to see. The drawer in the bedside table revealed indigestion tablets, a flashlight and a paperback, John D. MacDonald. No gadgets and no treasure maps.

With a sigh I went into the only other room on that floor and found it unfurnished and papered with garish metallic silvery roses which had been half ripped off at one point. So much for the decorator.

There was another flight of stairs going upward, but I didn't climb them. There would only be, by the looks of things, unused rooms to find there, and I thought I would go and look later when stairs weren't such a sweat. Anything deeply interesting in that house seemed likely to be found in the small back sitting room, so it was to there that I returned.

I sat for a while in the chair that was clearly Greville's favorite, from where he could see the television and the view over the garden. Places that people had left forever should be seen through their eyes, I thought. His presence was strong in that room, and in me.

Beside his chair there was a small antique table with, on its polished top, a telephone and an answering machine. A red light for messages received was shining on the machine, so after a while I pressed a button marked "rewind," followed by another marked "play."

A woman's voice spoke without preamble.

"Darling, where are you? Do call me."

There was a series of between-message clicks, then the same voice again, this time packed with anxiety.

"Darling, please please call. I'm very worried. Where are you, darling? *Please* call. I love you."

Again the clicks, but no more messages.

Poor lady, I thought. Grief and tears waiting in the wings.

I got up and explored the room more fully, pausing by two drawers in a table beside the window. They contained two small black unidentified gadgets which baffled me and which I stowed in my pockets, and also a slotted tray containing a rather nice collection of small bears, polished and carved from shaded pink, brown and charcoal stone. I laid the tray on top of the table beside some chrysanthemums and came next to a box made of greenish stone, also polished, which, true to Greville's habit, was firmly locked. Thinking perhaps that one of the keys fitted it, I brought out the bunch again and began to try the smallest.

I was facing the window with my back to the room, balancing on one foot and leaning a thigh against the table, my arms out of the crutches, intent on what I was doing and disastrously unheeding. The first I knew of anyone else in the house was a muffled exclamation behind me, and I turned to see a dark-haired woman coming through the doorway, her wild glance rigidly fixing on the green stone box. Without pause she came fast toward me, pulling out of a pocket a black object like a long fat cigar.

STRAIGHT

I opened my mouth to speak but she brought her hand round in a strong swinging arc, and in that travel the short black cylinder more than doubled its length into a thick silvery flexible stick which crashed with shattering force against my left upper arm, enough to stop a heavyweight in round one.

6

MY fingers went numb and dropped the box. I swayed and spun from the force of the impact and overbalanced, toppling, thinking sharply that I mustn't this time put my foot on the ground. I dropped the bunch of keys and grabbed at the back of an upright black leather chair with my right hand to save myself, but it turned over under my weight and came down on top of me onto the carpet in a tangle of chair legs, table legs and crutches, the green box underneath and digging into my back.

In a spitting fury I tried to orient myself and finally got enough breath for one single choice, charming and heartfelt word.

"*Bitch.*"

She gave me a baleful glare and picked up the telephone, pressing three fast buttons.

"Police," she said, and in as short a time as it took the emergency service to connect her, "Police, I want to report a burglary. I've caught a burglar."

"I'm Greville's brother," I said thickly, from the floor.

For a moment it didn't seem to reach her. I said again, more loudly, "I'm Greville's brother."

"What?" she said vaguely.

"For Christ's sake, are you deaf? I'm not a burglar, I'm Greville Franklin's brother." I gingerly sat up into an L shape and found no strength anywhere.

She put the phone down. "Why didn't you say so?" she demanded.

"What chance did you give me? And who the hell are you, walking into my brother's house and belting people?"

She held at the ready the fearsome thing she'd hit me with, looking as if she thought I'd attack her in my turn, which I certainly felt like. In the last six days I'd been crunched by a horse, a mugger and a woman. All I needed was a toddler to amble up with a coup de grâce. I pressed the fingers of my right hand on my forehead and the palm against my mouth and considered the blackness of life in general.

"What's the matter with you?" she said after a pause.

I slid the hand away and drawled, "Absolutely bloody nothing."

"I only tapped you," she said with criticism.

"Shall I give you a hefty clip with that thing so you can feel what it's like?"

"You're angry." She sounded surprised.

"Dead right."

I struggled up off the floor, straightened the fallen chair and sat on it. "Who are you?" I repeated. But I knew who she was: the woman on the answering machine. The same voice. The cut-crystal accent. Darling, where are you. I love you.

"Did you ring his office?" I said. "Are you Mrs. Williams?"

She seemed to tremble and crumple inwardly and she walked past me to the window to stare out into the garden.

"Is he really dead?" she asked.

"Yes."

She was forty, I thought, perhaps more. Nearly my height. In no way tiny or delicate. A woman of decision and power, sorely troubled.

She wore a leather-belted raincoat, though it hadn't rained for weeks, and plain black businesslike shoes. Her hair, thick and dark, was combed smoothly back from her forehead to curl under on her collar, a cool groomed look achieved only by expert cutting. There was no visible jewelry, little remaining lipstick, no trace of scent.

[93]

"How?" she said eventually.

I had a strong impulse to deny her the information, to punish her for her precipitous attack, to hurt her and get even. But there was no point in it, and I knew I would end up with more shame than satisfaction, so after a struggle I explained briefly about the scaffolding.

"Friday afternoon," I said. "He was unconscious at once. He died early on Sunday."

She turned her head slowly to look at me directly. "Are you Derek?" she said.

"Yes."

"I'm Clarissa Williams."

Neither of us made any attempt to shake hands. It would have been incongruous, I thought.

"I came to fetch some things of mine," she said. "I didn't expect anyone to be here."

It was an apology of sorts, I supposed: and if I had indeed been a burglar she would have saved the bric-à-brac.

"What things?" I asked.

She hesitated, but in the end said, "A few letters, that's all." Her gaze strayed to the answering machine and there was a definite tightening of muscles round her eyes.

"I played the messages," I said.

"Oh God."

"Why should it worry you?"

She had her reasons, it seemed, but she wasn't going to tell me what they were: or not then, at any rate.

"I want to wipe them off," she said. "It was one of the purposes of coming."

She glanced at me, but I couldn't think of any urgent reason why she shouldn't, so I didn't say anything. Tentatively, as if asking my forbearance every step of the way, she walked jerkily to the machine, rewound the tape and pressed the record button, recording silence over what had gone before. After a while she rewound the tape again and played it, and there were no desperate appeals anymore.

"Did anyone else hear . . . ?"

"I don't think so. Not unless the cleaner was in the habit of listening. She came today, I think."

"Oh God."

"You left no name." Why the hell was I reassuring her, I wondered. I still had no strength in my fingers. I could still feel that awful blow like a shudder.

"Do you want a drink?" she said abruptly. "I've had a dreadful day." She went over to the tray of bottles and poured vodka into a heavy tumbler. "What do you want?"

"Water," I said. "Make it a double."

She tightened her mouth and put down the vodka bottle with a clink. "Soda or tonic?" she asked starchily.

"Soda."

She poured soda into a glass for me and tonic into her own, diluting the spirit by not very much. Ice was downstairs in the kitchen. No one mentioned it.

I noticed she'd left her lethal weapon lying harmlessly beside the answering machine. Presumably I no longer represented any threat. As if avoiding personal contact, she set my soda water formally on the table beside me between the little stone bears and the chrysanthemums and drank deeply from her own glass. Better than tranquilizers, I thought. Alcohol loosened the stress, calmed the mental pain. The world's first anesthetic. I could have done with some myself.

"Where are your letters?" I asked.

She switched on a table light. The on-creeping dusk in the garden deepened abruptly toward night and I wished she would hurry because I wanted to go home.

She looked at a bookcase which covered a good deal of one wall.

"In there, I think. In a book."

"Do start looking, then. It could take all night."

"You don't need to wait."

"I think I will," I said.

"Don't you trust me?" she demanded.

[95]

"No."

She stared at me hard. "Why not?"

I didn't say that because of the diamonds I didn't trust anyone. I didn't know who I could safely ask to look out for them, or who would search to steal them, if they knew they might be found.

"I don't know you," I said neutrally.

"But I . . ." She stopped and shrugged. "I suppose I don't know you either." She went over to the bookshelves. "Some of these books are hollow," she said.

Oh Greville, I thought. How would I ever find anything he had hidden? I liked straight paths. He'd had a mind like a labyrinth.

She began pulling out books from the lower shelves and opening the front covers. Not methodically book by book along any row but always, it seemed to me, those with predominantly blue spines. After a while, on her knees, she found a hollow one which she laid open on the floor with careful sarcasm, so that I could see she wasn't concealing anything.

The interior of the book was in effect a blue velvet box with a close-fitting lid that could be pulled out by a tab. When she pulled the lid out, the shallow blue-velvet–lined space beneath was revealed as being entirely empty.

Shrugging, she replaced the lid and closed the book, which immediately looked like any other book, and returned it to the shelves: and a few seconds later found another hollow one, this time with red velvet interiors. Inside this one lay an envelope.

She looked at it without touching it, and then at me.

"It's not my letters," she said. "Not my writing paper."

I said, "Greville made a will leaving everything he possessed to me."

She didn't seem to find it extraordinary, although I did: he had done it that way for simplicity when he was in a hurry, and he would certainly have changed it, given time.

"You'd better see what's in here, then," she said calmly,

and she picked the envelope out and stretched across to hand it to me.

The envelope, which hadn't been stuck down, contained a single ornate key, about four inches long, the top flattened and pierced like metal lace, the business end narrow with small but intricate teeth. I laid it on my palm and showed it to her, asking her if she knew what it unlocked.

She shook her head. "I haven't seen it before." She paused. "He was a man of secrets," she said.

I listened to the wistfulness in her voice. She might be strongly controlled at that moment, but she hadn't been before Annette told her Greville was dead. There had been raw panicky emotion on the tape. Annette had simply confirmed her frightful fears and put what I imagined was a false calmness in place of escalating despair. A man of secrets . . . Greville had apparently not opened his mind to her much more than he had to me.

I put the key back into its envelope and handed it across.

"It had better stay in the book for now," I said, "until I find a keyhole it fits."

She put the key into the book and returned it to the shelves, and shortly afterward found her letters. They were fastened not with romantic ribbons but held together by a prosaic rubber band; not a great many of them by the look of things but carefully kept.

She stared at me from her knees. "I don't want you to read them," she said. "Whatever Greville left you, they're mine, not yours."

I wondered why she needed so urgently to remove all traces of herself from the house. Out of curiosity I'd have read the letters with interest if I'd found them myself, but I could hardly demand now to see her love letters . . . if they were love letters.

"Show me just a short page," I said.

She looked bitter. "You really don't trust me, do you? I'd like to know why."

"Someone broke into Greville's office over the weekend,"
I said, "and I'm not quite sure what they were looking for."

"Not my letters," she said positively.

"Show me just a page," I said, "so I know they're what you
say."

I thought she would refuse altogether, but after a moment's
thought she slid the rubber band off the letters and fingered
through them, finally, with all expression repressed, handing
me one small sheet.

It said,

> . . . and until next Monday my life will be a desert. What
> am I to do? After your touch I shrink from him. It's dread-
> ful. I am running out of headaches. I adore you.
>
> C.

I handed the page back in silence, embarrassed at having
intruded.

"Take them," I said.

She blinked a few times, snapped the rubber band back
round the small collection, and put them into a plain black
leather handbag which lay beside her on the carpet.

I felt down onto the floor, collected the crutches and stood
up, concentrating on at least holding the hand support of the
left one, even if not putting much weight on it. Clarissa Williams watched me go over toward Greville's chair with a touch
of awkwardness.

"Look," she said. "I didn't realize . . . I mean, when I came
in here and saw you stealing things . . . I thought you were
stealing things . . . I didn't notice the crutches."

I supposed that was the truth. Bona fide burglars didn't go
around peg-legged, and I'd laid the supports aside at the time
she'd come storming in. She'd been too fired up to ask questions: propelled no doubt by grief, anxiety and fear of the
intruder. None of which lessened my contrary feeling that she
damned well *ought* to have asked questions before waging
war.

I wondered how she would have explained her presence to the police, if they had arrived, when she was urgent to remove all traces of herself from the house. Perhaps she would have realized her mistake and simply departed, leaving the incapacitated burglar on the floor.

I went over to the telephone table and picked up the brutal little man-tamer. The heavy handle, a black cigar-shaped cylinder, knurled for a good grip, was under an inch in diameter and about seven inches long. Protruding beyond that was a short length of solidly thick chromium-plated closely-coiled spring, with a similar but narrower spring extending beyond that, the whole tipped with a black metal knob, fifteen or sixteen inches overall. A kick as hard as a horse.

"What is this?" I said, holding it, feeling its weight.

"Greville gave it to me. He said the streets aren't safe. He wanted me to carry it always ready. He said all women should carry them because of muggers and rapists . . . as a magistrate he heard so much about women being attacked. He said one blow would render the toughest man helpless and give me time to escape."

I hadn't much difficulty in believing it. I bent the black knob to one side and watched the close heavy spring flex and straighten fast when I let it go. She got to her feet and said, "I'm sorry. I've never used it before, not in anger. Greville showed me how . . . he just said to swing as hard as I could so that the springs would shoot out and do the maximum damage."

My dear brother, I thought. Thank you very much.

"Does it go back into its shell?" I asked.

She nodded. "Twist the bigger spring clockwise . . . it'll come loose and slide into the casing." I did that, but the smaller spring with the black knob still stuck out. "You have to give the knob a bang against something, then it will slide in."

I banged the knob against the wall, and like a meek lamb the narrower spring slid smoothly into the wider, and the end of the knob became the harmless-looking end of yet another gadget.

"What makes it work?" I asked, but she didn't know.

I found that the end opposite the knob unscrewed if one tried, so I unscrewed it about twenty turns until the inch-long piece came off, and I discovered that the whole end section was a very strong magnet.

Simple, I thought. Ordinarily the magnet held the heavy springs inside the cylinder. Make a strong flicking arc, in effect throw the springs out, and the magnet couldn't hold them, but let them go, letting loose the full whipping strength of the thing.

I screwed back the cap, held the cylinder, swung it hard. The springs shot out, flexible, shining, horrific.

Wordlessly I closed the thing up again and offered it to her.

"It's called a kiyoga," she said.

I didn't care what it was called. I didn't care if I never saw it again. She put it familiarly into her raincoat pocket, Everywoman's ultimate reply to footpads, maniacs and assorted misogynists.

She looked unhappily and uncertainly at my face.

"I suppose I can't ask you to forget I came here?" she said.

"It would be impossible."

"Could you just . . . not speak of it?"

If I'd met her in another way I suppose I might have liked her. She had generous eyes that would have looked better smiling, and an air of basic good humor which persisted despite her jumbling emotions.

With an effort she said, "Please."

"Don't beg," I said sharply. It made me uncomfortable and it didn't suit her.

She swallowed. "Greville told me about you. I guess . . . I'll have to trust to his judgment."

She felt in the opposite pocket to the one with the kiyoga and brought out a plain key ring with three keys on it.

"You'd better have these," she said. "I won't be using them anymore." She put them down by the answering machine and in her eyes I saw the shininess of sudden tears.

"He died in Ipswich," I said. "He'll be cremated there on Friday afternoon. Two o'clock."

She nodded speechlessly in acknowledgment, not looking at me, and went past me, through the doorway and down the hall and out of the front door, closing it with a quiet finality behind her.

With a sigh, I looked round the room. The book box that had contained her letters still lay open on the floor and I bent down, picked it up, and restored it to the shelves. I wondered just how many books were hollow. Tomorrow evening, I thought, after Elliot Trelawney, I would come and look.

Meanwhile I picked up the fallen green stone box and put it on the table by the chrysanthemums, reflecting that the ornate key in the red-lined book-box was far too large to fit its tiny lock. Greville's bunch of keys was down on the carpet also. I returned to what I'd been doing before being so violently interrupted, but found that the smallest of the bunch was still too big for the green stone.

A whole load of no progress, I thought moodily.

I drank the soda water, which had lost its fizz.

I rubbed my arm, which didn't make it much better.

I wondered what judgment Greville had passed on me, that could be trusted.

There was a polished cupboard that I hadn't investigated underneath the television set and, not expecting much, I bent down and pulled one of the doors open by its brass ring handle. The other door opened of its own accord and the contents of the cupboard slid outward as a unit: a video machine on top with, on two shelves below, rows of black boxes holding recording tapes. There were small uniform labels on the boxes bearing, not formulas this time, but dates.

I pulled one of the boxes out at random and was stunned to see the larger label stuck to its front: "Race Video Club," it said in heavy print, and underneath, in typing, "July 7th, Sandown Park, Dozen Roses."

The Race Video Club, as I knew well, sold tapes of races to

[101]

owners, trainers and anyone else interested. Greville, I thought in growing amazement as I looked further, must have given them a standing order: every race his horses had run in for the past two years, I judged, was there on his shelves to be watched.

He'd told me once, when I asked why he didn't go to see his runners, that he saw them enough on television; and I'd thought he meant on the ordinary scheduled programs, live from the racetracks in the afternoons.

The front doorbell rang, jarring and unexpected. I went along and looked through a small peephole and found Brad standing on the doorstep, blinking and blinded by two spotlights shining on his face. The lights came from above the door and lit up the whole path and the gate. I opened the door as he shielded his eyes with his arm.

"Hello," I said. "Are you all right?"

"Turn the lights off. Can't see."

I looked for a switch beside the front door, found several, and by pressing them all upward indiscriminately, put out the blaze.

"Came to see you were OK," Brad explained. "Those lights just went on."

Of their own accord, I realized. Another manifestation of Greville's security, no doubt. Anyone who came up the path after dark would get illuminated for his pains.

"Sorry I've been so long," I said. "Now you're here, would you carry a few things?"

He nodded as if he'd let out enough words already to last the evening, and followed me silently, when I beckoned him, toward the small sitting room.

"I'm taking that green stone box and as many of those video tapes as you can carry, starting from that end," I said, and he obligingly picked up about ten recent tapes, balancing the box on top.

I found a hall light, switched that on, and turned off the lamp in the sitting room. It promptly turned itself on again, unasked.

"Cor," Brad said.

I thought that maybe it was time to leave before I tripped any other alarms wired direct after dark to the local constabulary. I closed the sitting room door and we went along the hall to the outer world. Before leaving I pressed all the switches beside the front door downward, and maybe I turned more on than I'd turned off: the spotlights didn't go on, but a dog started barking noisily behind us.

"Strewth," Brad said, whirling round and clutching the video tapes to his chest as if they would defend him.

There was no dog. There was a loudspeaker like a bullhorn on a low hall table emitting the deep-throated growls and barks of a determined German shepherd.

"Bleeding hell," Brad said.

"Let's go," I said in amusement, and he could hardly wait.

The barking stopped of its own accord as we stepped out into the air. I pulled the door shut, and we set off to go down the steps and along the path. We'd gone barely three paces when the spotlights blazed on again.

"Keep going," I said to Brad. "I daresay they'll turn themselves off in time."

It was fine by him. He'd managed to park the car not far away, and I spent the swift journey to Hungerford wondering about Clarissa Williams; her life, love and adultery.

During the evening I failed both to open the green stone box and to understand the gadgets.

Shaking the box gave me no impression of contents and I supposed it could well be empty. A cigarette box, I thought, though I couldn't remember ever seeing Greville smoking. Perhaps a box to hold twin packs of cards. Perhaps a box for jewelry. Its tiny keyhole remained impervious to probes from nail scissors, suitcase keys and a piece of wire, and in the end I surrendered and laid it aside.

Neither of the gadgets opened or shut. One was a small black cylindrical object about the size of a thumb, with one end narrowly ridged, like a coin. Turning the ridged end a quarter-turn clockwise, its full extent of travel, produced a thin, faint high-pitched whine which proved to be the unexciting sum of the thing's activity. Shrugging, I switched the whine off again and stood the small tube upright on the green box.

The second gadget didn't even produce a whine. It was a flat black plastic container about the size of a pack of cards with a single square red button placed centrally on the front. I pressed the button: no results. A round chromiumed knob set into one of the sides of the cover revealed itself on further inspection as the end of a telescopic aerial. I pulled it out as far as it would go, about ten inches, and was rewarded with what I presumed was a small transmitter which transmitted I didn't know what to I didn't know where.

Sighing, I pushed the aerial back into its socket and added the transmitter to the top of the green box, and after that I fed Greville's tapes one by one into my video machine and watched the races.

Alfie's comment about in-and-out running had interested me more than I would have wanted him to know. Dozen Roses, from my own reading of the results, had had a long doldrum period followed by a burst of success, suggestive of the classic "cheating" pattern of running a horse to lose and go on losing until he was low in the handicap and unbacked, then setting him off to win at long odds in a race below his latent abilities and wheeling away the winnings in a barrow.

All trainers did that in a mild way sometimes, whatever the rules might say about always running flat out. Young and inexperienced horses could be ruined by being pressed too hard too soon: one had to give them a chance to enjoy themselves, to let their racing instinct develop fully.

That said, there was a point beyond which no modern trainer dared go. In the bad old days before universal camera coverage it had been harder to prove a horse hadn't been trying: many jockeys had been artists at waving their whips while hauling on the reins. Under the eagle lenses and fierce discipline of the current scene even natural and unforeseen

[104]

fluctuations in a horse's form could find the trainer yanked in before the Stewards for an explanation, and if the trainer couldn't explain why his short-priced favorite had turned leaden-footed it could cost him a depressing fine.

No trainer, however illustrious, was safe from suspicion, yet I'd never read or heard of Nicholas Loder getting himself into that sort of trouble. Maybe Alfie, I thought dryly, knew something the Stewards didn't. Maybe Alfie could tell me why Loder had all but panicked when he'd feared Dozen Roses might not run on Saturday next.

Brad had picked up the six most recent outings of Dozen Roses, interspersed by four of Gemstones'. I played all six of Dozen Roses first, starting with the earliest, back in May, checking the details with what Greville had written in his diary.

On the screen there were shots of the runners walking round the parade ring and going down to the start, with Greville's pink and orange colors bright and easy to see. The May race was a ten-furlong handicap for three-year-olds and upward, run at Newmarket on a Friday. Eighteen runners. Dozen Roses ridden by a second-string jockey because Loder's chief retained jockey was riding the stable's other runner, which started favorite.

Down at the start there was some sort of fracas involving Dozen Roses. I rewound the tape and played it through in slow motion and couldn't help laughing. Dozen Roses, his mind far from racing, had been showing unseemly interest in a mare.

I remembered Greville saying once that he thought it a shame and unfair to curb a colt's enthusiasm: no horse of his would ever be gelded. I remembered him vividly, leaning across a small table and saying it over a glass of brandy with a gleam in which I'd seen his own enjoyment of sex. So many glimpses of him in my mind, I thought. Too few, also. I couldn't really believe I would never eat with him again, whatever my senses said.

Trainers didn't normally run mares that had come into

season, but sometimes one couldn't tell early on. Horses knew, though. Dozen Roses had been aroused. The mare was loaded into the stalls in a hurry and Dozen Roses had been walked around until the last minute to cool his ardor. After that, he had run without sparkle and finished midfield, the mare to the rear of him trailing in last. Loder's other runner, the favorite, had won by a length.

Too bad, I thought, smiling, and watched Dozen Roses' next attempt three weeks later.

No distracting attractions, this time. The horse had behaved quietly, sleepily almost, and had turned in the sort of moderate performance which set owners wondering if the game was worth it. The next race was much the same, and if I'd been Greville I would have decided it was time to sell.

Greville, it seemed, had had more faith. After seven weeks' rest Dozen Roses had gone bouncing down to the start, raced full of zest and zoomed over the finishing line in front, netting 14/1 for anyone ignorant enough to have backed him. Like Greville, of course.

Watching the sequence of tapes I did indeed wonder why the Stewards hadn't made a fuss, but Greville hadn't mentioned anything except his pleasure in the horse's return to his three-year-old form.

Dozen Roses had next produced two further copybook performances of stamina and determination which brought us up to date. I rewound and removed the last tape and could see why Loder thought it would be another trot-up on Saturday.

Gemstones' tapes weren't as interesting. Despite his name he wasn't of much value, and the one race he'd won looked more like a fluke than constructive engineering. I would sell them both, I decided, as Loder wanted.

7

B RAD came early on Wednesday and drove me to Lambourn. The ankle was sore in spite of Distalgesic but less of a constant drag that morning and I could have driven the car myself if I'd put my mind to it. Having Brad around, I reflected on the way, was a luxury I was all too easily getting used to.

Clarissa Williams's attentions had worn off completely except for a little stiffness and a blackening bruise like a bar midway between shoulder and elbow. That didn't matter. For much of the year I had bruises somewhere or other, result of the law of averages operating in steeplechasing. Falls occurred about once every fourteen races, sometimes oftener, and while a few of the jockeys had bodies that hardly seemed to bruise at all, mine always did. On the other hand I healed everywhere fast, bones, skin and optimism.

Milo Shandy, striding about in his stable yard as if incapable of standing still, came over to my car as it rolled to a stop and yanked open the driver's door. The words he was about to say didn't come out as he stared first at Brad, then at me on the back seat, and what he eventually said was, "A chauffeur, by God. Coddling yourself, aren't you?"

Brad got out of the car, gave Milo a Neanderthal look and handed me the crutches as usual.

Milo, dark, short and squarely built, watched the proceedings with disgust.

"I want you to ride Datepalm," he said.

"Well, I can't."

"The Ostermeyers will want it. I told them you'd be here."

"Gerry rides Datepalm perfectly well," I said, Gerry being the lad who rode the horse at exercise as a matter of course most days of the week.

"Gerry isn't you."

"He's better than me with a groggy ankle."

Milo glared. "Do you want to keep the horse here or don't you?"

I did.

Milo and I spent a fair amount of time arguing at the best of times. He was pugnacious by nature, mercurial by temperament, full of instant opinions that could be reversed the next day, didactic, dynamic and outspoken. He believed absolutely in his own judgment and was sure that everything would turn out all right in the end. He was moderately tactful to the owners, hard on his work force and full of swearwords for his horses, which he produced as winners by the dozen.

I'd been outraged by the way he'd often spoken to me when I first started to ride for him three years earlier, but one day I lost my temper and yelled back at him and he burst out laughing and told me we would get along just fine, which in fact we did, though seldom on the surface.

I knew people thought ours an unlikely alliance, I neat and quiet, he restless and flamboyant, but in fact I liked the way he trained horses and they seemed to run well for him, and we had both prospered.

The Ostermeyers arrived at that point and they too had a chauffeur, which Milo took for granted. The bullishness at once disappeared from his manner to be replaced by the jocular charm that had owners regularly mesmerized, that morning being no exception. The Ostermeyers responded immediately, she with a roguish wiggle of the hips, he with a big handshake and a wide smile.

They were not so delighted about my crutches.

"Oh dear," Martha Ostermeyer exclaimed in dismay. "What have you done? Don't say you can't ride Datepalm. We only came, you know, because dear Milo said you'd be here to ride it."

"He'll ride it," Milo said before I had a chance of answering, and Martha Ostermeyer clapped her small gloved hands with relief.

"If we're going to buy him," she said, smiling, "we want to see him with his real jockey up, not some exercise rider."

Harley Ostermeyer nodded in agreement, benignly.

Not really my week, I thought.

The Ostermeyers were all sweetness and light while people were pleasing them, and I'd never had any trouble liking them, but I'd also seen Harley Ostermeyer's underlying streak of ruthless viciousness once in a racecourse car-park where he'd verbally reduced to rubble an attendant who had allowed someone to park behind him, closing him in. He had had to wait half an hour. The attendant had looked genuinely scared. "Goodnight, Derek," he'd croaked as I went past, and Ostermeyer had whirled round and cooled his temper fifty percent, inviting my sympathy in his trouble. Harley Ostermeyer liked to be thought a good guy, most of the time. He was the boss, as I understood it, of a giant supermarket chain. Martha Ostermeyer was also rich, a fourth-generation multimillionaire in banking. I'd ridden for them often in the past years and been well rewarded, because generosity was one of their pleasures.

Milo drove them and me up to the Downs where Datepalm and the other horses were already circling, having walked up earlier. The day was bright and chilly, the Downs rolling away to the horizon, the sky clear, the horses' coats glossy in the sun. A perfect day for buying a champion 'chaser.

Milo sent three other horses down to the bottom of the gallop to work fast so that the Ostermeyers would know where to look and what to expect when Datepalm came up and passed them. They stood out on the grass, looking where Milo pointed, intent and happy.

Milo had brought a spare helmet with us in the big-wheeled vehicle that rolled over the mud and ruts on the Downs, and with an inward sigh I put it on. The enterprise was stupid really, as my leg wasn't strong enough and if anything wild happened to upset Datepalm, he might get loose and injure himself and we'd lose him surely one way or another.

On the other hand, I'd ridden races now and then with cracked bones, not just exercise gallops, and I knew one jockey who in the past had broken three bones in his foot and won races with it, sitting with it in an ice bucket in the changing room between times and literally hopping out to the parade ring, supported by friends. The authorities had later brought in strict medical rules to stop that sort of thing as being unfair to the betting public, but one could still get away with it sometimes.

Milo saw me slide out of the vehicle with the helmet on and came over happily and said, "I knew you would."

"Mm," I said. "When you give me a leg up, put both hands round my knee and be careful, because if you twist my foot there'll be no sale."

"You're such a wimp," he said.

Nevertheless he was circumspect and I landed in the saddle with little trouble. I was wearing jeans, and that morning for the first time I'd managed to get a shoe on, or rather one of the wide soft black leather moccasins I used as bedroom slippers. Milo threaded the stirrup over the moccasin with unexpected gentleness and I wondered if he were having last-minute doubts about the wisdom of all this.

One look at the Ostermeyers' faces dispelled both his doubts and mine. They were beaming at Datepalm already with proprietary pride.

Certainly he looked good. He filled the eye, as they say. A bay with black points, excellent head, short sturdy legs with plenty of bone. The Ostermeyers always preferred handsome animals, perhaps because they were handsome themselves, and Datepalm was well-mannered besides, which made him a peach of a ride.

He and I and two others from the rest of the string set off at a walk toward the far end of the gallop but were presently trotting, which I achieved by standing in the stirrups with all my weight on my right foot while cursing Milo imaginatively for the sensations in my left. Datepalm, who knew how horses should be ridden, which was not lopsided like this, did a good deal of head and tail shaking but otherwise seemed willing to trust me. He and I knew each other well as I'd ridden him in all his races for the past three years. Horses had no direct way of expressing recognition, but occasionally he would turn his head to look at me when he heard my voice, and I also thought he might know me by scent as he would put his muzzle against my neck sometimes and make small whiffling movements of his nostrils. In any case we did have a definite rapport and that morning it stood us in good stead.

At the far end the two lads and I sorted out our three horses ready to set off at a working gallop back toward Milo and the Ostermeyers, a pace fast enough to be interesting but not flat out like racing.

There wasn't much finesse in riding a gallop to please customers, one simply saw to it that one was on their side of the accompanying horses, to give them a clear view of the merchandise, and that one finished in front to persuade them that that's what would happen in future.

Walking him around to get in position, I chatted quietly as I often did to Datepalm, because in common with many racehorses he was always reassured by a calm human voice, sensing from one's tone that all was well. Maybe horses heard the lower resonances: one never knew.

"Just go up there like a pro," I told him, "because I don't want to lose you, you old bugger. I want us to win the National one day, so shine, boy. Dazzle. Do your bloody best."

I shook up the reins as we got the horses going, and in fact Datepalm put up one of his smoothest performances, staying with his companions for most of the journey, lengthening his stride when I gave him the signal, coming away alone and then sweeping collectedly past the Ostermeyers with fluid power; and if the jockey found it an acutely stabbing discomfort all the way, it was a fair price for the result. Even before I'd pulled up, the Ostermeyers had bought the horse and shaken hands on the deal.

"Subject to a veterinarian's report, of course," Harley was saying as I walked Datepalm back to join them. "Otherwise, he's superb."

Milo's smile looked as if it would split his face. He held the reins while Martha excitedly patted the new acquisition, and went on holding them while I took my feet out of the stirrups and lowered myself very carefully to the ground, hopping a couple of steps to where the crutches lay on the grass.

"What did you do to your foot?" Martha asked unworriedly.

"Wrenched it," I said, slipping the arm cuffs on with relief. "Very boring."

She smiled, nodded and patted my arm. "Milo said it was nothing much."

Milo gave me a gruesome look, handed Datepalm back to his lad, Gerry, and helped the Ostermeyers into the big-wheeled vehicle for the drive home. We bumped down the tracks and I took off the helmet and ran my fingers through my hair, reflecting that although I wouldn't care to ride gallops like that every day of the week, I would do it again for as good an outcome.

We all went into Milo's house for breakfast, a ritual there as in many other racing stables, and over coffee, toast and scrambled eggs Milo and the Ostermeyers planned Datepalm's future program, including all the top races with of course another crack at the Gold Cup.

"What about the Grand National?" Martha said, her eyes like stars.

"Well, now, we'll have to see," Milo said, but his dreams too were as visible as searchlights. First thing on our return, he'd telephoned to Datepalm's former owner and got confirmation that she agreed to the sale and was pleased by it, and since then one had almost needed to pull him down from the ceiling with a string, like a helium-filled balloon. My own feelings weren't actually much lower. Datepalm really was a horse to build dreams on.

After the food and a dozen repetitions of the horse's virtues Milo told the Ostermeyers about my inheriting Dozen Roses and about the probate saga, which seemed to fascinate them. Martha sat up straighter and exclaimed, "Did you say York?"

Milo nodded.

"Do you mean this Saturday? Why, Harley and I are going to York races on Saturday, aren't we, Harley?"

Harley agreed that they were. "Our dear friends Lord and Lady Knightwood have asked us to lunch."

Martha said, "Why don't we give Derek a ride up there to see his horse run? What do you say, Harley?"

"Be glad to have you along," Harley said to me genuinely. "Don't give us no for an answer."

I looked at their kind, insistent faces and said lamely, "I thought of going by train, if I went at all."

"No, no," Martha said. "Come to London by train and we'll go up together. Do say you will."

Milo was looking at me anxiously: pleasing the Ostermeyers was still an absolute priority. I said I'd be glad to accept their kindness and Martha, mixing gratification with sudden alarm, said she hoped the inheritance wouldn't persuade me to stop riding races.

"No," I said.

"That's positive enough." Harley was pleased. "You're part of the package, fella. You and Datepalm together."

Brad and I went on to London, and I was very glad to have him drive.

"Office?" he asked, and I said "Yes," and we traveled there in silent harmony.

He'd told me the evening before that Greville's car wasn't parked anywhere near Greville's house: or rather he'd handed me back the piece of paper with the car's number on it and said, "Couldn't find it." I thought I'd better get on to the police and other towers-away in Ipswich, and I'd better start learning the company's finances and Greville's as well, and I had two-thirds of the vault still to check and I could feel the suction of the quicksand inexorably.

I took the two baffling little gadgets from Greville's sitting room upstairs to Greville's office and showed them to June.

"That one," she said immediately, pointing to the thumb-sized tube with the whine "is a device to discourage mosquitoes. Mr. Franklin said it's the noise of a male mosquito, and it frightens the blood-sucking females away." She laughed. "He said every man should have one."

She picked up the other gadget and frowned at it, pressing the red button with no results.

"It has an aerial," I said.

"Oh yes." She pulled it out to its full extent. "I think . . ." She paused. "He used to have a transmitter which started his car from a distance, so he could warm the engine up in cold weather before he left his house, but the receiver bit got stolen with his Porsche. Then he bought the old Rover, and he said a car-starter wouldn't work on it because it only worked with direct transmission or fuel injection, or something, which the Rover doesn't have."

"So this is the car-starter?"

"Well . . . no. This one doesn't do so much. The car-starter had buttons that would also switch on the headlights so that you could see where your car was, if you'd left it in a dark car-park." She pushed the aerial down again. "I think this one only switches the lights on, or makes the car whistle, if I remember right. He was awfully pleased with it when he got it, but I haven't seen it for ages. He had so many gadgets, he couldn't take them all in his pockets and I think he'd got a bit tired of carrying them about. He used to leave them in this desk, mostly."

"You just earned your twenty percent all over again," I said.

"What?"

"Let's just check that the batteries work," I said.

She opened the battery compartment and discovered it was empty. As if it were routine, she then pulled open a drawer in one of the other tiers of the desk and revealed a large open box containing packet after packet of new batteries in every possible size. She pulled out a packet, opened it and fed the necessary power packs into the slots, and although pressing the red button still provided no visible results, I was pretty confident we were in business.

June said suddenly, "You're going to take this to Ipswich, aren't you? To find his car? Isn't that what you mean?"

I nodded. "Let's hope it works."

"Oh, it must."

"It's quite a big town, and the car could be anywhere."

"Yes," she said, "but it must be *somewhere*. I'm sure you'll find it."

"Mm." I looked at her bright, intelligent face. "June," I said slowly, "don't tell anyone else about this gadget."

"Whyever not?"

"Because," I said, "someone broke into this office looking for something and we don't know if they found it. If they didn't, and it is by any chance in the car, I don't want anyone to realize that the car is still lost." I paused. "I'd much rather you said nothing."

"Not even to Annette?"

"Not to anyone."

"But that means you think . . . you think . . ."

"I don't really think anything. It's just for security."

Security was all right with her. She looked less troubled and agreed to keep quiet about the car-finder; and I hadn't needed to tell her about the mugger who had knocked me down to steal Greville's bag of clothes, which to me, in hindsight, was looking less and less a random hit and more and more a shot at a target.

Someone must have known Greville was dying, I thought.

Someone who had organized or executed a mugging. I hadn't the faintest idea who could have done either, but it did seem to me possible that one of Greville's staff might have unwittingly chattered within earshot of receptive ears. Yet what could they have said? Greville hadn't told any of them he was buying diamonds. And why hadn't he? Secretive as he was, gems were his business.

The useless thoughts squirreled around and got me nowhere. The gloomiest of them was that someone could have gone looking for Greville's car at any time since the scaffolding fell, and although I might find the engine and the wheels, the essential cupboard would be bare.

Annette came into the office carrying a fistful of papers which she said had come in the morning mail and needed to be dealt with—by me, her manner inferred.

"Sit down, then," I said, "and tell me what they all mean."

There were letters from insurance people, fund-raisers, dissatisfied customers, gemology forecasters, and a cable from a supplier in Hong Kong saying he didn't have enough African 12mm amethyst AA quality round beads to fill our order and would we take Brazilian amethyst to make it up.

"What's the difference?" I asked. "Does it matter?"

Annette developed worry lines over my ignorance. "The best amethyst is found in Africa," she said. "Then it goes to Hong Kong or Taiwan for cutting and polishing into beads, then comes here. The amethyst from Brazil isn't such a good deep color. Do you want me to order the Brazilian amethyst or wait until he has more of the African?"

"What do you think?" I said.

"Mr. Franklin always decided."

She looked at me anxiously. It's hopeless, I thought. The simplest decision was impossible without knowledge.

"Would the customers take the Brazilian instead?" I asked.

"Some would, some wouldn't. It's much cheaper. We sell a lot of the Brazilian anyway, in all sizes."

"Well," I said, "if we run out of the African beads, offer the customers Brazilian. Or offer a different size of African. Cable the Chinese supplier to send just the African AA 12mm he's got now and the rest as soon as he can."

She looked relieved. "That's what I'd have said."

Then why didn't you, I thought, but it was no use being angry. If she gave me bad advice I'd probably blame her for it: it was safer from her viewpoint, I supposed, not to stick her neck out.

"Incidentally," she said, "I did reach Prospero Jenks. He said he'd be in his Knightsbridge shop at two-thirty today, if you wanted to see him."

"Great."

She smiled. "I didn't mention horses."

I smiled back. "Fine."

She took the letters off to her own office to answer them, and I went from department to department on a round trip to the vault, watching everyone at work, all of them capable, willing and beginning to settle obligingly into the change of regime, keeping their inner reservations to themselves. I asked if one of them would go down and tell Brad I'd need him at two, not before: June went and returned like a boomerang.

I unlocked the vault and started on topaz: thousands of brilliant translucent slippery stones in a rainbow of colors, some bigger than acorns, some like peas.

No diamonds.

After that, every imaginable shape and size of garnet, which could be yellow and green, I found, as well as red, and boxes of citrine.

Two and a half hours of unfolding and folding glossy white packets, and no diamonds.

June swirled in and out at one point with a long order for faceted stones which she handed to me without comment, and I remembered that only Greville and Annette packed orders from the vault. I went in search of Annette and asked if I might watch while she worked down the list, found what was needed from twenty or more boxes and assembled the total on the shelf. She was quick and sure, knowing exactly where to find everything. It was quite easy, she said, reassuring me. I would soon get the hang of it. God help me, I thought.

At two, after another of June's sandwich lunches, I went down to the car and gave Prospero Jenks's address to Brad. "It's a shop somewhere near Harrods," I said, climbing in.

He nodded, drove through the traffic, found the shop.

"Great," I said. "Now this time you'll have to answer the car phone whether you like it or not, because there's nowhere here to park."

He shook his head. He'd resisted the suggestion several times before.

"Yes," I said. "It's very easy. I'll switch it on for you now. When it rings pick it up and press this button, SND, and you'll be able to hear me. OK? I'll ring when I'm ready to leave, then you just come back here and pick me up."

He looked at the telephone as if it were contaminated.

It was a totally portable phone, not a fixture in the car, and it didn't receive calls unless one switched it on, which I quite often forgot to do and sometimes didn't do on purpose. I put the phone ready on the passenger seat beside him, to make it easy, and hoped for the best.

Prospero Jenks's shopwindow glittered with the sort of intense lighting that makes jewelry sparkle, but the lettering of his name over the window was neat and plain, as if ostentation there would have been superfluous.

I looked at the window with a curiosity I would never have felt a week earlier and found it filled not with conventional displays of rings and wristwatches but with joyous toys: model cars, airplanes, skiing figures, racing yachts, pheasants and horses, all gold and enamel and shining with gems. Almost every passerby, I noticed, paused to look.

Pushing awkwardly through the heavy glass front door, I stepped into a deep carpeted area with chairs at the ready before every counter. Apart from the plushness, it was basically an ordinary shop, not very big, quiet in decor, all the excitement in the baubles.

There was no one but me in there and I swung over to one of the counters to see what was on display. Rings, I found, but not simple little circles. These were huge, often asymmetric, all colorful eye-catchers supreme.

"Can I help you?" a voice said.

A neutral man, middle-aged, in a black suit, coming from a doorway at the rear.

"My name's Franklin," I said. "Came to see Prospero Jenks."

"A minute."

He retreated, returned with a half smile and invited me through the doorway to the privacies beyond. Shielded from customers' view by a screening partition lay a much longer space which doubled as office and workroom and contained a fearsome-looking safe and several tiers of little drawers like the ones in Saxony Franklin. On one wall a large framed sign read NEVER TURN YOUR BACK TO CUSTOMERS. ALWAYS WATCH THEIR HANDS. A fine statement of no trust, I thought in amusement.

Sitting on a stool by a workbench, a jeweler's lens screwed into one eye, was a hunched man in pale pink and white striped shirtsleeves fiddling intently with a small gold object fixed into a vise. Patience and expert workmanship were much on view, all of it calm and painstaking.

He removed the lens with a sigh and rose to his feet, turning to inspect me from crown to crutches to toecaps with growing surprise. Whatever he'd been expecting, I was not it.

The feeling, I supposed, was mutual. He was maybe fifty but looked younger in a Peter Pan sort of way; a boyish face with intense bright blue eyes and a lot of lines developing across the forehead. Fairish hair, no beard, no mustache, no personal display. I had expected someone fancier, more extravagant, temperamental.

"Grev's brother?" he said. "What a turn-up. There I was, thinking you'd be his age, his height." He narrowed his eyes. "He never said he had a brother. How do I know you're legit?"

"His assistant, Annette Adams, made the appointment."

"Yes, so she did. Fair enough. Told me Grev was dead, long live the King. Said his brother was running the shop, life would go on. But I'll tell you, unless you know as much as Grev, I'm in trouble."

"I came to talk to you about that."

"It don't look like tidings of great joy," he said, watching me judiciously. "Want a seat?" He pointed at an office chair for me and took his place on the stool. His voice was a long way from cut-glass. More like East-end London tidied up for west; the sort that came from nowhere with no privileges and made it to the top from sheer undeniable talent. He had the confident manner of long success, a creative spirit who was also a tradesman, an original artist without airs.

"I'm just learning the business," I said cautiously. "I'll do what I can."

"Grev was a genius," he said explosively. "No one like him with stones. He'd bring me oddities, one-of-a-kinds from all over the world, and I've made pieces . . ." He stopped and spread his arms out. "They're in palaces," he said, "and museums and mansions in Palm Beach. Well, I'm in business. I sell them to wherever the money's coming from. I've got my pride, but it's in the pieces. They're good, I'm expensive, it works a treat."

"Do you make everything you sell?" I asked.

He laughed. "No, not myself personally, I couldn't. I design everything, don't get me wrong, but I have a workshop making them. I just make the special pieces myself, the unique ones. In between, I invent for the general market. Grev said he had some decent spinel, have you still got it?"

"Er," I said, "red?"

"Red," he affirmed. "Three, four or five carats. I'll take all you've got."

"We'll send it tomorrow."

"By messenger," he said. "Not post."

"All right."

"And a slab of rock crystal like the Eiger. Grev showed me a photo. I've got a commission for a fantasy. Send the crystal too."

"All right," I said again, and hid my doubts. I hadn't seen any slab of rock crystal. Annette would know, I thought.

He said casually, "What about the diamonds?"

I let the breath out and into my lungs with conscious control.

"What about them?" I said.

"Grev was getting me some. He'd got them, in fact. He told me. He'd sent a batch off to be cut. Are they back yet?"

"Not yet," I said, hoping I wasn't croaking. "Are those the diamonds he bought a couple of months ago from the Central Selling Organisation that you're talking about?"

"Sure. He bought a share in a sight from a sightholder. I asked him to. I'm still running the big chunky rings and necklaces I made my name in, but I'm setting some of them now with bigger diamonds, making more profit per item since the market will stand it, and I wanted Grev to get them because I trust him. Trust is like gold dust in this business, even though diamonds weren't his thing, really. You wouldn't want to buy two-to-three-carat stones from just anyone, even if they're not D or E flawless, right?"

"Er, right."

"So he bought the share of the sight and he's having them cut in Antwerp as I need them, as I expect you know."

I nodded. I did know, but only since he'd just told me.

"I'm going to make stars of some of them to shine from the rock crystal . . ." He broke off, gave a self-deprecating shrug of the shoulders, and said, "And I'm making a mobile, with diamonds on gold trembler wires that move in the

[121]

lightest air. It's to hang by a window and flash fire in the sunlight." Again the self-deprecation, this time in a smile. "Diamonds are ravishing in sunlight, they're at their best in it, and all the social snobs in this city scream that it's so frightfully vulgar, darling, to wear diamond earrings or bracelets in the daytime. It makes me sick, to be honest. Such a waste."

I had never thought about diamonds in sunlight before, though I supposed I would in future. Vistas opened could never be closed, as maybe Greville would have said.

"I haven't caught up with everything yet," I said, which was the understatement of the century. "Have any of the diamonds been delivered to you so far?"

He shook his head. "I haven't been in a hurry for them before."

"And . . . er . . . how many are involved?"

"About a hundred. Like I said, not the very best color in the accepted way of things but they can look warmer with gold sometimes if they're not ultra blue-white. I work with gold mostly. I like the feel."

"How much," I said slowly, doing sums, "will your rock crystal fantasy sell for?"

"Trade secret. But then, I guess you're trade. It's commissioned, I've got a contract for a quarter of a million if they like it. If they don't like it, I get it back, sell it somewhere else, dismantle it, whatever. In the worst event I'd lose nothing but my time in making it, but don't you worry, they'll like it."

His certainty was absolute, built on experience.

I said, "Do you happen to know the name of the Antwerp cutter Grev sent the diamonds to? I mean, it's bound to be on file in the office, but if I know who to look for . . ." I paused. "I could try to hurry him up for you, if you like."

"I'd like you to, but I don't know who Grev knew there, exactly."

I shrugged. "I'll look it up, then."

Exactly where was I going to look it up? I wondered. Not in the missing address book, for sure.

"Do you know the name of the sightholder?" I asked.

"Nope."

"There's a ton of paper in the office," I said in explanation. "I'm going through it as fast as I can."

"Grev never said a word he didn't have to," Jenks said unexpectedly. "I'd talk, he listened. We got on fine. He understood what I do better than anybody."

The sadness of his voice was my brother's universal accolade, I thought. He'd been liked. He'd been trusted. He would be missed.

I stood up and said, "Thank you, Mr. Jenks."

"Call me Pross," he said easily. "Everyone does."

"My name's Derek."

"Right," he said, smiling. "Now I'll keep on dealing with you, I won't say I won't, but I'm going to have to find me another traveler like Grev, with an eye like his. He's been supplying me ever since I started on my own, he gave me credit when the banks wouldn't, he had faith in what I could do. Near the beginning he brought me two rare sticks of watermelon tourmaline that were each over two inches long and were half pink, half green mixed all the way up and transparent with the light shining through them and changing while you watched. It would have been a sin to cut them for jewelry. I mounted them in gold and platinum to hang and twist in sunlight." He smiled his deprecating smile. "I like gemstones to have life. I didn't have to pay Grev for that tourmaline ever. It made my name for me, the piece was reviewed in the papers and won prizes, and he said the trade we'd do together would be his reward." He clicked his mouth. "I do go on a bit."

"I like to hear it," I said. I looked down the room to his workbench and said, "Where did you learn all this? How does one start?"

"I started in metalwork classes at the local high school," he said frankly. "Then I stuck bits of glass in gold-plated wire to give to my mum. Then her friends wanted some. So when I left school I took some of those things to show to a jewelry manufacturer and asked for a job. Costume jewelry, they made. I was soon designing for them, and I never looked back."

8

I borrowed Prospero's telephone to get Brad, but although
I could hear the ringing tone in the car, he didn't answer.
Cursing slightly, I asked Pross for a second call and got
through to Annette.

"Please keep on trying this number," I said, giving it to her.
"When Brad answers, tell him I'm ready to go."

"Are you coming back here?" she asked.

I looked at my watch. It wasn't worth going back as I had
to return to Kensington by five-thirty. I said no, I wasn't.

"Well, there are one or two things . . ."

"I can't really tie this phone up," I said. "I'll go to my
brother's house and call you from there. Just keep trying
Brad."

I thanked Pross again for the calls. Any time, he said
vaguely. He was sitting again in front of his vise, thinking and
tinkering, producing his marvels.

There were customers in the shop being attended to by the
black-suited salesman. He glanced up very briefly in acknowledgment as I went through and immediately returned to
watching the customers' hands. A business without trust;
much worse than racing. But then, it was probably impossible
to slip a racehorse into a pocket when the trainer wasn't
looking.

I stood on the pavement and wondered pessimistically how

long it would take Brad to answer the telephone but in the event he surprised me by arriving within a very few minutes. When I opened the car door, the phone was ringing.

"Why don't you answer it?" I asked, wriggling my way into the seat.

"Forgot which button."

"But you came," I said.

"Yerss."

I picked up the phone myself and talked to Annette. "Brad apparently reckoned that if the phone rang it meant I was ready, so he saw no need to answer it."

Brad gave a silent nod.

"So now we're setting off to Kensington." I paused. "Annette, what's a sightholder, and what's a sight?"

"You're back to diamonds again!"

"Yes. Do you know?"

"Of course I do. A sightholder is someone who is permitted to buy rough diamonds from the C.S.O. There aren't so many sightholders, only about a hundred and fifty world-wide, I think. They sell the diamonds then to other people. A sight is what they call the sales C.S.O. hold every five weeks, and a sight-box is a packet of stones they sell, though that's often called a sight too."

"Is a sightholder the same as a diamantaire?" I asked.

"All sightholders are diamantaires, but all diamantaires are not sightholders. Diamantaires buy from the sightholders, or share in a sight, or buy somewhere else, not from de Beers."

Ask a simple question, I thought.

Annette said, "A consignment of cultured pearls has come from Japan. Where shall I put them?"

"Um . . . Do you mean where because the vault is locked?"

"Yes."

"Where did you put things when my brother was traveling?"

She said doubtfully, "He always said to put them in the stockroom under 'miscellaneous beads.'"

[126]

"Put them in there, then."

"But the drawer is full with some things that came last week. I wouldn't want the responsibility of putting the pearls anywhere Mr. Franklin hadn't approved." I couldn't believe she needed direction over the simplest thing, but apparently she did. "The pearls are valuable," she said. "Mr. Franklin would never leave them out in plain view."

"Aren't there any empty drawers?"

"Well, I . . ."

"Find an empty drawer or a nearly empty drawer and put them there. We'll see to them properly in the morning."

"Yes, all right."

She seemed happy with it and said everything else could wait until I came back. I switched off the telephone feeling absolutely swamped by the prospect she'd opened up: if Greville hid precious things under "miscellaneous beads," where else might he not have hidden them? Would I find a hundred diamonds stuffed in at the back of rhodochrosite or jasper, if I looked?

The vault alone was taking too long. The four big stockrooms promised a nightmare.

Brad miraculously found a parking space right outside Greville's house, which seemed obscurely to disappoint him.

"Twenty past five," he said, "for the pub?"

"If you wouldn't mind. And . . . er . . . would you just stand there now while I take a look-see?" I had grown cautious, I found.

He ducked his head in assent and watched me maneuver the few steps up to the front door. No floodlights came on and no dog barked, presumably because it was daylight. I opened the three locks and pushed the door.

The house was still. No movements of air. I propped the door open with a bronze horse clearly lying around for the purpose and went down the passage to the small sitting room.

No intruders. No mess. No amazons waving riot sticks, no wrecking balls trying to get past the grilles on the windows.

[127]

If anyone had attempted to penetrate Greville's fortress, they hadn't succeeded.

I returned to the front door. Brad was still standing beside the car, looking toward the house. I gave him a thumbs-up sign, and he climbed into the driver's seat while I closed the heavy door and in the little sitting room started taking all of the books off the shelves methodically, riffling the pages and putting each back where I found it.

There were ten hollow books altogether, mostly with titles like "Tales of the Outback" and "With a Mule in Patagonia." Four were empty, including the one which had held Clarissa Williams's letters. One held the big ornate key. One held an expensive-looking gold watch, the hands pointing to the correct time.

The watch Greville had been wearing in Ipswich was one of those affairs with more knobs than instructions. It lay now beside my bed in Hungerford emitting bleeps at odd intervals and telling me which way was north. The slim gold elegance in the hollow box was for a different mood, a different man, and when I turned it over on my palm I found the inscription on the back: G, my love, C.

She couldn't have known it was there, I thought. She hadn't looked for it. She'd looked only for the letters, and by chance had come to them first. I put the watch back into the box and back on the shelf. There was no way I could return it to her, and perhaps she wouldn't want it, not with that inscription.

Two of the remaining boxes contained keys, again unspecified, and one contained a folded instruction leaflet detailing how to set a safe in a concrete nest. The last revealed two very small plastic cases containing baby recording tapes, each adorned with the printed legend "microcassette." The cassette cases were all of two inches long by one and a half wide, the featherweight tapes inside a fraction smaller.

I tossed one in my hand indecisively. Nowhere among Greville's tidy belongings had I so far found a microcassette player, which didn't mean I wouldn't in time. Sufficient to the day, I thought in the end, and left the tiny tapes in the book.

With the scintillating titles and their secrets all back on the shelves I stared at them gloomily. Not a diamond in the lot.

Instructions for concrete nests were all very well, but where was the safe? Tapes were OK, but where was the player? Keys were fine, but where were the keyholes? The most frustrating thing about it all was that Greville hadn't meant to leave such puzzles. For him, the answers were part of his fabric.

I'd noticed on my way in and out of the house that mail was accumulating in the wire container fixed inside the letter box, so to fill in the time before I was due at the pub I took the letters along to the sitting room and began opening the envelopes.

It seemed all wrong. I kept telling myself it was necessary but I still felt as if I were trespassing on ground Greville had surrounded with keep-out fences. There were bills, requests from charities, a bank statement for his private account, a gemology magazine and two invitations. No letters from sightholders, diamantaires or cutters in Antwerp. I put the letters into the gemology magazine's large envelope and added to them some similar unfinished business that I'd found in the drawer under the telephone, and reflected ruefully, putting it all ready to take to Hungerford, that I loathed paperwork at the best of times. My own had a habit of mounting up into increasingly urgent heaps. Perhaps having to do Greville's would teach me some sense.

Brad whisked us round to the Rook and Castle at five-thirty and pointed to the phone to let me know how I could call him when I'd finished, and I saw from his twitch of a smile that he found it a satisfactory amusement.

The Rook and Castle was old-fashioned inside as well as out, an oasis of drinking peace without a juke-box. There was a lot of dark wood and Tiffany lampshades and small tables with beer mats. An office-leaving clientele of mostly business-suited men was beginning to trickle in and I paused inside the door both to get accustomed to the comparative darkness and to give anyone who was interested a plain view of the crutches.

The interest level being nil, I judged Elliot Trelawney to be absent. I went over to the bar, ordered some Perrier and swallowed a Distalgesic, as it was time. The morning's gallop had done no good to the ankle department but it wasn't to be regretted.

A bulky man of about fifty came into the place as if familiar with his surroundings and looked purposefully around, sharpening his gaze on the crutches and coming without hesitation to the bar.

"Mr. Franklin?"

I shook his offered hand.

"What are you drinking?" he said briskly, eying my glass.

"Perrier. That's temporary also."

He smiled swiftly, showing white teeth. "You won't mind if I have a double Glenlivet? Greville and I drank many of them together here. I'm going to miss him abominably. Tell me what happened."

I told him. He listened intently, but at the end he said merely, "You look very uncomfortable propped against that stool. Why don't we move to a table?" And without more ado he picked up my glass along with the one the bartender had fixed for him, and carried them over to two wooden armchairs under a multicolored lampshade by the wall.

"That's better," he said, taking a sip and eying me over the glass. "So you're the brother he talked about. You're Derek."

"I'm Derek. His only brother, actually. I didn't know he talked about me."

"Oh, yes. Now and then."

Elliot Trelawney was big, almost bald, with half-moon glasses and a face that was fleshy but healthy-looking. He had thin lips but laugh lines around his eyes, and I'd have said on a snap judgment that he was a realist with a sense of humor.

"He was proud of you," he said.

[130]

"Proud?" I was surprised.

He glimmered. "We often played golf together on Saturday mornings and sometimes he would be wanting to finish before the two o'clock race at Sandown or somewhere, and it would be because you were riding and it was on the box. He liked to watch you. He liked you to win."

"He never told me," I said regretfully.

"He wouldn't, would he? I watched with him a couple of times and all he said after you'd won was, 'That's all right, then.' "

"And when I lost?"

"When you lost?" He smiled. "Nothing at all. Once you had a crashing fall and he said he'd be glad on the whole when you retired, as race-riding was so dangerous. Ironic, isn't it?"

"Yes."

"By God, I'll miss him." His voice was deep. "We were friends for twenty years."

I envied him. I wanted intolerably what it was too late to have, and the more I listened to people remembering Greville the worse it got.

"Are you a magistrate?" I asked.

He nodded. "We often sat together. Greville introduced me to it, but I've never had quite his gift. He seemed to know the truth of things by instinct. He said goodness was visible, therefore in its absence one sought for answers."

"What sort of cases did . . . do you try?"

"All sorts." He smiled again briefly. "Shoplifters. Vagrants. Possession of drugs. TV license fee evaders. Sex offenders . . . that's prostitution, rape, sex with minors, curb crawlers. Greville always seemed to know infallibly when those were lying."

"Go on," I said, when he stopped. "Anything else?"

"Well, there are a lot of diplomats in West London, in all the embassies. You'd be astonished what they get away with by claiming diplomatic immunity. Greville hated diplomatic immunity, but we have to grant it. Then we have a lot of small

[131]

businessmen who 'forget' to pay the road tax on the company vehicles, and there are TDA's by the hundreds—that's Taking and Driving Away cars. Other motoring offenses, speeding and so on, are dealt with separately, like domestic offenses and juveniles. And then occasionally we get the preliminary hearings in a murder case, but of course we have to refer those to the Crown Court."

"Does it all ever depress you?" I said.

He took a sip and considered me. "It makes you sad," he said eventually. "We see as much inadequacy and stupidity as downright villainy. Some of it makes you laugh. I wouldn't say it's depressing, but one learns to see the world from underneath, so to speak. To see the dirt and the delusions, to see through the offenders' eyes and understand their weird logic. But one's disillusion is sporadic because we don't have a bench every day. Twice a month, in Greville's and my cases, plus a little committee work. And that's what I really want from you: the notes Greville was making on the licensing of a new-style gaming club. He said he'd learned disturbing allegations against one of the organizers and he was going to advise turning down the application at the next committee meeting even though it was a project we'd formerly looked on favorably."

"I'm afraid," I said, "that I haven't so far found any notes like that."

"Damn . . . Where would he have put them?"

"I don't know. I'll look for them, though." No harm in keeping an eye open for notes while I searched for C.

Elliot Trelawney reached into an inner jacket pocket and brought out two flat black objects, one a notebook, the other a folded black case a bit like a cigarette case.

"These were Greville's," he said. "I brought them for you." He put them on the small table and moved them toward me with plump and deliberate fingers. "He lent me that one," he pointed, "and the notebook he left on the table after a committee meeting last week."

[132]

"Thank you," I said. I picked up the folded case and opened it and found inside a miniature electronic chess set, the sort that challenged a player to beat it. I looked up. Trelawney's expression, unguarded, was intensely sorrowful. "Would you like it?" I said. "I know it's not much, but would you like to keep it?"

"If you mean it."

I nodded and he put the chess set back into his pocket. "Greville and I used to play . . . *dammit* . . ." he finished explosively. "Why should such a futile thing happen?"

No answer was possible. I regretfully picked up the black notebook and opened it at random.

"The bad scorn the good," I read aloud, "and the crooked despise the straight."

"The thoughts of Chairman Mao," Trelawney said dryly, recovering himself. "I used to tease him. He said it was a habit he'd had from university when he'd learned to clarify his thoughts by writing them down. When I knew he was dead I read that notebook from cover to cover. I've copied down some of the things in it, I hope you won't mind." He smiled. "You'll find parts of it especially interesting."

"About his horses?"

"Those too."

I stowed the notebook in a trousers pocket which was already pretty full and brought out from there the racing diary, struck by a thought. I explained what the diary was, showing it to Trelawney.

"I phoned that number," I said, turning pages and pointing, "and mentioned Greville's name, and a woman told me in no uncertain terms never to telephone again as she wouldn't have the name Greville Franklin spoken in her house."

Elliot Trelawney blinked. "Greville? Doesn't sound like Greville."

"I didn't think so, either. So would it have had something to do with one of your cases? Someone he found guilty of something?"

"Hah. Perhaps." He considered. "I could probably find out whose number it is, if you like. Strange he would have had it in his diary, though. Do you want to follow it up?"

"It just seemed so odd," I said.

"Quite right." He unclipped a gold pencil from another inner pocket and in a slim notebook of black leather with gold corners wrote down the number.

"Do you make enemies much, because of the court?" I asked.

He looked up and shrugged. "We get cursed now and then. Screamed at, one might say. But usually not. Mostly they plead guilty because it's so obvious they are. The only real enemy Greville might have had is the gambling club organizer who's not going to get his license. A drugs baron is what Greville called him. A man suspected of murder but not tried through lack of evidence. He might have had very hard feelings." He hesitated. "When I heard Greville was dead, I even wondered about Vaccaro. But it seems clear the scaffolding was a sheer accident . . . wasn't it?"

"Yes, it was. The scaffolding broke high up. One man working on it fell three stories to his death. Pieces just rained down on Greville. A minute earlier, a minute later . . ." I sighed. "Is Vaccaro the gambling-license man?"

"He is. He appeared before the committee and seemed perfectly straightforward. Subject to screening, we said. And then someone contacted Greville and uncovered the muck. But we don't ourselves have any details, so we need his notes."

"I'll look for them," I promised again. I turned more pages in the diary. "Does Koningin Beatrix mean anything to you?" I showed him the entry. "Or CZ equals C times one point seven?"

C, I thought, looking at it again, stood for diamond.

"Nothing," Elliot Trelawney said. "But as you know, Greville could be as obscure as he was clear-headed. And these were private notes to himself, after all. Same as his notebook. It was never for public consumption."

[134]

I nodded and put away the diary and paid for Elliot Trelawney's repeat Glenlivet but felt waterlogged myself. He stayed for a while, seeming to be glad to talk about Greville, as I was content to listen. We parted eventually on friendly terms, he giving me his card with his phone number for when I found Greville's notes.

If, I silently thought. If I find them.

When he'd gone I used the pub's telephone to call the car, and after five unanswered *brr-brrs* disconnected and went outside, and Brad with almost a grin reappeared to pick me up.

"Home," I said, and he said, "Yerss," and that was that.

On the way I read bits of Greville's notebook, pausing often to digest the passing thoughts which had clearly been chiefly prompted by the flotsam drifting through the West London Magistrates Court.

"Goodness is sickening to the evil," he wrote, "as evil is sickening to the good. Both the evil and the good may be complacent."

"In all income groups you find your average regulation slob who sniggers at anarchy but calls the police indignantly to his burglarized home, who is actively anti-authority until he needs to be saved from someone with a gun."

"The palm outstretched for a handout can turn in a flash into a cursing fist. A nation's palm, a nation's fist."

"Crime to many is not crime but simply a way of life. If laws are inconvenient, ignore them, they don't apply to you."

"Infinite sadness is not to trust an old friend."

"Historically, more people have died of religion than cancer."

"I hate rapists. I imagine being anally assaulted myself, and the anger overwhelms me. It's essential to make my judgment cold."

Further on I came unexpectedly to what Elliot Trelawney must have meant.

Greville had written, "Derek came to dinner very stiff with broken ribs. I asked him how he managed to live with all those

[135]

injuries. 'Forget the pain and get on with the party,' he said. So we drank fizz."

I stopped reading and stared out at the autumn countryside which was darkening now, lights going on. I remembered that evening very well, up to a point. Greville had been good fun. I'd got pretty high on the cocktail of champagne and painkillers and I hadn't felt a thing until I'd woken in the morning. I'd driven myself seventy miles home and forgotten it, which frightening fact was roughly why I was currently and obediently sticking to water.

It was almost too dark to read more, but I flicked over one more page and came to what amounted to a prayer, so private and impassioned that I felt my mouth go dry. Alone on the page were three brief lines:

May I deal with honour.
May I act with courage.
May I achieve humility.

I felt as if I shouldn't have read it; knew he hadn't meant it to be read. May I achieve humility . . . that prayer was for saints.

When we reached my house I told Brad I would go to London the next day by train, and he looked devastated.

"I'll drive you for nowt," he said, hoarsely.

"It isn't the money." I was surprised by the strength of his feelings. "I just thought you'd be tired of all the waiting about."

He shook his head vigorously, his eyes positively pleading.

"All right, then," I said. "London tomorrow, Ipswich on Friday. OK?"

"Yerss," he said with obvious relief.

"And I'll pay you, of course."

He looked at me dumbly for a moment, then ducked his head into the car to fetch the big brown envelope from Greville's house, and he waited while I unlocked my door and made sure that there were no unwelcome visitors lurking.

Everything was quiet, everything orderly. Brad nodded at my all-clear, gave me the envelope and loped off into the night more tongue-tied than ever. I'd never wondered very much about his thoughts during all the silent hours; had never tried, I supposed, to understand him. I wasn't sure that I wanted to. It was restful the way things were.

I ate a microwaved chicken pie from the freezer and made an unenthusiastic start on Greville's letters, paying his bills for him, closing his accounts, declining his invitations, saying sorry, sorry, very sorry.

After that, in spite of good resolutions, I did not attack my own backlog but read right through Greville's notebook looking for diamonds. Maybe there were some solid gold nuggets, maybe some pearls of wisdom, but no helpful instructions like turn right at the fourth apple tree, walk five paces and dig.

I did however find the answer to one small mystery, which I read with wry amusement.

"The green soapstone box pleases me as an exercise in misdirection and deviousness. The keyhole has no key because it has no lock. It's impossible to unlock men's minds with keys, but guile and pressure will do it, as with the box."

Even with the plain instruction to be guileful and devious it took me ages to find the secret. I tried pressing each of the two hinges, pressing the lock, twisting, pressing everything again with the box upside down. The green stone stayed stubbornly shut.

Misdirection, I thought. If the keyhole wasn't a lock, maybe the hinges weren't hinges. Maybe the lid wasn't a lid. Maybe the whole thing was solid.

I tried the box upside down again, put my thumb on its bottom surface with firm pressure and tried to push it out endways, like a slide. Nothing happened. I reversed it and pushed the other way and as if with a sigh for the length of my stupidity the bottom of the box slid out reluctantly to halfway, and stopped.

It was beautifully made, I thought. When it was shut one

couldn't see the bottom edges weren't solid stone, so closely did they fit. I looked with great curiosity to see what Greville had hidden in his ingenious hiding place, not really expecting diamonds, and brought out two well-worn chamois leather pouches with drawstrings, the sort jewelers use, with the name of the jeweler indistinctly stamped on the front.

Both of the pouches were empty, to my great disappointment. I stuffed them back into the hole and shut the box, and it sat on the table beside the telephone all evening, an enigma solved but useless.

It wasn't until I'd decided to go to bed that some switch or other clicked in my brain and a word half-seen became suddenly a conscious thought. Van Ekeren, stamped in gold. Perhaps the jeweler's name stamped on the chamois pouches was worth another look.

I opened the box and pulled the pouches out again and in the rubbed and faded lettering read the full name and address.

JACOB VAN EKEREN
PELIKANSTRAAT 70
ANTWERP

There had to be, I thought, about ten thousand jewelers in Antwerp. The pouches were far from new, certainly not only a few weeks old. All the same . . . better find out.

I took one and left one, closing the box again, and in the morning bore the crumpled trophy to London and through international telephone inquiries found Jacob van Ekeren's number.

The voice that answered from Antwerp spoke either Dutch or Flemish, so I tried in French, "Je veux parler avec Monsieur Jacob van Ekeren, s'il vous plaît."

"Ne quittez pas."

I held on as instructed until another voice spoke, this time in French, of which I knew far too little.

[138]

"Monsieur van Ekeren n'est pas ici maintenant, monsieur."

"Parlez-vous anglais?" I asked. "I'm speaking from England."

"Attendez."

I waited again and was rewarded with an extremely English voice asking if he could help.

I explained that I was speaking from Saxony Franklin Ltd., gemstone importers in London.

"How can I help you?" He was courteous and noncommittal.

"Do you," I said baldly, "cut and polish rough diamonds?"

"Yes, of course," he answered. "But before we do business with any new client we need introductions and references."

"Um," I said. "Wouldn't Saxony Franklin Limited be a client of yours already? Or Greville Saxony Franklin, maybe? Or just Greville Franklin? It's really important."

"May I have your name?"

"Derek Franklin. Greville's brother."

"One moment." He returned after a while and said he would call me back shortly with an answer.

"Thank you very much," I said.

"Pas du tout." Bilingual besides.

I put down the phone and asked both Annette and June, who were busily moving around, if they could find Jacob van Ekeren anywhere in Greville's files. "See if you can find any mention of Antwerp in the computer," I added to June.

"Diamonds again!"

"Yup. The van Ekeren address is 70 Pelikanstraat."

Annette wrinkled her brow. "That's the Belgian equivalent of Hatton Garden," she said.

It disrupted their normal work and they weren't keen, but Annette was very soon able to say she had no record of any Jacob van Ekeren, but the files were kept in the office for only six years, and any contact before that would be in storage in the basement. June whisked in to confirm that she couldn't find van Ekeren or Pelikanstraat or Antwerp in the computer.

It wasn't exactly surprising. If Greville had wanted his diamond transaction to be common knowledge in the office he would have conducted it out in the open. Very odd, I thought, that he hadn't. If it had been anyone but Greville one would have suspected him of something underhanded, but as far as I knew he always had dealt with honor, as he'd prayed.

The telephone rang and Annette answered it. "Saxony Franklin, can I help you?" She listened. "Derek Franklin? Yes, just a moment." She handed me the receiver and I found it was the return of the smooth French-English voice from Belgium. I knew as well as he did that he had spent the time between the two calls getting our number from international inquiries so that he could check back and be sure I was who I'd said. Merely prudent. I'd have done the same.

"Mr. Jacob van Ekeren has retired," he said. "I am his nephew Hans. I can tell you now after our researches that we have done no business with your firm within the past six or seven years, but I can't speak for the time before that, when my uncle was in charge."

"I see," I said. "Could you, er, ask your uncle?"

"I will if you like," he said civilly. "I did telephone his house, but I understand that he and my aunt will be away from home until Monday, and their maid doesn't seem to know where they went." He paused. "Could I ask what all this is about?"

I explained that my brother had died suddenly, leaving a good deal of unfinished business which I was trying to sort out. "I came across the name and address of your firm. I'm following up everything I can."

"Ah," he said sympathetically. "I will certainly ask my uncle on Monday, and let you know."

"I'm most grateful."

"Not at all."

The uncle, I thought morosely, was a dead-end.

I went along and opened the vault, telling Annette that

Prospero Jenks wanted all the spinel. "And he says we have a piece of rock crystal like the Eiger."

"The what?"

"Sharp mountain. Like Mont Blanc."

"Oh." She moved down the rows of boxes and chose a heavy one from near the bottom of the far end. "This is it," she said, humping it onto the shelf and opening the lid. "Beautiful."

The Eiger, filling the box, was lying on its side and had a knobbly base so that it wouldn't stand up, but I supposed one could see in the lucent faces and angled planes that, studded with diamond stars and given the Jenks' sunlight treatment, it could make the basis of a fantasy worthy of the name.

"Do we have a price for it?" I asked.

"Double what it cost," she said cheerfully. "Plus tax, plus packing and transport."

"He wants everything sent by messenger."

She nodded. "He always does. Jason takes them in a taxi. Leave it to me, I'll see to it."

"And we'd better put the pearls away that came yesterday."

"Oh, yes."

She went off to fetch them and I moved down to where I'd given up the day before, feeling certain that the search was futile but committed to it all the same. Annette returned with the pearls, which were at least in plastic bags on strings, not in the awkward open envelopes, so while she counted and stored the new intake, I checked my way through the old.

Boxes of pearls, all sizes. No diamonds.

"Does CZ mean anything to you?" I asked Annette idly.

"CZ is cubic zirconia," she said promptly. "We sell a fair amount of it."

"Isn't that, um, imitation diamond?"

"It's a manufactured crystal very like diamond," she said, "but about ten thousand times cheaper. If it's in a ring, you can't tell the difference."

"Can't anyone?" I asked. "They must do."

[141]

"Mr. Franklin said that most jewelers can't at a glance. The best way to tell the difference, he said, is to take the stones out of their setting and weigh them."

"Weigh them?"

"Yes. Cubic zirconia's much heavier than diamond, so one carat of cubic zirconia is smaller than a one-carat diamond."

"CZ equals C times one point seven," I said slowly.

"That's right," she said, surprised. "How did you know?"

9

FROM noon on, when I closed the last box-lid unproductively on the softly changing colors of rainbow opal from Oregon, I sat in Greville's office reading June's print-out of a crash course in business studies, beginning to see the pattern of a cash flow that ended on the side of the angels. Annette, who as a matter of routine had been banking the receipts daily, produced a sheaf of checks for me to sign, which I did, feeling that it was the wrong name on the line, and she brought the day's post for decisions, which I strugglingly made.

Several people in the jewelry business telephoned in response to the notices of Greville's death which had appeared in the papers that morning. Annette, reassuring them that the show would go on, sounded more confident than she looked. "They all say Ipswich is too far, but they'll be there in spirit," she reported.

At four there was a phone call from Elliot Trelawney, who said he'd cracked the number of the lady who didn't want Greville's name spoken in her house.

"It's sad, really," he said with a chuckle. "I suppose I shouldn't laugh. That lady can't and won't forgive Greville because he sent her upper-crust daughter to jail for three months for selling cocaine to a friend. The mother was in court, I remember her, and she talked to the press afterward.

[143]

She couldn't believe that selling cocaine to a friend was an offense. Drug peddlers were despicable, of course, but that wasn't the same as selling to a friend."

"If a law is inconvenient, ignore it, it doesn't apply to you."

"What?"

"Something Greville wrote in his notebook."

"Oh yes. It seems Greville got the mother's phone number to suggest ways of rehabilitation for the daughter, but Mother wouldn't listen. Look." He hesitated. "Keep in touch now and then, would you? Have a drink in the Rook and Castle occasionally?"

"All right."

"And let me know as soon as you find those notes."

"Sure," I said.

"We want to stop Vaccaro, you know."

"I'll look everywhere," I promised.

When I put the phone down I asked Annette.

"Notes about his cases?" she said. "Oh no, he never brought those to the office."

Like he never bought diamonds, I thought dryly. And there wasn't a trace of them in the spreadsheets or the ledgers.

The small insistent alarm went off again, muffled inside the desk. Twenty past four, my watch said. I reached over and pulled open the drawer and the alarm stopped, as it had before.

"Looking for something?" June said, breezing in.

"Something with an alarm like a digital watch."

"It's bound to be the world clock," she said. "Mr. Franklin used to set it to remind himself to phone suppliers in Tokyo, and so on."

I reflected that as I wouldn't know what to say to suppliers in Tokyo I hardly needed the alarm.

"Do you want me to send a fax to Tokyo to say the pearls arrived OK?" she said.

"Do you usually?"

She nodded. "They worry."

[144]

"Then please do."

When she'd gone Jason with his orange hair appeared through the doorway and without any trace of insolence told me he'd taken the stuff to Prospero Jenks and brought back a check, which he'd given to Annette.

"Thank you," I said neutrally.

He gave me an unreadable glance, said, "Annette said to tell you," and took himself off. An amazing improvement, I thought.

I stayed behind that evening after they'd all left and went slowly round Greville's domain looking for hiding places that were guileful and devious and full of misdirection.

It was impossible to search the hundreds of shallow drawers in the stockrooms and I concluded he wouldn't have used them, because Lily or any of the others might easily have found what they weren't meant to. That was the trouble with the whole place, I decided in the end. Greville's own policy of not encouraging private territories had extended also to himself, as all of his staff seemed to pop in and out of his office familiarly whenever the need arose.

Hovering always was the uncomfortable thought that if any pointer to the diamonds' whereabouts had been left by Greville in his office, it could have vanished with the break-in artist, leaving nothing for me to find; and indeed I found nothing of any use. After a fruitless hour I locked everything that locked and went down to the yard to find Brad and go home.

The day of Greville's funeral dawned cold and clear and we were heading east when the sun came up. The run to Ipswich taking three hours altogether, we came into the town with generous time to search for Greville's car.

Inquiries from the police had been negative. They hadn't towed, clamped or ticketed any ancient Rover. They hadn't spotted its number in any public road or car-park, but that wasn't conclusive, they'd assured me. Finding the car had no priority with them as it hadn't been stolen but they would let me know if, if.

I explained the car-finder to Brad en route, producing a street map to go with it.

"Apparently when you press this red button the car's lights switch on and a whistle blows," I said. "So you drive and I'll press, OK?"

He nodded, seeming amused, and we began to search in this slightly bizarre fashion, starting in the town center near to where Greville had died and very slowly rolling up and down the streets, first to the north, then to the south, checking them off on the map. In many of the residential streets there were cars parked nose to tail outside houses, but nowhere did we get a whistle. There were public car-parks and shop car-parks and the station car-park, but nowhere did we turn lights on. Rover 3500s in any case were sparse: when we saw one we stopped to look at the plates, even if the paint wasn't gray, but none of them was Greville's.

Disappointment settled heavily. I'd seriously intended to find that car. As lunchtime dragged toward two o'clock I began to believe that I shouldn't have left it so long, that I should have started looking as soon as Greville died. But last Sunday, I thought, I hadn't been in any shape to, and anyway it wasn't until Tuesday that I knew there was anything valuable to look for. Even now I was sure he wouldn't have left the diamonds themselves vulnerable, but some reason for being in Ipswich at all . . . given luck, why not?

The crematorium was set in a garden with neatly planted rose trees: Brad dropped me at the door and drove away to find some food. I was met by two black-suited men, both with suitable expressions, who introduced themselves as the undertaker I'd engaged and one of the crematorium's officials. A lot of flowers had arrived, they said, and which did I want on the coffin.

In some bemusement I let them show me where the flowers were, which was in a long covered cloister beside the building, where one or two weeping groups were looking at wreaths of their own.

"These are Mr. Franklin's," the official said, indicating two long rows of bright bouquets blazing with colorful life in that place of death.

"All of these?" I said, astonished.

"They've been arriving all morning. Which do you want inside, on the coffin?"

There were cards on the bunches, I saw.

"I sent some from myself and our sisters," I said doubtfully. "The card has Susan, Miranda and Derek on it. I'll have that."

The official and the undertaker took pity on the crutches and helped me find the right flowers; and I came first not to the card I was looking for but to another that shortened my breath.

> I think of you every day at four-twenty.
> Love, C.

The flowers that went with it were velvety red roses arranged with ferns in a dark green bowl. Twelve sweet-smelling blooms. Dozen Roses, I thought. Heavens above.

"I've found them," the undertaker called, picking up a large display of pink and bronze chrysanthemums. "Here you are."

"Great. Well, we'll have these roses as well, and this wreath next to them, which is from the staff in his office. Is that all right?"

It appeared to be. Annette and June had decided on all-white flowers after agonizing and phoning from the office, and they'd made me promise to notice and tell them that they were pretty. We had decided that all the staff should stay behind and keep the office open as trade was so heavy, though I'd thought from her downcast expression that June would have liked to have made the journey.

I asked the official where all the other flowers had come

from: from businesses, he said, and he would collect all the cards afterward and give them to me.

I supposed for the first time that perhaps I should have taken Greville back to London to be seen off by colleagues and friends, but during the very quiet half-hour that followed had no single regret. The clergyman engaged by the undertakers asked if I wanted the whole service read as I appeared to be the only mourner, and I said yes, go ahead, it was fitting.

His voice droned a bit. I half-listened and half-watched the way the sunshine fell onto the flowers on the coffin from the high windows along one wall and thought mostly not of Greville as he'd been alive but what he had become to me during the past week.

His life had settled on my shoulders like a mantle. Through Monday, Tuesday, Wednesday and Thursday I'd learned enough of his business never to forget it. People who'd relied on him had transferred their reliance onto me, including in a way his friend Elliot Trelawney who wanted me as a Greville substitute to drink with. Clarissa Williams had sent her flowers knowing I would see them, wanting me to be aware of her, as if I weren't already. Nicholas Loder aimed to manipulate me for his own stable's ends. Prospero Jenks would soon be pressing hard for the diamonds for his fantasy, and the bank loan hung like a thundercloud in my mind.

Greville, lying cold in the coffin, hadn't meant any of it to happen.

A man of honor, I thought. I mentally repeated his own prayer for him, as it seemed a good time for it. May I deal with honor. May I act with courage. May I achieve humility. I didn't know if he'd managed that last one; I knew that I couldn't.

The clergyman droned to a halt. The official removed the three lots of flowers from the coffin to put them on the floor and, with a whirring and creaking of machinery that sounded loud in the silence, the coffin slid away forward, out of sight, heading for fire.

Goodbye, pal, I said silently. Goodbye, except that you are with me now more than ever before.

[148]

I went outside into the cold fresh air and thanked everyone and paid them and arranged for all of the flowers to go to St. Catherine's Hospital, which seemed to be no problem. The official gave me the severed cards and asked what I wanted to do with my brother's ashes, and I had a ridiculous urge to laugh, which I saw from his hushed face would be wildly inappropriate. The business of ashes had always seemed to me an embarrassment.

He waited patiently for a decision. "If you have any tall red rose trees," I said finally, "I daresay that would do, if you plant one along there with the others. Put the ashes there."

I paid for the rose tree and thanked him again, and waited for a while for Brad to return, which he did looking smug and sporting a definite grin.

"I found it," he said.

"What?" I was still thinking of Greville.

"Your brother's wheels."

"You didn't!"

He nodded, highly pleased with himself.

"Where?"

He wouldn't say. He waited for me to sit and drove off in triumph into the center of town, drawing up barely three hundred yards from where the scaffolding had fallen. Then, with his normal economy, he pointed to the forecourt of a used car sales business where under strips of fluttering pennants rows of offerings stood with large white prices painted on their windshields.

"One of those?" I asked in disbelief.

Brad gurgled; no other word for the delight in his throat. "Round the back," he said.

He drove into the forecourt, then along behind the cars, and turned a corner, and we found ourselves outside the wide-open doors of a garage advertising repairs, oil changes, MOT tests and Ladies and Gents. Brad held the car-finder out of his open window and pressed the red button, and somewhere in the shadowy depths of the garage a pair of headlights began flashing on and off and a piercing whistle shrieked.

A cross-looking mechanic in oily overalls came hurrying out. He told me he was the foreman in charge and he'd be glad to see the back of the Rover 3500, and I owed him a week's parking besides the cleaning of the spark plugs of the V8 engine, plus a surcharge for inconvenience.

"What inconvenience?"

"Taking up space for a week when it was meant to be for an hour, and having that whistle blast my eardrums three times today."

"Three times?" I said, surprised.

"Once this morning, twice this afternoon. This man came here earlier, you know. He said he'd bring the Rover's new owner."

Brad gave me a bright glance. The car-finder had done its best for us early on in the morning, it seemed: it was our own eyes and ears that had missed it, out of sight as the car had been.

I asked the foreman to make out a bill and, getting out of my own car, swung over to Greville's. The Rover's doors would open, I found, but the trunk was locked.

"Here," said the foreman, coming over with the account and the ignition keys. "The trunk won't open. Some sort of fancy lock. Custom made. It's been a bloody nuisance."

I mollifyingly gave him a credit card in settlement and he took it off to his cubbyhole of an office.

I looked at the Rover. "Can you drive that?" I asked Brad.

"Yerss," he said gloomily.

I smiled and pulled Greville's keys out of my pocket to see if any of them would unlock the trunk; and one did, to my relief, though not a key one would normally have associated with cars. More like the keys to a safe, I thought; and the lock revealed was intricate and steel. Its installation was typically Greville, ultra security-conscious after his experiences with the Porsche.

The treasure so well guarded included an expensive-looking set of golf clubs, with a trolley and a new box of golf balls, a large brown envelope, an overnight bag with pajamas, clean shirt, toothbrush and a scarlet can of shaving cream, a portable telephone like my own, a personal computer, a portable fax machine, an opened carton of spare fax paper, a polished wooden box containing a beautiful set of brass scales with feather-light weights, an anti-thief device for locking onto the steering wheel, a huge flashlight, and a heavy complicated-looking orange metal contraption that I recognized from Greville's enthusiastic description as a device for sliding under flat tires so that one could drive to a garage on it instead of changing a wheel by the roadside.

"Cor," Brad said, looking at the haul, and the foreman too, returning with the paperwork, was brought to an understanding of the need for the defenses.

I shut the trunk and locked it again, which seemed a very Greville-like thing to do, and took a quick look round inside the body of the car, seeing the sort of minor clutter which defies the tidiest habit: matchbooks, time-clock parking slips, blue sunglasses, and a cellophane packet of tissues. In the door pocket on the driver's side, jammed in untidily, a map.

I picked it out. It was a road map of East Anglia, the route from London to Ipswich drawn heavily in black with, written down one side, the numbers of the roads to be followed. The marked route, I saw with interest, didn't stop at Ipswich but went on beyond, to Harwich.

Harwich, on the North Sea, was a ferry port. Harwich to the Hook of Holland; the route of one of the historic crossings, like Dover to Calais, Folkestone to Ostend. I didn't know if the Harwich ferries still ran, and I thought that if Greville had been going to Holland he would certainly have gone by air. All the same he had, presumably, been going to Harwich.

I said abruptly to the foreman, who was showing impatience for our departure, "Is there a travel agent near here?"

"Three doors along," he said, pointing, "and you can't park here while you go there."

I gave him a tip big enough to change his mind, and left

[151]

Brad keeping watch over the cars while I peg-legged along the street. Right on schedule the travel agents came up, and I went in to inquire about ferries for the Hook of Holland.

"Sure," said an obliging girl. "They run every day and every night. Sealink operates them. When do you want to go?"

"I don't know, exactly."

She thought me feeble. "Well, the Saint Nicholas goes over to Holland every morning, and the Koningin Beatrix every night."

I must have looked as stunned as I felt. I closed my open mouth.

"What's the matter?" she said.

"Nothing at all. Thank you very much."

She shrugged as if the lunacies of the traveling public were past comprehension, and I shunted back to the garage with my chunk of new knowledge which had solved one little conundrum but posed another, such as what was Greville doing with Queen Beatrix, not a horse but a boat.

Brad drove the Rover to London and I drove my own car, the pace throughout enough to make a snail weep. Whatever the Ipswich garage had done to Greville's plugs hadn't cured any trouble, the V8 running more like a V4 or even a V1½ as far as I could see. Brad stopped fairly soon after we'd left the town and, cursing, cleaned the plugs again himself, but to no avail.

"Needs new ones," he said.

I used the time to search thoroughly through the golf bag, the box of golf balls, the overnight bag and all the gadgets.

No diamonds.

We set off again, the Rover going precariously slowly in very low gear up hills, with me staying on its tail in case it petered out altogether. I didn't much mind the slow progress except that resting my left foot on the floor sent frequent jabs up my leg and eventually reawoke the overall ache in the ankle, but in comparison with the ride home from Ipswich five days earlier it was chickenfeed. I still mended fast, I thought gratefully. By Tuesday at the latest I'd be walking. Well, limping, maybe, like Greville's car.

There was no joy in reflecting, as I did, that if the spark plugs had been efficient he wouldn't have stopped to have them fixed and he wouldn't have been walking along a street in Ipswich at the wrong moment. If one could foresee the future, accidents wouldn't happen. "If only" were wretched words.

We reached Greville's road eventually and found two spaces to park, though not outside the house. I'd told Brad in the morning that I would sleep in London that night to be handy for going to York with the Ostermeyers the next day. I'd planned originally that if we found the Rover he would take it on the orbital route direct to Hungerford and I would drive into London and go on home from there after I got back from York. The plugs having changed that plan near Ipswich, it was now Brad who would go to Hungerford in my car, and I would finish the journey by train. Greville's car, ruin that it was, could decorate the street.

We transferred all the gear from Greville's trunk into the back of my car, or rather Brad did the transferring while I mostly watched. Then, Brad carrying the big brown envelope from the Rover and my own overnight grip, we went up the path to the house in the dark and set off the lights and the barking. No one in the houses around paid any attention. I undid the three locks and went in cautiously but, as before, once I'd switched the dog off, the house was quiet and deserted. Brad, declining food and drink, went home to his mum, and I, sitting in Greville's chair, opened the big brown envelope and read all about Vaccaro, who had been a very bad boy indeed.

Most of the envelope's contents were a copy of Vaccaro's detailed application, but on an attached sheet in abbreviated prose Greville had handwritten:

[153]

Ramón Vaccaro, wanted for drug-running, Florida, U.S.A. Suspected of several murders, victims mostly pilots, wanting out from flying drug crates. Vaccaro leaves no mouths alive to chatter. My info from scared-to-death pilot's widow. She won't come to the committee meeting but gave enough insider details for me to believe her.

Vaccaro seduced private pilots with a big pay-off, then when they'd done one run to Colombia and got away with it, they'd be hooked and do it again and again until they finally got rich enough to have cold feet. Then the poor sods would die from being shot on their own doorsteps from passing cars, no sounds because of silencers, no witnesses and no clues. But all were pilots owning their own small planes, too many for coincidence. Widow says her husband scared stiff but left it too late. She's remarried, lives in London, always wanted revenge, couldn't believe it was same man when she saw local newspaper snippet, Vaccaro's Family Gaming, with his photo. Family! She went to Town Hall anonymously, they put her on to me.

We don't have to find Vaccaro guilty. We just don't give him a gaming license. Widow says not to let him know who turned his application down, he's dangerous and vengeful, but how can he silence a whole committee? The Florida police might like to know his whereabouts. Extradition?

I telephoned Elliot Trelawney at his weekend home, told him I'd found the red-hot notes and read them to him, which brought forth a whistle and a groan.

"But Vaccaro didn't kill Greville," I said.

"No." He sighed. "How did the funeral go?"

"Fine. Thank you for your flowers."

"Just sorry I couldn't get there, but on a working day, and so far . . ."

"It was fine," I said again, and it had been. I'd been relieved, on the whole, to be alone.

"Would you mind," he said, diffidently, "if I arranged a

memorial service for him? Sometime soon. Within a month?"

"Go right ahead," I said warmly. "A great idea."

He hoped I would send the Vaccaro notes by messenger on Monday to the Magistrates Court, and he asked if I played golf.

In the morning, after a dream-filled night in Greville's black and white bed, I took a taxi to the Ostermeyers' hotel, meeting them in the lobby as arranged on the telephone the evening before.

They were in very good form, Martha resplendent in a red wool tailored dress with a mink jacket, Harley with a new English-looking hat over his easy grin, binoculars and racing paper ready. Both of them seemed determined to enjoy whatever the day brought forth and Harley's occasional ill-humor was far out of sight.

The driver, a different one from Wednesday, brought a huge super-comfortable Daimler to the front door exactly on time, and with all auspices pointing to felicity, the Ostermeyers arranged themselves on the rear seat, I sitting in front of them beside the chauffeur.

The chauffeur, who announced his name as Simms, kindly stowed my crutches in the trunk and said it was no trouble at all, sir, when I thanked him. The crutches themselves seemed to be the only tiny cloud on Martha's horizon, bringing a brief frown to the proceedings.

"Is that foot still bothering you? Milo said it was nothing to worry about."

"No, it isn't, and it's much better," I said truthfully.

"Oh, good. Just as long as it doesn't stop you riding Datepalm."

"Of course not," I assured her.

"We're so pleased to have him. He's just darling."

I made some nice noises about Datepalm, which wasn't very difficult, as we nosed through the traffic to go north on the M1 highway.

[155]

Harley said, "Milo says Datepalm might go for the Charisma 'Chase at Kempton next Saturday. What do you think?"

"A good race for him," I said calmly. I would kill Milo, I thought. A dicey gallop was one thing, but no medic on earth was going to sign my card in one week to say I was fit; and I wouldn't be, because half a ton of horse over jumps at thirty-plus miles an hour was no puffball matter.

"Milo might prefer to save him for the Mackeson at Cheltenham next month," I said judiciously, sowing the idea. "Or of course for the Hennessy Cognac Gold Cup two weeks later." I'd definitely be fit for the Hennessy, six weeks ahead. The Mackeson, at four weeks, was a toss-up.

"Then there's that big race the day after Christmas." Martha sighed happily. "It's all so exciting. Harley promises we can come back to see him run."

They talked about horses for another half hour and then asked if I knew anything about a Dick Turpin.

"Oh, sure."

"Some guy said he was riding to York. I didn't understand any part of it."

I laughed. "It happened a couple of centuries ago. Dick Turpin was a highwayman, a real villain, who rode his mare Black Bess north to escape the law. They caught him in York and flung him in jail, and for a fortnight he held a sort of riotous court in his cell, making jokes and drinking with all the notables of the city who came to see the famous thief in his chains. Then they took him out and hanged him on a piece of land called the Knavesmire, which is now the racecourse."

"Oh, my," Martha said, ghoulishly diverted. "How perfectly grisly."

In time we left the M1 and traveled northeast to the difficult old A1, and I thought that no one in their senses would drive from London to York when they could go by train. The Ostermeyers, of course, weren't doing the driving.

Harley said as we neared the city, "You're expected at lunch with us, Derek."

Expected, in Ostermeyer speech, meant invited. I protested mildly that it wasn't so.

"It sure is. I talked with Lord Knightwood yesterday evening, told him we'd have you with us. He said right away to have you join us for lunch. They're giving their name to one of the races, it'll be a big party."

"Which race?" I asked with curiosity. Knightwood wasn't a name I knew.

"Here it is." Harley rustled the racing newspaper. "The University of York Trophy. Lord Knightwood is the University's top man, president or governor, some kind of figurehead. A Yorkshire VIP. Anyway, you're expected."

I thanked him. There wasn't much else to do, though a sponsor's lunch on top of no exercise could give me weight problems if I wasn't careful. However, I could almost hear Milo's agitated voice in my ear: "Whatever the Ostermeyers want, for Christ's sake give it to them."

"There's also the York Minster Cup," Harley said, reading his paper, "and the Civic Pride Challenge. Your horse Dozen Roses is in the York Castle Champions."

"My brother's horse," I said.

Harley chuckled. "We won't forget."

Simms dropped us neatly at the Club entrance. One could get addicted to chauffeurs, I thought, accepting the crutches gravely offered. No parking problems. Someone to drive one home on crunch days. But no spontaneity, no real privacy . . . No thanks, not even long-term Brad.

Back the first horse you see, they say. Or the first jockey. Or the first trainer.

The first trainer we saw was Nicholas Loder. He looked truly furious and, I thought in surprise, alarmed when I came face to face with him after he'd watched our emergence from the Daimler.

"What are *you* doing here?" he demanded brusquely. "You've no business here."

"Do you know Mr. and Mrs. Ostermeyer?" I asked politely,

introducing them. "They've just bought Datepalm. I'm their guest today."

He glared; there wasn't any other word for it. He had been waiting for a man, perhaps one of his owners, to collect a Club badge from the allotted window and, the transaction achieved, the two of them marched off into the racecourse without another word.

"Well!" Martha said, outraged. "If Milo ever behaved like that we'd whisk our horses out of his yard before he could say goodbye."

"It isn't my horse," I pointed out. "Not yet."

"When it is, what will you do?"

"The same as you, I think, though I didn't mean to."

"Good," Martha said emphatically.

I didn't really understand Loder's attitude or reaction. If he wanted a favor from me, which was that I'd let him sell Dozen Roses and Gemstones to others of his owners either for the commission or to keep them in his yard, he should at least have shown an echo of Milo's feelings for the Ostermeyers.

If Dozen Roses had been cleared by the authorities to run, why was Loder scared that I was there to watch it?

Crazy, I thought. The only thing I'd wholly learned was that Loder's ability to dissimulate was underdeveloped for a leading trainer.

Harley Ostermeyer said the York University's lunch was to be held at one end of the Club members' dining room in the grandstand, so I showed the way there, reflecting that it was lucky I'd decided on a decent suit for that day, not just a sweater. I might have been a last-minute addition to the party but I was happy not to look it.

There was already a small crowd of people, glasses in hand, chatting away inside a temporary white-lattice-fenced area, a long buffet set out behind them with tables and chairs to sit at for eating.

"There are the Knightwoods," said the Ostermeyers, clucking contentedly, and I found myself being introduced presently to a tall white-haired kindly looking man who had benevolence shining from every perhaps seventy-year-old wrinkle. He shook my hand amicably as a friend of the Ostermeyers with whom, it seemed, he had dined on a reciprocal visit to Harley's alma mater, the University of Pennsylvania. Harley was endowing a Chair there. Harley was a VIP in Pittsburgh, Pennsylvania.

I made the right faces and listened to the way the world went round, and said I thought it was great of the city of York to support its industry on the turf.

"Have you met my wife?" Lord Knightwood said vaguely. "My dear," he touched the arm of a woman with her back to us, "you remember Harley and Martha Ostermeyer? And this is their friend Derek Franklin that I told you about."

She turned to the Ostermeyers, smiling and greeting them readily, and she held out a hand for me to shake, saying, "How do you do. So glad you could come."

"How do you do, Lady Knightwood," I said politely.

She gave me a very small smile, in command of herself.

Clarissa Williams was Lord Knightwood's wife.

10

S HE had known I would be there, it was clear, and if she hadn't wanted me to find out who she was she could have developed a strategic illness in plenty of time.

She was saying graciously, "Didn't I see you on television winning the Gold Cup?" and I thought of her speed with that frightful kiyoga and the tumult of her feelings on Tuesday, four days ago. She seemed to have no fear that I would give her away, and indeed, what could I say? Lord Knightwood, my brother was your wife's lover? Just the right sort of thing to get the happy party off to a good start.

The said Lord was introducing the Ostermeyers to a professor of physics who with twinkles said that as he was the only true aficionado of horse racing among the teaching academics, he had been pressed into service to carry the flag, although there were about fifty undergraduates out on the course ready to bet their socks off in the cause.

"Derek has a degree," Martha said brightly, making conversation.

The professorial eyeballs swiveled my way speculatively. "What university?"

"Lancaster," I said dryly, which raised a laugh. Lancaster and York had fought battles of the red and white roses for many a long year.

"And subject?"

"Independent Studies."

His desultory attention sharpened abruptly.

"What are Independent Studies?" Harley asked, seeing his interest.

"The student designs his own course and invents his own final subject," the professor said. "Lancaster is the only university offering such a course and they let only about eight students a year do it. It's not for the weak-willed or the feeble-minded."

The Knightwoods and the Ostermeyers listened in silence and I felt embarrassed. I had been young then, I thought.

"What did you choose as your subject?" asked the professor, intent now on an answer. "Horses, in some way?"

I shook my head. "No . . . er . . . 'Roots and Results of War.' "

"My dear chap," Lord Knightwood said heartily, "sit next to the professor at lunch." He moved away benignly, taking his wife and the Ostermeyers with him, and the professor, left behind, asked what I fancied for the races.

Clarissa, by accident or design, remained out of talking distance throughout the meal and I didn't try to approach her. The party broke up during and after the first race, although everyone was invited to return for tea, and I spent most of the afternoon, as I'd spent so many others, watching horses stretch and surge and run as their individual natures dictated. The will to win was born and bred in them all, but some cared more than others: it was those with the implacable impulse to lead a wild herd who fought hardest and won most often. Sportswriters tended to call it courage but it went deeper than that, right down into the gene pool, into instinct, into the primordial soup, on the same evolutionary level as the belligerence so easily aroused in *Homo sapiens* that was the taproot of war.

I was no stranger to the thought that I sought battle on the turf because though the instinct to fight and conquer ran strong I was averse to guns. Sublimation, the pundits would no doubt call it. Datepalm and I both, on the same primitive plane, wanted to win.

"What are you thinking?" someone asked at my shoulder.

I would have known her voice anywhere, I thought. I turned to see her half-calm, half-anxious expression, the Lady Knightwood social poise explicit in the smooth hair, the patrician bones and the tailoring of her clothes, the passionate woman merely a hint in the eyes.

"Thinking about horses," I said.

"I suppose you're wondering why I came today, after I learned last night that you'd not only be at the races, which I expected you might be anyway because of Dozen Roses, but actually be coming to our lunch . . ." She stopped, sounding uncertain.

"I'm not Greville," I said. "Don't think of me as Greville."

Her eyelids flickered. "You're too damned perceptive." She did a bit of introspection. "Yes, all right, I wanted to be near you. It's a sort of comfort."

We were standing by the rails of the parade ring watching the runners for the next race walk round, led by their lads. It was the race before the University Trophy, two races before that of Dozen Roses, a period without urgency for either of us. There were crowd noises all around and the clip-clop of horses walking by, and we could speak quietly as in an oasis of private space without being overheard.

"Are you still angry with me for hitting you?" she said a shade bitterly, as I'd made no comment after her last remark.

I half-smiled. "No."

"I did think you were a burglar."

"And what would you have explained to the police, if they'd come?"

She said ruefully, "I hope I would have come to my senses and done a bunk before they got there." She sighed. "Greville said if I ever had to use the kiyoga in earnest to escape at once and not worry what I'd done to my attacker, but he never thought of a burglar in his own house."

"I'm surprised he gave you a weapon like that," I said mildly. "Aren't they illegal? And him a magistrate."

"I'm a magistrate too," she said unexpectedly. "That's how we originally met, at a magistrates' conference. I've not inquired into the legality of kiyogas. If I were prosecuted for carrying and using an offensive weapon, well, that would be much preferable to being a victim of the appalling assaults that come before us every week."

"Where did he get it?" I asked curiously.

"America."

"Do you have it with you here?"

She nodded and touched her handbag. "It's second nature, now."

She must have been thirty years younger than her husband, I thought inconsequently, and I knew what she felt about him. I didn't know whether or not I liked her, but I did recognize there was a weird sort of intimacy between us and that I didn't resent it.

The jockeys came out and stood around with the owners in little groups. Nicholas Loder was there with the man he'd come in with, a thickset powerful-looking man in a dark suit, the pink cardboard Club badge fluttering from his lapel.

"Dozen Roses," I said, watching Loder talking to the owner and his jockey, "was he named for you?"

"Oh, God," she said, disconcerted. "How ever . . . ?"

I said, "I put your roses on the coffin for the service."

"Oh . . ." she murmured with difficulty, her throat closing, her mouth twisting, "I . . . I can't . . ."

"Tell me how York University came to be putting its name to a race." I made it sound conversational, to give her composure time.

She swallowed, fighting for control, steadying her breathing. "I'm sorry. It's just that I can't even mourn for him except inside; can't let it show to anyone except you, and it sweeps over me, I can't help it." She paused and answered my unimportant question. "The Clerk of the Course wanted to involve the city. Some of the bigwigs of the University were against joining in, but Henry persuaded them. He and I have always come here to meetings now and then. We both like it, for a day out with friends."

"Your husband doesn't actually lecture at the University, does he?"

"Oh no, he's just a figurehead. He's chairman of a fair number of things in York. A public figure here."

Vulnerable to scandal, I thought: as she was herself, and Greville also. She and he must have been unwaveringly discreet.

"How long since you first met Greville?" I asked noncommittally.

"Four years." She paused. "Four marvelous years. Not enough."

The jockeys swung up onto the horses and moved away to go out onto the course. Nicholas Loder and his owner, busily talking, went off to the stands.

"May I watch the race with you?" Clarissa said. "Do you mind?"

"I was going to watch from the grass." I glanced down apologetically at the crutches. "It's easier."

"I don't mind the grass."

So we stood side by side on the grass in front of the grandstand and she said, "Whenever we could be together, he bought twelve red roses. It just . . . well . . ." She stopped, swallowing again hard.

"Mm," I said. I thought of the ashes and the red rose tree and decided to tell her about that another time. It had been for him, anyway, not for her.

Nicholas Loder's two-year-old won the sprint at a convincing clip and I caught a glimpse of the owner afterward looking heavily satisfied but unsmiling. Hardly a jolly character, I thought.

Clarissa went off to join her husband for the University race and after that, during their speeches and presentations, I went in search of Dozen Roses who was being led round in the pre-parade ring before being taken into a box or a stall to have his saddle put on.

Dozen Roses looked docile to dozy, I thought. An unremarkable bay, he had none of the looks or presence of Date-palm, nor the 'chaser's alert interest in his surroundings. He was a good performer, of that there was no question, but he didn't at that moment give an impression of going to be a "trot-up" within half an hour, and he was vaguely not what I'd expected. Was this the colt that on the video tapes had won his last three races full of verve? Was this the young buck who had tried to mount a filly at the starting gate at Newmarket Park?

No, I saw with a sense of shock, he was not. I peered under his belly more closely, as it was sometimes difficult to tell, but there seemed to be no doubt that he had lost the essential tackle; that he had in fact been gelded.

I was stunned, and I didn't know whether to laugh or be furious. It explained so much: the loss of form when he had his mind on procreation rather than racing, and the return to speed once the temptation was removed. It explained why the Stewards hadn't called Loder in to justify the difference in running: horses very often did better after the operation.

I unfolded my race-card at Dozen Roses' race, and there, sure enough, against his name stood not *c* for colt or *h* for horse, but *g* for gelding.

Nicholas Loder's voice, vibrating with fury, spoke from not far behind me, "That horse is not your horse. Keep away from him."

I turned. Loder was advancing fast with Dozen Roses' saddle over his arm and full-blown rage in his face. The heavily unjoyful owner, still for some reason in tow, was watching the proceedings with puzzlement.

"Mine or not, I'm entitled to look at him," I said. "And look at him I darned well have, and either he is not Dozen Roses or you have gelded him against my brother's express wishes."

[165]

His mouth opened and snapped shut.

"What's the matter, Nick?" the owner said. "Who is this?"

Loder failed to introduce us. Instead he said to me vehemently, "You can't do anything about it. I have an Authority to Act. I am the registered agent for this horse and what I decide is none of your business."

"My brother refused to have any of his horses gelded. You knew it well. You disobeyed him because you were sure he wouldn't find out, as he never went to the races."

He glared at me. He was aware that if I lodged a formal complaint he would be in a good deal of trouble, and I thought he was certainly afraid that as my brother's executor I could and quite likely would do just that. Even if I only talked about it to others, it could do him damage: it was the sort of tidbit the hungry racing press would pounce on for a giggle, and the owners of all the princely colts in his prestigious stable would get cold feet that the same might happen to their own property without their knowledge or consent.

He had understood all that, I thought, in the moment I'd told him on the telephone that it was I who would be inheriting Dozen Roses. He'd known that if I ever saw the horse I would realize at once what had been done. No wonder he'd lost his lower resonances.

"Greville was a fool," he said angrily. "The horse has done much better since he was cut."

"That's true," I agreed, "but it's not the point."

"How much do you want, then?" he demanded roughly.

My own turn, I thought, to gape like a fish. I said feebly, "It's not a matter of money."

"Everything is," he declared. "Name your price and get out of my way."

I glanced at the attendant owner who looked more phlegmatic than riveted, but might remember and repeat this conversation, and I said merely, "We'll discuss it later, OK?" and hitched myself away from them without aggression.

Behind me the owner was saying, "What was that all about,

Nick?" and I heard Loder reply, "Nothing, Rollo. Don't worry about it," and when I looked back a few seconds later I saw both of them stalking off toward the saddling boxes followed by Dozen Roses in the grasp of his lad.

Despite Nicholas Loder's anxious rage, or maybe because of it, I came down on the side of amusement. I would myself have had the horse gelded several months before the trainer had done it out of no doubt unbearable frustration: Greville had been pigheaded on the subject from both misplaced sympathy and not knowing enough about horses. I thought I would make peace with Loder that evening on the telephone, whatever the outcome of the race, as I certainly didn't want a fight on my hands for so rocky a cause. Talk about the roots of war, I thought wryly: there had been sillier reasons for bloody strife in history than the castration of a thoroughbred.

At York some of the saddling boxes were open to public view, some were furnished with doors. Nicholas Loder seemed to favor the privacy and took Dozen Roses inside away from my eyes.

Harley and Martha Ostermeyer, coming to see the horses saddled, were full of beaming anticipation. They had backed the winner of the University Trophy and had wagered all the proceeds on my, that was to say, my brother's horse.

"You won't get much return," I warned them. "It's favorite."

"We know that, dear," Martha said happily, looking around. "Where is he? Which one?"

"He's inside that box," I pointed, "being saddled."

"Harley and I have had a marvelous idea," she said sweetly, her eyes sparkling.

"Now, Martha," Harley said. He sounded faintly alarmed as if Martha's marvelous ideas weren't always the best possible news.

"We want you to dine with us when we get back to London," she finished.

Harley relaxed, relieved. "Yes. Hope you can." He clearly

meant that this particular marvelous idea was passable, even welcome. "London at weekends is a graveyard."

With a twitching of an inward grin I accepted my role as graveyard alleviator and, in the general good cause of cementing Ostermeyer-Shandy-Franklin relations, said I would be very pleased to stay to dinner. Martha and Harley expressed such gratification as to make me wonder whether when they were alone they bored each other to silence.

Dozen Roses emerged from his box with his saddle on and was led along toward the parade ring. He walked well, I thought, his good straight hocks encouraging lengthy strides, and he also seemed to have woken up a good deal, now that the excitement was at hand.

In the horse's wake hurried Nicholas Loder and his friend Rollo, and it was because they were crowding him, I thought, that Dozen Roses swung round on his leading rein and pulled backward from his lad, and in straightening up again hit the Rollo man a hefty buffet with his rump and knocked him to his knees.

Martha with instinctive kindness rushed forward to help him, but he floundered to his feet with a curse that made her blink. All the same she bent and picked up a thing like a blue rubber ball which had fallen out of his jacket and held it toward him, saying "You dropped this, I think."

He ungraciously snatched it from her, gave her an unnecessarily fierce stare as if she'd frightened the horse into knocking him over, which she certainly hadn't, and hurried into the parade ring after Nicholas Loder. He, looking back and seeing me still there, reacted with another show of fury.

"What perfectly horrid people," Martha said, making a face. "Did you hear what that man said? Disgusting! Fancy saying it aloud!"

Dear Martha, I thought, that word was everyday coinage on racecourses. The nicest people used it: it made no one a villain. She was brushing dust off her gloves fastidiously as if getting rid of contamination and I half-expected her to go up to Rollo and in the tradition of the indomitable American female to tell him to wash his mouth out with soap.

Harley had meanwhile picked something else up off the grass and was looking at it helplessly. "He dropped this too," he said. "I think."

Martha peered at his hands and took the object out of them.

"Oh, yes," she said with recognition, "that's the other half of the baster. You'd better have it, Derek, then you can give it back to that obnoxious friend of your trainer, if you want to."

I frowned at what she'd given me, which was a rigid plastic tube, semitransparent, about an inch in diameter, nine inches long, open at one end and narrowing to half the width at the other.

"A baster," Martha said again. "For basting meat when it's roasting. You know them, don't you? You press the bulb thing and release it to suck up the juices which you then squirt over the meat."

I nodded. I knew what a baster was.

"What an extraordinary thing to take to the races," Martha said wonderingly.

"Mm," I agreed. "He seems an odd sort of man altogether." I tucked the plastic tube into an inside jacket pocket, from which its nozzle end protruded a couple of inches, and we went first to see Dozen Roses joined with his jockey in the parade ring and then up onto the stands to watch him race.

The jockey was Loder's chief stable jockey, as able as any, as honest as most. The stable money was definitely on the horse, I thought, watching the forecast odds on the information board change from 2/1 on to 5/2 on. When a gambling stable didn't put its money up front, the whisper went round and the price eased dramatically. The whisper where it mattered that day had to be saying that Loder was in earnest about the "trot-up," and Alfie's base imputation would have to wait for another occasion.

Perhaps as a result of his year-by-year successes, Loder's

stable always, it was well-known in the racing world, attracted as owners serious gamblers whose satisfaction was more in winning money than in winning races: and that wasn't the truism it seemed, because in steeplechasing the owners tended to want to win the races more than the money. Stee-plechasing owners only occasionally made a profit overall and realistically expected to have to pay for their pleasure.

Wondering if the Rollo man was one of the big Loder gamblers, I flicked back the pages of the race-card and looked up his name beside the horse of his that had won the sprint. Owner, Mr. T. Rollway, the card read. Rollo for short to his friends. Never heard of him, I thought, and wondered if Gre-ville had.

Dozen Roses cantered down to the start with at least as much energy and enthusiasm as any of the seven other run-ners and was fed into the stalls without fuss. He'd been strid-ing out well, I thought, and taking a good hold of the bit. An old hand at the game by now, of course, as I was also, I thought dryly.

I'd ridden in several Flat races in my teens as an amateur, learning that the hardest and most surprising thing about the unrelenting Flat race crouch over the withers was the way it cramped one's lungs and affected one's breathing. The first few times I'd almost fallen off at the finish from lack of oxy-gen. A long time ago, I thought, watching the gates fly open in the distance and the colors spill out, long ago when I was young and it all lay ahead.

If I could find Greville's diamonds, I thought, I would in due course be able to buy a good big yard in Lambourn and start training free of a mortgage and on a decent scale, provid-ing of course I could get owners to send me horses, and I had no longer any doubt that one of these years, when my body packed up mending fast, as everyone's did in the end, that I would be content with the new life, even though the consum-ing passion I still felt for race-riding couldn't be replaced by anything tamer.

[170]

Dozen Roses was running with the pack, all seven bunched after the first three furlongs, flying along the far side of the track at more than cruising speed but with acceleration still in reserve.

If I didn't find Greville's diamonds, I thought, I would just scrape together whatever I could and borrow the rest, and still buy a place and set my hand to the future. But not yet, not yet.

Dozen Roses and the others swung left-handed into the long bend round the far end of the track, the bunch coming apart as the curve element hit them. Turning into the straight five furlongs from the winning post, Dozen Roses was in fourth place and making not much progress. I wanted him quite suddenly to win and was surprised by the strength of the feeling; I wanted him to win for Greville, who wouldn't care anyway, and perhaps also for Clarissa, who would. Sentimental fool, I told myself. Anyway, when the crowd started yelling home their fancy I yelled for mine also, and I'd never done that before as far as I could remember.

There was not going to be a trot-up, whatever Nicholas Loder might have thought. Dozen Roses was visibly struggling as he took second place at a searing speed a furlong from home and he wouldn't have got the race at all if the horse half a length in front, equally extended and equally exhausted, hadn't veered from a straight line at the last moment and bumped into him.

"Oh dear," Martha exclaimed sadly, as the two horses passed the winning post. "Second. Oh well, never mind."

"He'll get the race on an objection," I said. "Which I suppose is better than nothing. Your winnings are safe."

"Are you sure?"

"Certain," I said, and almost immediately the loudspeakers were announcing "Stewards' inquiry."

More slowly than I would have liked to be able to manage, the three of us descended to the area outside the weighing room where the horse that was not my horse stood in the

[171]

place for the unsaddling of the second, a net rug over his back and steam flowing from his sweating skin. He was moving about restlessly, as horses often do after an all-out effort, and his lad was holding tight to the reins, trying to calm him.

"He ran a great race," I said to Martha, and she said, "Did he, dear?"

"He didn't give up. That's really what matters."

Of Nicholas Loder there was no sign: probably inside the Stewards' room putting forward his complaint. The Stewards would show themselves the views from the side camera and the head-on camera, and at any moment now . . .

"Result of the Stewards' inquiry," said the loudspeakers. "Placing of first and second reversed." Hardly justice, but inevitable: the faster horse had lost. Nicholas Loder came out of the weighing room and saw me standing with the Oster-meyers, but before I could utter even the first conciliatory words like, "Well done," he'd given me a sick look and hur-ried off in the opposite direction. No Rollo in his shadow, I noticed.

Martha, Harley and I returned to the luncheon room for the University's tea where the Knightwoods were being gracious hosts and Clarissa, at the sight of me, developed renewed trouble with the tear glands. I left the Ostermeyers taking cups and saucers from a waitress and drifted across to her side.

"So silly," she said crossly, blinking hard as she offered me a sandwich. "But wasn't he great?"

"He was."

"I wish . . ." She stopped. I wished it too. No need at all to put it into words. But Greville never went to the races.

"I go to London fairly often," she said. "May I phone you when I'm there?"

"Yes, if you like." I wrote my home number on my race-card and handed it to her. "I live in Berkshire," I said, "not in Greville's house."

She met my eyes, hers full of confusion.

"I'm not Greville," I said.

"My dear chap," said her husband boomingly, coming to a halt beside us, "delighted your horse finally won. Though, of course, not technically your horse, what?"

"No, sir."

He was shrewd enough, I thought, looking at the intelligent eyes amid the bonhomie. Not easy to fool. I wondered fleetingly if he'd ever suspected his wife had a lover, even if he hadn't known who. I thought that if he had known who, he wouldn't have asked me to lunch.

He chuckled. "The professor says you tipped him three winners."

"A miracle."

"He's very impressed." He looked at me benignly. "Join us at any time, my dear chap." It was the sort of vague invitation, not meant to be accepted, that was a mild seal of approval, in its way.

"Thank you," I said, and he nodded, knowing he'd been understood.

Martha Ostermeyer gushed up to say how marvelous the whole day had been, and gradually from then on, as such things always do, the University party evaporated.

I shook Clarissa's outstretched hand in farewell, and also her husband's, who stood beside her. They looked good together, and settled, a fine couple on the surface.

"We'll see you again," she said to me, and I wondered if it were only I who could hear her smothered desperation.

"Yes," I said positively. "Of course."

"My dear chap," her husband said. "Any time."

Harley, Martha and I left the racecourse and climbed into the Daimler, Simms following Brad's routine of stowing the crutches.

Martha said reproachfully, "Your ankle's broken, not twisted. One of the guests told us. I said you'd ridden a gallop for us on Wednesday and they couldn't believe it."

"It's practically mended," I said weakly.

"But you won't be able to ride Datepalm in that race next Saturday, will you?"

"Not really. No."

She sighed. "You're very naughty. We'll simply have to wait until you're ready."

I gave her a fast smile of intense gratitude. There weren't many owners who would have dreamed of waiting. No trainer would; they couldn't afford to. Milo was currently putting up one of my arch-rivals on the horses I usually rode, and I just hoped I would get all of them back once I was fit. That was the main trouble with injuries, not the injury itself but losing one's mounts to other jockeys. Permanently, sometimes, if they won.

"And now," Martha said as we set off south toward London, "I have had another simply marvelous idea, and Harley agrees with me."

I glanced back to Harley who was sitting behind Simms. He was nodding indulgently. No anxiety this time.

"We think," she said happily, "that we'll buy Dozen Roses and send him to Milo to train for jumping. That is," she laughed, "if your brother's executor will sell him to us."

"Martha!" I was dumbstruck and used her Christian name without thinking, though I'd called her Mrs. Ostermeyer before, when I'd called her anything.

"There," she said, gratified at my reaction, "I told you it was a marvelous idea. What do you say?"

"My brother's executor is speechless."

"But you will sell him?"

"I certainly will."

"Then let's use the car phone to call Milo and tell him." She was full of high good spirits and in no mood for waiting, but when she reached Milo he apparently didn't immediately catch fire. She handed the phone to me with a frown, saying, "He wants to talk to you."

"Milo," I said, "what's the trouble?"

"That horse is an entire. They don't jump well."

"He's a gelding," I assured him.

"You told me your brother wouldn't ever have it done."

"Nicholas Loder did it without permission."

"You're kidding!"

"No," I said. "Anyway the horse got the race today on a Stewards' inquiry but he ran gamely, and he's fit."

"Has he ever jumped?"

"I shouldn't think so. But I'll teach him."

"All right then. Put me back to Martha."

"Don't go away when she's finished. I want another word."

I handed the phone to Martha who listened and spoke with a return to enthusiasm, and eventually I talked to Milo again.

"Why," I asked, "would one of Nicholas Loder's owners carry a baster about at the races?"

"A what?"

"Baster. Thing that's really for cooking. You've got one. You use it as an inhaler for the horses."

"Simple and effective."

He used it, I reflected, on the rare occasions when it was the best way to give some sort of medication to a horse. One dissolved or diluted the medicine in water and filled the rubber bulb of the baster with it. Then one fitted the tube onto that, slid the tube up the horse's nostril, and squeezed the bulb sharply. The liquid came out in a vigorous spray straight onto the mucous membranes and from there passed immediately into the bloodstream. One could puff out dry powder with the same result. It was the fastest way of getting some drugs to act.

"At the races?" Milo was saying. "An owner?"

"That's right. His horse won the five-furlong sprint."

"He'd have to be mad. They dope test two horses in every race, as you know. Nearly always the winner, and another at random. No owner is going to pump drugs into his horse at the races."

"I don't know that he did. He had a baster with him, that's all."

[175]

"Did you tell the Stewards?"

"No, I didn't. Nicholas Loder was with his owner and he would have exploded as he was angry with me already for spotting Dozen Roses' alteration."

Milo laughed. "So that was what all the heat was about this past week?"

"You've got it."

"Will you kick up a storm?"

"Probably not."

"You're too soft," he said, "and oh yes, I almost forgot. There was a phone message for you. Wait a tick. I wrote it down." He went away for a bit and returned. "Here you are. Something about your brother's diamonds." He sounded doubtful. "Is that right?"

"Yes. What about them?"

He must have heard the urgency in my voice because he said, "It's nothing much. Just that someone had been trying to call you last night and all day today, but I said you'd slept in London and gone to York."

"Who was it?"

"He didn't say. Just said that he had some info for you. Then he hummed and hahed and said if I talked to you would I tell you he would telephone your brother's house, in case you went there, at about ten tonight, or later. Or it might have been a she. Difficult to tell. One of those middle-range voices. I said I didn't know if you would be speaking to me, but I'd tell you if I could."

"Well, thanks."

"I'm not a message service," he said testily. "Why don't you switch on your answer phone like everyone else?"

"I do sometimes."

"Not enough."

I switched off the phone with a smile and wondered who'd been trying to reach me. It had to be someone who knew Greville had bought diamonds. It might even be Annette, I thought: her voice had a mid-range quality.

I would have liked to have gone to Greville's house as soon as we got back to London, but I couldn't exactly renege on the dinner after Martha's truly marvelous idea, so the three of us ate together as planned and I tried to please them as much as they'd pleased me.

Martha announced yet another marvelous idea during dinner. She and Harley would get Simms or another of the car firm's chauffeurs to drive us all down to Lambourn the next day to take Milo out to lunch, so that they could see Datepalm again before they went back to the States on Tuesday. They could drop me at my house afterward, and then go on to visit a castle in Dorset they'd missed last time around. Harley looked resigned. It was Martha, I saw, who always made the decisions, which was maybe why the repressed side of him needed to lash out sometimes at car-park attendants who boxed him in.

Milo, again on the telephone, told me he'd do practically anything to please the Ostermeyers, definitely including Sunday lunch. He also said that my informant had rung again and he had told him/her that I'd got the message.

"Thanks," I said.

"See you tomorrow."

I thanked the Ostermeyers inadequately for everything and went to Greville's house by taxi. I did think of asking the taxi driver to stay, like Brad, until I'd reconnoitered, but the house was quiet and dark behind the impregnable grilles, and I thought the taxi driver would think me a fool or a coward or both, so I paid him off and, fishing out the keys, opened the gate in the hedge and went up the path until the lights blazed on and the dog started barking.

Everyone can make mistakes.

11

I didn't get as far as the steps up to the front door. A dark figure, dimly glimpsed in the floodlights' glare, came launching itself at me from behind in a cannonball rugger tackle and when I reached the ground something very hard hit my head.

I had no sensation of blacking out or of time passing. One moment I was awake, and the next moment I was awake also, or so it seemed, but I knew in a dim way that there had been an interval.

I didn't know where I was except that I was lying facedown on grass. I'd woken up concussed on grass several times in my life, but never before in the dark. They couldn't have all gone home from the races, I thought, and left me alone out on the course all night.

The memory of where I was drifted back quietly. In Greville's front garden. Alive. Hooray for small mercies.

I knew from experience that the best way to deal with being knocked out was not to hurry. On the other hand, this time I hadn't come off a horse, not on Greville's pocket handkerchief turf. There might be urgent reasons for getting up quickly, if I could think of them.

I remembered a lot of things in a rush and groaned slightly, rolling up onto my knees, wincing and groping about for the crutches. I felt stupid and went on behaving stupidly, acting on fifty percent brain power. Looking back afterward, I thought that what I ought to have done was slither silently away through the gate to go to any neighboring house and call the police. What I actually did was to start toward Greville's front door, and of course the lights flashed on again and the dog started barking and I stood rooted to the spot expecting another attack, swaying unsteadily on the crutches, absolutely dim and pathetic.

The door was ajar, I saw, with lights on in the hall, and while I stood dithering it was pulled wide open from inside and the cannonball figure shot out.

The cannonball was a motorcycle helmet, shiny and black, its transparent visor pulled down over the face. Behind the visor the face also seemed to be black, but a black balaclava, I thought, not black skin. There was an impression of jeans, denim jacket, gloves, black running shoes, all moving fast. He turned his head a fraction and must have seen me standing there insecurely, but he didn't stop to give me another un-balancing shove. He vaulted the gate and set off at a run down the street and I simply stood where I was in the garden waiting for my head to clear a bit more and start working.

When that happened to some extent, I went up the short flight of steps and in through the front door. The keys, I found, were still in the lowest of the locks; the small bunch of three keys that Clarissa had had, which I'd been using instead of Greville's larger bunch as they were easier. I'd made things simple for the intruder, I thought, by having them ready in my hand.

With a spurt of alarm I felt my trousers pocket to find if Greville's main bunch had been stolen, but to my relief they were still there, clinking.

I switched off the floodlights and the dog and in the sudden silence closed the front door. Greville's small sitting room, when I reached it, looked like the path of a hurricane. I sur-veyed the mess in fury rather than horror and picked the tumbled phone off the floor to call the police. A burglary, I said. The burglar had gone.

Then I sat in Greville's chair with my head in my hands and

said "shit" aloud with heartfelt rage and gingerly felt the sore bump swelling on my scalp. A bloody pushover, I thought. Like last Sunday. Too like last Sunday to be a coincidence. The cannonball had known both times that I wouldn't be able to stand upright against a sudden unexpected rush. I supposed I should be grateful he hadn't smashed my head in altogether this time while he had the chance. No knife, this time, either.

After a bit I looked wearily round the room. The pictures were off the walls, most of the glass smashed. The drawers had been yanked out of the tables and the tables themselves overturned. The little pink and brown stone bears lay scattered on the floor, the chrysanthemum plant and its dirt were trampled into the carpet, the chrysanthemum pot itself was embedded in the smashed screen of the television, the video recorder had been torn from its unit and dropped, the video cassettes of the races lay pulled out in yards of ruined tape. The violence of it all angered me as much as my own sense of failure in letting it happen.

Many of the books were out of the bookshelves, but I saw with grim satisfaction that none of them lay open. Even if none of the hollow books had contained diamonds, at least the burglar hadn't known the books were hollow. A poor consolation, I thought.

The police arrived eventually, one in uniform, one not. I went along the hall when they rang the doorbell, checked through the peephole and let them in, explaining who I was and why I was there. They were both of about my own age and they'd seen a great many break-ins.

Looking without emotion at Greville's wrecked room, they produced notebooks and took down an account of the assault in the garden. (Did I want a doctor for the bump? No, I didn't.) They knew of this house, they said. The new owner, my brother, had installed all the window grilles and had them wired on a direct alarm to the police station so that if anyone tried to enter that way they would be nicked. Police specialists had given their advice over the defenses and had considered the house as secure as was possible, up to now: but shouldn't there have been active floodlights and a dog alarm? They'd worked well, I said, but before they came I'd turned them off.

"Well, sir," they said, not caring much, "what's been stolen?"

I didn't know. Nothing large, I said, because the burglar had had both hands free, when he vaulted the gate.

Small enough to go into a pocket, they wrote.

What about the rest of the house? Was it in the same state?

I said I hadn't looked yet. Crutches. Bang on head. That sort of thing. They asked about the crutches. Broken ankle, I said. Paining me, perhaps? Just a bit.

I went with them on a tour of the house and found the tornado had blown through all of it. The long drawing room on the ground floor was missing all the pictures from the walls and all the drawers from chests and tables.

"Looking for a safe," one of the policemen said, turning over a ruined picture. "Did your brother have one here, do you know?"

"I haven't seen one," I said.

They nodded and we went upstairs. The black and white bedroom had been ransacked in the same fashion and the bathroom also. Clothes were scattered everywhere. In the bathroom, aspirins and other pills were scattered on the floor. A toothpaste tube had been squeezed flat by a shoe. A can of shaving cream lay in a washbasin, with some of the contents squirted out in loops on the mirror. They commented that as there was no graffiti and no excrement smeared over everything, I had got off lightly.

"Looking for something small," the nonuniformed man said. "Your brother was a gem merchant, wasn't he?"

"Yes."

"Have you found any jewels here yourself?"

"No, I haven't."

They looked into the empty bedroom on that floor, still

empty, and went up the stairs to look around above, but coming down reported nothing to see but space. It's one big attic room, they explained, when I said I hadn't been up there. Might have been a studio once, perhaps.

We all descended to the semibasement where the mess in the kitchen was indescribable. Every packet of cereal had been poured out, sugar and flour had been emptied and apparently sieved in a strainer. The fridge's door hung open with the contents gutted. All liquids had been poured down the sinks, the cartons and bottles either standing empty or smashed by the draining boards. The ice cubes I'd wondered about were missing, presumably melted. Half of the floor of carpet tiles had been pulled up from the concrete beneath.

The policemen went phlegmatically round looking at things but touching little, leaving a few footprints in the floury dust.

I said uncertainly, "How long was I unconscious? If he did all this . . ."

"Twenty minutes, I'd say," one said, and the other nodded. "He was working fast, you can see. He was probably longest down here. I'd say he was pulling up these tiles looking for a floor safe when you set the alarms off again. I'd reckon he panicked then, he'd been here long enough. And also, if it's any use to you, I'd guess that if he was looking for anything particular, he didn't find it."

"Good news, is that?" asked the other, shrewdly, watching me.

"Yes, of course." I explained about the Saxony Franklin office being broken into the previous weekend. "We weren't sure what had been stolen, apart from an address book. In view of this," I gestured to the shambles, "probably nothing was."

"Reasonable assumption," one said.

"When you come back here another time in the dark," the other advised, "shine a good big torch all around the garden before you come through the gate. Sounds as if he was waiting there for you, hiding in the shadow of the hedge, out of range of the body-heat-detecting mechanism of the lights."

"Thank you," I said.

"And switch all the alarms on again, when we leave."

"Yes."

"And draw all the curtains. Burglars sometimes wait about outside, if they haven't found what they're after, hoping that the householders, when they come home, will go straight to the valuables to check if they're there. Then they come rampaging back to steal them."

"I'll draw the curtains," I said.

They looked around in the garden on the way out and found half a brick lying on the grass near where I'd woken up. They showed it to me. Robbery with violence, that made it.

"If you catch the robber," I said.

They shrugged. They were unlikely to, as things stood. I thanked them for coming and they said they'd be putting in a report, which I could refer to for insurance purposes when I made a claim. Then they retreated to the police car double-parked outside the gate and presently drove away, and I shut the front door, switched on the alarms, and felt depressed and stupid and without energy, none of which states was normal.

The policemen had left lights on behind them everywhere. I went slowly down the stairs to the kitchen meaning merely to turn them off, but when I got there I stood for a while contemplating the mess and the reason for it.

Whoever had come had come because the diamonds were still somewhere to be found. I supposed I should be grateful at least for that information; and I was also inclined to believe the policeman who said the burglar hadn't found what he was looking for. But could I find it, if I looked harder?

I hadn't particularly noticed on my first trip downstairs that the kitchen's red carpet was in fact carpet tiles, washable squares that were silent and warmer underfoot than conventional tiles. I'd been brought up on such flooring in our parents' house.

The big tiles, lying flat and fitting snugly, weren't stuck to the hard surface beneath, and the intruder had had no trouble in pulling them up. The intruder hadn't been certain there was a safe, I thought, or he wouldn't have sieved the sugar. And if he'd been successful and found a safe, what then? He hadn't given himself time to do anything about it. He hadn't killed me. Hadn't tied me. Must have known I would wake up.

All it added up to, I thought, was a frantic and rather unintelligent search, which didn't make the bump on my head or my again knocked-about ankle any less sore. Grinding machines had no brains either. Nor, I thought dispiritedly, had the ground product.

I drew the curtains as advised and bent down and pulled up another of the red tiles, thinking about Greville's security complex. It would be just like him to build a safe into the solid base of the house and cover it with something deceptive. Setting a safe in concrete, as the pamphlet had said. People tended to think of safes as being built into walls: floors were less obvious and more secure, but far less convenient. I pulled up a few more tiles, doubting my conclusions, doubting my sanity.

The same sort of feeling as in the vaults kept me going. I didn't expect to find anything but it would be stupid not to make sure, just in case. This time it took half an hour, not three days, and in the end the whole area was up except for a piece under a serving table on wheels. Under that carpet square, when I'd moved the table, I found a flat circular piece of silvery metal flush with the hard base floor, with a recessed ring in it for lifting.

Amazed and suddenly unbearably hopeful, I knelt and pulled the ring up and tugged, and the flat piece of metal came away and off like the lid of a biscuit tin, revealing another layer of metal beneath: an extremely solid-looking circular metal plate the size of a dinner plate in which there was a single keyhole and another handle for lifting.

I pulled the second handle. As well try to pull up the house by its roots. I tried all of Greville's bunch of keys in the keyhole but none of them came near to fitting.

Even Greville, I thought, must have kept the key reasonably handy, but the prospect of searching anew for anything at all filled me with weariness. Greville's affairs were a maze with more blind alleys than Hampton Court.

There were keys in the hollow books, I remembered. Might as well start with those. I shifted upstairs and dug out "With a Mule in Patagonia" and the others, rediscovering the two businesslike keys and also the decorative one which looked too flamboyant for sensible use. True to Greville's mind, however, it was that one whose wards slid easily into the keyhole of the safe and under pressure turned the mechanism inside.

Even then the circular lid wouldn't pull out. Seesawing between hope and frustration I found that, if one turned instead of pulling, the whole top of the safe went round like a wheel until it came against stops; and at that point it finally gave up the struggle and came up loose in my grasp.

The space below was big enough to hold a case of champagne but to my acute disappointment it contained no nest-egg, only a clutch of businesslike brown envelopes. Sighing deeply I took out the top two and found the first contained the freehold deeds of the house and the second the paperwork involved in raising a mortgage to buy it. I read the latter with resignation: Greville's house belonged in essence to a finance company, not to me.

Another of the envelopes contained a copy of his will, which was as simple as the lawyers had said, and in another there was his birth certificate and our parents' birth and marriage certificates. Another yielded an endowment insurance policy taken out long ago to provide him with an income at sixty-five: but inflation had eaten away its worth and he had apparently not bothered to increase it. Instead, I realized, remembering what I'd learned of his company's finances, he had plowed back his profits into expanding his business which would itself ride on the tide of inflation and provide him with a munificent income when he retired and sold.

A good plan, I thought, until he'd knocked the props out by throwing one point five million dollars to the winds. Only he hadn't, of course. He'd had a sensible plan for a sober profit. Deal with honor . . . He'd made a good income, lived a comfortable life and run his racehorses, but he had stacked away no great personal fortune. His wealth, whichever way one looked at it, was in the stones.

Hell and damnation, I thought. If I couldn't find the damned diamonds I'd be failing him as much as myself. He would long for me to find them, but where the bloody *hell* had he put them?

I stuffed most of the envelopes back into their private basement, keeping out only the insurance policy, and replaced the heavy circular lid. Turned it, turned the key, replaced the upper piece of metal and laid a carpet tile on top. Fireproof the hiding place undoubtedly was, and thiefproof it had proved, and I couldn't imagine why Greville hadn't used it for jewels.

Feeling defeated, I climbed at length to the bedroom where I found my own overnight bag had, along with everything else, been tipped up and emptied. It hardly seemed to matter. I picked up my sleeping shorts and changed into them and went into the bathroom. The mirror was still half covered with shaving cream and by the time I'd wiped that off with a face cloth and swallowed a Distalgesic and brushed my teeth and swept a lot of the crunching underfoot junk to one side with a towel, I had used up that day's ration of stamina pretty thoroughly.

Even then, though it was long past midnight, I couldn't sleep. Bangs on the head were odd, I thought. There had been one time when I'd dozed for a week afterward, going to sleep in midsentence as often as not. Another time I'd apparently walked and talked rationally to a doctor but hadn't any recollection of it half an hour later. This time, in Greville's bed, I felt shivery and unsettled, and thought that that had probably as much to do with being attacked as concussed.

[186]

I lay still and let the hours pass, thinking of bad and good and of why things happened, and by morning felt calm and much better. Sitting on the lid of the loo in the bathroom, I unwrapped the crepe bandage and by hopping and holding on to things took a long, luxurious and much needed shower, washing my hair, letting the dust and debris and the mental tensions of the week run away in the soft bombardment of water. After that, loinclothed in a bath towel, I sat on the black and white bed and more closely surveyed the ankle scenery.

It was better than six days earlier, one could confidently say that. On the other hand it was still black, still fairly swollen and still sore to the touch. Still vulnerable to knocks. I flexed my calf and foot muscles several times: the bones and ligaments still violently protested, but none of it could be helped. To stay strong the muscles had to move, and that was that. I kneaded the calf muscle a bit to give it some encouragement and thought about borrowing an apparatus called Electrovet which Milo had tucked away somewhere, which he used on his horses' legs to give their muscles electrical stimuli to bring down swelling and get them fit again. What worked on horses should work on me, I reckoned.

Eventually I wound the bandage on again, not as neatly as the surgeon, but I hoped as effectively. Then I dressed, borrowing one of Greville's clean white shirts and, down in the forlorn little sitting room, telephoned to Nicholas Loder.

He didn't sound pleased to hear my voice.

"Well done with Dozen Roses," I said.

He grunted.

"To solve the question of who owns him," I continued, "I've found a buyer for him."

"Now look here!" he began angrily. "I . . ."

"Yes, I know," I interrupted, "you'd ideally like to sell him to one of your own owners and keep him in your yard, and I do sympathize with that, but Mr. and Mrs. Ostermeyer, the people I was with yesterday at York, they've told me they would like the horse themselves."

[187]

"I strongly protest," he said.

"They want to send him to Milo Shandy to be trained for jumping."

"You owe it to me to leave him here," he said obstinately. "Four wins in a row . . . it's downright dishonorable to take him away."

"He's suitable for jumping, now that he's been gelded." I said it without threat, but he knew he was in an awkward position. He'd had no right to geld the horse. In addition, there was in fact nothing to stop Greville's executor selling the horse to whomever he pleased, as Milo had discovered for me, and which Nicholas Loder had no doubt discovered for himself, and in the racing world in general the sale to the Ostermeyers would make exquisite sense as I would get to ride the horse even if I couldn't own him.

Into Loder's continued silence I said, "If you find a buyer for Gemstones, though, I'll give my approval."

"He's not as good."

"No, but not useless. No doubt you'd take a commission, I wouldn't object to that."

He grunted again, which I took to mean assent, but he also said grittily, "Don't expect any favors from me, ever."

"I've done one for you," I pointed out, "in not lodging a complaint. Anyway, I'm lunching with the Ostermeyers at Milo's today and we'll do the paperwork of the sale. So Milo should be sending a box to collect Dozen Roses sometime this week. No doubt he'll fix a day with you."

"Rot you," he said.

"I don't want to quarrel."

"You're having a damn good try." He slammed down his receiver and left me feeling perplexed as much as anything else by his constant rudeness. All trainers lost horses regularly when owners sold them and, as he'd said himself, it wasn't as if Dozen Roses were a Derby hope. Nicholas Loder's stable held far better prospects than a five-year-old gelding, prolific winner though he might be.

Shrugging, I picked up my overnight bag and felt vaguely guilty at turning my back on so much chaos in the house. I'd done minimum tidying upstairs, hanging up Greville's suits and shirts and so on, and I'd left my own suit and some other things with them because it seemed I might spend more nights there, but the rest was physically difficult and would have to wait for the anonymous Mrs. P., poor woman, who was going to get an atrocious shock.

I went by taxi to the Ostermeyers' hotel and again found them in champagne spirits, and it was again Simms, fortyish, with a mustache, who turned up as chauffeur. When I commented on his working Sunday as well as Saturday he smiled faintly and said he was glad of the opportunity to earn extra; Monday to Friday he developed films in the dark.

"Films?" Martha asked. "Do you mean movies?"

"Family snapshots, madam, in a one-hour photo shop."

"Oh." Martha sounded as if she couldn't envisage such a life. "How interesting."

"Not very, madam," Simms said resignedly, and set off smoothly into the sparse Sunday traffic. He asked me for directions as we neared Lambourn and we arrived without delay at Milo's door, where Milo himself greeted me with the news that Nicholas Loder wanted me to phone him at once.

"It sounded to me," Milo said, "like a great deal of agitation pretending to be casual."

"I don't understand him."

"He doesn't want me to have Dozen Roses, for some reason."

"Oh, but," Martha said to him anxiously, overhearing, "you are going to, aren't you?"

"Of course, yes, don't worry. Derek, get it over with while we go and look at Datepalm." He bore the Ostermeyers away, dazzling them with twinkling charm, and I went into his kitchen and phoned Nicholas Loder, wondering why I was bothering.

"Look," he said, sounding persuasive. "I've an owner

[189]

who's very interested in Dozen Roses. He says he'll top whatever your Ostermeyers are offering. What do you say?"

I didn't answer immediately, and he said forcefully, "You'll
make a good clear profit that way. There's no guarantee the
horse will be able to jump. You can't ask a high price for him,
because of that. My owner will top their offer and add a cash
bonus for you personally. Name your figure."

"Um," I said slowly, "this owner wouldn't be yourself,
would it?"

He said sharply, "No, certainly not."

"The horse that ran at York yesterday," I said even more
slowly, "does he fit Dozen Roses' passport?"

"That's slanderous!"

"It's a question."

"The answer is yes. The horse is Dozen Roses. Is that good
enough for you?"

"Yes."

"Well, then," he sounded relieved, "name your figure."

I hadn't yet discussed any figure at all with Martha and
Harley and I'd been going to ask a bloodstock agent friend for
a snap valuation. I said as much to Nicholas Loder who,
sounding exasperated, repeated that his owner would offer
more, plus a tax-free sweetener for myself.

I had every firm intention of selling Dozen Roses to the
Ostermeyers and no so-called sweetener that I could think of
would have persuaded me otherwise.

"Please tell your owner I'm sorry," I said, "but the Ostermeyers have bought Datepalm, as I told you, and I am obli-
gated to them, and loyalty to them comes first. I'm sure
you'll find your owner another horse as good as Dozen
Roses."

"What if he offered double what you'd take from the Ostermeyers?"

"It's not a matter of money."

"Everyone can be bought," he said.

"Well, no. I'm sorry, but no."

"Think it over," he said, and slammed the receiver down

again. I wondered in amusement how often he broke them. But he hadn't in fact been amusing, and the situation as a whole held no joy. I was going to have to meet him on racecourses forever once I was a trainer myself, and I had no appetite for chronic feuds.

I went out into the yard where, seeing me, Milo broke away from the Ostermeyers, who were feasting their eyes as Datepalm was being led round on the gravel to delight them.

"What did Loder want?" Milo demanded, coming toward me.

"He offered double whatever I was asking the Ostermeyers to pay for Dozen Roses."

Milo stared. "Double? Without knowing what it was?"

"That's right."

"What are you going to do?"

"What do you think?" I asked.

"If you've accepted, I'll flatten you."

I laughed. Too many people that past week had flattened me and no doubt Milo could do it with the best.

"Well?" he said belligerently.

"I told him to stuff it."

"Good."

"Mm, perhaps. But you'd better arrange to fetch the horse here at once. Like tomorrow morning, as we don't want him having a nasty accident and ending up at the knackers, do you think?"

"Christ!" He was appalled. "He wouldn't! Not Nicholas Loder."

"One wouldn't think so. But no harm in removing the temptation."

"No." He looked at me attentively. "Are you all right?" he asked suddenly. "You don't look too well."

I told him briefly about being knocked out in Greville's garden. "Those phone calls you took," I said, "were designed to make sure I turned up in the right place at the right time. So I walked straight into an ambush and, if you want to know, I feel a fool."

[191]

"Derek!" He was dumbfounded, but also of course practical. "It's not going to delay your getting back on a horse?"

"No, don't worry."

"Did you tell the Ostermeyers?"

"No, don't bother them. They don't like me being unfit."

He nodded in complete understanding. To Martha, and to Harley to a lesser but still considerable extent, it seemed that proprietorship in the jockey was as important as in the horse. I'd met that feeling a few times before and never undervalued it: they were the best owners to ride for, even if often the most demanding. The quasi-love relationship could however turn to dust and damaging rejection if one ever put them second, which was why I would never jeopardize my place on Datepalm for a profit on Dozen Roses. It was hard to explain to more rational people, but I rode races, as every jump jockey did, from a different impetus than making money, though the money was nice enough and thoroughly earned besides.

When Martha and Harley at length ran out of questions and admiration of Datepalm we all returned to the house, where over drinks in Milo's comfortable sitting room we telephoned to the bloodstock agent for an opinion and then agreed on a price which was less than he'd suggested. Milo beamed. Martha clapped her hands together with pleasure. Harley drew out his checkbook and wrote in it carefully, "Saxony Franklin Ltd."

"Subject to a vet's certificate," I said.

"Oh yes, dear," Martha agreed, smiling. "As if you would ever sell us a lemon."

Milo produced the 'Change of Ownership' forms, which Martha and Harley and I all signed, and Milo said he would register the new arrangements with Weatherby's in the morning.

"Is Dozen Roses ours, now?" Martha asked, shiny-eyed.

"Indeed he is," Milo said, "subject to his being alive and in good condition when he arrives here. If he isn't the sale is void and he still belongs to Saxony Franklin."

I wondered briefly if he were insured. Didn't want to find out the hard way.

With the business concluded Milo drove us all out to lunch at a nearby restaurant which as usual was crammed with Lambourn people: Martha and Harley held splendid court as the new owners of Gold Cup winner Datepalm and were pink with gratification over the compliments to their purchase. I watched their stimulated faces, hers rounded and still pretty under the blonde-rinsed gray hair, his heavily handsome, the square jaw showing the beginning of jowls. Both now looking sixty, they still displayed enthusiasms and enjoyments that were almost childlike in their simplicity, which did no harm in the weary old world.

Milo drove us back to rejoin the Daimler and Simms, who'd eaten his lunch in a village pub, and Martha in farewell gave Milo a kiss with flirtation but also real affection. Milo had bound the Ostermeyers to his stable with hoops of charm and all we needed now was for the two horses to carry on winning.

Milo said "Thanks" to me briefly as we got into the car, but in truth I wanted what he wanted, and securing the Ostermeyers had been a joint venture. We drove out of the yard with Martha waving and then settling back into her seat with murmurs and soft remarks of pleasure.

I told Simms the way to Hungerford so that he could drop me off there, and the big car purred along with Sunday afternoon somnolence.

Martha said something I didn't quite catch and I turned my face back between the headrests, looking toward her and asking her to say it again. I saw a flash of raw horror begin on Harley's face, and then with a crash and a bang the car rocketed out of control across the road toward a wall and there was blood and shredded glass everywhere and we careered off the wall back onto the road and into the path of a fifty-seater touring coach which had been behind us and was now bearing down on us like a runaway cliff.

[193]

12

IN the split second before the front of the bus hit the side of the car where I was sitting, in the freeze-frame awareness of the tons of bright metal thundering inexorably toward us, I totally believed I would be mangled to pulp within a breath.

There was no time for regrets or anger or any other emotion. The bus plunged into the Daimler and turned it again forward and both vehicles screeched along the road together, monstrously joined wheel to wheel, the white front wing of the coach buried deep in the black Daimler's engine, the noise and buffeting too much for thinking, the speed of everything truly terrifying and the nearness of death an inevitability merely postponed.

Inertia dragged the two vehicles toward a halt, but they were blocking the whole width of the road. Toward us, round a bend, came a family car traveling too fast to stop in the space available. The driver in a frenzy braked so hard that his rear end swung round and hit the front of the Daimler broadside with a sickening jolt and a crunching bang and behind us, somewhere, another car ran into the back of the bus.

About that time I stopped being clear about the sequence of events. Against all catastrophe probability I was still alive and that seemed enough. After the first stunned moments of silence when the tearing of metal had stopped, there were voices shouting everywhere, and people screaming and a sharp petrifying smell of raw petrol.

The whole thing was going to burn, I thought. Explode. Fireballs coming. Greville had burned two days ago. Greville had at least been dead at the time. Talk about delirious. I had half a car in my lap and in my head the warmed-up leftovers of yesterday's concussion.

The heat of the dead engine filled the cracked-open body of the car, forewarning of worse. There would be oil dripping out of it. There were electrical circuits . . . sparks . . . there was dread and despair and a vision of hell.

I couldn't escape. The glass had gone from the window beside me and from the windshield, and what might have been part of the frame of the door had bent somehow across my chest, pinning me deep against the seat. What had been the fascia and the glove compartment seemed to be digging into my waist. What had been ample room for a dicky ankle was now as constricting as any cast. The car seemed to have wrapped itself around me in an iron-maiden embrace and the only parts free to move at all were my head and the arm nearest Simms. There was intense pressure rather than active agony, but what I felt most was fear.

Almost automatically, as if logic had gone on working on its own, I stretched as far as I could, got my fingers on the keys, twisted and pulled them out of the ignition. At least, no more sparks. At most, I was breathing.

Martha, too, was alive, her thoughts probably as abysmal as my own. I could hear her whimpering behind me, a small moaning without words. Simms and Harley were silent; and it was Simms's blood that had spurted over everything, scarlet and sticky. I could smell it under the smell of petrol; it was on my arm and face and clothes and in my hair.

The side of the car where I sat was jammed tight against the bus. People came in time to the opposite side and tried to open the doors, but they were immovably buckled. Dazed people emerged from the family car in front, the children weeping. People from the coach spread along the roadside, all of them elderly, most of them, it seemed to me, with their mouths open. I wanted to tell them all to keep away, to go farther to safety, far from what was going to be a conflagration at any second, but I didn't seem to be able to shout, and the croak I achieved got no farther than six inches.

Behind me Martha stopped moaning. I thought wretchedly that she was dying, but it seemed to be the opposite. In a quavery small voice she said, "Derek?"

"Yes." Another croak.

"I'm frightened."

So was I, by God. I said futilely, hoarsely, "Don't worry."

She scarcely listened. She was saying "Harley? Harley, honey?" in alarm and awakening anguish. "Oh, get us out, please, someone get us out."

I turned my head as far as I could and looked back sideways at Harley. He was cold to the world but his eyes were closed, which was a hopeful sign on the whole.

Simms's eyes were half open and would never blink again. Simms, poor man, had developed his last one-hour photo. Simms wouldn't feel any flames.

"Oh God, honey. Honey, wake up." Her voice cracked, high with rising panic. "Derek, get us out of here, can't you smell the gas?"

"People will come," I said, knowing it was of little comfort. Comfort seemed impossible, out of reach.

People and comfort came, however, in the shape of a works foreman-type of man, used to getting things done. He peered through the window beside Harley and was presently yelling to Martha that he was going to break the rear window to get her out and she should cover her face in case of flying glass.

Martha hid her face against Harley's chest, calling to him and weeping, and the rear window gave way to determination and a metal bar.

"Come on, Missis," encouraged the best of British workmen. "Climb up on the seat, we'll have you out of there in no time."

"My husband . . ." she wailed.

"Him too. No trouble. Come on, now."

It appeared that strong arms hauled Martha out bodily. Almost at once her rescuer was himself inside the car, lifting the still-unconscious Harley far enough to be raised by other hands outside. Then he put his head forward near to mine, and took a look at me and Simms.

"Christ," he said.

He was smallish, with a mustache and bright brown eyes.

"Can you slide out of there?" he asked.

"No."

He tried to pull me, but we could both see it was hopeless.

"They'll have to cut you out," he said, and I nodded. He wrinkled his nose. "The smell of petrol's very strong in here. Much worse than outside."

"It's vapor," I said. "It ignites."

He knew that, but it hadn't seemed to worry him until then.

"Clear all those people farther away," I said. I raised perhaps a twitch of a smile. "Ask them not to smoke."

He gave me a sick look and retreated through the rear window, and soon I saw him outside delivering a warning which must have been the quickest crowd control measure on record.

Perhaps because with more of the glass missing there was a through current of air, the smell of petrol did begin to abate, but there was still, I imagined, a severed fuel line somewhere beneath me, with freshly released vapor continually seeping through the cracks. How much liquid bonfire, I wondered numbly, did a Daimler's tank hold?

There were a great many more cars now ahead in the road, all stopped, their occupants out and crash-gazing. No doubt to the rear it would be the same thing. Sunday afternoon entertainment at its worst.

Simms and I sat on in our silent immobility and I thought of the old joke about worrying, that there was no point in it. If one worried that things would get bad and they didn't, there was no point in worrying. If they got bad and one worried they would get worse, and they didn't, there was no point in worrying. If they got worse and one worried that one might die, and one didn't, there was no point in worrying, and if one died one could no longer worry, so why worry.

For worry read fear, I thought; but the theory didn't work. I went straight on being scared silly.

It was odd, I thought, that for all the risks I took I very seldom felt any fear of death. I thought about physical pain, as indeed one often had to in a trade like mine, and remembered things I'd endured, and I didn't know why the imagined pain of burning should fill me with a terror hard to control. I swallowed and felt lonely, and hoped that if it came it would be over quickly.

There were sirens at length in the distance and the best sight in the world, as far as I was concerned, was the red fire engine which slowly forced its way forward, scattering spectator cars to either side of the road. There was room, just, for three cars abreast; a wall on one side of the road, a row of trees on the other. Behind the fire engine I could see the flashing blue light of a police car and beyond that another flashing light which might betoken an ambulance.

Figures in authority uniforms appeared from the vehicles, the best being in flameproof suits lugging a hose. They stopped in front of the Daimler, seeing the bus wedged into one side of it and the family car on the other, and one of them shouted to me through the space where the windshield should have been.

"There's petrol running from these vehicles," he said. "Can't you get out?"

What a damn silly question, I thought. I said, "No."

"We're going to spray the road underneath you. Shut your eyes and hold something over your mouth and nose."

I nodded and did as I was bid, managing to shield my face inside the neck of my jersey. I listened to the long whooshing of the spray and thought no sound could be sweeter. Incineration faded progressively from near certainty to diminishing probability to unlikely outcome, and the release from fear was almost as hard to manage as the fear itself. I wiped blood and sweat off my face and felt shaky.

After a while some of the firemen brought up metal-cutting gear and more or less tore out of its frame the buckled door next to where Harley had been sitting. Into this new entrance edged a policeman who took a preliminary look at Simms and me and then perched on the rear seat where he could see my head. I turned it as far as I could toward him, seeing a serious face under the peaked cap: about my own age, I judged, and full of strain.

"A doctor's coming," he said, offering crumbs. "He'll deal with your wounds."

"I don't think I'm bleeding," I said. "It's Simms's blood that's on me."

"Ah." He drew out a notebook and consulted it. "Did you see what caused this . . . all this?"

"No," I said, thinking it faintly surprising that he should be asking at this point. "I was looking back at Mr. and Mrs. Ostermeyer, who were sitting where you are now. The car just seemed to go out of control." I thought back, remembering. "I think Harley . . . Mr. Ostermeyer . . . may have seen something. For a second he looked horrified . . . then we hit the wall and rebounded into the path of the bus."

He nodded, making a note.

"Mr. Ostermeyer is now conscious," he said, sounding carefully noncommittal. "He says you were shot."

"We were *what?*"

"Shot. Not all of you. You, personally."

"No." I must have sounded as bewildered as I felt. "Of course not."

"Mr. and Mrs. Ostermeyer are very distressed but he is quite clear he saw a gun. He says the chauffeur had just pulled out to pass a car that had been in front of you for some way, and the driver of that car had the window down and was pointing a gun out of it. He says the gun was pointing at you, and you were shot. Twice at least, he says. He saw the spurts of flame."

I looked from the policeman to Simms, and at the chauffeur's blood over everything and at the solidly scarlet congealed mess below his jaw.

"No," I protested, not wanting to believe it. "It can't be right."

"Mrs. Ostermeyer is intensely worried that you are sitting here bleeding to death."

"I feel squeezed, not punctured."

"Can you feel your feet?"

I moved my toes, one foot after another. There wasn't the slightest doubt, particularly about the left.

"Good," he said. "Well, sir, we are treating this from now on as a possible murder inquiry, and apart from that I'm afraid the firemen say it may be some time before they can get you loose. They need more gear. Can you be patient?" He didn't wait for a reply, but went on, "As I said, a doctor is here and will come to you, but if you aren't in urgent need of him there are two other people back there in a very bad way, and I hope you can be patient about that also."

I nodded slightly. I could be patient for hours if I wasn't going to burn.

"Why," I asked, "would anyone shoot at us?"

"Have you no idea?"

"None at all."

"Unfortunately," he said, "there isn't always an understandable reason."

I met his eyes. "I live in Hungerford," I said.

"Yes, sir, so I've been told." He nodded and slithered out of the car, and left me thinking about the time in Hungerford when a berserk man had gunned down many innocent people, including some in cars, and turned the quiet country town into a place of horror. No one who lived in Hungerford would ever discount the possibility of being randomly slaughtered.

The bullet that had torn into Simms would have gone

through my own neck or head, I thought, if I hadn't turned round to talk to Martha. I'd put my head between the headrests, the better to see her. I tried to sort out what had happened next, but I hadn't seen Simms hit, I'd heard only the bang and crash of the window breaking and felt the hot spray of the blood that had fountained out of his smashed main artery in the time it had taken him to die. He had been dead, I thought, before anyone had started screaming: the jet of blood had stopped by then.

The steering wheel was now rammed hard against his chest with the instrument panel slanting down across his knees, higher my end than his. The edge of it pressed uncomfortably into my stomach, and I could see that if it had traveled back another six inches, it would have cut me in half.

A good many people arrived looking official with measuring tapes and cameras, taking photographs of Simms particularly and consulting in low tones. A police surgeon solemnly put a stethoscope to Simms's chest and declared him dead, and without bothering with the stethoscope declared me alive.

How bad was the compression, he wanted to know. Uncomfortable, I said.

"I know you, don't I?" he said, considering me. "Aren't you one of the local jockeys? The jumping boys?"

"Mm."

"Then you know enough about being injured to give me an assessment of your state."

I said that my toes, fingers and lungs were OK and that I had cramp in my legs, the trapped arm was aching and the instrument panel was inhibiting the digestion of a good Sunday lunch.

"Do you want an injection?" he asked, listening.

"Not unless it gets worse."

He nodded, allowed himself a small smile and wriggled his way out onto the road. It struck me that there was much less legroom for the back seat than there had been when we set

[201]

out. A miracle Martha's and Harley's legs hadn't been broken. Three of us, I thought, had been incredibly lucky.

Simms and I went on sitting quietly side by side for what seemed several more ages but finally the extra gear to free us appeared in the form of winches, cranes and an acetylene torch, which I hoped they would use around me with discretion.

Large mechanics scratched their heads over the problems. They couldn't get to me from my side of the car because it was tight against the bus. They decided that if they tried to cut through the support under the front seats and pull them backward they might upset the tricky equilibrium of the engine and instead of freeing my trapped legs bring the whole weight of the front of the car down to crush them. I was against the idea, and said so.

In the end, working from inside the car in fireproof suits with thick fresh foam pumped all around, using a scorching acetylene flame which roared and threw out terrifying sparks, they cut away most of the driver's side, and after that, since he couldn't feel or protest, they forcefully pulled Simm's stiffening body out and laid it on a stretcher. I wondered grayly if he had a wife, who wouldn't know yet.

With Simms gone, the mechanics began fixing chains and operating jacks and I sat and waited without bothering them with questions. From time to time they said, "You all right, mate?" and I answered "Yes," and was grateful to them.

After a while they fastened chains and a winch to the family car still impacted broadside on the Daimler's wing and with inching care began to pull it away. There was almost instantly a fearful shudder through the Daimler's crushed body and also through mine, and the pulling stopped immediately. A little more head-scratching went on, and one of them explained to me that their crane couldn't get a good enough stabilizing purchase on the Daimler because the family car was in the way, and they would have to try something else. Was I all right? Yes, I said.

One of them began calling me Derek. "Seen you in Hungerford, haven't I," he said, "and on the telly?" He told the others, who made jolly remarks like, "Don't worry, we'll have you out in time for the three-thirty tomorrow. Sure to." One of them seriously told me that it sometimes did take hours to free people because of the dangers of getting it wrong. Lucky, he said, that it was a Daimler I was in, with its tanklike strength. In anything less I would have been history.

They decided to rethink the rear approach. They wouldn't disturb the seat anchorages from their pushed-back position: the seats were off their runners, they said, and had dug into the floor. Also the recliner-mechanism had jammed and broken. However, they were going to cut off the back of Simms's seat to give themselves more room to work. They were then going to extract the padding and springs from under my bottom and see if they could get rid of the back of my seat also, and draw me out backward so that they wouldn't have to maneuver me out sideways past the steering column, which they didn't want to remove as it was the anchor for one of the chief stabilizing chains. Did I understand? Yes, I did.

They more or less followed this plan, although they had to dismantle the back of my seat before the cushion, the lowering effect of having the first spring removed from under me having jammed me even tighter against the fascia and made breathing difficult. They yanked padding out from behind me to relieve that, and then with a hacksaw took the back of the seat off near the roots; and, finally, with one of them supporting my shoulders, another pulled out handfuls of springs and other seat innards, and the bear-hug pressure on my abdomen and arm and legs lessened and went away, and I had only blessed pins and needles instead.

Even then the big car was loath to let me go. With my top half free the two men began to pull me backward, and I grunted and stiffened, and they stopped at once.

"What's the matter?" one asked anxiously.

"Well, nothing. Pull again."

[203]

In truth the pulling hurt the left ankle but I'd sat there long enough. It was at least an old, recognizable pain, nothing threateningly new. Reassured, my rescuers hooked their arms under my armpits and used a bit of strength, and at last extracted me from the car's crushing embrace like a breeched calf from a cow.

Relief was an inadequate word. They gave me a minute's rest on the back seat, and sat each side of me, all three of us breathing deeply.

"Thanks," I said briefly.

"Think nothing of it."

I guessed they knew the depths of my gratitude, as I knew the thought and care they'd expended. Thanks, think nothing of it: it was enough.

One by one we edged out onto the road, and I was astonished to find that after all that time there was still a small crowd standing around waiting: policemen, firemen, mechanics, ambulance men and assorted civilians, many with cameras. There was a small cheer and applause as I stood up free, and I smiled and moved my head in a gesture of both embarrassment and thanksgiving.

I was offered a stretcher but said I'd much rather have the crutches that might still be in the trunk, and that caused a bit of general consternation, but someone brought them out unharmed, about the only thing still unbent in the whole mess. I stood for a bit with their support simply looking at all the intertwined wreckage: at the bus and the family car and above all at the Daimler's buckled up roof, at its sheared-off hood, its dislodged engine awry at a tilted angle, its gleaming black paintwork now unrecognizable scrap, its former shape mangled and compressed like a stamped-on toy. I thought it incredible that I'd sat where I'd sat and lived. I reckoned that I'd used up a lifetime's luck.

The Ostermeyers had been taken to Swindon Hospital and treated for shock, bruises and concussion. From there, recovering a little, they had telephoned Milo and told him what had happened and he, reacting I guessed with spontaneous generosity but also with strong business sense, had told them they must stay with him for the night and he would collect them. All three were on the point of leaving when I in my turn arrived.

There was a predictable amount of fussing from Martha over my rescue, but she herself looked as exhausted as I felt and she was pliably content to be supported on Harley's arm on their way to the door.

Milo, coming back a step, said, "Come as well, if you like. There's always a bed."

"Thanks, I'll let you know."

He stared at me. "Is it true Simms was shot?"

"Mm."

"It could have been you."

"Nearly was."

"The police took statements here from Martha and Harley, it seems." He paused, looking toward them as they reached the door. "I'll have to go. How's the ankle?"

"Be back racing as scheduled."

"Good."

He bustled off and I went through the paperwork routines, but there was nothing wrong with me that a small application of time wouldn't fix and I got myself discharged pretty fast as a patient and was invited instead to give a more detailed statement to the police. I couldn't add much more than I'd told them in the first place, but some of their questions were in the end disturbing.

Could we have been shot at for any purpose?

I knew of no purpose.

How long had the car driven by the man with the gun been in front of us?

I couldn't remember: hadn't noticed.

Could anyone have known we would be on that road at that time?

I stared at the policeman. Anyone, perhaps, who had been in the restaurant for lunch. Anyone there could have followed us from there to Milo's house, perhaps, and waited for us to leave, and passed us, allowing us then to pass again. But why ever should they?

Who else might know?

Perhaps the car company who employed Simms.

Who else?

Milo Shandy, and he'd have been as likely to shoot himself as the Ostermeyers.

Mr. Ostermeyer said the gun was pointing at you, sir.

With all due respect to Mr. Ostermeyer, he was looking through the car and both cars were moving, and at different speeds presumably, and I didn't think one could be certain.

Could I think of any reason why anyone should want to kill me?

Me, personally? No . . . I couldn't.

They pounced on the hesitation I could hear in my own voice, and I told them I'd been attacked and knocked out the previous evening. I explained about Greville's death. I told them he had been dealing in precious stones as he was a gem merchant and I thought my attacker had been trying to find and steal part of the stock. But I had no idea why the would-be thief should want to shoot me today when he could easily have bashed my head in yesterday.

They wrote it down without comment. Had I any idea who had attacked me the previous evening?

No, I hadn't.

They didn't say they didn't believe me, but something in their manner gave me the impression they thought anyone attacked twice in two days had to know who was after him.

I would have liked very much to be able to tell them. It had just occurred to me, if not to them, that there might be more to come.

I'd better find out soon, I thought.

I'd better not find out too late.

13

I didn't go to Milo's house nor to my own bed, but stayed in an anonymous hotel in Swindon where unknown enemies wouldn't find me.

The urge simply to go home was strong, as if one could retreat to safety into one's den, but I thought I would probably be alarmed and wakeful all night there, when what I most wanted was sleep. All in all it had been a rough ten days, and however easily my body usually shook off bumps and bangs, the accumulation was making an insistent demand for rest.

RICE, I thought wryly, RICE being the acronym of the best way to treat sports injuries: rest, ice, compression, elevation. I rarely seemed to be managing all of them at the same time, though all, in one way or another, separately. With elevation in place, I phoned Milo from the hotel to say I wouldn't be coming and asked how Martha and Harley were doing.

"They're quavery. It must have been some crash. Martha keeps crying. It seems a car ran into the back of the bus and two people in the car were terribly injured. She saw them, and it's upsetting her almost as much as knowing Simms was shot. Can't you come and comfort her?"

"You and Harley can do it better."

"She thought you were dying too. She's badly shocked. You'd better come."

"They gave her a sedative at the hospital, didn't they?"

"Yes," he agreed grudgingly. "Harley too."

"Look . . . persuade them to sleep. I'll come in the morning and pick them up and take them back to their hotel in London. Will that do?"

He said unwillingly that he supposed so.

"Say goodnight to them from me," I said. "Tell them I think they're terrific."

"Do you?" He sounded surprised.

"It does no harm to say it."

"Cynic."

"Seriously," I said, "they'll feel better if you tell them."

"All right then. See you at breakfast."

I put down the receiver and on reflection a few minutes later got through to Brad.

"Cor," he said, "you were in that crash."

"How did you hear about it?" I asked, surprised.

"Down the pub. Talk of Hungerford. Another madman. It's shook everyone up. My mum won't go out."

It had shaken his tongue loose, I thought in amusement.

"Have you still got my car?" I said.

"Yerss." He sounded anxious. "You said keep it here."

"Yes. I meant keep it there."

"I walked down your house earlier. There weren't no one there then."

"I'm not there now," I said. "Do you still want to go on driving?"

"Yerss." Very positive. "Now?"

"In the morning." I said I would meet him at eight outside the hotel near the railway station at Swindon, and we would be going to London. "OK?"

"Yerss," he said again, signing off, and it sounded like a cat purring over the resumption of milk.

Smiling and yawning, a jaw-cracking combination, I ran a bath, took off my clothes and the bandage and lay gratefully in hot water, letting it soak away the fatigue along with

[208]

Simms's blood. Then, my overnight bag having survived unharmed along with the crutches, I scrubbed my teeth, put on sleeping shorts, rewrapped the ankle, hung a "Do not disturb" card outside my door and was in bed by nine and slept and dreamed of crashes and fire and hovering unidentified threats.

Brad came on the dot in the morning and we went first to my place in a necessary quest for clean clothes. His mum, Brad agreed, would wash the things I'd worn in the crash.

My rooms were still quiet and unransacked and no dangers lurked outside in daylight. I changed uneventfully and repacked the traveling bag and we drove in good order to Lambourn, I sitting beside Brad and thinking I could have done the driving myself, except that I found his presence reassuring and I'd come to grief on both of the days he hadn't been with me.

"If a car passes us and sits in front of us," I said, "don't pass it. Fall right back and turn up a side road."

"Why?"

I told him that the police thought we'd been caught in a deliberate moving ambush. Neither the Ostermeyers nor I, I pointed out, would be happy to repeat the experience, and Brad wouldn't be wanting to double for Simms. He grinned, an unnerving sight, and gave me to understand with a nod that he would follow the instruction.

The usual road to Lambourn turned out to be still blocked off, and I wondered briefly, as we detoured, whether it was because of the murder inquiry or simply technical difficulties in disentangling the omelette.

Martha and Harley were still shaking over breakfast, the coffee cups trembling against their lips. Milo with relief shifted the burden of their reliance smartly from himself to me, telling them that now Derek was here, they'd be safe. I wasn't so sure about that, particularly if both Harley and the police were right about me personally being yesterday's target. Neither Martha nor Harley seemed to suffer such qualms and gave me the instant status of surrogate son/nephew, the one to be naturally leaned on, psychologically if not physically, for succor and support.

I looked at them with affection. Martha had retained enough spirit to put on lipstick. Harley was making light of an adhesive bandage on his temple. They couldn't help their nervous systems' reaction to mental trauma, and I hoped it wouldn't be long before their habitual preference for enjoyment resurfaced.

"The only good thing about yesterday," Martha said with a sigh, "was buying Dozen Roses. Milo says he's already sent a van for him."

I'd forgotten about Dozen Roses. Nicholas Loder and his tizzies seemed a long way off and unimportant. I said I was glad they were glad, and that in about a week or so, when he'd settled down in his new quarters, I would start teaching him to jump.

"I'm sure he'll be brilliant," Martha said bravely, trying hard to make normal conversation. "Won't he?"

"Some horses take to it better than others," I said neutrally. "Like humans."

"I'll believe he'll be brilliant."

Averagely good, I thought, would be good enough for me: but most racehorses could jump if started patiently over low obstacles like logs.

Milo offered fresh coffee and more toast, but they were ready to leave and in a short while we were on the road to London. No one passed us and slowed, no one ambushed or shot us, and Brad drew up with a flourish outside their hotel, at least the equal of Simms.

Martha with a shine of tears kissed my cheek in goodbye, and I hers: Harley gruffly shook my hand. They would come back soon, they said, but they were sure glad to be going home tomorrow. I watched them go shakily into the hotel and thought uncomplicated thoughts, like hoping Datepalm would cover himself with glory for them, and Dozen Roses also, once he could jump.

"Office?" I suggested to Brad, and he nodded, and made the now familiar turns toward the environs of Hatton Garden.

Little in Saxony Franklin appeared to have changed. It seemed extraordinary that it was only a week since I'd walked in there for the first time, so familiar did it feel on going back. The staff said "Good morning, Derek" as if they'd been used to me for years, and Annette said there were letters left over from Friday which needed decisions.

"How was the funeral?" she asked sadly, laying out papers on the desk.

A thousand light-years ago, I thought. "Quiet," I said. "Good. Your flowers were good. They were on top of his coffin."

She looked pleased and said she would tell the others, and received the news that there would be a memorial service with obvious satisfaction. "It didn't seem right, not being at his funeral, not on Friday. We had a minute's silence here at two o'clock. I suppose you'll think us silly."

"Far from it." I was moved and let her see it. She smiled sweetly in her heavy way and went off to relay to the others and leave me floundering in the old treacle of deciding things on a basis of no knowledge.

June whisked in looking happy with a pink glow on both cheeks and told me we were low in blue lace agate chips and snowflake obsidian and amazonite beads.

"Order some more, same as before."

"Yes, right."

She turned and was on her way out again when I called her back and asked her if there was an alarm clock among all the gadgets. I pulled open the deep drawer and pointed downward.

"An alarm clock?" She was doubtful and peered at the assorted black objects. "Telescopes, dictionaries, Geiger counter, calculators, spy juice . . ."

[211]

"What's spy juice?" I asked, intrigued.

"Oh, this." She reached in and extracted an aerosol can. "That's just my name for it. You squirt this stuff on anyone's envelopes and it makes the paper transparent so you can read the private letters inside." She looked at my face and laughed. "Banks have got round it by printing patterns all over the insides of their envelopes. If you spray their envelopes, all you see is the pattern."

"Whatever did Greville use it for?"

"Someone gave it to him, I think. He didn't use it much, just to check if it was worth opening things that looked like advertisements."

She put a plain sheet of paper over one of the letters lying on the desk and squirted a little liquid over it. The plain paper immediately became transparent so that one could read the letter through it, and then slowly went opaque again as it dried.

"Sneaky," she said, "isn't it?"

"Very."

She was about to replace the can in the drawer but I said to put it on top of the desk, and I brought out all the other gadgets and stood them around in plain sight. None of them, as far as I could see, had an alarm function.

"You mentioned something about a world clock," I said, "but there isn't one here."

"I've a clock with an alarm in my room," she said helpfully. "Would you like me to bring that?"

"Um, yes, perhaps. Could you set it to four-fifteen?"

"Sure, anything you like."

She vanished and returned fiddling with a tiny thing like a black credit card which turned out to be a highly versatile timepiece.

"There you are," she said. "Four-fifteen. P.M., I suppose you mean." She put the clock on the desk.

"This afternoon, yes. There's an alarm somewhere here that goes off every day at four-twenty. I thought I might find it."

Her eyes widened. "Oh, but that's Mr. Franklin's watch."
"Which one?" I asked.
"He only ever wore one. It's a computer itself, a calendar and a compass."
That watch, I reflected, was beside my bed in Hungerford.
"I think," I said, "that he may have had more than one alarm set to four-twenty."
The fair eyebrows lifted. "I did sometimes wonder why," she said. "I mean, why four-twenty? If he was in the stockroom and his watch alarm went off he would stop doing whatever it was for a few moments. I sort of asked him once, but he didn't really answer, he said it was a convenient time for communication, or something like that. I didn't understand what he meant, but that was all right, he didn't mean me to."
She spoke without resentment and with regret. I thought that Greville must have enjoyed having June around him as much as I did. All that bright intelligence and unspoiled good humor and common sense. He'd liked her enough to make puzzles for her and let her share his toys.
"What's this one?" I asked, picking up a small gray contraption with black ear sponges on a headband with a cord like a walkabout cassette player, but with no provision for cassettes in what might have been a holder.
"That's a sound-enhancer. It's for deaf people, really, but Mr. Franklin took it away from someone who was using it to listen to a private conversation he was having with another gem merchant. In Tucson, it was. He said he was so furious at the time that he just snatched the amplifier and headphones off the man who was listening and walked away with them uttering threats about commercial espionage, and he said the man hadn't even tried to get them back." She paused. "Put the earphones on. You can hear everything anyone's saying anywhere in the office. It's pretty powerful. Uncanny, really."
I put on the ultralight earphones and pressed the on switch on the cigarette packet–sized amplifier, and sure enough, I could straightaway hear Annette across the hallway talking to

[213]

Lily about remembering to ask Derek for time off for the dentist.

I removed the earphones and looked at June.

"What did you hear?" she asked. "Secrets?"

"Not that time, no."

"Scary, though?"

"As you say."

The sound quality was in fact excellent, astonishingly sensitive for so small a microphone and amplifier. Some of Greville's toys, I thought, were decidedly unfriendly.

"Mr. Franklin was telling me that there's a voice transformer that you can fix on the telephone that can change the pitch of your voice and make a woman sound like a man. He said he thought it was excellent for women living alone so that they wouldn't be bothered by obscene phone calls and no one would think they were alone and vulnerable."

I smiled. "It might disconcert a bona fide boyfriend innocently calling."

"Well, you'd have to warn them," she agreed. "Mr. Franklin was very keen on women taking precautions."

"Mm," I said wryly.

"He said the jungle came into his court."

"Did you get a voice-changer?" I asked.

"No. We were only talking about it just before . . ." She stopped. "Well . . . anyway, do you want a sandwich for lunch?"

"Yes, please."

She nodded and was gone. I sighed and tried to apply myself to the tricky letters and was relieved at the interruption when the telephone rang.

It was Elliot Trelawney on the line, asking if I would messenger round the Vaccaro notes at once if I wouldn't mind as they had a committee meeting that afternoon.

"Vaccaro notes," I repeated. I'd clean forgotten about them. I couldn't remember, for a moment, where they were.

"You said you would send them this morning," Trelawney

said with a tinge of civilized reproach. "Do you remember?"

"Yes." I did, vaguely.

Where the hell were they? Oh yes, in Greville's sitting room. Somewhere in all that mess. Somewhere there, unless the thief had taken them.

I apologized. I didn't actually say I'd come near to being killed twice since I'd last spoken to him and it was playing tricks with my concentration. I said things had cropped up. I was truly sorry. I would try to get them to the court by . . . when?

"The committee meets at two and Vaccaro is first on the agenda," he said.

"The notes are still in Greville's house," I replied, "but I'll get them to you."

"Awfully good of you." He was affable again. "It's frightfully important we turn this application down."

"Yes, I know."

Vaccaro, I thought uncomfortably, replacing the receiver, was alleged to have had his wanting-out cocaine-smuggling pilots murdered by shots from moving cars.

I stared into space. There was no reason on earth for Vaccaro to shoot me, even supposing he knew I existed. I wasn't Greville, and I had no power to stand in the way of his plans. All I had, or probably had, were the notes on his transgressions, and how could he know that? And how could he know I would be in a car between Lambourn and Hungerford on Sunday afternoon? And couldn't the notes be gathered again by someone else besides Greville, even if they were now lost?

I shook myself out of the horrors and went down to the yard to see if Brad was sitting in the car, which he was, reading a magazine about fishing.

Fishing? "I didn't know you fished," I said.

"I don't."

End of conversation.

Laughing inwardly I invited him to go on the journey. I

gave him the simple key ring of three keys and explained about the upheaval he would find. I described the Vaccaro notes in and out of their envelope and wrote down Elliot Trelawney's name and the address of the court.

"Can you do it?" I asked, a shade doubtfully.

"Yerss." He seemed to be slighted by my tone and took the paper with the address with brusqueness.

"Sorry," I said.

He nodded without looking at me and started the car, and by the time I'd reached the rear entrance to the offices he was driving out of the yard.

Upstairs, Annette said there had just been a phone call from Antwerp and she had written down the number for me to ring back.

Antwerp.

With an effort I thought back to Thursday's distant conversations. What was it I should remember about Antwerp?

Van Ekeren. Jacob. His nephew, Hans.

I got through to the Belgian town and was rewarded with the smooth bilingual voice telling me that he had been able now to speak to his uncle on my behalf.

"You're very kind," I said.

"I'm not sure that we will be of much help. My uncle says he knew your brother for a long time, but not very well. However, about six months ago your brother telephoned my uncle for advice about a sightholder." He paused. "It seems your brother was considering buying diamonds and trusted my uncle's judgment."

"Ah," I said hopefully. "Did your uncle recommend anyone?"

"Your brother suggested three or four possible names. My uncle said they were all trustworthy. He told your brother to go ahead with any of them."

I sighed. "Does he possibly remember who they were?"

Hans said, "He knows one of them was Guy Servi here in Antwerp, because we ourselves do business with him often. He can't remember the others. He doesn't know which one your brother decided on, or if he did business at all."

"Well, thank you, anyway."

"My uncle wishes to express his condolences."

"Very kind."

He disconnected with politeness, having dictated to me carefully the name, address and telephone number of Guy Servi, the one sightholder Greville had asked about that his uncle remembered.

I dialed the number immediately and again went through the rigmarole of being handed from voice to voice until I reached someone who had both the language and the information.

Mr. Greville Saxony Franklin, now deceased, had been my brother? They would consult their files and call me back.

I waited without much patience while they went through whatever security checks they considered necessary but finally, after a long hour, they came back on the line.

What was my problem, they wanted to know.

"My problem is that our offices were ransacked and a lot of paperwork is missing. I've taken over since Greville's death, and I'm trying to sort out his affairs. Could you please tell me if it was your firm who bought diamonds for him?"

"Yes," the voice said matter-of-factly. "We did."

Wow, I thought. I quietened my breath and tried not to sound eager.

"Could you, er, give me the details?" I asked.

"Certainly. We purchased a sight-box of color H diamonds of average weight three point two carats at the July sight at the CSO in London and we delivered one hundred stones, total weight three hundred and twenty carats, to your brother."

"He . . . er . . . paid for them in advance, didn't he?"

"Certainly. One point five million United States dollars in cash. You don't need to worry about that."

[217]

"Thank you," I said, suppressing irony. "Um, when you delivered them, did you send any sort of, er, packing note?"

It seemed he found the plebeian words "packing note" faintly shocking.

"We sent the diamonds by personal messenger," he said austerely. "Our man took them to your brother at his private residence in London. As is our custom, your brother inspected the merchandise in our messenger's presence and weighed it, and when he was satisfied he signed a release certificate. He would have the carbon copy of that release. There was no other, uh, packing note."

"Unfortunately I can't find the carbon copy."

"I assure you, sir . . ."

"I don't doubt you," I said hastily. "It's just that the tax people have a habit of wanting documentation."

"Ah." His hurt feelings subsided. "Yes, of course."

I thought a bit and asked, "When you delivered the stones to him, were they rough or faceted?"

"Rough, of course. He was going to get them cut and polished over a few months, as he needed them, I believe, but it was more convenient for us and for him to buy them all at once."

"You don't happen to know who he was getting to polish them?"

"I understood they were to be cut for one special client who had his own requirements, but no, he didn't say who would be cutting them."

I sighed. "Well, thank you anyway."

"We'll be happy to send you copies of the paperwork of the transaction, if it would be of any use?"

"Yes, please," I said. "It would be most helpful."

"We'll put them in the post this afternoon."

I put the receiver down slowly. I might now know where the diamonds had come *from* but was no nearer knowing where they'd gone *to*. I began to hope that they were safely sitting somewhere with a cutter who would kindly write to tell me they were ready for delivery. Not an impossible dream, really. But if Greville had sent them to a cutter, why was there no record?

Perhaps there had been a record, now stolen. But if the record had been stolen the thief would know the diamonds were with a cutter, and there would be no point in searching Greville's house. Unprofitable thoughts, chasing their own tails.

I straightened my neck and back and eased a few of the muscles which had developed small aches since the crash.

June came in and said, "You look fair knackered," and then put her hand to her mouth in horror and said, "I'd never have said that to Mr. Franklin."

"I'm not him."

"No, but . . . you're the boss."

"Then think of someone who could supply a list of cutters and polishers of diamonds, particularly those specializing in unusual requirements, starting with Antwerp. What we want is a sort of Yellow Pages directory. After Antwerp, New York, Tel Aviv and Bombay, isn't that right? Aren't those the four main centers?" I'd been reading his books.

"But we don't deal . . ."

"Don't say it," I said. "We do. Greville bought some for Prospero Jenks who wants them cut to suit his sculptures or fantasy pieces, or whatever one calls them."

"Oh." She looked first blank and then interested. "Yes, all right, I'm sure I can do that. Do you want me to do it now?"

"Yes, please."

She went as far as the door and looked back with a smile. "You still look fair . . ."

"Mm. Go and get on with it."

I watched her back view disappear. Gray skirt, white shirt. Blonde hair held back with combs behind the ears. Long legs. Flat shoes. Exit June.

The day wore on. I assembled three orders in the vault by myself and got Annette to check they were all right, which it

[219]

seemed they were. I made a slow tour of the whole place, calling in to see Alfie pack his parcels, watching Lily with her squashed governess air move endlessly from drawer to little drawer collecting orders, seeing Jason manhandle heavy boxes of newly arrived stock, stopping for a moment beside strong-looking Tina, whom I knew least, as she checked the new intake against the packing list and sorted it into trays.

None of them paid me great attention. I was already wallpaper. Alfie made no more innuendos about Dozen Roses, and Jason, though giving me a dark sideways look, again kept his cracks to himself. Lily said, "Yes, Derek," meekly, Annette looked anxious, June was busy. I returned to Greville's office and made another effort with the letters.

By four o'clock, in between her normal work with the stock movements on the computer, June had received answers to her "feelers," as she described them, in the shape of a long list of Antwerp cutters and a shorter one so far for New York. Tel Aviv was "coming" but had language difficulties and she had nothing for Bombay, though she didn't think Mr. Franklin would have sent anything to Bombay because with Antwerp so close there was no point. She put the lists down and departed.

At the rate all the cautious diamond-dealers worked, I thought, picking up the roll call, it would take a week just to get yes or no answers from the Antwerp list. Maybe it would be worth trying. I was down to straws. One of the letters was from the bank, reminding me that interest on the loan was now due.

June's tiny alarm clock suddenly began bleeping. All the other mute gadgets on top of the desk remained unmoved. June returned through my doorway at high speed and paid them vivid attention.

"Five minutes to go," I said calmingly. "Is every single gadget in sight?"

She checked all the drawers swiftly and peered into filing cabinets, leaving everything wide open, as I asked.

"Can't find any more," she said. "Why does it matter?"

"I don't know," I said. "I try everything."

She stared. I smiled lopsidedly.

"Greville left me a puzzle too," I said. "I try to solve it, though I don't know where to look."

"Oh." It made a sort of sense to her, even without more explanation. "Like my raise?"

I nodded. "Something like that." But not so positive, I thought. Not so certain. He had at least assured her that the solution was there to find.

The minutes ticked away and at four-twenty by June's clock the little alarm duly sounded. Very distant, not at all loud. Insistent. June looked rather wildly at the assembled gadgets and put her ear down to them.

"I will think of you every day at four-twenty."

Clarissa had written it on her card at the funeral. Greville had apparently done it every day in the office. It had been their own private language, a long way from diamonds. I acknowledged with regret that I would learn nothing from whatever he'd used to jog his awareness of loving and being loved.

The muffled alarm stopped. June raised her head, frowning.

"It wasn't any of these," she said.

"No. It was still inside the desk."

"But it can't have been." She was mystified. "I've taken everything out."

"There must be another drawer."

She shook her head, but it was the only reasonable explanation.

"Ask Annette," I suggested.

Annette, consulted, said with a worried frown that she knew nothing at all about another drawer. The three of us looked at the uninformative three-inch-deep slab of black grainy wood that formed the enormous top surface. There was no way it could be a drawer, but there wasn't any other possibility.

[221]

I thought back to the green stone box. To the keyhole that wasn't a keyhole, to the sliding base.

To the astonishment of Annette and June I lowered myself to the floor and looked upward at the desk from under the kneehole part. The wood from there looked just as solid, but in the center, three inches in from the front, there was what looked like a sliding switch. With satisfaction I regained the black leather chair and felt under the desk top for the switch. It moved away from one under pressure, I found. I pressed it, and absolutely nothing happened.

Something had to have happened, I reasoned. The switch wasn't there for nothing. Nothing about Greville was for nothing. I pressed it back hard again and tried to raise, slide or otherwise move anything else I could reach. Nothing happened. I banged my fist with frustration down on the desk top, and a section of the front edge of the solid-looking slab fell off in my lap.

Annette and June gasped. The piece that had come off was like a strip of veneer furnished with metal clips for fastening it in place. Behind it was more wood, but this time with a keyhole in it. Watched breathlessly by Annette and June, I brought out Greville's bunch of keys and tried those that looked the right size: and one of them turned obligingly with hardly a click. I pulled the key, still in the hole, toward me, and like silk a wide shallow drawer slid out.

We all looked at the contents. Passport. Little flat black gadgets, four or five of them.

No diamonds.

June was delighted. "That's the Wizard," she said.

14

"WHICH is the Wizard?" I asked.

"That one."

She pointed at a black rectangle a good deal smaller than a paperback, and when I picked it up and turned it over, sure enough, it had "Wizard" written on it in gold. I handed it to June who opened it like a book, laying it flat on the desk. The right-hand panel was covered with buttons and looked like an ultraversatile calculator. The left-hand side had a small screen at the top and a touch panel at the bottom with headings like "expense record," "time accounting," "reports" and "reference."

"It does everything," June said. "It's a diary, a phone directory, a memo pad, an appointments calendar, an accounts keeper . . ."

"And does it have an alarm set to four-twenty?"

She switched the thing on, pressed three keys and showed me the screen. "Daily alarm," it announced. "4:20 P.M., set."

"Fair enough."

For Annette the excitement seemed to be over. There were things she needed to see to, she said, and went away. June suggested she should tidy away all the gadgets and close all the drawers, and while she did that I investigated further the contents of the one drawer we left open.

I frowned a bit over the passport. I'd assumed that in going to Harwich, Greville had meant to catch the ferry. The Koningin Beatrix sailed every night . . .

If one looked at it the other way round, the Koningin Beatrix must sail from Holland to Harwich every day. If he hadn't taken the passport with him, perhaps he'd been going to *meet* the Koningin Beatrix, not leave on her.

Meet *who?*

I looked at his photograph, which like all passport photographs wasn't very good but good enough to bring him vividly into the office; his office, where I sat in his chair.

June looked over my shoulder and said, "Oh," in a small voice. "I do miss him, you know."

"Yes."

I put the passport with regret back into the drawer and took out a flat square object hardly larger than the Wizard, that had a narrow curl of paper coming out of it.

"That's the printer," June said.

"A printer? So small?"

"It'll print everything stored in the Wizard."

She plugged the printer's short cord into a slot in the side of the Wizard and dexterously pressed a few keys. With a whir the tiny machine went into action and began printing out a strip of half the telephone directory, or so it seemed.

"Lovely, isn't it?" June said, pressing another button to stop it. "When he was away on trips, Mr. Franklin would enter all his expenses on here and we would print them out when he got home, or sometimes transfer them from the Wizard to our main computer through an interface . . . oh, dear." She smothered the uprush of emotion and with an attempt at controlling her voice said, "He would note down in there a lot of things he wanted to remember when he got home. Things like who had offered him unusual stones. Then he'd tell Prospero Jenks, and quite often I'd be writing to the addresses to have the stones sent."

I looked at the small black electronic marvel. So much information quiescent in its circuits.

"Is there an instruction manual?" I asked.

"Of course. All the instruction manuals for everything are in this drawer." She opened one on the outer right-hand stack. "So are the warranty cards, and everything." She sorted through a rank of booklets. "Here you are. One for the Wizard, one for the printer, one for the expenses organizer."

"I'll borrow them," I said.

"They're yours now," she replied blankly. "Aren't they?"

"I can't get used to it any more than you can."

I laid the manuals on top of the desk next to the Wizard and the printer and took a third black object out of the secret drawer.

This one needed no explanation. This was the microcassette recorder that went with the tiny tapes I'd found in the hollowed-out books.

"That's voice activated," June said, looking at it. "It will sit quietly around doing nothing for hours, then when anyone speaks it will record what's said. Mr. Franklin used it sometimes for dictating letters or notes because it let him say a bit, think a bit, and say a bit more, without using up masses of tape. I used to listen to the tapes and type straight onto the word processor."

Worth her weight in pearls, Greville had judged. I wouldn't quarrel with that.

I put the microcassette player beside the other things and brought out the last two gadgets. One was a tiny Minolta camera which June said Greville used quite often for pictures of unusual stones for Prospero Jenks, and the last was a gray thing one could hold in one's hand that had an on/off switch but no obvious purpose.

"That's to frighten dogs away," June said with a smile. "Mr. Franklin didn't like dogs, but I think he was ashamed of not liking them, because at first he didn't want to tell me what that was, when I asked him."

I hadn't known Greville didn't like dogs. I fiercely wanted him back, if only to tease him about it. The real trouble with death was what it left unsaid: and knowing that that thought was a more or less universal regret made it no less sharp.

I put the dog frightener back beside the passport and also the baby camera, which had no film in it. Then I closed and locked the shallow drawer and fitted the piece of veneer back in place, pushing it home with a click. The vast top again looked wholly solid, and I wondered if Greville had bought that desk simply because of the drawer's existence, or whether he'd had the whole piece specially made.

"You'd never know that drawer was there," June said. "I wonder how many fortunes have been lost by people getting rid of hiding places they didn't suspect?"

"I read a story about that once. Something about money stuffed in an old armchair that was left to someone." I couldn't remember the details: but Greville had left me more than an old armchair, and more than one place to look, and I too could get rid of the treasure from not suspecting the right hiding place, if there were one at all to find.

Meanwhile there was the problem of staying healthy while I searched. There was the worse problem of sorting out ways of taking the war to the enemy, if I could identify the enemy in the first place.

I asked June if she could find something I could carry the Wizard and the other things in and she was back in a flash with a soft plastic bag with handles. It reminded me fleetingly of the bag I'd had snatched at Ipswich but this time, I thought, when I carried the booty to the car, I would take with me an invincible bodyguard, a long-legged, flat-chested twenty-one-year-old blonde half in love with my brother.

The telephone rang. I picked up the receiver and said, "Saxony Franklin" out of newly acquired habit.

"Derek? Is that you?"

"Yes, Milo, it is."

"I'm not satisfied with this horse." He sounded aggressive, which wasn't unusual, and also apologetic, which was.

"Which horse?" I asked.

"Dozen Roses, of course. What else?"

"Oh."

"What do you mean, oh? You knew damn well I was fetching it today. The damn thing's half asleep. I'm getting the vet round at once and I'll want urine and blood tests. The damn thing looks doped."

"Maybe they gave him a tranquilizer for the journey."

"They've no right to, you know that. If they have, I'll have Nicholas Loder's head on a platter, like you should, if you had any sense. The man does what he damn well likes. Anyway, if the horse doesn't pass my vet he's going straight back, Ostermeyers or no Ostermeyers. It's not fair on them if I accept shoddy goods."

"Um," I said calmingly, "perhaps Nicholas Loder wants you to do just that."

"What? What do you mean?"

"Wants you to send him straight back."

"Oh."

"And," I said, "Dozen Roses was the property of Saxony Franklin Limited, not Nicholas Loder, and if you think it's fair to the Ostermeyers to void the sale, so be it, but my brother's executor will direct you to send the horse anywhere else but back to Loder."

There was a silence. Then he said with a smothered laugh, "You always were a bright tricky bastard."

"Thanks."

"But get down here, will you? Take a look at him. Talk to the vet. How soon can you get here?"

"Couple of hours. Maybe more."

"No, come on, Derek."

"It's a long way to Tipperary," I said. "It never gets any nearer."

"You're delirious."

"I shouldn't wonder."

"Soon as you can, then," he said. "See you."

I put down the receiver with an inward groan. I did not want to go belting down to Lambourn to a crisis, however easily resolved. I wanted to let my aches unwind.

I telephoned the car and heard the ringing tone, but Brad, wherever he was, didn't answer. Then, as the first step toward leaving, I went along and locked the vault. Alfie in the packing room was stretching his back, his day's load finished. Lily, standing idle, gave me a repressed look from under her lashes. Jason goosed Tina in the doorway to the stockrooms, which she didn't seem to mind. There was a feeling of afternoon ending, of abeyance in the offing, of corporate activity drifting to suspense. Like the last race on an October card.

Saying goodnights and collecting the plastic bag, I went down to the yard and found Brad there waiting.

"Did you find those papers OK?" I asked him, climbing in beside him after storing the crutches on the back seat.

"Yerss," he said.

"And delivered them?"

"Yerss."

"Thanks. Great. How long have you been back?"

He shrugged. I left it. It wasn't important.

"Lambourn," I said, as we turned out of the yard. "But on the way, back to my brother's house to collect something else. OK?"

He nodded and drove to Greville's house skillfully, but slowed just before we reached it and pointed to Greville's car, still standing by the curb.

"See?" he said. "It's been broken into."

He found a parking place and we went back to look. The heavily locked trunk had been jimmied open and now wouldn't close again.

"Good job we took the things out," I said. "I suppose they are still in my car."

He shook his head. "In our house, under the stairs. Our mum said to do it with your car outside our door all night. Dodgy neighborhood, round our part."

"Very thoughtful," I said.

He nodded. "Smart, our mum."

He came with me into Greville's garden, holding the gate open.

"They done this place over proper," he said, producing the three keys from his pocket. "Want me to?"

He didn't wait for particular assent but went up the steps and undid the locks. Daylight: no floods, no dog.

He waited in the hall while I went along to the little sitting room to collect the tapes. It all looked forlorn in there, a terrible mess made no better by time. I put the featherweight cassettes into my pocket and left again, thinking that tidying up was a long way down my urgency list. When the ankle had altogether stopped hurting; maybe then. When the insurance people had seen it, if they wanted to.

I had brought with me a note which I left prominently on the lowest step of the staircase, where anyone coming into the house would see it.

"Dear Mrs. P. I'm afraid there is bad news for you. Don't clean the house. Telephone Saxony Franklin Ltd. instead."

I'd added the number in case she didn't know it by heart, and I'd warned Annette to go gently with anyone calling. Nothing else I could do to cushion the shock.

Brad locked the front door and we set off again to Lambourn. He had done enough talking for the whole journey and we traveled in customary silence, easy if not comrades.

Milo was striding about in the yard, expending energy to no purpose. He yanked the passenger-side door of my car open and scowled in at Brad, more as a reflection of his general state of mind, I gathered, than from any particular animosity.

I retrieved the crutches and stood up, and he told me it was high time I threw them away.

"Calm down," I said.

"Don't patronize me."

"Is Phil here?"

Phil was Phil Urquhart, veterinary surgeon, pill pusher to the stable.

"No, he isn't," Milo said crossly, "but he's coming back. The damned horse won't give a sample. And for a start, you can tell me whether it is or isn't Dozen Roses. His passport matches, but I'd like to be sure."

He strode away toward a box in one corner of the yard and I followed and looked where he looked, over the bottom half of the door.

Inside the box were an obstinate-looking horse and a furious red-faced lad. The lad held a pole which had on one end of it an open plastic bag on a ring, like a shrimping net. The plastic bag was clean and empty.

I chuckled.

"It's all right for you," Milo said sharply. "You haven't been waiting for more than two hours for the damned animal to stale."

"On Singapore racecourse, one time," I said, "they got a sample with nicotine in it. The horse didn't smoke, but the lad did. He got tired of waiting for the horse and just supplied the sample himself."

"Very funny," Milo said repressively.

"This often takes hours, though, so why the rage?"

It sounded always so simple, of course, to take a regulation urine sample from two horses after every race, one nearly always from the winner. In practice it meant waiting around for the horses to oblige. After two hours of nonperformance, blood samples were taken instead, but blood wasn't as easy to come by. Many tempers were regularly lost while the horses made up their minds.

"Come away," I said, "he'll do it in the end. And he's definitely the horse that ran at York. Dozen Roses without doubt."

He followed me away reluctantly and we went into the kitchen where Milo switched lights on and asked me if I'd like a drink.

"Wouldn't mind some tea," I said.

"Tea? At this hour? Well, help yourself." He watched me fill the kettle and set it to boil. "Are you off booze forever?"

"No."

"Thank God."

Phil Urquhart's car scrunched into the yard and pulled up outside the window, and he came breezing into the kitchen asking if there were any results. He read Milo's scowl aright and laughed.

"Do you think the horse is doped?" I asked him.

"Me? No, not really. Hard to tell. Milo thinks so."

He was small and sandy-haired, and about thirty, the grandson of a three-generation family practice, and to my mind the best of them. I caught myself thinking that when I in the future trained here in Lambourn, I would want him for my horses. An odd thought. The future planning itself behind my back.

"I hear we're lucky you're still with us," he said. "An impressive crunch, so they say." He looked at me assessingly with friendly professional eyes. "You've a few rough edges, one can see."

"Nothing that will stop him racing," Milo said crisply.

Phil smiled. "I detect more alarm than sympathy."

"Alarm?"

"You've trained more winners since he came here."

"Rubbish," Milo said.

He poured drinks for himself and Phil, and I made my tea; and Phil assured me that if the urine passed all tests he would give the thumbs-up to Dozen Roses.

"He may just be showing the effects of the hard race he had at York," he said. "It might be that he's always like this. Some horses are, and we don't know how much weight he lost."

"What will you get the urine tested for?" I asked.

He raised his eyebrows. "Barbiturates, in this case."

"At York," I said thoughtfully, "one of Nicholas Loder's owners was walking around with an inhaler in his pocket. A kitchen baster, to be precise."

"An owner?" Phil asked, surprised.

"Yes. He owned the winner of the five-furlong sprint. He was also in the saddling box with Dozen Roses."

Phil frowned. "What are you implying?"

"Nothing. Merely observing. I can't believe he interfered with the horse. Nicholas Loder wouldn't have let him. The stable money was definitely on. They wanted to win, and they knew if it won it would be tested. So the only question is, what could you give a horse that wouldn't disqualify it? Give it via an inhaler just before a race?"

"Nothing that would make it go faster. They test for all stimulants."

"What if you gave it, say, sugar? Glucose? Or adrenaline?"

"You've a criminal mind!"

"I just wondered."

"Glucose would give energy, as to human athletes. It wouldn't increase speed, though. Adrenaline is more tricky. If it's given by injection you can see it, because the hairs stand up all round the puncture. But straight into the mucous membranes . . . well, I suppose it's possible."

"And no trace."

He agreed. "Adrenaline pours into a horse's bloodstream naturally anyway, if he's excited. If he wants to win. If he feels the whip. Who's to say how much? If you suspected a booster you'd have to take a blood sample in the winner's enclosure, practically, and even then you'd have a hard job proving any reading was excessive. Adrenaline levels vary too much. You'd even have a hard job proving extra adrenaline made any difference at all." He paused and considered me soberly. "You do realize that you're saying that if anything was done, Nicholas Loder condoned it?"

"Doesn't seem likely, does it?"

"No, it doesn't," he said. "If he were some tin-pot little crook, well then, maybe, but not Nicholas Loder with his Classic winners and everything to lose."

"Mm." I thought a bit. "If I asked, I could get some of the urine sample that was taken from Dozen Roses at York. They always make it available to owners for private checks. To my brother's company, that is to say, in this instance." I thought a bit more. "When Nicholas Loder's friend dropped his baster, Martha Ostermeyer handed the bulb part back to him, but then Harley Ostermeyer picked up the tube part and gave it to me. But it was clean. No trace of liquid. No adrenaline. So I suppose it's possible he might have used it on his own horse and still had it in his pocket, but did nothing to Dozen Roses."

They considered it.

"You could get into a lot of trouble making unfounded accusations," Phil said.

"So Nicholas Loder told me."

"Did he? I'd think twice, then, before I did. It wouldn't do you much good generally in the racing world, I shouldn't think."

"Wisdom from babes," I said, but he echoed my thoughts.

"Yes, old man."

"I kept the baster tube," I said, shrugging, "but I guess I'll do just what I did at the races, which was nothing."

"As long as Dozen Roses tests clean both at York and here, that's likely best," Phil said, and Milo, for all his earlier pugnaciousness, agreed.

A commotion in the darkening yard heralded the success of the urine mission and Phil went outside to unclip the special bag and close its patented seal. He wrote and attached the label giving the horse's name, the location, date and time and signed his name.

"Right," he said, "I'll be off. Take care." He loaded himself, the sample and his gear into his car and with economy of movement scrunched away. I followed soon after with Brad still driving but decided again not to go home.

"You saw the mess in London," I said. "I got knocked out by whoever did that. I don't want to be in if they come to Hungerford. So let's go to Newbury instead, and try The Chequers."

Brad slowed, his mouth open.

"A week ago yesterday," I said, "you saved me from a man

[233]

with a knife. Yesterday someone shot at the car I was in and killed the chauffeur. It may not have been your regulation madman. So last night I slept in Swindon, tonight in Newbury."

"Yerss," he said, understanding.

"If you'd rather not drive me anymore, I wouldn't blame you."

After a pause, with a good deal of stalwart resolution, he made a statement. "You need me."

"Yes," I said. "Until I can walk properly, I do."

"I'll drive you, then."

"Thanks," I said, and meant it wholeheartedly, and he could hear that, because he nodded twice to himself emphatically and seemed even pleased.

The Chequers Hotel having a room free, I booked in for the night. Brad took himself home in my car, and I spent most of the evening sitting in an armchair upstairs learning my way round the Wizard.

Computers weren't my natural habitat like they were Greville's and I hadn't the same appetite for them. The Wizard's instructions seemed to take it for granted that everyone reading them would be computer-literate, so it probably took me longer than it might have done to get results.

What was quite clear was that Greville had used the gadget extensively. There were three separate telephone and address lists, a world-time clock, a system for entering daily appointments, a prompt for anniversaries, a calendar flashing with the day's date, and provision for storing oddments of information. By plugging in the printer, and after a few false starts, I ended with long printed lists of everything held listed under all the headings, and read them with growing frustration.

None of the addresses or telephone numbers seemed to have anything to do with Antwerp or with diamonds, though the "Business Overseas" list contained many gem merchants' names from all round the world. None of the appointments scheduled, which stretched back six weeks or more, seemed to be relevant, and there were no entries at all for the Friday he'd gone to Ipswich. There was no reference to Koningin Beatrix.

I thought of my question to June the day she'd found her way to "pearl": what if it were all in there, stored in secret.

The Wizard's instruction manual, two hundred pages long, certainly did give lessons in how to lock things away. Entries marked "secret" could be retrieved only by knowing the password, which could be any combination of numbers and letters up to seven in all. Forgetting the password meant bidding farewell to the entries: they could never be seen again. They could be deleted unseen, but not printed or brought to the screen.

One could tell if secret files were present, the book said, by the small symbol *s,* which could be found on the lower right-hand side of the screen. I consulted Greville's screen and found the *s* there, sure enough.

It would be, I thought. It would have been totally unlike him to have had the wherewithal for secrecy and not used it.

Any combination of numbers or letters up to seven . . .

The book suggested 1 2 3 4, but once I'd sorted out the opening moves for unlocking and entered 1 2 3 4 in the space headed "Secret Off," all I got was a quick dusty answer, "Incorrect Password."

Damn him, I thought, wearily defeated. Why couldn't he make any of it easy?

I tried every combination of letters and numbers I thought he might have used but got absolutely nowhere. Clarissa was too long, 12Roses should have been right but wasn't. To be right the password had to be entered exactly as it had been set, whether in capital letters or lower case. It all took time. In the end I was ready to throw the confounded Wizard across the room, and stared at its perpetual "Incorrect Password" with hatred.

I finally laid it aside and played the tiny tape recorder instead. There was a lot of office chat on the tapes and I couldn't

[235]

think why Greville should have bothered to take them home and hide them. Long before I reached the end of the fourth side, I was asleep.

I woke stiffly after a while, unsure for a second where I was. I rubbed my face, looked at my watch, thought about all the constructive thinking I was supposed to be doing and wasn't, and rewound the second of the baby tapes to listen to what I'd missed. Greville's voice, talking business to Annette.

The most interesting thing, the only interesting thing about those tapes, I thought, was Greville's voice. The only way I would ever hear him again.

". . . going out to lunch," he was saying. "I'll be back by two-thirty."

Annette's voice said, "Yes, Mr. Franklin."

A click sounded on the tape.

Almost immediately, because of the concertina-ing of time by the voice-activated mechanism, a different voice said, "I'm in his office now and I can't find them. He hides everything, he's security mad, you know that." Click. "I can't ask. He'd never tell me, and I don't think he trusts me." Click. "Po-faced Annette doesn't sneeze unless he tells her to. She'd never tell me anything." Click. "I'll try. I'll have to go, he doesn't like me using this phone, he'll be back from lunch any second." Click.

End of tape.

Bloody hell, I thought. I rewound the end of the tape and listened to it again. I knew the voice, as Greville must have done. He'd left the recorder on, I guessed by mistake, and he'd come back and listened, with I supposed sadness, to treachery. It opened up a whole new world of questions and I went slowly to bed groping toward answers.

I lay a long time awake. When I slept, I dreamed the usual surrealist muddle and found it no help, but around dawn, awake again and thinking of Greville, it occurred to me that there was one password I hadn't tried because I hadn't thought of him using it.

The Wizard was across the room by the armchair. Impelled by curiosity I turned on the light, rolled out of bed and hopped over to fetch it. Taking it back with me, I switched it on, pressed the buttons, found "Secret Off" and into the offered space typed the word Greville had written on the last page of his racing diary, below the numbers of his passport and national insurance.

DEREK, all in capital letters.

I typed DEREK and pressed "Enter," and the Wizard with resignation let me into its data.

15

I began printing out everything in the secret files as it seemed from the manual that, particularly as regarded the expense organizer, it was the best way to get at the full information stored there.

Each category had to be printed separately, the baby printer clicking away line by line and not very fast. I watched its steady output with fascination, hoping the small roll of paper would last to the end, as I hadn't any more.

From the Memo section, which I printed first, came a terse note, "Check, don't trust."

Next came a long list of days and dates which seemed to bear no relation to anything. Monday, Jan. 30, Wednesday, March 8 . . . Mystified I watched the sequence lengthen, noticing only that most of them were Mondays, Tuesdays or Wednesdays, five or six weeks apart, sometimes less, sometimes longer. The list ended five weeks before his death, and it began . . . it began, I thought blankly, four years earlier. Four years ago; when he first met Clarissa.

I felt unbearable sadness for him. He'd fallen in love with a woman who wouldn't leave home for him, whom he hadn't wanted to compromise: he'd kept a record, I was certain, of every snatched day they'd spent together, and hidden it away as he had hidden so much else. A whole lot of roses, I thought.

The Schedule section, consulted next, contained appointments not hinted at earlier, including the delivery of the diamonds to his London house. For the day of his death there were two entries: the first, "Ipswich. Orwell Hotel, P. 3:30 P.M.," and the second, "Meet Koningin Beatrix 6:30 P.M., Harwich." For the following Monday he had noted "Meet C King's Cross 12:10 Lunch Luigi's."

Meet C at King's Cross . . . He hadn't turned up, and she'd telephoned his house, and left a message on his answering machine, and sometime in the afternoon she'd telephoned his office to ask for him. Poor Clarissa. By Monday night she'd left the ultra-anxious second message, and on Tuesday she had learned he was dead.

The printer whirred and produced another entry, for the Saturday after. "C and Dozen Roses both at York! Could I go? Not wise. Check TV."

The printer stopped, as Greville's life had done. No more appointments on record.

Next I printed the Telephone sections, Private, Business and Business Overseas. Private contained only Knightwood. Business was altogether empty, but from Business Overseas I watched with widening eyes the emergence of five numbers and addresses in Antwerp. One was van Ekeren, one was Guy Servi: three were so far unknown to me. I breathed almost painfully with exultation, unable to believe Greville had entered them there for no purpose.

I printed the Expense Manager's secret section last as it was the most complicated and looked the least promising, but the first item that emerged was galvanic.

ANTWERP SAYS 5 OF THE FIRST
BATCH OF ROUGH ARE CZ.
DON'T WANT TO BELIEVE IT,
INFINITE SADNESS.
PRIORITY 1.
ARRANGE MEETINGS. IPSWICH?
UNDECIDED. DAMNATION!

[239]

I wished he had been more explicit, more specific, but he'd seen no need to be. It was surprising he'd written so much. His feelings must have been strong to have been entered at all. No other entries afterward held any comment but were short records of money spent on courier services with a firm called Euro-Securo, telephone number supplied. In the middle of those the paper ran out. I brought the rest of the stored information up onto the screen and scrolled through it, but there was nothing else disturbing.

I switched off both baby machines and reread the long curling strip of printing from the beginning, afterward flattening it out and folding it to fit a shirt pocket. Then I dressed, packed, breakfasted, waited for Brad and traveled to London hopefully.

The telephone calls to Antwerp had to be done from the Saxony Franklin premises because of the precautionary checking back. I would have preferred more privacy than Greville's office but couldn't achieve it, and one of the first things I asked Annette that morning was whether my brother had had one of those gadgets that warned you if someone was listening to your conversation on an extension. The office phones were all interlinked.

"No, he didn't," she said, troubled.

"He could have done with one," I said.

"Are you implying that we listened when he didn't mean us to?"

"Not you," I assured her, seeing her resentment of the suggestion. "But yes, I'd think it happened. Anyway, at some point this morning I want to make sure of not being overheard, so when that call comes through perhaps you'll all go into the stockroom and sing 'Rule Britannia.'"

Annette never made jokes. I had to explain I didn't mean sing literally. She rather huffily agreed that when I wanted it, she would go round the extensions checking against eavesdroppers.

I asked her why Greville hadn't had a private line in any

case, and she said he had had one earlier but they now used that for the fax machine.

"If he wanted to be private," she said, "he went down to the yard and telephoned from his car."

There, I supposed, he would have been safe also from people with sensitive listening devices, if he'd suspected their use. He had been conscious of betrayal, that was for sure.

I sat at Greville's desk with the door closed and matched the three unknown Antwerp names from the Wizard with the full list June had provided, and found that all three were there.

The first and second produced no results, but from the third, once I explained who I was, I got the customary response about checking their files and calling back. They did call back, but the amorphous voice on the far end was cautious to the point of repression.

"We at Maarten-Pagnier cannot discuss anything at all with you, monsieur," he said. "Monsieur Franklin gave express orders that we were not to communicate with anyone in his office except himself."

"My brother is dead," I said.

"So you say, monsieur. But he warned us to beware of any attempt to gain information about his affairs and we cannot discuss them."

"Then please will you telephone to his lawyers and get their assurance that he's dead and that I am now managing his business?"

After a pause the voice said austerely, "Very well, monsieur. Give us the name of his lawyers."

I did that and waited for ages during which time three customers telephoned with long orders which I wrote down, trying not to get them wrong from lack of concentration.

Then there was a frantic call from a nearly incoherent woman who wanted to speak to Mr. Franklin urgently.

"Mrs. P.?" I asked tentatively.

Mrs. P. it was. Mrs. Patterson, she said. I gave her the abysmal news and listened to her telling me what a fine nice gentleman my brother had been, and oh dear, she felt faint, had I seen the mess in the sitting room?

I warned her that the whole house was the same. "Just leave it," I said. "I'll clean it up later. Then if you could come after that to vacuum and dust, I'd be very grateful."

Calming a little, she gave me her phone number. "Let me know, then," she said. "Oh dear, oh dear.'

Finally the Antwerp voice returned and, begging him to hold on, I hopped over to the door, called Annette, handed her the customers' orders and said this was the moment for securing the defenses. She gave me a disapproving look as I again closed the door.

Back in Greville's chair I said to the voice, "Please, monsieur, tell me if my brother had any dealings with you. I am trying to sort out his office but he has left too few records."

"He asked us particularly not to send any records of the work we were doing for him to his office."

"He, er, what?" I said.

"He said he could not trust everyone in his office as he would like. Instead, he wished us to send anything necessary to the fax machine in his car, but only when he telephoned from there to arrange it."

"Um," I said, blinking, "I found the fax machine in his car but there were no statements or invoices or anything from you."

"I believe if you ask his accountants, you may find them there."

"Good grief."

"I beg your pardon, monsieur?"

"I didn't think of asking his accountants," I said blankly.

"He said for tax purposes . . ."

"Yes, I see." I hesitated. "What exactly were you doing for him?"

"Monsieur?"

"Did he," I asked a shade breathlessly, "send you a hundred diamonds, color H, average uncut weight three point two carats, to be cut and polished?"

"No, monsieur."

"Oh." My disappointment must have been audible.

"He sent twenty-five stones, monsieur, but five of them were not diamonds."

"Cubic zirconia," I said, enlightened.

"Yes, monsieur. We told Monsieur Franklin as soon as we discovered it. He said we were wrong, but we were not, monsieur."

"No," I agreed. "He did leave a note saying five of the first batch were CZ."

"Yes, monsieur. He was extremely upset. We made several inquiries for him, but he had bought the stones from a sightholder of impeccable honor and he had himself measured and weighed the stones when they were delivered to his London house. He sent them to us in a sealed Euro-Securo courier package. We assured him that the mistake could not have been made here by us, and it was then, soon after that, that he asked us not to send or give any information to anyone in his . . . your . . . office." He paused. "He made arrangements to receive the finished stones from us, but he didn't meet our messenger."

"Your messenger?"

"One of our partners, to be accurate. We wished to deliver the stones to him ourselves because of the five disputed items, and Monsieur Franklin thought it an excellent idea. Our partner dislikes flying, so it was agreed he should cross by boat and return the same way. When Monsieur Franklin failed to meet him he came back here. He is elderly and had made no provision to stay away. He was . . . displeased . . . at having made a tiring journey for nothing. He said we should wait to hear from Monsieur Franklin. Wait for fresh instructions. We have been waiting, but we've been puzzled. We didn't try to reach Monsieur Franklin at his office as he had forbidden us to do that, but we were considering asking someone else to try on our behalf. We are very sorry to hear of his death. It explains everything, of course."

I said, "Did your partner travel to Harwich on the Koningin Beatrix?"

"That's right, monsieur."

"He brought the diamonds with him."

"That's right, monsieur. And he brought them back. We will now wait your instructions instead."

I took a deep breath. Twenty of the diamonds at least were safe. Five were missing. Seventy-five were . . . *where?*

The Antwerp voice said, "It's to be regretted that Monsieur Franklin didn't see the polished stones. They cut very well. Twelve teardrops of great brilliance, remarkable for that color. Eight were not suitable for teardrops, as we told Monsieur Franklin, but they look handsome as stars. What shall we do with them, monsieur?"

"When I've talked to the jeweler they were cut for, I'll let you know."

"Very good, monsieur. And our account? Where shall we send that?" He mentioned considerately how much it would be.

"To this office," I said, sighing at the prospect. "Send it to me marked 'Personal.' "

"Very good, monsieur."

"And thank you," I said. "You've been very helpful."

"At your service, monsieur."

I put the receiver down slowly, richer by twelve glittering teardrops destined to hang and flash in sunlight, and by eight handsome stars that might twinkle in a fantasy of rock crystal. Better than nothing, but not enough to save the firm.

Using the crutches, I went in search of Annette and asked her if she would please find Prospero Jenks, wherever he was, and make another appointment for me, that afternoon if possible. Then I went down to the yard, taking a tip from Greville, and on the telephone in my car put a call through to his accountants.

Brad, reading a golfing magazine, paid no attention.

Did he play golf? I asked.

No, he didn't.

The accountants helpfully confirmed that they had received envelopes both from my brother and from Antwerp, and were holding them unopened, as requested, pending further instructions.

"You'll need them for the general accounts," I said. "So would you please just keep them?"

Absolutely no problem.

"On second thought," I said, "please open all the envelopes and tell me who all the letters from Antwerp have come from."

Again no problem: but the letters were all either from Guy Servi, the sightholder, or from Maarten-Pagnier, the cutters. No other firms. No other safe havens for seventy-five rocks.

I thanked them, watched Brad embark on a learned comparison of Ballesteros and Faldo, and thought about disloyalty and the decay of friendship.

It was restful in the car, I decided. Brad went on reading. I thought of robbery with violence and violence without robbery, of being laid out with a brick and watching Simms die of a bullet meant for me, and I wondered whether, if I were dead, anyone could find what I was looking for, or whether they reckoned they now couldn't find it if I were alive.

I stirred and fished in a pocket and gave Brad a check I'd written out for him upstairs.

"What's this?" he said, peering at it.

I usually paid him in cash, but I explained I hadn't enough for what I owed him, and cash dispensers wouldn't disgorge enough all at once and we hadn't recently been in Hungerford when the banks were open, as he might have noticed.

"Give me cash later," he said, holding the check out to me. "And you paid me double."

"For last week and this week." I nodded. "When we get to the bank I'll swap it for cash. Otherwise, you could bring it back here. It's a company check. They'd see you got cash for it."

[245]

He gave me a long look. "Is this because of guns and such? In case you never get to the bank?"

I shrugged. "You might say so."

He looked at the check, folded it deliberately and stowed it away. Then he picked up the magazine and stared blindly at a page he'd just read. I was grateful for the absence of comment or protest, and in a while said matter-of-factly that I was going upstairs for a bit, and why didn't he get some lunch.

He nodded.

"Have you got enough money for lunch?"

"Yerss."

"You might make a list of what you've spent. I've enough cash for that."

He nodded again.

"OK, then," I said. "See you."

Upstairs, Annette said she had opened the day's mail and put it ready for my attention, and she'd found Prospero Jenks and he would be expecting me in the Knightsbridge shop any time between three and six.

"Great."

She frowned. "Mr. Jenks wanted to know if you were taking him the goods Mr. Franklin bought for him. Grev—he always calls Mr. Franklin Grev. I do wish he wouldn't. I asked what he meant about goods and he said you would know."

"He's talking about diamonds," I said.

"But we haven't . . ." She stopped and then went on with a sort of desperate vehemence. "I *wish* Mr. Franklin was here. Nothing's the same without him."

She gave me a look full of her insecurity and doubt of my ability and plodded off into her own domain and I thought that with what lay ahead I'd have preferred a vote of confidence: and I too, with all my heart, wished Greville back.

The police from Hungerford telephoned, given my number by Milo's secretary. They wanted to know if I had remembered anything more about the car driven by the gunman.

They had asked the family in the family car if they had noticed the make and color of the last car they'd seen coming toward them before they rounded the bend and crashed into the Daimler, and one of the children, a boy, had given them a description. They had also, while the firemen and others were trying to free me, walked down the row of spectator cars asking them about the last car they'd seen coming toward them. Only the first two drivers had seen a car at all, that they could remember, and they had no helpful information. Had I any recollection, however vague, as they were trying to piece together all the impressions they'd been given.

"I wish I could help," I said, "but I was talking to Mr. and Mrs. Ostermeyer, not concentrating on the road. It winds a bit, as you know, and I think Simms had been waiting for a place where he could pass the car in front, but all I can tell you, as on Sunday, is that it was a grayish color and fairly large. Maybe a Mercedes. It's only an impression."

"The child in the family car says it was a gray Volvo travel- ing fast. The bus driver says the car in question was traveling slowly before the Daimler tried to pass it, and he was aiming to pass also at that point, and was accelerating to do so, which was why he rammed the Daimler so hard. He says the car was silver gray and accelerated away at high speed, which matched what the child says."

"Did the bus driver," I asked, "see the gun or the shots?"

"No, sir. He was looking at the road ahead and at the Daimler, not at the car he intended to pass. Then the Daimler veered sharply, and bounced off the wall straight into his path. He couldn't avoid hitting it, he said. Do you confirm that, sir?"

"Yes. It happened so fast. He hadn't a chance."

"We are asking in the neighborhood for anyone to come forward who saw a gray four-door sedan, possibly a Volvo, on that road on Sunday afternoon, but so far we have heard nothing new. If you remember anything else, however minor, let us know."

I would, I said.

I put the phone down wondering if Vaccaro's shot-down pilots had seen the make of car from which their deaths had come spitting. Anyone seeing those murders would, I supposed, have been gazing with uncomprehending horror at the falling victims, not dashing into the road to peer at a fast-disappearing license plate.

No one had heard any shots on Sunday. No one had heard the shots, the widow had told Greville, when her husband was killed. A silencer on a gun in a moving car . . . a swift *pffit* . . . curtains.

It couldn't have been Vaccaro who shot Simms. Vaccaro didn't make sense. Someone with the same antisocial habits, as in Northern Ireland and elsewhere. A copycat. Plenty of precedent.

Milo's secretary had been busy and given my London number also to Phil Urquhart, who came on the line to tell me that Dozen Roses had tested clean for barbiturates and he would give a certificate of soundness for the sale.

"Fine," I said.

"I've been to examine the horse again this morning. He's still very docile. It seems to be his natural state."

"Mm."

"Do I hear doubt?"

"He's excited enough every time cantering down to the start."

"Natural adrenaline," Phil said.

"If it was anyone but Nicholas Loder . . ."

"He would never risk it," Phil said, agreeing with me. "But look . . . there are things that potentiate adrenaline, like caffeine. Some of them are never tested for in racing, as they are not judged to be stimulants. It's your money that's being spent on the tests I've had done for you. We have some more of that sample of urine. Do you want me to get different tests done, for things not usually looked for? I mean, do you really think Nicholas Loder gave the horse something, and if you do, do you want to know about it?"

"It was his owner, a man called Rollway, who had the baster, not Loder himself."

"Same decision. Do you want to spend more, or not bother? It may be money down the drain, anyway. And if you get any results, what then? You don't want to get the horse disqualified, that wouldn't make sense."

"No . . . it wouldn't."

"What's your problem?" he asked. "I can hear it in your voice."

"Fear," I said. "Nicholas Loder was afraid."

"Oh." He was briefly silent. "I could get the tests done anonymously, of course."

"Yes. Get them done, then. I particularly don't want to sell the Ostermeyers a lemon, as she would say. If Dozen Roses can't win on his own merits, I'll talk them out of the idea of owning him."

"So you'll pray for negative results."

"I will indeed."

"While I was at Milo's this morning," he said, "he was talking to the Ostermeyers in London, asking how they were and wishing them a good journey. They were still a bit wobbly from the crash, it seems."

"Surprising if they weren't."

"They're coming back to England, though, to see Datepalm run in the Hennessy. How's your ankle?"

"Good as new by then."

"Bye, then." I could hear his smile. "Take care."

He disconnected and left me thinking that there still were good things in the world, like the Ostermeyers' faith and riding Datepalm in the Hennessy, and I stood up and put my left foot flat on the floor for a progress report.

It wasn't so bad if I didn't lean any weight on it, but there were still jabbingly painful protests against attempts to walk. Oh well, I thought, sitting down again, give it another day or two. It hadn't exactly had a therapeutic week and was no doubt doing its best against odds. On Thursday, I thought, I would get rid of the crutches. By Friday, definitely. Any day after that I'd be running. Ever optimistic. It was the belief that cured.

The overworked telephone rang again, and I answered it with "Saxony Franklin?" as routine.

"Derek?"

"Yes," I said.

Clarissa's unmistakable voice said, "I'm in London. Could we meet?"

I hadn't expected her so soon, I thought. I said, "Yes, of course. Where?"

"I thought . . . perhaps . . . Luigi's. Do you know Luigi's bar and restaurant?"

"I don't," I said slowly, "but I can find it."

"It's in Swallow Street near Piccadilly Circus. Would you mind coming at seven, for a drink?"

"And dinner?"

"Well . . ."

"And dinner," I said.

I heard her sigh, "Yes. All right," as she disconnected, and I was left with a vivid understanding both of her compulsion to put me where she had been going to meet Greville and of her awareness that perhaps she ought not to.

I could have said no, I thought. I could have, but hadn't. A little introspection revealed ambiguities in my response to her also, like did I want to give comfort, or to take it.

By three-thirty I'd finished the paperwork and filled an order for pearls and another for turquoise and relocked the vault and got Annette to smile again, even if faintly. At four, Brad pulled up outside Prospero Jenks's shop in Knightsbridge and I put the telephone ready to let him know when to collect me.

Prospero Jenks was where I'd found him before, sitting in shirtsleeves at his workbench. The discreet dark-suited man, serving customers in the shop, nodded me through.

"He's expecting you, Mr. Franklin."

Pross stood up with a smile on his young-old Peter Pan face

and held out his hand, but let it fall again as I waggled a crutch handle at him instead.

"Glad to see you," he said, offering a chair, waiting while I sat. "Have you brought my diamonds?" He sat down again on his own stool.

"No. Afraid not."

He was disappointed. "I thought that was what you were coming for."

"No, not really."

I looked at his long efficient workroom with its little drawers full of unset stones and thought of the marvels he produced. The big notice on the wall still read NEVER TURN YOUR BACK TO CUSTOMERS. ALWAYS WATCH THEIR HANDS.

I said, "Greville sent twenty-five rough stones to Antwerp to be cut for you."

"That's right."

"Five of them were cubic zirconia."

"No, no."

"Did you," I asked neutrally, "swap them over?"

The half-smile died out of his face, which grew stiff and expressionless. The bright blue eyes stared at me and the lines deepened across his forehead.

"That's rubbish," he said. "I'd never do anything stupid like that."

I didn't say anything immediately and it seemed to give him force.

"You can't come in here making wild accusations. Go on, get out, you'd better leave." He half-rose to his feet.

I said, not moving, "When the cutters told Greville five of the stones were cubic zirconia, he was devastated. Very upset."

I reached into my shirt pocket and drew out the print-out from the Wizard.

"Do you want to see?" I asked. "Read there."

After a hesitation he took the paper, sat back on the stool and read the entry:

ANTWERP SAYS 5 OF THE FIRST
BATCH OF ROUGH ARE CZ.
DON'T WANT TO BELIEVE IT.
INFINITE SADNESS.
PRIORITY 1.
ARRANGE MEETINGS. IPSWICH?
UNDECIDED. DAMNATION!

"Greville used to write his thoughts in a notebook," I said. "In there, it says 'Infinite sadness is not to trust an old friend.'"

"So what?"

"Since Greville died," I said, "someone has been trying to find his diamonds, to steal them from me. That someone had to be someone who knew they were there to be found. Greville kept the fact that he'd bought them very quiet for security reasons. He didn't tell even his staff. But of course you yourself knew, as it was for you he bought them."

He said again, "So what?"

"If you remember," I said, still conversationally, "someone broke into Greville's office after he died and stole things like an address book and an appointments diary. I began to think the thief had also stolen any other papers which might point to where the diamonds were, like letters or invoices. But I know now there weren't any such papers to be found there, because Greville was full of distrust. His distrust dated from the day the Antwerp cutters told him five of his stones were cubic zirconia, which was about three weeks before he died."

Pross, Greville's friend, said nothing.

"Greville bought the diamonds," I went on, "from a sightholder based in Antwerp who sent them by messenger to his London house. There he measured them and weighed them and signed for them. Then it would be reasonable to suppose that he showed them to you, his customer. Or showed you twenty-five of them, perhaps. Then he sent that twenty-five back to Antwerp by the Euro-Secure couriers. Five diamonds had mysteriously become cubic zirconia, and yes, it was an entirely stupid thing to do, because the substitution was bound to be discovered almost at once, and you knew it would be. Had to be. I'd think you reckoned Greville would never believe it of you, but would swear the five stones had to have been swapped by someone in the couriers or the cutters in Antwerp, and he would collect the insurance in due course, and that would be that. You would be five diamonds to the good, and he would have lost nothing."

"You can't prove it," he said flatly.

"No, I can't prove it. But Greville was full of sorrow and distrust, and why should he be if he thought his stones had been taken by strangers?"

I looked with some of Greville's own sadness at Prospero Jenks. A likable, entertaining genius whose feelings for my brother had been strong and long-lasting, whose regret at his death had been real.

"I'd think," I said, "that after your long friendship, after all the treasures he'd brought you, after the pink and green tourmaline, after your tremendous success, that he could hardly bear your treachery."

"Stop it," he said sharply. "It's bad enough . . ."

He shut his mouth tight and shook his head, and seemed to sag internally.

"He forgave me," he said.

He must have thought I didn't believe him.

He said wretchedly, "I wished I hadn't done it almost from the beginning, if you want to know. It was just an impulse. He left the diamonds here while he went off to do a bit of shopping, and I happened to have some rough CZ the right size in those drawers, as I often do, waiting for when I want special cutting, and I just . . . exchanged them. Like you said. I didn't think he'd lose by it."

"He knew, though," I said. "He knew you, and he knew a lot about thieves, being a magistrate. Another of the things he wrote was 'If laws are inconvenient, ignore them, they don't apply to you.' "

"Stop it. Stop it. He forgave me."

"When?"

"In Ipswich. I went to meet him there."

I lifted my head. "Ipswich. Orwell Hotel, P. three-thirty P.M.," I said.

"What? Yes." He seemed unsurprised that I should know. He seemed to be looking inward to an unendurable landscape.

"I saw him die," he said.

16

" "I saw the scaffolding fall on him," he said.
He'd stunned me to silence.

"We talked in the hotel. In the lounge there. It was almost empty . . . then we walked down the street to where I'd left my car. We said goodbye. He crossed the road and walked on, and I watched him. I wanted him to look back and wave . . . but he didn't."

Forgiveness was one thing, I thought, but friendship had gone. What did he expect? Absolution and comfort? Perhaps Greville in time would have given those too, but I couldn't.

Prospero Jenks with painful memory said, "Grev never knew what happened . . . There wasn't any warning. Just a clanging noise and metal falling and men with it. Crashing down fast. It buried him. I couldn't see him. I ran across the road to pull him out and there were bodies . . . and he . . . he . . . I thought he was dead already. His head was bleeding . . . there was a metal bar in his stomach and another had ripped into his leg . . . it was . . . I can't . . . I try to forget but I see it all the time."

I waited and in a while he went on.

"I didn't move him. Couldn't. There was so much blood . . . and a man lying over his legs . . . and another man groaning. People came running . . . then the police . . . it was just chaos . . ."

He stopped again, and I said, "When the police came, why didn't you stay with Greville and help him? Why didn't you identify him to them, even?"

His genuine sorrow was flooded with a shaft of alarm. The dismay was momentary, and he shrugged it off.

"You know how it is." He gave me a little-boy shamefaced look, much the same as when he'd admitted to changing the stones. "Don't get involved. I didn't want to be dragged in . . . I thought he was dead."

Somewhere along the line, I thought, he was lying to me. Not about seeing the accident: his description of Greville's injuries had been piercingly accurate.

"Did you simply . . . drive off?" I asked bleakly.

"No, I couldn't. Not for ages. The police cordoned off the street and took endless statements. Something about criminal responsibility and insurance claims. But I couldn't help them. I didn't see why the scaffolding fell. I felt sick because of the blood. I sat in my car till they let us drive out. They'd taken Grev off in an ambulance before that . . . and the bar was still sticking out of his stomach . . ."

The memory was powerfully reviving his nausea.

"You knew by then that he was still alive," I said.

He was shocked. "How? How could I have known?"

"They hadn't covered his face."

"He was dying. Anyone could see. His head was dented . . . and bleeding . . ."

Dead men don't bleed, I thought, but didn't say it. Prospero Jenks already looked about to throw up, and I wondered how many times he actually had, in the past eleven days.

Instead, I said, "What did you talk about in the Orwell Hotel?"

He blinked. "You know what."

"He accused you of changing the stones."

"Yes." He swallowed. "Well, I apologized. Said I was sorry. Which I was. He could see that. He said why did I do it when I was bound to be found out, but when I did it, it was an impulse, and I didn't think I'd be found out, like I told you."

"What did he say?"

"He shook his head as if I were a baby. He was sad more than angry. I said I would give his diamonds back, of course, and I begged him to forgive me."

"Which he did?"

"Yes, I told you. I asked if we could go on trading together. I mean, no one was as good as Grev at finding marvelous stones, and he always loved the things I made. It was good for both of us. I wanted to go back to that."

Going back was one of life's impossibilities, I thought. Nothing was ever the same.

"Did Greville agree?" I asked.

"Yes. He said he had the diamonds with him but he had arrangements to make. He didn't say what. He said he would come here to the shop at the beginning of the week and I would give him his five stones and pay for the teardrops and stars. He wanted cash for them, and he was giving me a day or two to find the money."

"He didn't usually want cash for things, did he? You sent a check for the spinel and rock crystal."

"Yes, well . . ." Again the quick look of shame. "He said cash in future, as he couldn't trust me. But you didn't know that."

Greville certainly hadn't trusted him, and it sounded as if he'd said he had the diamonds with him when he knew they were at that moment on a boat crossing the North Sea. Had he said that, I wondered? Perhaps Prospero Jenks had misheard or misunderstood, but he'd definitely believed Greville had had the diamonds with him.

"If I give you those diamonds now, then that will be the end of it?" he said. "I mean, as Grev had forgiven me, you won't go back on that and make a fuss, will you? Not the police . . . Grev wouldn't have wanted that, you know he wouldn't."

I didn't answer. Greville would have to have balanced his betrayed old friendship against his respect for the law, and I supposed he wouldn't have had Prospero prosecuted, not for a first offense, admitted and regretted.

Prospero Jenks gave my silence a hopeful look, rose from his stool and crossed to the ranks of little drawers. He pulled one open, took out several apparently unimportant packets and felt deep inside with a searching hand. He brought out a twist of white gauze fastened with a band of sticky tape and held it out to me.

"Five diamonds," he said. "Yours."

I took the unimpressive little parcel, which most resembled the muslin bag of herbs cooks put in stews, and weighed it in my hand. I certainly couldn't myself tell CZ from C and he could see the doubt in my face.

"Have them appraised," he said with unjustified bitterness, and I said we would weigh them right there and then and he would write out the weight and sign it.

"Grev didn't . . ."

"More fool he. He should have done. But he trusted you. I don't."

"Come on, Derek." He was cajoling: but I was not Greville.

"No. Weigh them," I said.

With a sigh and an exaggerated shrug he cut open the little bag when I handed it back to him, and on small fine scales weighed the contents.

It was the first time I'd actually seen what I'd been searching for, and they were unimposing, to say the least. Five dull-looking grayish pieces of crystal the size of large misshapen peas without a hint of the fire waiting within. I watched the weighing carefully and took them myself off the scales, wrapping them in a fresh square of gauze which Prospero handed me and fastening them safely with sticky tape.

"Satisfied?" he said with a touch of sarcasm, watching me stow the bouquet garni in my trousers pocket.

"No. Not really."

"They're the genuine article," he protested. He signed the paper on which he'd written their combined weight, and gave it to me. "I wouldn't make that mistake again." He studied me. "You're much harder than Grev."

"I've reason to be."

"What reason?"

"Several attempts at theft. Sundry assaults."

His mouth opened.

"Who else?" I said.

"But I've never . . . I didn't . . ." He wanted me to believe him. He leaned forward with earnestness. "I don't know what you're talking about."

I sighed slightly. "Greville hid the letters and invoices dealing with the diamonds because he distrusted someone in his office. Someone that he guessed was running to you with little snippets of information. Someone who would spy for you."

"Nonsense." His mouth seemed dry, however.

I pulled out of a pocket the microcassette recorder and laid it on his workbench.

"This is voice activated," I said. "Greville left it switched on one day when he went to lunch, and this is what he found on the tape when he returned." I pressed the switch and the voice that was familiar to both of us spoke revealing forth:

"I'm in his office now and I can't find them. He hides everything, he's security mad, you know that. I can't ask. He'd never tell me, and I don't think he trusts me. Po-faced Annette doesn't sneeze unless he tells her to . . ."

Jason's voice, full of the cocky street-smart aggression that went with the orange spiky hair, clicked off eventually into silence. Prospero Jenks worked some saliva into his mouth and carefully made sure the recorder was not still alive and listening.

"Jason wasn't talking to me," he said unconvincingly. "He was talking to someone else."

"Jason was the regular messenger between you and Greville," I said. "I sent him round here myself last week. Jason wouldn't take much seducing to bring you information along with the merchandise. But Greville found out. It compounded his sense of betrayal. So when you and he were talking in the Orwell at Ipswich, what was his opinion of Jason?"

He made a gesture of half-suppressed fury.

"I don't know how you know all this," he said.

It had taken nine days and a lot of searching and a good deal of guessing at possibilities and probabilities, but the pattern was now a reliable path through at least part of the maze, and no other interpretation that I could think of explained the facts.

I said again, "What did he say about Jason?"

Prospero Jenks capitulated. "He said he'd have to leave Saxony Franklin. He said it was a condition of us ever doing business again. He said I was to tell Jason not to turn up for work on the Monday."

"But you didn't do that," I said.

"Well, no."

"Because when Greville died, you decided to try to steal not only five stones but the lot."

The blue eyes almost smiled. "Seemed logical, didn't it?" he said. "Grev wouldn't know. The insurance would pay. No one would lose."

Except the underwriters, I thought. But I said, "The diamonds weren't insured. Are not now insured. You were stealing them directly from Greville."

He was almost astounded, but not quite.

"Greville told you that, didn't he?" I guessed.

Again the little-boy shame. "Well, yes, he did."

"In the Orwell?"

"Yes."

"Pross," I said, "did you ever grow up?"

"You don't know what growing up is. Growing up is being ahead of the game."

"Stealing without being found out?"

"Of course. Everyone does it. You have to make what you can."

"But you have this marvelous talent," I said.

[260]

"Sure. But I make things for money. I make what people like. I take their bread, whatever they'll pay. Sure, I get a buzz when what I've made is brilliant, but I wouldn't starve in a garret for art's sake. Stones sing to me. I give them life. Gold is my paintbrush. All that, sure. But I'll laugh behind people's backs. They're gullible. The day I understood all customers are suckers is the day I grew up."

I said, "I'll bet you never said all that to Greville."

"Do me a favor. Grev was a saint, near enough. The only truly good person through and through I've ever known. I wish I hadn't cheated him. I regret it something rotten."

I listened to the sincerity in his voice and believed him, but his remorse had been barely skin deep, and nowhere had it altered his soul.

"Jason," I said, "knocked me down outside St. Catherine's Hospital and stole the bag containing Greville's clothes."

"No." The Jenks denial was automatic, but his eyes were full of shock.

I said, "I thought at the time it was an ordinary mugging. The attacker was quick and strong. A friend who was with me said the mugger wore jeans and a woolly hat, but neither of us saw his face. I didn't bother to report it to the police because there was nothing of value in the bag."

"So how can you say it was Jason?"

I answered his question obliquely.

"When I went to Greville's firm to tell them he was dead," I said, "I found his office had been ransacked. As you know. The next day I discovered that Greville had bought diamonds. I began looking for them, but there was no paperwork, no address book, no desk diary, no reference to or appointments with diamond dealers. I couldn't physically find the diamonds either. I spent three days searching in the vault, with Annette and June, her assistant, telling me that there never were any diamonds in the office, Greville was far too security conscious. You yourself told me the diamonds were intended for you, which I didn't know until I came here.

[261]

Everyone in the office knew I was looking for diamonds, and at that point Jason must have told you I was looking for them, which informed you that I didn't know where they were."

He watched my face with his mouth slightly open, no longer denying, showing only the stunned disbelief of the profoundly found out.

"The office staff grew to know I was a jockey," I said, "and Jason behaved to me with an insolence I thought inappropriate, but I now think his arrogance was the result of his having had me facedown on the ground under his foot. He couldn't crow about that, but his belief in his superiority was stamped all over him. I asked the office staff not to unsettle the customers by telling them that they were now trading with a jockey, not a gemologist, but I think it's certain that Jason told *you.* "

"What makes you think that?" He didn't say it hadn't happened.

"You couldn't get into Greville's house to search it," I said, "because it's a fortress. You couldn't swing any sort of wrecking ball against the windows because the grilles inside made it pointless, and anyway they're wired on a direct alarm to the police station. The only way to get into that house is by key, and I had the keys. So you worked out how to get me there, and you set it up through the trainer I ride for, which is how I know you were aware I was a jockey. Apart from the staff, no one else who knew I was a jockey knew I was looking for diamonds, because I carefully didn't tell them. Come to the telephone in Greville's house for information about the diamonds, you said, and I obediently turned up, which was foolish."

"But I never went to Greville's house . . ." he said.

"No, not you, Jason. Strong and fast in the motorcycle helmet which covered his orange hair, butting me over again just like old times. I saw him vault the gate on the way out. That couldn't have been you. He turned the house upside down but the police didn't think he'd found what he was looking for, and I'm sure he didn't."

"Why not?" he asked, and then said, "That's to say . . ."

"Did you mean Jason to kill me?" I asked flatly.

"No! Of course not!" The idea seemed genuinely to shock him.

"He could have done," I said.

"I'm not a murderer!" His indignation, as far as I could tell, was true and without reservation, quite different to his reaction to my calling him a thief.

"What were you doing two days ago, on Sunday afternoon?" I said.

"What?" He was bewildered by the question but not alarmed.

"Sunday afternoon," I said.

"What about Sunday afternoon? What are you talking about?"

I frowned. "Never mind. Go back to Saturday night. To Jason giving me a concussion with half a brick."

The knowledge of that was plain to read. We were again on familiar territory.

"You can kill people," I said, "hitting them with bricks."

"But he said . . ." He stopped dead.

"You might as well go on," I said reasonably, "we both know that what I've said is what happened."

"Yes, but . . . what are you going to do about it?"

"I don't know yet."

"I'll deny everything."

"What did Jason say about the brick?"

He gave a hopeless little sigh. "He said he knew how to knock people out for half an hour. He'd seen it done in street riots, he said, and he'd done it himself. He said it depended on where you hit."

"You can't time it," I objected.

"Well, that's what he said."

He hadn't been so wrong, I supposed. I'd beaten his estimate by maybe ten minutes, not more.

"He said you'd be all right afterward," Pross said.

[263]

"He couldn't be sure of that."

"But you are, aren't you?" There seemed to be a tinge of regret that I hadn't emerged punch-drunk and unable to hold the present conversation. Callous and irresponsible, I thought, and unforgivable, really. Greville had forgiven treachery; and which was worse?

"Jason knew which office window to break," I said, "and he came down from the roof. The police found marks up there." I paused. "Did he do that alone, or were you with him?"

"Do you expect me to tell you?" he said incredulously.

"Yes, I do. Why not? You know what plea bargaining is, you just tried it with five diamonds."

He gave me a shattered look and searched his common sense; not that he had much of it, when one considered.

Eventually, without shame, he said, "We both went."

"When?"

"That Sunday. Late afternoon. After he brought Grev's things back from Ipswich and they were a waste of time."

"You found out which hospital Greville was in," I said, "and you sent Jason to steal his things because you believed they would include the diamonds which Greville had told you he had with him, is that right?"

He rather miserably nodded. "Jason phoned me from the hospital on the Saturday and said Grev wasn't dead yet but that his brother had turned up, some frail old creature on crutches, and it was good because he'd be an easy mark . . . which you were."

"Yes."

He looked at me and repeated, "Frail old creature," and faintly smiled, and I remembered his surprise at my physical appearance when I'd first come into this room. Jason, I supposed, had seen only my back view and mostly at a distance. I certainly hadn't noticed anyone lurking, but I probably wouldn't at the time have noticed half a ship's company standing at attention. Being with the dying, seeing the death, had made ordinary life seem unreal and unimportant, and it had taken me until hours after Jason's attack to lose that feeling altogether.

"All right," I said, "so Jason came back empty-handed. What then?"

He shrugged. "I thought I'd probably got it wrong. Grev couldn't have meant he had the diamonds with him." He frowned. "I thought that was what he said, though."

I enlightened him. "Greville was on his way to Harwich to meet a diamond cutter coming from Antwerp by ferry, who was bringing your diamonds with him. Twelve teardrops and eight stars."

"Oh." His face cleared momentarily with pleasure but gloom soon returned. "Well, I thought it was worth looking in his office, though Jason said he never kept anything valuable there. But for diamonds . . . so many diamonds . . . it was worth a chance. Jason didn't take much persuading. He's a violent young bugger . . ."

I wondered fleetingly if that description mightn't be positively and scatologically accurate.

"So you went up to the roof in the service lift," I said, "and swung some sort of pendulum at the packing room window."

He shook his head. "Jason brought grappling irons and a rope ladder and climbed down that to the window, and broke the glass with a baseball bat. Then when he was inside I threw the hooks and the ladder down into the yard, and went down in the lift to the eighth floor, and Jason let me in through the staff door. But we couldn't get into the stock-rooms because of Grev's infernal electronic locks, or into the showroom, same reason. And that vault . . . I wanted to try to beat it open with the bat but Jason said the door is six inches thick." He shrugged. "So we had to make do with papers . . . and we couldn't find anything about diamonds. Jason got angry . . . we made quite a mess."

"Mm."

"And it was all a waste of time. Jason said what we really needed was something called a Wizard, but we couldn't find that either. In the end, we simply left. I gave it up. Grev had been too careful. I got resigned to not having the diamonds unless I paid for them. Then Jason said you were hunting high and low for them, and I got interested again. Very. You can't blame me."

I could and did, but I didn't want to switch off the fountain.

"And then," he said, "like you guessed, I inveigled you into Grev's garden, and Jason had been waiting ages there getting furious you took so long. He let his anger out on the house, he said."

"He made a mess there too, yes."

"Then you woke up and set the alarms off and Jason said he was getting right nervous by then and he wasn't going to wait around for the handcuffs. So Grev had beaten us again . . . and he's beaten you too, hasn't he?" He looked at me shrewdly. "You haven't found the diamonds either."

I didn't answer him. I said, "When did Jason break into Greville's car?"

"Well . . . when he finally found it in Greville's road. I'd looked for it at the hotel and round about in Ipswich, but Grev must have hired a car to drive there, because his own car won't start."

"When did you discover that?"

"Saturday. If the diamonds had been in it, we wouldn't have needed to search the house."

"He wouldn't have left a fortune in the street," I said.

Pross shook his head resignedly. "You'd already looked there, I suppose."

"I had." I considered him. "Why Ipswich?" I said.

"What?"

"Why the Orwell Hotel at Ipswich, particularly? Why did he want you to go there?"

"No idea," he said blankly. "He didn't say. He'd often ask me to meet him in odd places. It was usually because he'd found some heirloom or other and wanted to know if the stones would be of use to me. An ugly old tiara once, with a boring yellow diamond centerpiece filthy from neglect. I had the stone recut and set it as the crest of a rock crystal bird and hung it in a golden cage . . . it's in Florida, in the sun."

I was shaken with the pity of it. So much soaring priceless imagination and such grubby, perfidious greed.

I said, "Had he found you a stone in Ipswich?"

"No. He told me he'd asked me to come there because he didn't want us to be interrupted. Somewhere quiet, he said. I suppose it was because he was going to Harwich."

I nodded. I supposed so also, though it wasn't on the most direct route, which was farther south, through Colchester. But Ipswich was where Greville had chosen, by freak mischance.

I thought of all Pross had told me, and was struck by one unexplored and dreadful possibility.

"When the scaffolding fell," I said slowly, "when you ran across the road and found Greville lethally injured . . . when he was lying there bleeding with the metal bar in him . . . did you steal his wallet?"

Pross's little-boy face crumpled and he put his hands to cover it as if he would weep. I didn't believe in the tears and the remorse. I couldn't bear him any longer. I stood up to go.

"You thought he might have diamonds in his wallet," I said bitterly. "And then, even then, when he was dying, you were ready to rob him."

He said nothing. He in no way denied it.

I felt such anger on Greville's behalf that I wanted suddenly to hurt and punish the man before me with a ferocity I wouldn't have expected in myself, and I stood there trembling with the self-knowledge and the essential restraint, and felt my throat close over any more words.

Without thinking I put my left foot down to walk out and felt the pain as an irrelevance, but then after three steps used the crutches to make my way to his doorway and round the screen into the shop and through there out onto the sidewalk, and I wanted to yell and scream at the bloody injustice of Greville's death and the wickedness of the world and call down the rage of angels.

17

I stood blindly on the sidewalk oblivious to the passersby finding me an obstacle in their way. The swamping tidal wave of fury and desolation swelled and broke and gradually ebbed, leaving me still shaking from its force, a tornado in the spirit.

I loosened a jaw I hadn't realized was clamped tight shut and went on feeling wretched.

A grandmotherly woman touched my arm and said, "Do you need help?" and I shook my head at her kindness because the help I needed wasn't anyone's to give. One had to heal from the inside: to knit like bones.

"Are you all right?" she asked again, her eyes concerned.

"Yes." I made an effort. "Thank you."

She looked at me uncertainly, but finally moved on, and I took a few sketchy breaths and remembered with bathos that I needed a telephone if I were ever to move from that spot.

A hairdressing salon having (for a consideration) let me use their phone, Brad came within five minutes to pick me up. I shoved the crutches into the back and climbed wearily in beside him, and he said, "Where to?" giving me a repeat of the grandmotherly solicitude in his face if not his words.

"Uh," I said. "I don't know."

"Home?"

"No . . ." I gave it a bit of thought. I had intended to go to Greville's house to change into my suit that was hanging in his wardrobe before meeting Clarissa at seven, and it still seemed perhaps the best thing to do, even if my energy for the project had evaporated.

Accordingly we made our way there, which wasn't far, and when Brad stopped outside the door, I said, "I think I'll sleep here tonight. This house is as safe as anywhere. So you can go on to Hungerford now, if you like."

He didn't look as if he liked, but all he said was "I come back tomorrow?"

"Yes, please," I agreed.

"Pick you up. Take you to the office?"

"Yes, please."

He nodded, seemingly reassured that I still needed him. He got out of the car with me and opened the gate, brought my overnight bag and came in with me to see, upstairs and down, that the house was safely empty of murderers and thieves. When he'd departed I checked that all the alarms were switched on and went up to Greville's room to change.

I borrowed another of his shirts and a navy silk tie, and shaved with his electric razor which was among the things I'd picked up from the floor and put on his white chest of drawers, and brushed my hair with his brushes for the same reason, and thought with an odd frisson that all of these things were mine now, that I was in his house, in his room, in his clothes . . . in his life.

I put on my own suit, because his anyway were too long, and came across the tube of the baster, still there in an inner breast pocket. Removing it, I left it among the jumble on the dressing chest and checked in the looking glass on the wall that Franklin, Mark II, wouldn't entirely disgrace Franklin, Mark I. He had looked in that mirror every day for three months, I supposed. Now his reflection was my reflection and the man that was both of us had dark marks of tiredness under the eyes and a taut thinness in the cheeks, and looked as if he could do with a week's lying in the sun. I gave him a rueful smile and phoned for a taxi, which took me to Luigi's with ten minutes to spare.

She was there before me all the same, sitting at a small table in the bar area to one side of the restaurant, with an emptyish glass looking like vodka on a prim mat in front of her. She stood up when I went in and offered me a cool cheek for a polite social greeting, inviting me with a gesture to sit down.

"What will you drink?" she asked formally, but battling, I thought, with an undercurrent of diffidence.

I said I would pay for our drinks and she said no, no, this was her suggestion. She called the waiter and said, "Double water?" to me with a small smile and when I nodded ordered Perrier with ice and fresh lime juice for both of us.

I was down by then to only two or three Distalgesics a day and would soon have stopped taking them, though the one I'd just swallowed in Greville's house was still an inhibitor for the evening. I wondered too late which would have made me feel better, a damper for the ankle or a large scotch everywhere else.

Clarissa was wearing a blue silk dress with a double-strand pearl necklace, pearl, sapphire and diamond earrings and a sapphire and diamond ring. I doubted if I would have noticed those, in the simple old jockey days. Her hair, smooth as always, curved in the expensive cut and her shoes and hand-bag were quiet black calf. She looked as she was, a polished, well-bred woman of forty or so, nearly beautiful, slender, with generous eyes.

"What have you been doing since Saturday?" she asked, making conversation.

"Peering into the jaws of death. What have you?"

"We went to . . ." She broke off. "*What* did you say?"

"Martha and Harley Ostermeyer and I were in a car crash on Sunday. They're OK, they went back to America today, I believe. And I, as you see, am here in one piece. Well . . . almost one piece."

She was predictably horrified and wanted to hear all the details, and the telling at least helped to evaporate any awkwardness either of us had been feeling at the meeting.

"Simms was *shot?*"

"Yes."

"But . . . do the police know who did it?"

I shook my head. "Someone in a large gray Volvo, they think, and there are thousands of those."

"Good heavens." She paused. "I didn't like to comment, but you look . . ." She hesitated, searching for the word.

"Frazzled?" I suggested.

"Smooth." She smiled. "Frazzled underneath."

"It'll pass."

The waiter came to ask if we would be having dinner and I said yes, and no argument, the dinner was mine. She accepted without fuss, and we read the menus.

The fare was chiefly Italian, the decor cosmopolitan, the ambience faintly European tamed by London. A lot of dark red, lamps with glass shades, no wallpaper music. A comfortable place, nothing dynamic. Few diners yet, as the hour was early.

It was not, I was interested to note, a habitual rendezvous place for Clarissa and Greville: none of the waiters treated her as a regular. I asked her about it and, startled, she said they had been there only two or three times, always for lunch.

"We never went to the same place often," she said. "It wouldn't have been wise."

"No."

She gave me a slightly embarrassed look. "Do you disapprove of me and Greville?"

"No," I said again. "You gave him joy."

"Oh." She was comforted and pleased. She said with a certain shyness, "It was the first time I'd fallen in love. I suppose you'll think that silly. But it was the first time for him too, he said. It was . . . truly *wonderful.* We were like . . . as if twenty years younger . . . I don't know if I can explain. Laughing. Lit up."

"As far as I can see," I said, "the thunderbolt strikes at any age. You don't have to be teenagers."

[271]

"Has it . . . struck you?"

"Not since I was seventeen and fell like a ton of bricks for a trainer's daughter."

"What happened?"

"Nothing much. We laughed a lot. Slept together, a bit clumsily at first. She married an old man of twenty-eight. I went to college."

"I met Henry when I was eighteen. He fell in love with me . . . pursued me . . . I was flattered . . . and he was so very good looking . . . and kind."

"He still is," I said.

"He'd already inherited his title. My mother was ecstatic . . . she said the age difference didn't matter . . . so I married him." She paused. "We had a son and a daughter, both grown up now. It hasn't been a bad life, but before Greville, incomplete."

"A better life than most," I said, aiming to comfort.

"You're very like Greville," she said unexpectedly. "You look at things straight, in the same way. You've his sense of proportion."

"We had realistic parents."

"He didn't speak about them much, only that he became interested in gemstones because of the museums his mother took him to. But he lived in the present and he looked outward, not inward, and I loved him to distraction and in a way I didn't know him . . ." She stopped and swallowed and seemed determined not to let emotion intrude further.

"He was like that with me too," I said. "With everyone, I think. It didn't occur to him to give running commentaries on his actions and feelings. He found everything else more interesting."

"I do miss him," she said.

"What will you eat?" I asked.

She gave me a flick of a look and read the menu without seeing it for quite a long time. In the end she said with a sigh, "You decide."

[272]

"Did Greville?"

"Yes."

"If I order fried zucchini as a starter, then fillet steak in pepper sauce with linguine tossed in olive oil with garlic, will that do?"

"I don't like garlic. I like everything else. Unusual. Nice."

"Ok. No garlic."

We transferred to the dining room before seven-thirty and ate the proposed program, and I asked if she were returning to York that night: if she had a train to catch, if that was why we were eating early.

"No, I'm down here for two nights. Tomorrow I'm going to an old friend's wedding, then back to York on Thursday morning." She concentrated on twirling linguine onto her fork. "When Henry and I come to London together we always stay at the Selfridge Hotel, and when I come alone I stay there also. They know us well there. When I'm there alone they don't present me with an account, they send it to Henry." She ate the forkful of linguine. "I tell him I go to the cinema and eat in snack bars . . . and he knows I'm always back in the hotel before midnight."

There was a good long stretch of time between this dinner and midnight.

I said, "Every five weeks or so, when you came down to London alone, Greville met you at King's Cross, isn't that right, and took you to lunch?"

She said in surprise, "Did he tell you?"

"Not face to face. Did you ever see that gadget of his, the Wizard?"

"Yes, but . . ." She was horrified. "He surely didn't put me in it?"

"Not by name, and only under a secret password. You're quite safe."

She twiddled some more with the pasta, her eyes down, her thoughts somewhere else.

"After lunch," she said, with pauses, "if I had appointments, I'd keep them, or do some shopping . . . something

[273]

to take home. I'd register at the hotel and change, and go to Greville's house. He used to have the flat, of course, but the house was much better. When he came, we'd have drinks . . . talk . . . maybe make love. We'd go to dinner early, then back to his house." Her voice stopped. She still didn't look up.

I said, "Do you want to go to his house now, before midnight?"

After a while she said, "I don't know."

"Well . . . would you like coffee?"

She nodded, still not meeting my eyes, and pushed the linguine away. We sat in silence while waiters took away the plates and poured into cups, and if she couldn't make up her mind, nor could I.

In the end I said, "If you like, come to Greville's house now. I'm sleeping there tonight, but that's not a factor. Come if you like, just to be near him, to be with him as much as you can for maybe the last time. Lie on his bed. Weep for him. I'll wait for you downstairs . . . and take you safely to your hotel before the fairy coach changes back to a pumpkin."

"Oh!" She turned what was going to be a sob into almost a laugh. "Can I really?"

"Whenever you like."

"Thank you, then. Yes."

"I'd better warn you," I said, "it's not exactly tidy." I told her what she would find, but she was inconsolable at the sight of the reality.

"He would have hated this," she said. "I'm so glad he didn't see it."

We were in the small sitting room, and she went round picking up the pink and brown stone bears, restoring them to their tray.

"I gave him these," she said. "He loved them. They're rhodonite, he said."

"Take them to remember him by. And there's a gold watch you gave him, if you'd like that too."

She paused with the last bear in her hand and said, "You're very kind to me."

"It's not difficult. And he'd have been furious with me if I weren't."

"I'd love the bears. You'd better keep the watch, because of the engraving."

"OK," I said.

"I think," she said with diffidence, "I'll go upstairs now."

I nodded.

"Come with me," she said.

I looked at her. Her eyes were wide and troubled, but not committed, not hungry. Undecided. Like myself.

"All right," I said.

"Is there chaos up there too?"

"I picked some of it up."

She went up the stairs ahead of me at about four times my speed, and I heard her small moan of distress at the desecration of the bedroom. When I joined her, she was standing forlornly looking around, and with naturalness she turned to me and put her arms loosely round my waist, laying her head on my shoulder. I shed the confounded crutches and hugged her tight in grief for her and for Greville and we stood there for a long minute in mutual and much-needed comfort.

She let her arms fall away and went over to sit on the bed, smoothing a hand over the black and white checkerboard bedspread.

"He was going to change this room," she said. "All this drama . . ." She waved a hand at the white furniture, the black carpet, one black wall. "It came with the house. He wanted me to choose something softer, that I would like. But this is how I'll always remember it."

She lay down flat, her head on the pillows, her legs toward the foot of the bed, ankles crossed. I half-hopped, half-limped across the room and sat on the edge beside her.

She watched me with big eyes. I put my hand flat on her stomach and felt the sharp internal contraction of muscles.

[275]

"Should we do this?" she said.

"I'm not Greville."

"No . . . Would he mind?"

"I shouldn't think so." I moved my hand, rubbing a little. "Do you want to go on?"

"Do you?"

"Yes," I said.

She sat up fast and put her arms round my neck in a sort of released compulsion.

"I do want this," she said. "I've wanted it all day. I've been pretending to myself, telling myself I shouldn't, but yes, I do want this passionately, and I know you're not Greville, I know it will be different, but this is the only way I can love him . . . and can you bear it, can you understand it, if it's him I love?"

I understood it well, and I minded not at all.

I said, smiling, "Just don't *call* me Greville. It would be the turn-off of the century."

She took her face away from the proximity of my ear and looked me in the eyes, and her lips too, after a moment, were smiling.

"Derek," she said deliberately, "make love to me. Please."

"Don't beg," I said.

I put my mouth on hers and took my brother's place.

As a memorial service it was quite a success. I lay in the dark laughing in my mind at that disgraceful pun, wondering whether or not to share it with Clarissa.

The catharsis was over, and her tears. She lay with her head on my chest, lightly asleep, contented, as far as I could tell, with the substitute loving. Women said men were not all the same in the dark, and I knew both where I'd surprised her and failed her, known what I'd done like Greville and not done like Greville from the instinctive releases and tensions of her reactions.

Greville, I now knew, had been a lucky man, though whether he had himself taught her how to give exquisite pleasure was something I couldn't quite ask. She knew, though, and she'd done it, and the feeling of her featherlight tattooing fingers on the base of my spine at the moment of climax had been a revelation. Knowledge marched on, I thought. Next time, with anyone else, I'd know what to suggest.

Clarissa stirred and I turned my wrist over, seeing the fluorescent hands of my watch.

"Wake up," I said affectionately. "It's Cinderella time."

"Ohh . . ."

I stretched out a hand and turned on a bedside light. She smiled at me sleepily, no doubts remaining.

"That was all right," she said.

"Mm. Very."

"How's the ankle?"

"What ankle?"

She propped herself on one elbow, unashamed of nakedness, and laughed at me. She looked younger and sweeter, and I was seeing, I knew, what Greville had seen, what Greville had loved.

"Tomorrow," she said, "my friend's wedding will be over by six or so. Can I come here again?" She put her fingers lightly on my mouth to stop me answering at once. "This time was for him," she said. "Tomorrow for us. Then I'll go home."

"Forever?"

"Yes, I think so. What I had with Greville was unforgettable and unrepeatable. I decided on the train coming down here that whatever happened with you, or didn't happen, I would live with Henry, and do my best there."

"I could easily love you," I said.

"Yes, but don't."

I knew she was right. I kissed her lightly.

"Tomorrow for us," I agreed. "Then goodbye."

When I went into the office in the morning, Annette told me crossly that Jason hadn't turned up for work, nor had he telephoned to say he was ill.

Jason had been prudent, I thought. I'd have tossed him

down the elevator shaft, insolence, orange hair and all, given half an ounce of provocation.

"He won't be coming back," I said, "so we'll need a replacement."

She was astonished. "You can't sack him for not turning up. You can't sack him for anything without paying compensation."

"Stop worrying," I said, but she couldn't take that advice.

June came zooming into Greville's office waving a tabloid newspaper and looking at me with wide incredulous eyes.

"Did you know you're in the paper? Lucky to be alive, it says here. You didn't say anything about it!"

"Let's see," I said, and she laid the *Daily Sensation* open on the black desk.

There was a picture of the smash in which one could more or less see my head inside the Daimler, but not recognizably. The headline read "Driver shot, jockey lives," and the piece underneath listed the lucky-to-be-alive passengers as Mr. and Mrs. Ostermeyer of Pittsburgh, America, and ex-champion steeplechase jockey Derek Franklin. The police were reported to be interested in a gray Volvo seen accelerating from the scene, and also to have recovered two bullets from the bodywork of the Daimler. After that tidbit came a rehash of the Hungerford massacre and a query, "Is this a copycat killing?" and finally a picture of Simms looking happy: "Survived by wife and two daughters who were last night being comforted by relatives."

Poor Simms. Poor family. Poor every shot victim in Hungerford.

"It happened on Sunday," June exclaimed, "and you came here on Monday and yesterday as if nothing was wrong. No wonder you looked knackered."

"June!" Annette disapproved of the word.

"Well, he did. Still does." She gave me a critical, kindly, motherly-sisterly inspection. "He could have been killed, and then what would we all have done here?"

The dismay in Annette's face was a measure, I supposed, of the degree to which I had taken over. The place no longer felt like quicksand to me either and I was beginning by necessity to get a feel of its pulse.

But there was racing at Cheltenham that day. I turned the pages of the newspaper and came to the runners and riders. That was where my name belonged, not on Saxony Franklin checks. June looked over my shoulder and understood at least something of my sense of exile.

"When you go back to your own world," she said, rephrasing her thought and asking it seriously, "what will we do here?"

"We have a month," I said. "It'll take me that time to get fit." I paused. "I've been thinking about that problem, and, er, you might as well know, both of you, what I've decided."

They both looked apprehensive, but I smiled to reassure them.

"What we'll do," I said, "is this. Annette will have a new title, which will be Office Manager. She'll run things generally and keep the keys."

She didn't look displeased. She repeated "Office Manager" as if trying it on for size.

I nodded. "Then I'll start looking from now on for a business expert, someone to oversee the cash flow and do the accounts and try to keep us afloat. Because it's going to be a struggle, we can't avoid that."

They both looked shocked and disbelieving. Cash flow seemed never to have been a problem before.

"Greville did buy diamonds," I said regretfully, "and so far we are only in possession of a quarter of them. I can't find out what happened to the rest. They cost the firm altogether one and a half million dollars, and we'll still owe the bank getting on for three-quarters of that sum when we've sold the quarter we have."

Their mouths opened in unhappy unison.

"Unless and until the other diamonds turn up," I said, "we

[279]

have to pay interest on the loan and persuade the bank that somehow or other we'll climb out of the hole. So we'll want someone we'll call the Finance Manager, and we'll pay him out of part of what used to be Greville's own salary."

They began to understand the mechanics, and nodded.

"Then," I said, "we need a gemologist who has a feeling for stones and understands what the customers like and need. There's no good hoping for another Greville, but we will create the post of Merchandise Manager, and that," I looked at her, "will be June."

She blushed a fiery red. "But I can't . . . I don't know enough."

"You'll go on courses," I said. "You'll go to trade fairs. You'll travel. You'll do the buying."

I watched her expand her horizons abruptly and saw the sparkle appear in her eyes.

"She's too young," Annette objected.

"We'll see," I said, and to June I added, "You know what sells. You and the Finance Manager will work together to make us the best possible profit. You'll still work the computer, and teach Lily or Tina how to use it for when you're away."

"Tina," she said, "she's quicker."

"Tina, then."

"What about you?" she asked.

"I'll be General Manager. I'll come when I can, at least twice a week for a couple of hours. Everyone will tell me what's going on and we will all decide what is best to be done, though if there's a disagreement I'll have the casting vote. Right or wrong will be my responsibility, not yours."

Annette, nevertheless troubled, said, "Surely you yourself will need Mr. Franklin's salary."

I shook my head. "I earn enough riding horses. Until we're solvent here, we need to save every penny."

"It's an adventure!" June said, enraptured.

I thought it might be a very long haul and even in the end

impossible, but I couldn't square it with the consciousness of Greville all around me not to try.

"Well," I said, putting a hand in a pocket and bringing out a twist of gauze, "we have here five uncut diamonds which cost about seventy-five thousand dollars altogether."

They more or less gasped.

"How do we sell them?" I said.

After a pause, Annette said, "Interest a diamantaire."

"Do you know how to do that?"

After another moment's hesitation, she nodded.

"We can give provenance," I said. "Copies of the records of the original sale are on their way here from Guy Servi in Antwerp. They might be here tomorrow. Sight-box number and so on. We'll put these stones in the vault until the papers arrive, then you can get cracking."

She nodded, but fearfully.

"Cheer up," I said. "It's clear from the ledgers that Saxony Franklin is normally a highly successful and profitable business. We'll have to cut costs where we can, that's all."

"We could cut out Jason's salary," Annette said unexpectedly. "Half the time Tina's been carrying the heavy boxes, anyway, and I can do the vacuuming myself."

"Great," I said with gratitude. "If you feel like that, we'll succeed."

The telephone rang and Annette answered it briefly.

"A messenger has left a packet for you down at the front desk," she said.

"I'll go for it," June said, and was out of the door on the words, returning in her usual short time with a brown padded Jiffy bag, not very large, addressed simply to Derek Franklin in neat handwriting, which she laid before me with a flourish.

"Mind it's not a bomb," she said facetiously as I picked it up, and I thought with an amount of horror that it was a possibility I hadn't thought of.

"I didn't mean it," she said teasingly, seeing me hesitate. "Do you want me to open it?"

[281]

"And get your hands blown off instead?"

"Of course it's not a bomb," Annette said uneasily.

"Tell you what," June said, "I'll fetch the shears from the packing room." She was gone for a few seconds. "Alfie says," she remarked, returning, "we ought to put it in a bucket of water."

She gave me the shears, which were oversized scissors that Alfie used for cutting cardboard, and for all her disbelief she and Annette backed away across the room while I sliced the end off the bag.

There was no explosion. Complete anticlimax. I shook out the contents which proved to be two objects and one envelope.

One of the objects was the microcassette recorder that I'd left on Prospero Jenks's workbench in my haste to be gone.

The other was a long black leather wallet almost the size of the Wizard, with gold initials G.S.F. in one corner and an ordinary brown rubber band holding it shut.

"That's Mr. Franklin's," Annette said blankly, and June, coming to inspect it, nodded.

I peeled off the rubber band and laid the wallet open on the desk. There was a business card lying loose inside it with Prospero Jenks's name and shops on the front, and on the reverse the single word, "Sorry."

"Where did he get Mr. Franklin's wallet from?" Annette asked, puzzled, looking at the card.

"He found it," I said.

"He took his time sending it back," June said tartly.

"Mm."

The wallet contained a Saxony Franklin checkbook, four credit cards, several business cards and a small pack of banknotes, which I guessed were fewer in number than when Greville set out.

The small excitement over, Annette and June went off to tell the others the present and future state of the nation, and I was alone when I opened the envelope.

18

P ROSS had sent me a letter and a certified bank draft: instantly cashable money.

I blinked at the numbers on the check and reread them very carefully. Then I read the letter.

It said:

Derek,

This is a plea for a bargain, as you more or less said. The cheque is for the sum I agreed with Grev for the twelve teardrops and eight stars. I know you need the money, and I need those stones.

Jason won't be troubling you again. I'm giving him a job in one of my workrooms.

Grev wouldn't have forgiven the brick, though he might the wallet. For you it's the other way round. You're very like him. I wish he hadn't died.

Pross.

What a mess, I thought. I did need the money, yet if I accepted it I was implicitly agreeing not to take any action against him. The trouble about taking action against him was that however much I might want to I didn't know that I could. Apart from difficulties of evidence, I had more or less made a bargain that for information he would get inaction, but that had been before the wallet. It was perceptive of him, I thought, to see that it was betrayal and attacks on our *brother* that would anger both Greville and me most.

Would Greville want me to extend, if not forgiveness, then at least suspended revenge? Would Greville want me to confirm his forgiveness or to rise up in wrath and tear up the check. . . .

In the midst of these somber squirreling thoughts the telephone rang and I answered it.

"Elliot Trelawney here," the voice said.

"Oh, hello."

He asked me how things were going and I said life was full of dilemmas. Ever so, he said with a chuckle.

"Give me some advice," I said on impulse, "as a magistrate."

"If I can, certainly."

"Well. Listen to a story, then say what you think."

"Fire away."

"Someone knocked me out with a brick . . ." Elliot made protesting noises on my behalf, but I went on, "I know now who it was, but I didn't then, and I didn't see his face because he was masked. He wanted to steal a particular thing from me, but although he made a mess in the house searching, he didn't find it, and so didn't rob me of anything except consciousness. I guessed later who it was, and I challenged another man with having sent him to attack me. That man didn't deny it to me, but he said he would deny it to anyone else. So . . . what do I do?"

"Whew." He pondered. "What do you want to do?"

"I don't know. That's why I need the advice."

"Did you report the attack to the police at the time?"

"Yes."

"Have you suffered serious aftereffects?"

"No."

"Did you see a doctor?"

"No."

He pondered some more. "On a practical level you'd find it difficult to get a conviction, even if the prosecution service would bring charges of actual bodily harm. You couldn't swear to the identity of your assailant if you didn't see him at the time, and as for the other man, conspiracy to commit a crime is one of the most difficult charges to make stick. As you didn't consult a doctor, you're on tricky ground. So, hard as it may seem, my advice would be that the case wouldn't get to court."

I sighed. "Thank you," I said.

"Sorry not to have been more positive."

"It's all right. You confirmed what I rather feared."

"Fine then," he said. "I rang to thank you for sending the Vaccaro notes. We held the committee meeting and turned down Vaccaro's application, and now we find we needn't have bothered because on Saturday night he was arrested and charged with attempting to import illegal substances. He's still in custody, and America is asking for him to be extradited to Florida where he faces murder charges and perhaps execution. And we nearly gave him a gambling license! Funny old world."

"Hilarious."

"How about our drink in the Rook and Castle?" he suggested. "Perhaps one evening next week?"

"OK."

"Fine," he said. "I'll call you."

I put the phone down thinking that if Vaccaro had been arrested on Saturday evening and held in custody it was unlikely he'd shot Simms from a moving car in Berkshire on Sunday afternoon. But then, I'd never really thought he had.

Copycat. Copycat, that's what it had been.

Pross hadn't shot Simms either. Had never tried to kill me. The Peter Pan face upon which so many emotions could be read had shown a total blank when I'd asked him what he was doing on Sunday afternoon.

The shooting of Simms, I concluded, had been random

violence like the other murders in Hungerford. Pointless and vicious; malignant, lunatic and impossible to explain.

I picked up the huge check and looked at it. It would solve all immediate problems: pay the interest already due, the cost of cutting the diamonds and more than a fifth of the capital debt. If I didn't take it we would no doubt sell the diamonds later to someone else, but they had been cut especially for Prospero Jenks's fantasies and might not easily fit necklaces and rings.

A plea. A bargain. A chance that the remorse was at least half real. Or was he taking me again for a sucker?

I did some sums with a calculator and when Annette came in with the day's letters I showed her my figures and the check and asked her what she thought.

"That's the cost price," I pointed. "That's the cost of cutting and polishing. That's for delivery charges. That's for loan interest and tax. If you add those together and subtract them from the figure on this check, is that the sort of profit margin Greville would have asked?"

Setting prices was something she well understood, and she repeated my steps on the calculator.

"Yes," she said finally, "it looks about right. Not overgenerous, but Mr. Franklin would have seen this as a service for commission, I think. Not like the rock crystal, which he bought on spec, which had to help pay for his journeys." She looked at me anxiously. "You understand the difference?"

"Yes," I said. "Prospero Jenks says this is what he and Greville agreed on."

"Well then," she said, relieved, "he wouldn't cheat you."

I smiled with irony at her faith. "We'd better bank this check, I suppose," I said, "before it evaporates."

"I'll do it at once," she declared. "With a loan as big as you said, every minute costs us money."

She put on her coat and took an umbrella to go out with, as the day had started off raining and showed no signs of relenting.

It had been raining the previous night when Clarissa had been ready to leave, and I'd had to ring three times for a taxi, a problem Cinderella didn't seem to have encountered. Midnight had come and gone when the wheels had finally arrived, and I'd suggested meanwhile that I lend her Brad and my car for going to her wedding.

I didn't need to, she said. When she and Henry were in London, they were driven about by a hired car firm. The car was already ordered to take her to the wedding, which was in Surrey. The driver would wait for her and return her to the hotel, and she'd better stick to the plan, she said, because the bill for it would be sent to her husband.

"I always do what Henry expects," she said. "Then there are no questions."

"Suppose Brad picks you up from the Selfridge after you get back?" I said, packing the little stone bears and giving them to her in a carrier. "The forecast is lousy and if it's raining you'll have a terrible job getting a taxi at that time of day."

She liked the idea except for Brad's knowing her name. I assured her he never spoke unless he couldn't avoid it, but I told her I would ask Brad to park somewhere near the hotel. Then she could call the car phone's number when she was ready to leave, and Brad would beetle up at the right moment and not need to know her name or ask for her at the desk.

As that pleased her, I wrote down the phone number and the car's license plate so that she would recognize the right pumpkin, and described Brad to her; going bald, a bit morose, an open-necked shirt, a very good driver.

I couldn't tell Brad's own opinion of the arrangement. When I'd suggested it in the morning on the rainy way to the office he had merely grunted, which I'd taken as preliminary assent.

When he'd brought Clarissa, I thought as I looked through the letters Annette had given me, he could go on home, to Hungerford, and Clarissa and I might walk along to the restaurant at the end of Greville's street where he could have been known but I was not, and after an early dinner we would return to Greville's bed, this time for us, and we'd order the taxi in better time . . . perhaps.

I was awoken from this pleasant daydream by the ever-demanding telephone, this time with Nicholas Loder on the other end spluttering with rage.

"Milo says you had the confounded cheek," he said, "to have Dozen Roses dope-tested."

"For barbiturates, yes. He seemed very sleepy. Our vet said he'd be happier to know the horse hadn't been tranquilized for the journey before he gave him an all-clear certificate."

"I'd never give a horse tranquilizers," he declared.

"No, none of us really thought so," I said pacifyingly, "but we decided to make sure."

"It's shabby of you. Offensive. I expect an apology."

"I apologize," I said sincerely enough, and thought guiltily of the further checks going on at that moment.

"That's not good enough," Nicholas Loder said huffily.

"I was selling the horse to good owners of Milo, people I ride for," I said reasonably. "We all know you disapproved. In the same circumstances, confronted by a sleepy horse, you'd have done the same, wouldn't you? You'd want to be sure what you were selling."

Weigh the merchandise, I thought. Cubic zirconia, size for size, was one point seven times heavier than diamond. Greville had carried jewelers' scales in his car on his way to Harwich, presumably to check what the Koningin Beatrix was bringing.

"You've behaved disgustingly," Nicholas Loder said. "When did you see the horse last? And when next?"

"Monday evening, last. Don't know when next. As I told you, I'm tied up a bit with Greville's affairs."

"Milo's secretary said I'd find you in Greville's office," he grumbled. "You're never at home. I've got a buyer for Gemstones, I think, though you don't deserve it. Where will you be this evening, if he makes a definite offer?"

"In Greville's house, perhaps."

"Right, I have the number. And I want a written apology from you about those dope tests. I'm so angry I can hardly be civil to you."

He hardly was, I thought, but I was pleased enough about Gemstones. The money would go into the firm's coffers and hold off bankruptcy a little while longer. I still held the Ostermeyers' check for Dozen Roses, waiting for Phil Urquhart's final clearance before cashing it. The horses would make up for a few of the missing diamonds. Looking at it optimistically, saying it quickly, the millstone had been reduced to near one million dollars.

June out of habit brought me a sandwich for lunch. She was walking with an extra bounce, with unashamed excitement. Way down the line, I thought, if we made it through the crisis, what then? Would I simply sell the whole of Saxony Franklin as I'd meant or keep it and borrow against it to finance a stable, as Greville had financed the diamonds? I wouldn't hide the stable! Perhaps I would have learned enough by then to manage both businesses on a sound basis: I'd learned a good deal in ten days. I had also, though I found it surprising, grown fond of Greville's firm. If we saved it, I wouldn't want to let it go.

If I went on riding until solvency dawned I might be the oldest jump jockey in history . . .

Again the telephone interrupted the daydreams, and I'd barely made a start on the letters.

It was a man with a long order for cabochons and beads. I hopped to the door and yelled for June to pick up the phone and to put the order on the computer, and Alfie came along to complain we were running out of heavy-duty binding tape and to ask why we'd ever needed Jason. Tina did his work in half the time without the swear words.

Annette almost with gaiety vacuumed everywhere, though I thought I would soon ask Tina to do it instead. Lily came with downcast eyes to ask meekly if she could have a title also. Stockroom Manager? she suggested.

"Done!" I said with sincere pleasure; and before the day was out we had a Shipment Manager (Alfie) and an Enabling Manager (Tina), and it seemed to me that such a spirit had been released there that the enterprise was now flying. Whether the euphoria would last or not was next week's problem.

I telephoned Maarten-Pagnier in Antwerp and discussed the transit of twelve teardrops, eight stars and five fakes.

"Our customer has paid us for the diamonds," I said. "I'd like to be able to tell him when we could get them to him."

"Do you want them sent direct to him, monsieur?"

"No. Here to us. We'll pass them on." I asked if he would insure them for the journey and send them by Euro-Securo; no need to trouble his partner again personally as we did not dispute that five of the stones sent to him had been cubic zirconia. The real stones had been returned to us, I said.

"I rejoice for you, monsieur. And shall we expect a further consignment for cutting? Monsieur Franklin intended it."

"Not at the moment, I regret."

"Very well, monsieur. At any time, we are at your service."

After that I asked Annette if she could find Prospero Jenks to tell him his diamonds would be coming. She ran him to earth in one of his workrooms and appeared in my doorway saying he wanted to speak to me personally.

With inner reluctance I picked up the receiver. "Hello, Pross," I said.

"Truce, then?" he asked.

"We've banked the check. You'll get the diamonds."

"When?"

"When they get here from Antwerp. Friday, maybe."

"Thanks." He sounded fervently pleased. Then he said with hesitation, "You've got some light blue topaz, each fifteen carats or more, emerald cut, glittering like water . . . can I have it? Five or six big stones, Grev said. I'll take them all."

"Give it time," I said, and God, I thought, what unholy nerve.

"Yes, well, but you and I need each other," he protested.

"Symbiosis?" I said.

"What? Yes."

It had done Greville no harm in the trade, I'd gathered, to be known as the chief supplier of Prospero Jenks. His firm still needed the cachet as much as the cash. I'd taken the money once. Could I afford pride?

"If you try to steal from me one more time," I said, "I not only stop trading with you, I make sure everyone knows why. Everyone from Hatton Garden to Pelikanstraat."

"Derek!" He sounded hurt, but the threat was a dire one.

"You can have the topaz," I said. "We have a new gemologist who's not Greville, I grant you, but who knows what you buy. We'll still tell you what special stones we've imported. You can tell us what you need. We'll take it step by step."

"I thought you wouldn't!" He sounded extremely relieved. "I thought you'd never forgive me the wallet. Your face . . ."

"I don't forgive it. Or forget. But after wars, enemies trade." It always happened, I thought, though cynics might mock. Mutual benefit was the most powerful of bridge-builders, even if the heart remained bitter. "We'll see how we go," I said again.

"If you find the other diamonds," he said hopefully, "I still want them." Like a little boy in trouble, I thought, trying to charm his way out.

Disconnecting, I ruefully smiled. I'd made the same inner compromise that Greville had, to do business with the treacherous child, but not to trust him. To supply the genius in him, and look to my back.

June came winging in and I asked her to go along to the vault to look at the light blue, large stone topaz, which I well remembered. "Get to know it while it's still here. I've sold it to Prospero Jenks."

"But I don't go into the vault," she said.

"You do now. You'll go in there every day from now on at

spare moments to learn the look and feel of the faceted stones, like I have. Topaz is slippery, for instance. Learn the chemical formulas, learn the cuts and the weights, get to know them so that if you're offered unusual faceted stones anywhere in the world you can check them against your knowledge for probability."

Her mouth opened.

"You're going to buy the raw materials for Prospero Jenks's museum pieces," I said. "You've got to learn fast."

Her eyes stretched wide as well, and she vanished.

With Annette I finished the letters.

At four o'clock I answered the telephone yet again, and found myself talking to Phil Urquhart, whose voice sounded strained.

"I've just phoned the lab for the results of Dozen Roses' tests." He paused. "I don't think I believe this."

"What's the matter?" I asked.

"Do you know what a metabolite is?"

"Only vaguely."

"What, then?" he said.

"The result of metabolism, isn't it?"

"It is," he said. "It's what's left after some substance or other has broken down in the body."

"So what?"

"So," he said reasonably, "if you find a particular metabolite in the urine, it means a particular substance was earlier present in the body. Is that clear?"

"Like viruses produce special antibodies, so the presence of the antibodies proves the existence of the viruses?"

"Exactly," he said, apparently relieved I understood. "Well, the lab found a metabolite in Dozen Roses' urine. A metabolite known as benzyl ecognine."

"Go on," I urged, as he paused. "What is it the metabolite *of?*"

"Cocaine," he said.

* * *

I sat in stunned disbelieving silence.

"Derek?" he said.

'Yes."

"Racehorses aren't routinely tested for cocaine because it isn't a stimulant. Normally a racehorse could be full of cocaine and no one would know."

"If it isn't a stimulant," I said, loosening my tongue, "why give it to them?"

"If you *believed* it was a stimulant, you might. Knowing it wouldn't be tested for."

"How could you believe it?"

"It's one of the drugs that potentiates adrenaline. I particularly asked the lab to test for all drugs like that because of what you said about adrenaline yourself. What happens with a normal adrenaline surge is that after a while an enzyme comes along to control it. Cocaine blocks out that enzyme, so the adrenaline goes roaring round the body for much longer. When the cocaine decays, its chief metabolic product is benzyl ecognine, which is what the lab found in its gas chromatograph analyzer this afternoon."

"There were some cases in America . . ." I said vaguely.

"It's still not part of a regulation dope test even there."

"But my God," I said blankly, "Nicholas Loder must have known."

"Almost certainly, I should think. You'd have to administer the cocaine very soon before the race, because its effect is short lived. One hour, an hour and a half at most. It's difficult to tell, with a horse. There's no data. And although the metabolite would appear in the blood and the urine soon after that, the metabolite itself would be detectable for probably not much longer than forty-eight hours, but with a horse, that's still a guess. We took the sample from Dozen Roses on Monday evening about fifty-two hours after he'd raced. The lab said the metabolite was definitely present, but they could make no estimate of how much cocaine had been assimilated. They told me all this very very carefully. They have much more experience with humans. They say in humans the rush from cocaine is fast, lasts about forty minutes and brings little post-exhilaration depression."

"Nice," I said.

"In horses," he went on, "they think it would probably induce skittishness at once."

I thought back to Dozen Roses' behavior both at York and on the TV tapes. He'd certainly woken up dramatically between saddling box and starting gate.

"But," Phil added, "they say that at the most it might give more stamina, but not more speed. It wouldn't make the horse go faster, but just make the adrenaline push last longer."

That might be enough sometimes, I thought. Sometimes you could feel horses "die" under you near the finish, not from lack of ability, but from lack of perseverance, of fight. Some horses were content to be second. In them, uninhibited adrenaline might perhaps tip the balance.

Caffeine, which had the same potentiating effect, was a prohibited substance in racing.

"Why don't they test for cocaine?" I asked.

"Heaven knows," Phil said. "Perhaps because enough to wind up a horse would cost the doper too much to be practicable. I mean . . . more than one could be sure of winning back on a bet. But cocaine's getting cheaper, I'm told. There's more and more of it around."

"I don't know much about drugs," I said.

"Where have you been?"

"Not my scene."

"Do you know what they'd call you in America?"

"What?"

"Straight," he said.

"I thought that meant heterosexual."

He laughed. "That too. You're straight through and through."

"Phil," I said, "what do I do?"

He sobered abruptly. "God knows. My job ends with passing on the facts. The moral decisions are yours. All I can tell you is that some time before Monday evening Dozen Roses took cocaine into his bloodstream."

"Via a baster?" I said.

After a short silence he said, "We can't be sure of that."

"We can't be sure he didn't."

"Did I understand right, that Harley Ostermeyer picked up the tube of the baster and gave it to you?"

"That's right," I said. "I still have it, but like I told you, it's clean."

"It might look clean," he said slowly, "but if cocaine was blown up it in powder form, there may be particles clinging."

I thought back to before the race at York.

"When Martha Ostermeyer picked up the blue bulb end and gave it back to Rollway," I said, "she was brushing her fingers together afterwards. She seemed to be getting rid of dust from her gloves."

"Oh glory," Phil said.

I sighed and said, "If I give the tube to you, can you get it tested without anyone knowing where it came from?"

"Sure. Like the urine, it'll be anonymous. I'll get the lab to do another rush job, if you want. It costs a bit more, though."

"Get it done, Phil," I said. "I can't really decide anything unless I know for sure."

"Right. Are you coming back here soon?"

"Greville's business takes so much time. I'll be back at the weekend, but I think I'll send the tube to you by carrier, to be quicker. You should get it tomorrow morning."

"Right," he said. "We might get a result late tomorrow. Friday at the latest."

"Good, and er . . . don't mention it to Milo."

"No, but why not?"

"He told Nicholas Loder we tested Dozen Roses for tranquilizers and Nicholas Loder was on my phone hitting the roof."

[295]

"Oh God."

"I don't want him knowing about tests for cocaine. I mean, neither Milo nor Nicholas Loder."

"You may be sure," Phil said seriously, "they won't learn it from me."

It was the worst dilemma of all, I thought, replacing the receiver.

Was cocaine a stimulant or was it not? The racing authorities didn't think so: didn't test for it. If I believed it didn't affect speed then it was all right to sell Dozen Roses to the Ostermeyers. If I thought he wouldn't have got the race at York without help, then it wasn't all right.

Saxony Franklin needed the Ostermeyers' money.

The worst result would be that, if I banked the money and Dozen Roses never won again and Martha and Harley ever found out I knew the horse had been given cocaine, I could say goodbye to any future Gold Cups or Grand Nationals on Datepalm. They wouldn't forgive the unforgivable.

Dozen Roses had seemed to me to run gamely at York and to battle to the end. I was no longer sure. I wondered now if he'd won all his four races spaced out, as the orthopedist would have described it; as high as a kite.

At the best, if I simply kept quiet, banked the money and rode Dozen Roses to a couple of respectable victories, no one would ever know. Or I could inform the Ostermeyers privately, which would upset them.

There would be precious little point in proving to the world that Dozen Roses had been given cocaine (and of course I could do it by calling for a further analysis of the urine sample taken by the officials at York) because if cocaine weren't a specifically banned substance, neither was it a normal nutrient. Nothing that was not a normal nutrient was supposed to be given to thoroughbreds racing in Britain.

If I disclosed the cocaine, would Dozen Roses be disqualified for his win at York? If he were, would Nicholas Loder lose his license to train?

If I caused so much trouble, I would be finished in racing. Whistle-blowers were regularly fired from their jobs.

My advice to myself seemed to be, take the money, keep quiet, hope for the best.

Coward, I thought. Maybe stupid as well.

My thoughts made me sweat.

19

JUNE, her hands full of pretty pink beads from the stock-room, said, "What do we do about more rhodochrosite? We're running out and the suppliers in Hong Kong aren't reliable anymore. I was reading in a trade magazine that a man in Germany has some of good quality. What do you think?"

"What would Greville have done?" I asked.

Annette said regretfully, "He'd have gone to Germany to see. He'd never start buying from a new source without know-ing who he was trading with."

I said to June, "Make an appointment, say who we are, and book an airline ticket."

They both simultaneously said, "But . . ." and stopped.

I said mildly, "You never know whether a horse is going to be a winner until you race it. June's going down to the starting gate."

June blushed and went away. Annette shook her head doubtfully.

"I wouldn't know rhodochrosite from granite," I said. "June does. She knows its price, knows what sells. I'll trust that knowledge until she proves me wrong."

"She's too young to make decisions," Annette objected.

"Decisions are easier when you're young."

Isn't that the truth, I thought wryly, rehearing my own

words. At June's age I'd been full of certainties. At June's age, what would I have done about cocaine-positive urine tests? I didn't know. Impossible to go back.

I said I would be off for the day and would see them all in the morning. Dilemmas could be shelved, I thought. The evening was Clarissa's.

Brad, I saw, down in the yard, had been reading the *Racing Post,* which had the same photograph as the *Daily Sensation.* He pointed to the picture when I eased in beside him, and I nodded.

"That's your head," he said.

"Mm."

"Bloody hell," he said.

I smiled. "It seems a long time ago."

He drove to Greville's house and came in with me while I went upstairs and put the baster tube into an envelope and then into a Jiffy bag brought from the office for the purpose and addressed it to Phil Urquhart.

To Brad, downstairs again, I said, "The Euro-Securo couriers' main office is in Oxford Street not very far from the Selfridge Hotel. This is the actual address . . ." I gave it to him. "Do you think you can find it?"

"Yerss." He was again affronted.

"I phoned them from the office. They're expecting this. You don't need to pay, they're sending the bill. Just get a receipt. OK?"

"Yerss."

"Then pick up my friend from the Selfridge Hotel and bring her here. She'll phone for you, so leave it switched on."

"Yerss."

"Then go on home, if you like."

He gave me a glowering look but all he said was, "Same time tomorrow?"

"If you're not bored."

He gave me a totally unexpected grin. Unnerving, almost, to see that gloom-ridden face break up.

"Best time o' my life," he said, and departed, leaving me literally gasping.

In bemusement, I went along to the little sitting room and tidied up a bit more of the mess. If Brad enjoyed waiting for hours reading improbable magazines it was all right by me, but I no longer felt in imminent danger of assault or death, and I could drive my car myself if I cared to, and Brad's days as bodyguard/chauffeur were numbered. He must realize it, I thought: he'd clung on to the job several times.

By that Wednesday evening there was rapid improvement also in the ankle. Bones, as I understood it, always grew new soft tissue at the site of a fracture, as if to stick the pieces together with glue. After eight or nine days, the soft tissue began to harden, the bone getting progressively stronger from then on, and it was in that phase that I'd by then arrived. I laid one of the crutches aside in the sitting room and used the other like a walking stick, and put my left toe down to the carpet for balance if not to bear my full weight.

Distalgesic, I decided, was a thing of the past. I'd drink wine for dinner with Clarissa.

The front door bell rang, which surprised me. It was too early to be Clarissa: Brad couldn't have done the errand and got to the Selfridge and back in the time he'd been gone.

I hopped along to the door and looked through the peephole, and was astounded to see Nicholas Loder on the doorstep. Behind him, on the path, stood his friend Rollo Rollway, looking boredly around at the small garden.

In some dismay I opened the door and Nicholas Loder immediately said, "Oh, good. You're in. We happened to be dining in London so as we'd time to spare I thought we'd come round on the off-chance to discuss Gemstones, rather than negotiate on the telephone."

"But I haven't named a price," I said.

"Never mind. We can discuss that. Can we come in?"

I shifted backward reluctantly.

"Well, yes," I said, looking at my watch. "But not for long. I have another appointment pretty soon."

"So have we," he assured me. He turned round and waved a beckoning arm to his friend. "Come on, Rollo, he has time to see us."

Rollway, looking as if the enterprise were not to his liking, came up the steps and into the house. I turned to lead the way along the passage, ostentatiously not closing the front door behind them as a big hint to them not to stay long.

"The room's in a mess," I warned them over my shoulder. "We had a burglar."

"We?" Nicholas Loder said.

"Greville and I."

"Oh."

He said "Oh" again when he saw the chrysanthemum pot wedged in the television, but Rollway blinked around in an uninterested fashion as if he saw houses in chaos every day of the week.

Rollway at close quarters wasn't any more attractive than Rollway at a distance: a dull dark lump of a man, thickset, middle-aged and humorless. One could only explain his friendship with the charismatic Loder, I thought, in terms of trainer-owner relationship.

"This is Thomas Rollway," Nicholas Loder said to me, making belated introductions. "One of my owners. He's very interested in buying Gemstones."

Rollway didn't look very interested in anything.

"I'd offer you a drink," I said, "but the burglar broke all the bottles."

Nicholas Loder looked vaguely at the chunks of glass on the carpet. There had been no diamonds in the bottles. Waste of booze.

"Perhaps we could sit down," he said.

"Sure."

He sat in Greville's armchair and Rollway perched on the arm of the second armchair, which effectively left me the one upright hard one. I sat on the edge of it, wanting them to hurry, laying the second crutch aside.

I looked at Loder, big, light-haired with brownish eyes, full of ability and not angry with me as he had been in the recent past. It was almost with guilt that I thought of the cocaine analyses going on behind his back when his manner toward me was more normal than at any time since Greville's death. If he'd been like that from the beginning, I'd have seen no reason to have had the tests done.

"Gemstones," he said, "what do you want for him?"

I'd seen in the Saxony Franklin ledgers what Gemstones had cost as a yearling, but that had little bearing on his worth two years later. He'd won one race. He was no bright star. I doubled his cost and asked for that.

Nicholas Loder laughed with irony. "Come on, Derek. Half."

"Half is what he cost Greville originally," I said.

His eyes narrowed momentarily and then opened innocently. "So we've been doing our homework!" He actually smiled. "I've promised Rollo a reasonable horse at a reasonable price. We all know Gemstones is no world-beater, but there are more races in him. His cost price is perfectly fair. More than fair."

I thought it quite likely was indeed fair, but Saxony Franklin needed every possible penny.

"Meet me halfway," I said, "and he's yours."

Nicholas raised his eyebrows at his friend for a decision. "Rollo?"

Rollo's attention seemed to be focused more on the crutch I'd earlier propped unused against a wall rather than on the matter in hand.

"Gemstones is worth that," Nicholas Loder said to him judiciously, and I thought in amusement that he would get me as much as he could in order to earn himself a larger commission. Trade with the enemy, I thought: build mutual-benefit bridges.

"I don't want Gemstones at any price," Rollo said, and they were the first words he'd uttered since arriving. His voice was harsh and curiously flat, without inflection. Without emotion, I thought.

Nicholas Loder protested, "But that's why you wanted to come here! It was your idea to come here."

Thomas Rollway, as if absentmindedly, stood and picked up the abandoned crutch, turning it upside down and holding it by the end normally near the floor. Then, as if the thought had at that second occurred to him, he bent his knees and swung the crutch round forcefully in a scything movement a bare four inches above the carpet.

It was so totally unexpected that I wasn't quick enough to avoid it. The elbow-rest and cuff crashed into my left ankle and Rollway came after it like a bull, kicking, punching, over-balancing me, knocking me down.

I was flabbergasted more than frightened, and then furi-ous. It seemed senseless, without reason, unprovoked, out of any sane proportion. Over Rollway's shoulder I glimpsed Nicholas Loder looking dumbfounded, his mouth and eyes stretched open, uncomprehending.

As I struggled to get up, Thomas Rollway reached inside his jacket and produced a handgun; twelve inches of it at least, with the thickened shape of a silencer on the business end.

"Keep still," he said to me, pointing the barrel at my chest.

A gun . . . Simms . . . I began dimly to understand and to despair pretty deeply.

Nicholas Loder was shoving himself out of his armchair. "What are you doing?" His voice was high with alarm, with rising panic.

"Sit down, Nick," his friend said. "Don't get up." And such was the grindingly heavy tone of his unemotional voice that Nicholas Loder subsided, looking overthrown, not believing what was happening.

"But you came to buy his horse," he said weakly.

"I came to kill him."

[303]

Rollway said it dispassionately, as if it were nothing. But then, he'd tried to before.

Loder's consternation became as deep as my own.

Rollway moved his gun and pointed it at my ankle. I immediately shifted it, trying desperately to get up, and he brought the spitting end back fast into alignment with my heart.

"Keep still," he said again. His eyes coldly considered me as I half sat, half lay on the floor, propped on my elbow and without any weapon within reach, not even the one crutch I'd been using. Then, with as little warning as for his first attack, he stamped hard on my ankle and for good measure ground away with his heel as if putting out a cigarette butt. After that he left his shoe where it was, pressing down on it with his considerable weight.

I swore at him and couldn't move, and thought idiotically, feeling things give way inside there, that it would take me a lot longer now to get fit, and that took my mind momentarily off a bullet that I would feel a lot less, anyway.

"But *why?*" Nicholas Loder asked, wailing. "Why are you doing this?"

Good question.

Rollway answered it.

"The only successful murders," he said, "are those for which there appears to be no motive."

It sounded like something he'd learned on a course. Something surrealistic. Monstrous.

Nicholas Loder, sitting rigidly to my right in Greville's chair, said with an uneasy attempt at a laugh, "You're kidding, Rollo, aren't you? This is some sort of joke?"

Rollo was not kidding. Rollo, standing determinedly on my ankle between me and the door, said to me, "You picked up a piece of my property at York races. When I found it was missing I went back to look for it. An official told me you'd put it in your pocket. I want it back."

I said nothing.

Damn the official, I thought. So helpful. So deadly. I hadn't even noticed one watching.

Nicholas Loder, bewildered, said, "What piece of property?"

"The tube part of the inhaler," Rollway told him.

"But that woman, Mrs. Ostermeyer, gave it back to you."

"Only the bulb. I didn't notice the tube had dropped as well. Not until after the race. After the Stewards' inquiry."

"But what does it matter?"

Rollway pointed his gun unwaveringly at where it would do me fatal damage and answered the question without taking his gaze from my face.

"You yourself, Nick," he informed him, "told me you were worried about Franklin, he was observant and too bright."

"But that was because I gelded Dozen Roses."

"So when I found he had the inhaler, I asked one or two other people their opinion of Derek Franklin as a person, not a jockey, and they all said the same. Brainy. Intelligent. Bright." He paused. "I don't like that."

I was thinking that through the door, down the passage and in the street there was sanity and Wednesday and rain and rush hour all going on as usual. Saturn was just as accessible.

"I don't believe in waiting for trouble," Rollway said. "And dead men can't make accusations." He stared at me. "Where's the tube?"

I didn't answer for various reasons. If he took murder so easily in his stride and I told him I'd sent the tube to Phil Urquhart I could be sentencing Phil to death too, and besides, if I opened my mouth for any reason what might come out wasn't words at all but something between a yell and a groan, a noise I could hear loudly in my head but which wasn't important either, or not as important as getting out of the sickening prospect of the next few minutes.

"But he would never have suspected . . ." Loder feebly said.

"Of course he did. Anyone would. Why do you think he's had that bodyguard glued to him? Why do you think he's been

dodging about so I can't find him and not going home? And
he had the horse's urine taken in Lambourn for testing, and
there's the official sample too at York. I tell you, I'm not
waiting for him to make trouble. I'm not going to jail, I'll tell
you."

"But you wouldn't."

"Be your age, Nick," Rollway said caustically. "I import the
stuff. I take the risks. And I get rid of trouble as soon as I see
it. If you wait too long, trouble can destroy you."

Nicholas Loder said in wailing protest, "I told you it wasn't
necessary to give it to horses. It doesn't make them go faster."

"Rubbish. You can't tell, because it isn't much done. No
one can afford it except people like me. I'm swamped with the
stuff at the moment, it's coming in in bulk from the Medellín
cartel in Madrid . . . *Where's the tube?*" he finished, bouncing
his weight up and down.

If not telling him would keep me alive a bit longer, I wasn't
going to try telling him I'd thrown it away.

"You can't just shoot him," Nicholas Loder said despair-
ingly. "Not with me watching."

"You're no danger to me, Nick," Rollway said flatly.
"Where would you go for your little habit? One squeak from
you would mean your own ruin. I'd see you went down for
possession. For conniving with me to drug horses. They'd
take your license away for that. Nicholas Loder, trainer of
Classic winners, down in the gutter." He paused. "You'll keep
quiet, we both know it."

The threats were none the lighter for being uttered in a
measured unexcited monotone. He made my hair bristle.
Heaven knew what effect he had on Loder.

He wouldn't wait much longer, I thought, for me to tell him
where the tube was; and maybe the tube would in the end
indeed be his downfall, because Phil knew whose it was, and
that the Ostermeyers had been witnesses, and if I were found
shot perhaps he would light a long fuse . . . but it wasn't of
much comfort at that moment.

With the strength of desperation I rolled my body and with my right foot kicked hard at Rollway's leg. He grunted and took his weight off my ankle and I pulled away from him, shuffling backward, trying to reach the chair I'd been sitting on to use it as a weapon against him, or at least not to lie there supinely waiting to be slaughtered, and I saw him recover his rocked balance and begin to straighten his arm, aiming and looking along the barrel so as not to miss.

That unmistakable stance was going to be the last thing I would see: and the last emotion I would feel would be the blazing fury of dying for so pointless a cause.

Nicholas Loder, also seeing that it was the moment of irretrievable crisis, sprang with horror from the armchair and shouted urgently, "No, no. Rollo. No, don't do it!"

It might have been the droning of a gnat for all the notice Rollo paid him.

Nicholas Loder took a few paces forward and grabbed at Rollway and at his aiming arm.

I took the last opportunity to get my hands on something—anything—and got my fingers on a crutch.

"I won't let you," Nicholas Loder frantically persisted. "You mustn't!"

Rollo shook him off and swung his gun back to me.

"No!" Loder was terribly disturbed. Shocked. Almost frenzied. "It's wrong. I won't let you!" He put his body against Rollway's, trying to push him away.

Rollway shrugged him off, all bull-muscle and undeterrable. Then, very fast, he pointed the gun straight at Nicholas Loder's chest and without pausing pulled the trigger. Pulled it twice.

I heard the rapid *phut, phut.* Saw Nicholas Loder fall, saw the blankness on his face, the absolute astonishment.

There was no time to waste on terror, though I felt it. I gripped the crutch I'd reached and swung the heavier end of it at Rollway's right hand, and landed a blow fierce enough to make him drop the gun.

[307]

It fell out of my reach.

I stretched for it and rolled and scrambled but he was upright and much faster, and he bent down and took it into his hand again with a tight look of fury as hot as my own.

He began to lift his arm again in my direction and again I whipped at him with the crutch and again hit him. He didn't drop the gun that time but transferred it to his left hand and shook out the fingers of his right hand as if they hurt, which I hoped to God they did.

I slashed at his legs. Another hit. He retreated a couple of paces and with his left hand began to take aim. I slashed at him. The gun barrel wavered. When he pulled the trigger, the flame spat out and the bullet missed me.

He was still between me and the door.

Ankle or not, I thought, once I was on my feet I'd smash him down and out of the way and run, run . . . run into the street . . .

I had to get up. Got as far as my knees. Stood up on my right foot. Put down the left. It wasn't a matter of pain. I didn't feel it. It just buckled. It needed the crutch's help . . . and I needed the crutch to fight against his gun, to hop and shuffle forward and hack at him, to put off the inevitable moment, to fight until I was dead.

A figure appeared abruptly in the doorway, seen peripherally in my vision.

Clarissa.

I'd forgotten she was coming.

"Run," I shouted agonizedly, "Run. Get away."

It startled Rollway. I'd made so little noise. He seemed to think the instructions were for himself. He sneered. I kept my eyes on his gun and lunged at it, making his aim swing wide again at a crucial second. He pulled the trigger. Flame. *Phut.* The bullet zipped over my shoulder and hit the wall.

"Run," I yelled again with fearful urgency. "Quick. Oh, be quick."

Why didn't she run? He'd see her if he turned.

He would kill her.

Clarissa didn't run. She brought her hand out of her raincoat pocket holding a thing like a black cigar and she swung her arm in a powerful arc like an avenging fury. Out of the black tube sprang the fearsome telescopic silvery springs with a knob on the end, and the kiyoga smashed against the side of Rollway's skull.

He fell without a sound. Fell forward, cannoning into me, knocking me backward. I ended on the floor, sitting, his inert form stomach-down over my shins.

Clarissa came down on her knees beside me, trembling violently, very close to passing out. I was breathless, shattered, trembling like her. It seemed ages before either of us was able to speak. When she could, it was a whisper, low and distressed.

"Derek . . ."

"Thanks," I said jerkily, "for saving my life."

"Is he dead?" She was looking with fear at Rollway's head, strain in her eyes, in her neck, in her voice.

"I don't care if he is," I said truthfully.

"But I . . . I hit him."

"I'll say I did it. Don't worry. I'll say I hit him with the crutch."

She said waveringly, "You can't."

"Of course I can. I meant to, if I could."

I glanced over at Nicholas Loder, and Clarissa seemed to see him for the first time. He was on his back, unmoving.

"Dear God," she said faintly, her face even paler. "Who's that?"

I introduced her posthumously to Nicholas Loder, racehorse trainer and then to Thomas Rollway, drug baron. They'd squirted cocaine into Dozen Roses, I said, struggling for lightness. I'd found them out. Rollway wanted me dead rather than giving evidence against him. He'd said so.

Neither of the men contested the charges, though Rollway

at least was alive, I thought. I could feel his breathing on my legs. A pity, on the whole. I told Clarissa, which made her feel a shade happier.

Clarissa still held the kiyoga. I touched her hand, brushing my fingers over hers, grateful beyond expression for her courage. Greville had given her the kiyoga. He couldn't have known it would keep me alive. I took it gently out of her grasp and let it lie on the carpet.

"Phone my car," I said. "If Brad hasn't gone too far, he'll come back."

"But . . ."

"He'll take you safely back to the Selfridge. Phone quickly."

"I can't just . . . leave you."

"How would you explain being here, to the police?"

She looked at me in dismay and obstinacy. "I can't . . ."

"You must," I said. "What do you think Greville would want?"

"Oh . . ." It was a long sigh of grief, both for my brother and, I thought, for the evening together that she and I were not now going to have.

"Do you remember the number?" I said.

"Derek . . ."

"Go and do it, my dear love."

She got blindly to her feet and went over to the telephone. I told her the number, which she'd forgotten. When the impersonal voice of the radio-phone operator said as usual after six or seven rings that there was no reply, I asked her to dial the number again, and yet again. With luck, Brad would reckon three calls spelled emergency.

"When we got here," Clarissa said, sounding stronger, "Brad told me there was a gray Volvo parked not far from your gate. He was worried, I think. He asked me to tell you. Is it important?"

God in heaven . . .

"Will that phone stretch over here?" I said. "See if it will. Push the table over. Pull the phone over here. If I ring the

[310]

police from here, and they find me here, they'll take the scene for granted."

She tipped the table on its side, letting the answering machine fall to the floor, and pulled the phone to the end of its cord. I still couldn't quite reach it, and edged round a little in order to do so, and it hurt, which she saw.

"Derek!"

"Never mind." I smiled at her, twistedly, making a joke of it. "It's better than death."

"I can't leave you." Her eyes were still strained and she was still visibly trembling, but her composure was on the way back.

"You damned well can," I said. "You have to. Go out to the gate. If Brad comes, get him to toot the horn, then I'll know you're away and I'll phone the police. If he doesn't come . . . give him five minutes, then walk . . . walk and get a taxi. Promise?"

I picked up the kiyoga and fumbled with it, trying to concertina it shut. She took it out of my hands, twisted it, banged the knob on the carpet and expertly returned it closed to her pocket.

"I'll think of you, and thank you," I said, "every day that I live."

"At four-twenty," she said as if automatically, and then paused and looked at me searchingly. "It was the time I met Greville."

"Four-twenty," I said, and nodded. "Every day."

She knelt down again beside me and kissed me, but it wasn't passion. More like farewell.

"Go on," I said. "Time to go."

She rose reluctantly and went to the doorway, pausing there and looking back. Lady Knightwood, I thought, a valiant deliverer with not a hair out of place.

"Phone me," I said, "one day soon?"

"Yes."

She went quietly down the passage but wasn't gone long.

DICK FRANCIS

Brad himself came bursting into the room with Clarissa behind him like a shadow.

Brad almost skidded to a halt, the prospect before him
enough to shock even the garrulous to silence.

"Strewth," he said economically.

"As you say," I replied.

Rollway had dropped his gun when he fell but it still lay not
far from his left hand. I asked Brad to move it farther away
in case the drug man woke up.

"Don't touch it," I said sharply as he automatically reached
out a hand, bending down. "Your prints would be an embarrassment."

He made a small grunt of acknowledgment and Clarissa
wordlessly held out a tissue with which Brad gingerly took
hold of the silencer and slid the gun across the room to the
window.

"What if he does wake up?" he said, pointing to Rollway.

"I give him another clout with the crutch."

He nodded as if that were normal behavior.

"Thanks for coming back," I said.

"Didn't go far. You've got a Volvo . . ."

I nodded.

"Is it the one?"

"Sure to be," I said.

"Strewth."

"Take my friend back to the Selfridge," I said. "Forget she
was here. Forget you were here. Go home."

"Can't leave you," he said. "I'll come back."

"The police will be here."

As ever, the thought of policemen made him uneasy.

"Go on home," I said. "The dangers are over."

He considered it. Then he said hopefully, "Same time tomorrow?"

I moved my head in amused assent and said wryly, "Why
not?"

He seemed satisfied in a profound way, and he and Clarissa

went over to the doorway, pausing there and looking back, as she had before. I gave them a brief wave, and they waved back before going. They were both, incredibly, smiling.

"Brad!" I yelled after him.

He came back fast, full of instant alarm.

"Everything's fine," I said. "Just fine. But don't shut the front door behind you. I don't want to have to get up to let the police in. I don't want them smashing the locks. I want them to walk in here nice and easy."

20

IT was a long dreary evening, but not without humor.

I sat quietly apart most of the time in Greville's chair, largely ignored while relays of people came and efficiently measured, photographed, took fingerprints and dug bullets out of walls.

There had been a barrage of preliminary questions in my direction which had ended with Rollway groaning his way back to consciousness. Although the police didn't like advice from a civilian, they did, at my mild suggestion, handcuff him before he was fully awake, which was just as well, as the bullish violence was the first part of his personality to surface. He was on his feet, thrashing about, mumbling, before he knew where he was.

While a policeman on each side of him held his arms, he stared at me, his eyes slowly focusing. I was still at that time on the floor, thankful to have his weight off me. He looked as if he couldn't believe what was happening, and in the same flat uninflected voice as before, called me a bastard, among other things not as innocuous.

"I knew you were trouble," he said. He was still too groggy to keep a rein on his tongue. "You won't live to see evidence, I'll see to that."

The police phlegmatically arrested him formally, told him his rights and said he would get medical attention at the police station. I watched him stumble away, thinking of the irony of the decision I'd made earlier not to accuse him of anything at all, much less, as now, of shooting people. I hadn't known he'd shot Simms. I hadn't feared him at all. It didn't seem to have occurred to him that I might not act against him on the matter of cocaine. He'd been ready to kill to prevent it. Yet I hadn't suspected him even of being a large-scale dealer until he'd boasted of it.

While the investigating activity went on around me, I wondered if it were because drug runners cared so little for the lives of others that they came so easily to murder.

Like Vaccaro, I thought, gunning down his renegade pilots from a moving car. Perhaps that was a habitual mode of cleanup among drug kings. Copycat murder, everyone had thought about Simms, and everyone had been right.

People like Rollway and Vaccaro held other people's lives cheap because they aimed anyway at destroying them. They made addiction and corruption their business, willfully intended to profit from the collapse and unhappiness of countless lives, deliberately enticed young people onto a one-way misery trail. I'd read that people could snort cocaine for two or three years before the physical damage hit. The drug growers, shippers, wholesalers knew that. It gave them time for steady selling. Their greed had filthy feet.

The underlying immorality, the aggressive callousness had themselves to be corrupting; addictive. Rollway had self-destructed, like his victims.

I wondered how people grew to be like him. I might condemn them, but I didn't understand them. They weren't happy-go-lucky dishonest, like Pross. They were uncaring and cold. As Elliot Trelawney had said, the logic of criminals tended to be weird. If I ever added to Greville's notebook, I thought, it would be something like "The ways of the crooked are mysterious to the straight," or even "What makes the crooked crooked and the straight straight?" One couldn't trust the sociologists' easy answers.

I remembered an old story I'd heard sometime. A scorpion asked a horse for a ride across a raging torrent. Why not? said the horse, and obligingly started to swim with the scorpion on his back. Halfway across, the scorpion stung the horse. The horse, fatally poisoned, said, "We will both drown now. Why did you do that?" And the scorpion said, "Because it's my nature."

Nicholas Loder wasn't going to worry or wonder about anything anymore; and his morality, under stress, had risen up unblemished and caused his death. Injustice and irony everywhere, I thought, and felt regret for the man who couldn't acquiesce in my murder.

He had taken cocaine himself, that much was clear. He'd become perhaps dependent on Rollway, had perhaps been more or less blackmailed by him into allowing his horses to be tampered with. He'd been frightened I would find him out: but in the end he hadn't been evil, and Rollway had seen it, had seen he couldn't trust him to keep his mouth shut after all.

Through Loder, Rollway had known where to find me on Sunday afternoon, and through him he'd known where to find me this Wednesday evening. Yet Nicholas Loder hadn't knowingly set me up. He'd been used by his supposed friend; and I hadn't seen any danger in reporting on Sunday morning that I'd be lunching with Milo and the Ostermeyers or saying I would be in Greville's house ready for Gemstones bids.

I hadn't specifically been keeping myself safe from Rollway, whatever he might believe, but from an unidentified enemy, someone *there* and dangerous, but unrecognized.

Irony everywhere . . .

I thought about Martha and Harley and the cocaine in Dozen Roses. I would ask them to keep the horse and race him, and I'd promise that if he never did any good I would give them their money back and send him to auction. What the Jockey Club and the racing press would have to say about the whole mess boggled the mind. We might still lose the York race: would have to, I guessed.

I thought of Clarissa in the Selfridge Hotel struggling to behave normally with a mind filled with visions of violence. I hoped she would ring up her Henry, reach back to solid ground, mourn Greville peacefully, be glad she'd saved his brother. I would leave the Wizard's alarm set to 4:20 P.M., and remember them both when I heard it: and one could say it was sentimental, that their whole affair had been packed with sentimental behavior, but who cared, they'd enjoyed it, and I would endorse it.

At some point in the evening's proceedings a highly senior plainclothes policeman arrived whom everyone else deferred to and called sir.

He introduced himself as Superintendent Ingold and invited a detailed statement from me, which a minion wrote down. The superintendent was short, piercing, businesslike, and considered what I said with pauses before his next question, as if internally computing my answers. He was also, usefully, a man who liked racing: who sorrowed over Nicholas Loder and knew of my existence.

I told him pretty plainly most of what had happened, omitting only a few things: the precise way Rollway had asked for his tube, and Clarissa's presence, and the dire desperation of the minutes before she'd arrived. I made that hopeless fight a lot shorter, a lot easier, a rapid knockout.

"The crutches?" he inquired. "What are they for?"

"A spot of trouble with an ankle at Cheltenham."

"When was that?"

"Nearly two weeks ago."

He merely nodded. The crutch handles were quite heavy enough for clobbering villains, and he sought no other explanation.

It all took a fair while, with the pauses and the writing. I told him about the car crash near Hungerford. I said I thought it possible that it had been Rollway who shot Simms. I said that of course they would compare the bullets the Hungerford police had taken from the Daimler with those just now dug out of Greville's walls, and those no doubt to be retrieved from Nicholas Loder's silent form. I wondered innocently what sort of car Rollway drove. The Hungerford police, I told the superintendent, were looking for a gray Volvo.

After a pause a policeman was dispatched to search the street. He came back wide-eyed with his news and was told to put a cordon round the car and keep the public off.

It was by then well past dark. Every time the police or officials came into the house, the mechanical dog started barking and the lights repeatedly blazed on. I thought it amusing which says something for my lightheaded state of mind but it wore the police nerves to irritation.

"The switches are beside the front door," I said to one of them eventually. "Why don't you flip them all up?"

They did, and got peace.

"Who threw the flowerpot into the television?" the superintendent wanted to know.

"Burglars. Last Saturday. Two of your men came round."

"Are you ill?" he said abruptly.

"No. Shaken."

He nodded. Anyone would be, I thought.

One of the policemen mentioned Rollway's threat that I wouldn't live to give evidence. To be taken seriously, perhaps.

Ingold looked at me speculatively. "Does it worry you?"

"I'll try to be careful."

He smiled faintly. "Like on those horses?" The smile disappeared. "You could do worse than hire someone to mind your back for a while."

I nodded my thanks. Brad, I thought dryly, would be ecstatic.

They took poor Nicholas Loder away. I would emphasize his bravery, I thought, and save what could be saved of his reputation. He had given me, after all, a chance of life.

[318]

Eventually the police wanted to seal the sitting room, although the superintendent said it was a precaution only: the events of the evening seemed crystal clear.

He handed me the crutches and asked where I would be going.

"Upstairs to bed," I said.

"Here?" He was surprised. "In this house?"

"This house," I said, "is a fortress. Until one lowers the drawbridge, that is."

They sealed the sitting room, let themselves out, and left me alone in the newly quiet hallway.

I sat on the stairs and felt awful. Cold. Shivery. Old and gray. What I needed was a hot drink to get warm from inside, and there was no way I was going down to the kitchen. Hot water from the bathroom tap upstairs would do fine, I thought.

As happened in many sorts of battle, it wasn't the moment of injury that was worst, but the time a couple of hours later when the body's immediate natural anesthetic properties subsided and let pain take over: nature's marvelous system for allowing a wild animal to flee to safety before hiding to lick its wounds with healing saliva. The human animal was no different. One needed the time to escape, and one needed the pain afterward to say something was wrong.

At the moment of maximum adrenaline, fight-or-flight, I'd believed I could run on that ankle. It had been mechanics that had defeated me, not instinct, not willingness. Two hours later, the idea of even standing on it was impossible. Movement alone became breathtaking. I'd sat in Greville's chair for another two long hours after that, concentrating on policemen, blanking out feeling.

With them gone, there was no more pretending. However much I might protest in my mind, however much rage I might feel, I knew the damage to bones and ligaments was about as bad as before. Rollway had cracked them apart again. Back to square one . . . and the Hennessy only four and a half weeks away . . . and I was bloody well going to ride Datepalm in it, and I wasn't going to tell anyone about tonight's little stamping-ground, no one knew except Rollway and he wouldn't boast about that.

If I stayed away from Lambourn for two weeks, Milo wouldn't find out; not that he would himself care all that much. If he didn't know, though, he couldn't mention it to anyone else. No one expected me to be racing again for another four weeks. If I simply stayed in London for two of those and ran Greville's business, no one would comment. Then once I could walk I'd go down to Lambourn and ride every day, get physiotherapy, borrow the Electrovet . . . it could be done . . . piece of cake.

Meanwhile there were the stairs.

Up in Greville's bathroom, in a zipped bag with my washing things, I would find the envelope the orthopedic surgeon had given me, which I'd tucked into a waterproof pocket and traveled around with ever since. In the envelope, three small white tablets not as big as aspirins, more or less with my initials on: DF 118s. Only as a last resort, the orthopedist had said.

Wednesday evening, I reckoned, qualified.

I went up the stairs slowly, backward, sitting down, hooking the crutches up with me. If I dropped them, I thought, they would slither down to the bottom again. I wouldn't drop them.

It was pretty fair hell. I reminded myself astringently that people had been known to crawl down mountains with much worse broken bones: they wouldn't have made a fuss over one little flight upward. Anyway, there had to be an end to everything, and eventually I sat on the top step, with the crutches beside me, and thought that the DF 118s weren't going to fly along magically to my tongue. I still had to get them.

I shut my eyes and put both hands round my ankle on top of the bandage. I could feel the heat and it was swelling again already, and there was a pulse hammering somewhere.

Damn it, I thought. God bloody damn it. I was used to this sort of pain, but it never made it any better. I hoped Rollway's head was banging like crazy.

I made it to the bathroom, ran the hot water, opened the door of the medicine cabinet, pulled out and unzipped my bag.

One tablet, no pain, I thought. Two tablets, spaced out. Three tablets, unconscious.

Three tablets had definite attractions but I feared I might wake in the morning needing them again and wishing I'd been wiser. I swallowed one with a glassful of hot water and waited for miracles.

The miracle that actually happened was extraordinary but had nothing to do with the pills.

I stared at my gray face in the mirror over the basin. Improvement, I thought after a while, was a long time coming. Perhaps the damned things didn't work.

Be patient.

Take another . . .

No. Be patient.

I looked vaguely at the objects in the medicine cupboard. Talc. Deodorant. Shaving cream. Shaving cream. Most of one can of shaving cream had been squirted all over the mirror by Jason. A pale blue and gray can: "Unscented," it said.

Greville had an electric razor as well, I thought inconsequentially. It was on the dressing chest. I'd borrowed it that morning. Quicker than a wet shave, though not so long lasting.

The damn pill wasn't working.

I looked at the second one longingly.

Wait a bit.

Think about something else.

I picked up the second can of shaving cream which was scarlet and orange and said "Regular Fragrance." I shook the can and took off the cover and tried to squirt foam onto the mirror.

Nothing happened. I shook it. Tried again. Nothing at all.

Guile and misdirection, I thought. Hollow books and green stone boxes with keyholes but no keys. Safes in concrete, secret drawers in desks . . . Take nothing at face value. Greville's mind was a maze, . . . *and he wouldn't have used scented shaving cream.*

I twisted the shaving cream can this way and that and the bottom ring moved and began to turn in my hand. I caught my breath. Didn't really believe it. I went on turning . . . unscrewing.

It would be another empty hiding place, I told myself. Get a grip on hope. I unscrewed the whole bottom off the can, and from a nest of cotton wool a chamois leather pouch fell out into my hand.

Well, all right, I thought, but it wouldn't be diamonds.

With the help of the crutches I took the pouch into the bedroom and sat on Greville's bed, and poured onto the bedspread a little stream of dullish-looking pea-sized lumps of carbon.

I almost stopped breathing. Time stood still. I couldn't believe it. Not after everything . . .

With shaking fingers I counted them, setting them in small clumps of five.

Ten . . . fifteen . . . twenty . . . twenty-five.

Twenty-five meant I'd got fifty percent. Half of what Greville had bought. With half, Saxony Franklin would be safe. I offered heartbursting thanks to the fates. I came dangerously near to crying.

Then, with a sense of revelation, I knew where the rest were. Where they had to be. Greville really had taken them with him to Ipswich, as he'd told Pross. I guessed he'd taken them thinking he might give them to the Maarten-Pagnier partner to take back to Antwerp for cutting.

I'd searched through the things in his car and had found nothing, and I'd held his diamonds in my hand and not known it.

They were . . . they had to be . . . in that other scarlet and orange can, in the apparent can of shaving cream in his overnight bag, safe as Fort Knox now under the stairs of Brad's mum's house in Hungerford. She'd taken all Greville's things in off the street, out of my car, to keep them safe in a dodgy neighborhood. In memory I could hear Brad's pride in her.

"Smart, our mum . . ."

The DF 118 was at last taking the edge off the worst.

I rolled the twenty-five precious pebbles around under my fingers with indescribable joy and thought how relieved Greville would have been. Sleep easy, pal, I told him, uncontrollably smiling. I've finally found them.

He'd left me his business, his desk, his gadgets, his enemies, his horses, his mistress. Left me Saxony Franklin, the Wizard, the shaving cream cans, Prospero Jenks and Nicholas Loder, Dozen Roses, Clarissa.

I'd inherited his life and laid him to rest; and at that moment, though I might hurt and I might throb, I didn't think I had ever been happier.